Dear Reader:

During the most challenging times of my life I seem to be drawn to water. I always go to a special lake, where Canadian geese, blue herons, and snowy egrets also visit. Somehow, just watching the current of water enables me to calm down and think more clearly. One day, while pondering a situation, I was mesmerized by the sunlight dancing upon the water as it lapped the shore, and the beginning of this book played out in my mind.

I thought about traveling—my own traveling—and how I always seem to pack too much and how it's always such a drag to carry it around with me. Then I thought about time traveling and how the characters I write about also carry too much baggage, only theirs is emotional and, if you're having an adventure, the very last thing you need is excess baggage. It's way too heavy, slows you down, and you can't really enjoy the moment.

The hero and heroine in this book are weighed down with baggage. Each can see how to lighten the load of the other but is at a loss as to how to drop his/her own. There's such relief when they finally let go of their heavy burdens and take a deep breath. And maybe, in that breath, we realize they never really needed to carry it at all. Charlie and Suzanne begin as friends, needing each other, yet they quickly learn what an extraordinary expansive force love can be. I so enjoyed spending time with these characters and I hope you also will come to know them as I did . . . endearing, yet so very human in their flaws. From their experiences I have adopted a new motto: Travel lightly . . . in life and on my own adventures into the world.

See you on the next one!

Kindest regards,

Constance O'Day

Other Avon Books by
Constance O'Day-Flannery

ANYWHERE YOU ARE
ONCE AND FOREVER
HEAVEN ON EARTH
TIME AFTER TIME

CONSTANCE O'DAY-FLANNERY

Here and Now

AVON BOOKS
An Imprint of HarperCollinsPublishers

AVON BOOKS
An Imprint of HarperCollins*Publishers*
10 East 53rd Street
New York, New York 10022-5299

For Kristen and Ryan

For all the years together,
for all the love, the laughter,
the tears, and the growth.

Thank you for choosing me.

PROLOGUE

Charles Garrity knew he wasn't going to die. He'd bet his life on it.

Taking chances was something he was mighty familiar with and, so far, the odds had always seemed to be in his favor. This time it was obvious he'd trusted far too much, and now his options were narrowed down to two. Maybe it was Irish luck, but at only thirty-six he had a lifetime of hopes and dreams ahead of him and he wasn't about to give up now. Right now, he was too angry.

Perilously balanced on the edge of the bridge, his mind quickly played out his first gamble. He could jump, simply falling over one hundred feet like a puppet held aloft and then cut from its strings. There was a chance he'd be pummeled beyond recognition by the web of trestle beams before his limp body even smacked the water. Still, if his luck held out, he'd live through it.

A sudden shove from the barrel of the gun pointed at his chest declared his other option.

"I'm only going to ask one last time, Charlie. The deed. Where is it?"

Swallowing the dry lump in his throat, he clenched his teeth and refused to answer the man he once thought he knew. He and Mitch Davies had crossed the ocean together to come to this country. Now the man standing before him, his partner in business, the friend he'd asked to witness his forthcoming wedding, seemed crazed with greed.

Snippets of memories flashed through Charles's mind of everything the two of them had gone through since they'd set foot upon America's shore back in 1916—their struggle to survive and get out of the tenements, their brief adventures out west, fighting the Germans during the Great War, making it back home and collecting a small fortune in bootleg liquor and the stock market, then finally getting back to New Jersey with enough money to fulfill their dream. He'd been more a father to this boy than his drunken own had been to him, taking the young lad under his wing, protecting him, clothing him, caring for him when he was wounded in the trenches of France, and watching him grow into a man. How could Mitch have turned on him now?

"It always came so easy for you, Charlie. Money, women, everything. But I've worked damn hard too, and it's about time I got something for me. I want that deed now. Don't make me shoot, then search your body."

Picturing in his mind where he'd hidden it, Charles growled, "It's not on me." He wondered how long it would remain safe. With sudden insight, he realized what Mitch really wanted was his life, everything he had achieved. He would even kill him to get it.

"Then take me to it," Davies snapped. "I didn't come this far to—"

Instinctively, Charles shoved Mitch's arm away as he leapt out into the air. Looking down at the blinding reflection of sun on the water, he heard a shot ring out and felt searing pain wrack his skull. Blackness took over and, falling into what seemed oblivion, he felt lost, as though time and he had been suspended.

Only one thought kept repeating in his confused mind . . .
Why haven't I hit the water yet?

1

"This can't be happening," she whispered in numbed shock. Stuff like this just didn't happen in her life. This was like the craziness of tabloid television!

Breathing deeply of the late spring air, Suzanne McDermott looked out to the Rancocas Creek and then stared at the diamond-studded wedding band in the palm of her hand. Secretly, she'd always thought it was too heavy and gaudy for her taste. The sunlight glinted off the raised gold setting and she registered a moment of surprise that after six years of constant wear the ring still shined brightly—unlike the marriage.

A thick lump formed in her throat and her chest ached with an unbearable heaviness. She had stuck by the rules. She'd played fair her whole life, but she didn't get to live happily ever after.

An image of her husband and her dearest friend assaulted her mind, and she groaned with a bitter, heart-rending pain. Betrayal. She honestly didn't know which tore at her the deepest—the man with whom she had shared her life and planned for a future and a family, or the woman who had shared her intimate thoughts since she was a child in seventh grade. She had honestly thought they were each other's best cheerleaders in life. The two people in the world that she'd trusted most had just ripped apart the foundation of her belief system, and she had nothing to hold on to any longer. She felt as though everything was falling away and she was sinking. No matter how she tried, she couldn't seem to wipe away a mental picture of Ingrid and Kevin *together*. How could her brain make sense of it when her mind continued to haunt her with fantastic scenarios of them making love, while she . . . she . . .

Looking down at her extended stomach, she felt fresh tears begin to surge up within her. Eight and half months into a pregnancy was one hell of a time to have a husband walk out on her for her best friend.

Rules? There are no damn rules now!

She wanted to scream, pull her hair out, and pull out Kevin's hair and Ingrid's too! She wanted to fight, to make them hurt the way she was hurting. She wanted to shriek her denial that everything she had dreamed about was never going to happen—for in that one horrid conversation her world had tilted crazily and she couldn't seem to find her equilibrium. But she couldn't, wouldn't harm the baby. Somehow, by some miracle in the universe, she had to keep it together. She could not afford a nervous breakdown. Not with a baby soon to be born.

Taking a deep breath in a feeble attempt to calm down, she tenderly ran her fingers over her belly and mentally whispered, *We're going to be all right, you and I. I don't know how, but we'll get through this madness.*

Immediately her mind snuck past her best intentions and once more began to torture her with outrage. How could they go behind her back and betray her at a time like this? Sniffing through more tears, she looked out to the river and heard

Kevin's voice in her head. He was *sorry*, and the timing couldn't be worse, but he and Ingrid had been having an affair for over a year. He had to be *honest* and confess they were in love and now they wanted to be together. She'd listened carefully, yet at the time thought she was having an out-of-body experience as he went on and on about how sorry they both were. None of it felt real. It actually *was* like one of those tabloid shows! Her life had been so sane, so perfect . . . or so she'd thought. A great husband, a beautiful home, financial security, a baby on the way. What more could a woman want?

The truth, maybe?

She'd told him to get out, to leave the farmhouse, the only piece of land left after he'd sold over 150 acres to a land developer. And the kicker was that she'd been so damn liberated and so sure the marriage would last forever that she'd signed a prenup six years ago. What a fool she'd been. Why hadn't she seen even a hint of this coming? Had she been too self-absorbed with the pregnancy? What was wrong with her?

"Arrrgh!" The yell escaped her lips and she felt better for it. Why was she making excuses? Why was she blaming herself? Kevin was the one who was self-absorbed. He was the one who had broken the marriage vows, though he still claimed to care about their unborn child. And now here she was, standing at the edge of the Rancocas Creek, her favorite place since childhood, a place where she always came for peace of mind.

It wasn't working. Not this time.

This time there was no easy fix. Her brain spat out the facts: Her husband had made it clear he wanted out of the marriage. She was pregnant. He wanted to marry Ingrid. She had signed away her security. She was alone in the world.

As if in protest, she felt the baby move.

Okay, she wasn't alone.

Tears ran down her cheeks as she stared at her swelled body, encased in a blue knit maternity dress that looked like a gigantic sweatshirt. She felt so ugly, so unwanted, so pathetic. "I'm so sorry," she sniffled, wishing with all her heart that she could provide this child with a stable environment. At thirty-four, she was without extended family now. Her parents had died within a year of each other. First her father was killed in a car accident almost five years ago and her grief-stricken mother just didn't wake up one morning. There was nowhere to turn.

Kevin's parents were retired in Florida and even though they would be shocked, they would support their precious, spoiled son, just as they always had—even when he'd sold the family's land two years ago. His grandfather was kept alive by machines in a nursing home and didn't even know of the sale. The old man still thought the family farm was intact. There was no one to help her now. Maybe the worst part was she couldn't even turn to her best friend for support. Somehow, she had to handle this hideously nauseating drama herself.

Everything was heavy upon her, as if she were carrying the weight of the world, and she felt the muscles in her abdomen tense with resistence. Unconsciously, her hand caressed the side of her belly in response.

What was she going to do?

She wanted to go entirely numb. And why not? She felt abandoned by everything. She didn't believe in marriage anymore. She didn't believe in God anymore. She didn't believe in friendship. All of it, everything she had been taught, had backfired on her and she was left with the ugly lies.

Rubbing the moisture away from her eyes, she stared at the water, watching as the sun reflected off it and felt suddenly mesmerized by the bright dancing lights that seemed to move closer to her with the ebb of the tide. For a moment, Suzanne was almost blinded by the phenomenon and blinked several times to clear her vision. She glanced down to her palm and picked up the wedding ring.

Clutching the heavy band between her fingers, she looked

back out to the wide body of water where she'd made every major decision in her life. It was here that she had decided to marry Kevin, and now it was here she knew it had all ended.

When you've lost everything, what are you?

A tiny thought flickered across her brain, as though struggling to pierce through her sorrow.

Maybe you're free.

Freedom didn't feel so good. She still had too much hurt inside of her that was begging for release. It felt like a volcano of agony bubbling right below the surface, white, hot, and unbearably powerful. Somehow, she knew if she didn't find a way to get it out she would explode, have a stroke or something. What she needed was some help—from anywhere!

Gathering all her sorrow, she felt she had to do something, even if it were merely symbolic. With every ounce of strength and willpower she possessed, Suzanne McDermott threw that wedding band, that symbol of a lie, as far over the sparkling water as she could. Screw love. The only love she knew to be true was what she felt for the child she carried beneath her heart. As she tried to follow the path of the ring, again the sun almost blinded her as it reflected off the surface of the water and for just a moment she thought she saw something, a large fish or—

"What the hell is that?" she whispered in disbelief.

With no more time to wonder, she jumped with fright. Only a few yards from her, a creature suddenly lunged out of the water, gasped for breath and splashed back down. Instinctively, she retreated and almost tripped on an exposed root on the embankment. Regaining her balance, Suzanne caught her breath and squinted back out at the water. Shielding her eyes from the bright sun, she tried to find the place where she had just seen . . . whatever it was.

There! A dark lump was floating on the water and she craned her neck to see better. All thoughts of her own miserable situation fled as she began to make out the form.

It was a body!

"Hey," she yelled, trying to quell the panic escalating inside her. "Hey! Are you okay?"

Immediately she realized what a ridiculous question that was and slowly stepped to the water's edge. She could now see it was a man. He was floating closer to her with the tide and her heart started thudding harder against her rib cage. He was alive. She'd seen him gasp for breath. He'd probably been swimming by and her ring had struck him and—

Wait a minute. People don't go swimming fully clothed ... *Stop wondering and react!* If she didn't pull him out of there, he might drown, and with the way her luck was running, the last thing she needed was a dead man! With no thought for herself, Suzanne clumsily waded into the cool, shallow water until she could grab his boot.

She felt her sandals sink into the silty bottom and cold water lap around her exposed legs. Ignoring the sensations, she pulled with all her might on his pant leg and, as his body turned over, he choked for more breath. It was evident to her now that his time was running out, so she did the only thing she could and grabbed the front of his white shirt. Her brain barely registered that the man's complexion was pale gray and as soon as the water cleared from his face, a wound at his temple began to bleed.

"Shit!" She didn't mean to hit him with her ring! She hadn't seen him in the water; the sun had blinded her for a split second just as she threw the damn thing!

Grasping his collar, she dragged him toward the shore. She felt every muscle in her body straining with herculean effort. She barely noticed one of her sandals being suctioned off her foot in the muck as she struggled.

When she finally had his torso out of the water, she let him go and knelt next to him. Panting, Suzanne turned her head and tried to see if he was breathing. She couldn't tell. Immediately, she crawled closer to him and went into action as every TV emergency show she'd seen flashed through her brain. After wiping her mouth on her sleeve, she slid her hand behind his neck and tilted his head back. Pinching his nose with her other hand, she gasped in a deep breath and then blew into his mouth. Over and over she gulped air and blew into his passageway, watching his chest rise with each exchange. Okay, his airway was obviously clear. She didn't need to do CPR . . . or did she? Damn, she always meant to get it straight in her head.

With one more breath into his mouth, Suzanne felt his body spasm and she lifted her face just as the man gurgled water and started coughing. She pulled back and turned his face away to let him spit out the river water. Relief spread over her entire body and she gasped for air along with him.

"Thank goodness," she breathed. "You'll be all right now."

He slowly opened his eyes and looked up at her, before turning on his shoulder and coughing some more.

"What happened? What the hell happened?" he rasped out after several moments. "I'm alive?"

"Yes, very much alive."

"What were you doing?" He hung his head as he coughed more water onto the ground.

"Doing? You mean CPR?"

He gasped for breath to fill his lungs. "Kissing me."

Feeling a bit shocked, she sputtered, "I wasn't kissing you! I was saving your life."

"I'm sorry," he mumbled, as he again glanced up at her and after several moments added, "Thank you."

He coughed a few more times and she could see the color returning to his cheeks. In seconds her mind registered that he appeared to be in his mid-thirties, had a long, lean build, an attractive face, and the most startling green eyes she had ever seen. His wet hair had glints of auburn that were highlighted by the afternoon sun. His expression appeared sincere, even though blood was trickling down the side of his face. And if she wasn't mistaken, he also had a slight Irish accent.

"You're welcome," she answered, then added, "though maybe I should be apologizing to you." Suddenly, she was distracted by the sensation of something warm seeping down between her legs.

"Why would you need to—" He coughed.

Before he could finish, she interrupted, "I think I may have hit you with my ring."

"Your ring?" he gasped, still catching his breath.

She nodded, trying to ignore the tensing of her abdominal muscles. "My wedding ring. I . . . I threw it into the water when you were swimming. Listen, I've got to get out of this mud." Focusing on getting to drier land, she was vaguely aware of the man staring at her.

"Are you all right, ma'am?" He turned on his side and wiped his bloody temple on his shirtsleeve.

"I don't know," Suzanne sputtered, as she shuffled on all fours to the grass. A strange cramping began at the small of her back and was wrapping around her hanging belly. Turning her head to the man who was now crawling toward her, she muttered, "But you need to see a doctor."

"I think you may need one more than I do," he breathed back, collapsing on the lush green knoll. "You're bleeding too."

"I'm what?" Startled, Suzanne grabbed up the front of her dress and was shocked to see bloody water trickling down her legs. "Oh my God, this can't be happening now! It's . . . it's too early!"

"Early?"

She looked at him as though he were either blind or just stupid. "I'm pregnant! But my due date isn't until the twenty-ninth!"

Charles Garrity stared at the strange woman next to him who was kneeling on all fours, gasping for breath, and appearing as though she was about to become hysterical at any moment. He looked back out to the river and couldn't see the railroad bridge. Wondering how far he had floated before she'd found him, he glanced around at his surroundings and, as his gaze fell upon a piece of red machinery, he felt his jaw dropping in awe.

"What is that?" he whispered, lifting his hand and pointing to it.

The woman raised her head and looked in the direction of his hand. "It's my car, what do you think it is?" she demanded impatiently while glaring at him. "Look, I need some help here. You think you can make it to the car and get my purse? I have a cell phone. I need to call nine-one-one and get an ambulance here right away. I am not going to have my baby in the mud!"

He glanced back into her frightened blue eyes. "What are you talking about?"

"I'm talking about getting help! I'm in labor here!" She again pointed to the large red metal piece of machinery. "Get my purse!"

"Your purse?"

"In the car."

"The car? That's an automobile?"

Still kneeling on all fours, she appeared exasperated as she lifted one hand and pushed the short curly blond hair back from her face. She then spoke to him slowly and deliberately. "Just . . . go . . . in . . . the car . . . and get . . . my . . . purse." She took a deep breath before adding quickly, "or help me to stand and I'll damn well do it myself!"

"All right. I get it. I'm not lame," he muttered, pushing himself upright. Once on his feet, he couldn't seem to find his balance and nearly fell back down.

"Oh, geez . . . what a pair we are. You're worse off than I am!" the woman exclaimed. "Here, help me up."

He turned to her and grabbed her outstretched hand. Using all his strength, Charles managed to get her upright as they awkwardly balanced each other.

Grasping the front of his shirt, she looked into his eyes and whispered, "Who are you, anyway?"

"Charles Garrity, ma'am. And thank you again . . . for pulling me out of the river." He didn't know what else to say to this confusing female and he certainly had no idea what to do with a woman about to give birth.

She nodded, threading her arm through his and leaning against him as she used her other hand to cradle her extended belly. "I'm Suzanne. Suzanne McDermott. Now let's just make it to the car so both of us can get some help."

Charles kept looking at the odd automobile. He'd paid almost five hundred dollars for a Ford Model T, but this fantastic machine in front of him was like nothing he had ever seen or imagined. He couldn't contain his amazement any longer. "You drove this?"

"Of course I drove it," she shot back, suddenly stopping and bending forward again, obviously in a great deal of pain.

Instantly, Charles reached down behind her legs and, with a grunt, he swept her up into his arms.

"No! Wait! You'll drop me!" she yelped, clutching so tightly around his neck and shoulders that he nearly stumbled again. The two of them swayed back and forth, teetering on the edge of a fall, until he righted his shoulders.

"Just stay still, ease up, and we'll make it," he gritted out between clenched teeth as he lurched forward, concentrating on placing one foot in front of the other.

As they approached the machine, Charles took one last step and set her down as gently as he could next to it. She leaned over the hood and breathed deeply, as though she too was exhausted by the effort.

"Thanks. Okay, could you grab my purse? The cell phone is in it."

"Cell-phone?"

"My portable telephone?" She glanced up at him and impatiently waved her hand to the interior. "Just open the door and give me my purse, please."

Portable telephone? What the hell was she talking about?

He pulled on the metal latch and stared in wonder as the

door opened easily and exposed the luxurious interior. There were rich leather seats, a control panel that was absolutely fantastic, and large windows all around. A leather-encased lever between the—

"Look on the floor." She interrupted his survey.

He did as he was asked, running his hand over the thick pile carpeting. "I don't see it," he yelled back to her.

"Look in the back, behind the driver's seat."

Again, he did as asked, still marveling at the expansive room and comfort of this incredible vehicle. Where had this woman gotten such a thing? "There's nothing here," he said, coming back out to see her now leaning against the front fender, with arms cradling her belly, as though willing the baby to stay put.

"Shit, shit, shit! I ran out of the house without it," she gasped. "Now what am I going to do? How in the hell are we going to get help?"

Although startled by her language, he offered, "Ma'am, I'll help any way I can."

He watched as she stared at him.

"Okay," she quickly directed. "Get the keys and go into the trunk. There's a large, blue bag in there."

He simply stared right back at her. "The keys?"

"On the seat. I know I left them there."

He looked back into the car and saw a ring of keys on the driver's seat. Leaning in once again, he scooped them up and hurried to the rear of the vehicle. When he turned the key in the lock, the whole panel swung up and he quickly leaned back to avoid the metal lid. Still marveling at the construction of this exceptional machine, he spied the shiny fabric bag and grabbed the web straps. "Got it."

Bringing it around to the front of the vehicle, he placed it on the hood.

"Thank heavens I had enough sense to pack this thing last week," she muttered, opening the bag and rummaging through it. She took out something white and handed it to him. "Here, open this and use it on your head."

It was made out of a shiny white material he had never seen. Unfolding it, he touched something that had the softness of fabric, yet wasn't. "What is it?"

"What's it look like? A diaper."

"A diaper?"

"Why do you repeat everything I say? Yes, a disposable diaper. Just stick it on your head."

"My head? Stick a diaper on my head?"

"Ohh . . ." She waddled the three feet separating them and grabbed the thing out of his hands. Flipping it open, she pulled on some tabs and then wrapped the thing around his forehead, roughly patting the sticky tabs onto his wet hair. "There, that should hold for a while . . . at least to stop the bleeding. Now, you're going to have to drive us to the hospital."

"I am?" Pushing the damn diaper against his wound, he glanced away and hated to admit that he was intimidated by the sheer complexity of the machine.

In spite of everything, Suzanne couldn't hold back a giggle as she looked at the soaking wet man standing in front of her. He did look ridiculous. "Yes, you are. You have driven a car before, haven't you? Damn, that would just be my luck . . . dripping wet, filthy, in labor, with a wounded man who can't get me to a hospital!"

"I've driven an automobile," he insisted, straightening his backbone.

"Good," Suzanne answered, picking up the maternity bag and attempting to walk toward the back door of the SUV. She felt like her legs weren't working correctly and she had to waddle. Waddle! How much more bizarre and embarrassing could this get? "Let's get out of here. I want a doctor around when my baby arrives."

"Here, let me help you," he said, wrapping his arm around

what was left of her waist and assisting her. When they managed to get her onto the backseat, he stood panting.

Suzanne looked up at the man with a glazed expression on his face and a baby's diaper wrapped around his head. The two of them must truly be a sight and she almost laughed out loud at the mental image. The poor guy seemed frozen and quite unsure of the entire situation. She felt like she was instructing a child as she patiently began rattling off instructions. "Close the trunk and then get in the driver's seat. C'mon, let's go!"

He nodded and closed the door. She watched through the windows as he slammed the trunk and hurried to the driver's side. He opened the door and stared at the seat.

"Get in," she commanded, as another contraction captured her in a vise of pain.

"You mean I don't have to—"

"Get in!"

He did as he was instructed and then didn't move.

"Well?"

"Well, what?"

"Oh please, do not tell me you don't know what to do!" she gasped.

"Well, I've never driven an automobile like . . . well, like this before," he grumbled.

"Okay, what kind of car *have* you driven?" This was not possible! How could her luck be this bad?

"A Model T."

"What?"

"A Ford Model T."

"Oh, gimme a break here."

He swung around in the seat and glared at her. "Look, I'm trying to help. You could try too. Just tell me what to do!"

Suzanne held her lower abdomen with both hands and grunted through the next contraction. "Okay, just listen, we don't have much time. Put the key into the ignition and fire this thing up!"

"Where's the—"

"On the side of the steering column, there, on the right," she said, pointing as he fumbled for a moment then sat back once the key was inserted. "Okay, now turn it . . . toward the dashboard."

A wave of relief swept over her as the engine cranked and the motor began humming.

"This is astounding," he said with a breath of awe.

"Yeah, I'm astounded. I'm the textbook definition of *backseat driver* here," she muttered, hugging her belly.

"Huh?"

"Forget it. Just push down on the big pedal on the right." She watched as he did what he was told and the engine raced.

"Gently!" she shouted over the roar.

"Okay, okay. Now what?"

"I meant put your foot on the brake, shift it into reverse, and back outta here."

"Put what into reverse?"

Suzanne groaned with the realization that this man really didn't know how to drive a modern car. "That lever in the middle—right there at your side. Push the black button on top with your thumb and shift the stick back to where the red *R* is. That's reverse. Then use the gas pedal again to go." She grabbed a baby blanket from the bag and was stuffing it between her legs as the car was swiftly thrust backward.

"Stop! Hit the brakes, the brakes!" Suzanne yelped, pressing one hand against the back of the front seat.

The car immediately jerked to a halt, throwing her back against her seat.

"I'm sorry," he said, his face reddening as he adjusted the diaper at his temple. "Okay, how do I go forward now?"

Righting herself, she muttered, "Maybe I should drive. I don't need to be treated for whiplash too."

"No, really. I can do it," he insisted. "Just tell me."

The tone of his voice wasn't any real assurance, but what other choice did she have? Resigning herself to the situation, she sighed. "Fine. Just remember you have a very pregnant woman back here, so lighten up on the lead foot, okay?"

"Yeah, okay."

"Now, put the gear shift into drive—the *D*."

"Okay. *R* is for reverse, *D* is for drive, you say? Okay. That makes sense."

He sounded as though he was trying to convince himself, rather than her, of his driving skills.

"None of this makes sense, Charlie . . . none of it! How could you not know how to drive a car? Where have you been living? In a cave?"

"I told you I know how to drive, just not one like this where there's no clutch. Now, be quiet so I can concentrate."

Suzanne's mouth hung open at the statement. Now was not the time for an argument. Now she had to get to a hospital. The car moved forward in slow, broken lurches, at speeds of only ten miles an hour, and she found she just couldn't shut up.

"You know, you can go faster than this. You're going to *have* to go faster than this or I'll be having the baby on the backseat!"

He must have hit every single rut on the back country road. Suzanne grunted, gasped, grabbed his shoulder, and pleaded through it all. When they finally came to the main road, he stopped the car even though there were several times when he could have safely merged into traffic.

"What's wrong? Why aren't we going?" she demanded.

Charles Garrity stared at the unbelievable spectacle before him. Automobiles of every color and size whizzed past him with more speed than he'd ever imagined. White-knuckling the steering wheel, immense dread spread throughout his already tense body. Something was wrong. *Very* wrong, for this was no place he'd ever been before. Not in his day and age . . .

"Where the hell am I?" he demanded.

2

"**W**hat do you mean, where are you? You're in New Jersey."

"Where in New Jersey? What *is* all this?"

"This? It's Route Thirty-eight." She shoved his shoulder. "We're at a yield, not a stop. C'mon, there's people backing up behind us. Go."

"But they're all traveling so fast."

She stared at the back of his head as she held the blanket between her legs. If he didn't look ridiculous with a diaper slipping off it, she would have smacked his skull. "Step on it!" She looked to her left and saw the road was empty. *"Now!"*

He cautiously turned the car onto the highway and Suzanne breathed easier until she realized they were traveling at about twenty miles an hour. "Will you *please* drive faster? The speed limit is fifty here, and I really *need* to get to the hospital."

She felt the engine accelerate and took hope. Maybe his odd behavior had to do with his head wound and loss of blood. And maybe he was as much in need of a hospital visit as she was.

"What are those signs?" he asked, nodding toward the billboards.

"Advertisements." One was for a casino at the Jersey shore with the digital amounts of winnings blinking furiously. "You haven't ever seen them? How long have you been in this country?"

"I've been here for almost twenty years and I've never seen anything like that. How do the numbers keep changing so quickly?"

"I don't know. It's a computer chip, or something. Can you go faster?" she pleaded as another contraction wrapped around her even more tightly.

"I am going fast!" he protested.

She looked over his shoulder at the speedometer. "You're only going forty miles an hour. Do at least sixty-five."

"What? I thought the purpose of this was get you to a hospital safely."

"Please!"

He sped up and Suzanne gripped the front seat as the contraction eased. "Where are you from, Charlie? Ireland?" she asked, desperate to get her mind off her situation.

"Well, many years ago I was. I've just bought an fair-sized piece of land in Mount Laural."

"Really? What are you going to build, a house?" So many builders were streaming into the area and constructing executive homes. It's why Kevin had made a financial killing when he'd sold off their land.

"Eventually. My objective is to plant fruit trees, apple and peach, and market the harvest."

She stared at him. "Fruit trees?" All those acres of fruit trees that she had so loved were now plowed over by a steam shovel and big, carbon-copy houses with barren land took their place. "I wish you luck," she whispered, as they approached a traffic light. "Slow down. *Stop!* It's a red light!"

The car screeched to a stop and Suzanne was practically in the front seat with him when the momentum suddenly ended and she fell back onto her seat. "What were you thinking?" she demanded.

"I didn't know I was supposed to stop," he explained, looking back at her. "Are you all right?"

"What do you mean you didn't know? Where the hell are you from?"

"I'm from a place that certainly doesn't have any of this . . . these things, that's where! A place where there isn't this madness! Now, why don't you tell me something. Where in the hell am I?"

Something about the way he said it made the hairs on Suzanne's neck rise. "Okay, calm down. You're in Mount Laural, New Jersey. I thought you said you live here."

"I got here a few months ago, but when I arrived it looked nothing like this!"

"Well, I don't know what part you've seen, but this is how Mount Laural has looked for about the last forty years. Not a lot's changed, except for the shopping centers and all the housing developments."

Suzanne watched as the man's face became suddenly pale.

"Something is very wrong here," he mumbled as he peered out the windows. "This is all surreal."

"Look, Charlie," she began in a soothing tone, "this is all very real. There are no Model T Fords, except in museums and antique car shows. This is the modern world. You know . . . modern, as in the new millennium?"

Please, please let there be some sign of recognition, she mentally pleaded.

"What are you talking about?" he demanded. "The new century passed twenty-six years ago."

Wait a minute. Maybe that gash on his temple had given him amnesia or something. "Ah, I don't think so, Charlie. It's only two thousand one."

He stared back at her as though she were the demented one. "I beg to differ, ma'am. It's nineteen twenty-six by my calendar."

She took a deep breath, as she felt another contraction begin its slow grip on her. "Please, Charlie, you can't have a nervous breakdown on me now. If *anyone* on this planet deserves one, it's me, and if I can't have one, you can't either. Got it? Now, get ready, the light is about to change."

She watched as he blinked a few times, as though he were attempting to digest her words, and then he noticed the other cars on either side of them. "Got it?" she repeated, hoping he wasn't going to completely freak out on her. As the traffic light changed, the car behind them beeped its horn.

She nearly jumped with fright as he suddenly spun around, tore the diaper from his head, grabbed the steering wheel and slammed his foot onto the accelerator. The car raced ahead of the others and Suzanne, shocked by his sudden take-charge attitude, once more clutched the seat for balance and held her breath.

Charlie was right about one thing: This was definitely surreal.

As he maneuvered through three more traffic lights, weaving around cars and lane changes, and finally a jug handle that took them across the highway, she continuously reminded herself to remain calm and to keep breathing. Through all her instructions, he never said another word or even looked back at her. The man appeared almost automated and did only as he was directed. Within ten minutes they pulled in front of the hospital as a mixture of pain and relief spread over Suzanne and tears streamed down her cheeks. She had never in her life been on such a crazy ride, but he had done it. "Stop there, where it says 'Emergency,' " she instructed, feeling her heartbeat in her ears.

They came to a halt right by the door and he turned off the ignition. The car died without being put into park and he then sat frozen, just staring out the front window, as though in shock.

"Yo, Charlie?"

Her voice seemed to snap him out of it and he bolted out of the car to help her.

"Yes. We're here now. The doctors can help you."

As the car door opened, she looked into his green eyes and smiled with relief. "Thank you, Charles Garitty," she whispered with a sigh. "You did it. You're my hero."

He appeared slightly self-conscious as he held out his hand to her. "Come along now, don't turn all mushy on me. I was rather fond of that feisty side of you." His smile was almost tender and meant to be reassuring.

Suzanne awkwardly slid toward the door and nearly collapsed against his arm. She felt as though everything was rushing out of her when she stood upright. "I'm so sorry for all this," she gasped in embarrassment. "You know, you should have someone look at your head while you're here."

"Forget about my head. It's stopped bleeding anyway." He wrapped his arms around her and, practically holding her body up, he moved slowly with her exhausted pace. "Careful, there's a step up here."

Suzanne looked down to see the yellow painted curb and gingerly stepped up.

"Besides, I really think someone needs to take care of you," he added with a smile.

It was his last words, spoken so honestly, that did her in as everything she had been holding back came to the surface. She couldn't help it. She started crying, really crying. "Yes. I need somebody to take care of me, Charlie," she sobbed, knowing she sounded pathetic, yet unable to stop the fear from spreading through her body. "Right now I have no one."

His arm around her shoulder tightened. "Where's your husband?"

"Probably off with my best friend. He left me for her today. Just told me he's in love with my best friend and . . . oh God," she gasped, as another deep contraction took control of her body.

"Somebody help us here!" he yelled to the large glass doors.

He stopped and stared at them as they slid open and attendants rushed to close the space. "Amazing," he breathed.

Suzanne didn't have time to analyze his reaction as she was put into a wheelchair and rushed into the emergency area. Reaching behind, she shouted, "Don't leave, Charlie. Stay with me . . . for a while . . . please?"

A male nurse turned to him and said, "Everything's under control now, sir. But you're going to have to move your car. It's in an unloading zone."

"Charlie!" Suzanne hated that her voice sounded so scared. The moment she had been praying for was here, and now she was terrified of what awaited her. She always thought her husband and her best friend would be there for support. Neither of those choices were available now. She truly was all alone, except for this extremely strange man who had appeared out of nowhere. She turned in the chair and looked back for a friendly face.

When their eyes met it was as though he read her thoughts, for the knot in Charles's stomach tightened as he glared back at the man in the light green smock. "You move it. I'm not leaving her."

"Sir, you can be with your wife as soon as she's been examined and put in a labor room. Now you'll have to move your car immediately, or it will be towed."

Denied access to the building and left to watch dumbly as Suzanne was taken beyond another set of doors, Charles suddenly felt helpless. His mind raced back to when she'd found him by the water. She'd saved his life. Even though he'd only just met her, his integrity told him he owed Suzanne a lot more. Charles Garitty had never been the kind of man to leave anyone who'd asked for his help, and he wasn't about to start now. Ignoring the man in the doorway, Charles stepped forward.

"Wait. It seems you've been hurt yourself," the man said, raising his hand in an attempt to stop him.

Glancing down at the man's hand on his shoulder, Charles then stared hard at the man's face. "I'm fine. She needs my help. I'm going to her now."

"Please, sir," the man said sympathetically, dropping his hand, but still blocking the doorway. "Babies are born every day. It's going to take a little while to prep your wife, but she'll be fine. All you've got to do is park your car over there," he said, pointing in the direction, "where it says 'Visitor Parking,' and then come right back."

Charles looked over to where the man had instructed. It didn't seem too far away.

"And when you come back, I'll get you a bandage and you can use the men's room to clean up your wound. Afterward, you can be with her again, I promise."

Charles looked back at the man. "All right," he relented. After all, he mentally reasoned, she was in a hospital with doctors, and he really didn't want to cause any trouble since he was in *very* unfamiliar territory. He nodded his thanks and turned back to the car.

Within minutes he had managed to park between two white lines in a huge open area and was now standing at a sink with a faucet and no knobs in the men's room of the hospital. The male nurse had given him a thin bandage wrapped in paper, and another clear package with what appeared to be a cotton ball soaked in brown liquid. Ignoring his own disheveled reflection in the mirror, he tore open the cotton ball with antiseptic, at least that's what he hoped it was, as it began staining his fingers. Dabbing at his forehead, he grit his teeth and inhaled as the stinging sensation began.

Damn Mitch, he thought, and couldn't suppress the hiss as more medicine entered the cut. Dismissing the pain, he blot-

ted up the excess liquid around the gash and then tore open
the bandage. Before putting it on, he wouldn't mind wiping
his face to get some of the blood off it, but for the life of him
he couldn't figure out how to turn on the water without any
knobs. To his surprise when he simply touched the bottom of
the faucet to examine it, water came pouring out—all by itself!

He looked once more into the mirror and stared into his
eyes as a wave of dread spread through his body. Something
was really, really wrong here. He'd never seen or heard of
such inventions. Automobiles that were beyond mechanical
belief. Lights and signs on roads he'd never imagined. A hospital building, the likes of which he'd never seen, and now
water coming magically out of a faucet with no levers or
knobs. Everyone he'd met seemed to take it all for granted,
yet it was nothing he was accustomed to. Ever since Suzanne
had pulled him from the water nothing was the same. It was
all out of place. He'd already considered he might be hallucinating or maybe dreaming since he'd passed out when he
jumped from that bridge, but he'd never dreamed anything
this vividly before.

Shaking his head, he bent down and splashed water over
his face and neck, hoping it would provide some clarity to his
situation. Okay, he didn't know where he was, but maybe he
could rationalize how he'd gotten here. He mentally began
recounting the facts as he knew them to be. He and Mitch had
been taking some measurements on the land he'd just purchased, and were walking back to town. They were discussing how many trees to start with in the lower portion of
the orchard. Then, while crossing the trestle railroad bridge,
Mitch suddenly pulled a gun from his jacket and demanded
the property deed. Charles again shook his head with disbelief. If he weren't so confused now, he'd have the strength to
be angry. Splashing more water on his face, he closed his
eyes and exhaled deeply as the pain of his longtime friend's
betrayal began to sink in.

Slowly looking up at his reflection in the mirror, he saw beads of water dripping from his face as his mind flashed back to the Rancocas Creek. He remembered turning and jumping, all the while praying he wouldn't be torn to pieces by the beams before he hit the water. He heard a shot ring out and felt the searing pain in his head. He saw flashes of light, like brilliant explosions on the water that nearly blinded him. He recalled closing his eyes and . . . and then he guessed he'd blacked out.

"Shit. I can't remember anything after that." His whisper echoed in the sterile room. Suddenly feeling self-conscious, he looked around and was relieved to find he was still alone.

Immediately, he thought of the woman who had breathed life back into him. He was certainly grateful, and he would repay her somehow but, quite frankly, he had to conclude Suzanne was rather odd. Model Ts in museums? She had to have been overcome with delirium from labor pains, he mused. And when she had said it was the year 2001, she looked at him as though *he* were a lunatic!

Silence filled the room as the water stopped flowing and Charles stood, blankly staring at his own reflection. His eyes widened as though he'd heard a nagging voice from some unknown place and the words came back to him.

The year *2001!*

That's impossible.

Every muscle in his body became rigid as he felt his blood blast from his toes to his head and back down again. Each rapid beat of his heart sent sledgehammers to his brain. He felt rage beginning to boil inside him, and with every ounce of effort he could gather in an attempt to calm himself, he slowly unfurled his clenched hands. It wasn't enough. He wanted to scream out in denial for everything that was happening to him. Why had his best friend turned on him? Who were all these crazy people around him? Why was everything so different? Where in the hell had his life gone?

Breathe, Charles. Inhaling slowly and deeply, he obeyed

his conscience. With steel determination, he glared into the eyes of the opposing reflection. He knew he was on the brink, but this time, he wasn't going to jump. This time, he was going to stand his ground.

Don't think about it any longer, he mentally commanded himself. Just go out and do it. Just deny the insanity and simply go along with everyone and everything until you figure out a way to get back and take care of Mitch.

Right now he had to pull it together not only for himself, but for someone who'd asked for his help, someone to whom he owed a great deal. He might be precariously balanced on the edge of madness now, but being with Suzanne would be enough to take his mind off from his own pain and anger.

Okay, finish up here, make yourself somewhat presentable, and find her, he encouraged himself. He thought back to the moment when they'd stared at each other as she was being wheeled down the hall. He had to admit, he'd felt an unexplainable tug at his heart that was so strong, he knew he couldn't desert her while she was so alone and scared. The least he could do was not leave until he knew she was okay. He'd have time to figure out how to repay her later.

"Lady Luck has always been on your side, Charles Garrity," he said with a forced wink to the mirror.

His regained confidence nearly flew out the door when it swung open and a hospital worker walked in. The man hesitated for a moment, and Charles hoped he hadn't overheard his conceit. He looked down to where the man was staring. His blood-stained shirt. He wished he had a way to wash it too, but he didn't want to waste any more time. With his hands still held out and dripping, Charlie smiled and shrugged at the man, to convey there was nothing more he could do. The fellow said nothing and passed him to enter a stall.

Turning quickly to find something with which to dry his hands, he saw there were paper hand towels on the wall and he pulled out a few to wipe his hands and face. He picked up the bandage from the sink and played with it for a few moments until he figured out how to make it stick. Once it was in place, he ran his fingers through his hair and walked out.

"There you are," the male nurse exclaimed. "Here. Change into this and I'll direct you to the labor rooms. Don't want to miss the big moment, right?"

"Ah, right," Charles answered, holding the green paper shirt in his hand as he followed the fellow down a hallway.

"Hurry up, man. They're never going to let you into maternity with all that blood on you."

Charles began unbuttoning his soiled shirt as they continued their brisk walk. He'd been in a hospital once before. He'd gone to visit Mitch after the kid had taken some shrapnel in his side during the war and then had spent some time as a patient himself after being wounded. But like everything else he'd encountered so far today, this hospital was nothing like what he'd ever seen before. The amount of light was so overwhelming he had to squint. There were strange pinging noises coming from every room they passed. Insistent voices from the ceiling requested doctors by name and gave instructions for them to pick up lines. Charles looked down at the highly polished floor. At least it appeared very clean and the stench of sulphur wasn't wafting through the air.

"Hang on. You've got it backward. Here, let me help you."

He felt like a child as the man turned the paper shirt around and tied it behind him.

"So, what are you having, a boy or a girl?"

"Huh?" Charles gasped, trying to spin around to face the man.

"Do you know what the baby is?"

"I . . . I have no idea. In fact, it's not—"

"Careful, these things can rip pretty easily," the nurse interrupted. "They just don't make 'em like they used to," he continued almost absentmindedly before adding, "You seem pretty nervous. This must be your first."

"Yeah, you could say that," Charles sighed in resignation. What was the use in trying to explain the unexplainable?

"There," the man said with a pat to his back. "Okay, go through those doors and tell them your wife's name. They'll take you right to her."

"Um, sure. My wife. Yes, thank you," Charles mumbled, still in shock by what was happening so quickly.

"Hey, I've got two sons myself. Good luck."

Left for a moment standing idly in front of the double doors, he reached out to push one, when both seemed to open magically. One more marvel to add to the many he had already experienced. Shaking his head, he whispered under his breath, "Just do it." Stepping beyond the doors, he saw two women at a circular desk.

"Can I help you, sir?" one older woman asked.

He cleared his throat and tried to remember Suzanne's last name. "Yes, a woman was just brought here. Suzanne Mc . . . McDermott." There. That was it, wasn't it?

The nurse looked down to her desk. "Yes. She's in room three. I see from the preadmission forms that you're signed up for natural childbirth. Do you have her bag?"

"Her bag?" he asked stupidly.

"Yes, her maternity bag."

"Oh, yes. The bag. It's still in the car."

"Well, let me take you to her and see if she wants you to get it." The woman gently patted his shoulder as she passed. "Come along."

He followed her down the hallway and overheard a woman's voice groaning in pain. The blood seemed to drain from his head and he lectured himself to be strong. If he could make it through a world war in a foreign country, he could certainly make it through this!

"Here we are," the nurse cheerily proclaimed, holding open a door.

He walked through it and saw Suzanne lying upon the high bed with bars on the sides.

"Here's your handsome husband, Suzanne. He looks shell shocked. You might want to go over your breathing exercises to bring him back."

Suzanne, looking freshened and dressed in a yellow gown, smiled politely at the nurse. "I will," she said. "Thank you for bringing him."

"I'll be back to check you in a few minutes. You seem to be proceeding nicely."

"When will I see my doctor? I'm two weeks early, remember?"

"He's been beeped. He'll be here soon."

When they were left alone, they looked at each other for a few moments in silence. Charles smiled and asked, "How are you?"

"Better, now that I'm here. Look, I'm sorry for everything, for the way I acted, for yelling at you . . . all of it." She looked as if she was about to burst into tears again, before adding, "And for letting everyone think you're my husband. It's kind of childish of me not to tell the truth, but the truth is so ugly and . . ." Her words trailed off.

He shook his head and walked closer to the bed. "It's okay."

"I just don't want to be alone, you know?"

He nodded. "I said it's all right. Don't you think you should contact him, though?"

"I will not speak to him now," she gritted out between her teeth, as she wiped away a tear. "He doesn't deserve to know. If he cared so much he wouldn't have walked out and . . . oh God, here's another one!"

She reached out her hand and he took hold of it as he watched her being pulled into some great torrent of pain. Her pretty face became contorted and deep red. The veins in her neck strained with the effort as she moaned. It was reminiscent of the times he'd felt helpless watching soldiers who'd been shot in the gut as they waited in the muddy trenches for a medic. Her intense grip on his hand lessened as she seemed to crest over the worst of it and slide back to some amount of comfort.

"They're getting stronger," she gasped with a weak smile as she let go of his hand. "I guess I should try those breathing exercises with the next one."

"Good idea," he answered, wondering how she could be so strong. Her dark blond hair was damp with exertion and her wide blue eyes looked scared. His heart went out to her and he tried to smile reassuringly. "Women have been having babies since, well, forever. You'll do fine, Suzanne."

"You think?" she asked hopefully.

"I know," he replied, leaning on the metal railing. "That nurse said you might want me to get your bag. Should I?"

She grabbed his shirt. "Don't leave me, okay? I mean, you don't have to stay through the whole thing, but just don't go right now. I know I sound like a baby about all this, but nothing is turning out the way I'd planned." Releasing him, she ran her fingers through her hair. "Like who plans on having their husband tell them about his affair with their best friend and then hitting a man with their wedding ring and dragging him out of the river?" She looked up to him as she let him go. "How's your head?"

"It's fine," Charles said, deciding now was not the time to let this woman know it was a bullet that had grazed his temple, not her ring. "A man gave me a bandage and this shirt."

Suzanne looked to the green paper shirt and tears started once more. "I'm so sorry for getting you messed up with all this."

"Hey, you saved my life. Don't be sorry."

She appeared to shrug that off as she waved her hand. "Anybody would have done it. I'm glad you're okay."

Okay. He mentally refuted the word. He was definitely not okay. He had no idea *where* the hell he was and how he had gotten here, nor how to get back to normalcy. He had business to take care of and a score to settle.

"I'm really sorry about everything. I guess I didn't want to admit to anyone else that I'd been abandoned. Kinda cowardly, huh?"

"I'm indebted and grateful to you, Suzanne. And you shouldn't be worrying about what anyone else thinks right now. I'll stay with you as long as you want. I owe you that."

She stared into his eyes for the longest time and then started crying again. "You're a very nice man, Charles Garrity, even if you drive a car like a maniac."

He chuckled for the first time in a long while. "Hey, I got you here, didn't I?"

"Yes, you did and . . . oh God . . . it's starting again! I should be breathing and . . . and I can't!" She panted and blew air out of her mouth and then muttered, *"It's not working!"*

He continued to hold her hand, even though she was clutching him so hard he was sure his fingers would be numb when she let go. "You are breathing, Suzanne," he said, trying to reassure her and stop her near hysteria from escalating.

"Not . . . not the right breathing," she again muttered through the instances of pain, her face a grimace of agony before she gratefully collapsed back onto the pillow with relief.

When she released his hand, he too took a deep breath and began looking around at all the machines in the room. His mind was too overwhelmed to ask questions and he didn't think Suzanne would appreciate his curiosity at the moment. "You're all right?" he asked with concern.

She nodded. "I have to get this under control. I'm supposed to breathe in short gasps and concentrate on something. I bought this tiny angel and that was supposed to be my focal point and—" She started crying again.

"Tell me what to do," he said, patting her arm in a feeble attempt to comfort her. Shit, how could he be so useless? How the hell did he get to be in this room with a woman who was about to deliver a baby? He knew what to do in a war. He also knew what to do with that sonofabitch Mitch Davies. But here and now, he was more than completely lost.

"All right," the nurse announced, interrupting his thoughts as she burst back into the room. "Your doctor has been notified and is on his way. Now, let's get this IV started and then hook you up to the fetal monitor."

Charles stood back as the nurse took over and he glanced away with an inward shudder when she inserted a long needle into Suzanne's hand. When he looked back, the woman was sticking a long narrow tube to it that was attached to a clear bag on a pole. What were they doing to Suzanne? She didn't appear to be protesting, so it must be all right. The nurse adjusted something on the needle and then walked in front of him to a machine. She picked up a long black belt with several wires attached and brought them to Suzanne.

"Let's hook you up and then your husband can monitor your contractions."

Within minutes, the machine was beeping quickly and the nurse instructed him how to tell when another contraction would begin. "See the way it's rising now?" she asked, pointing to a small window on the thing as Suzanne began to moan.

He nodded stupidly.

"I'll turn down the baby's heartbeat so that won't distract you."

Again, he simply nodded and then saw Suzanne looking at him with a panicked expression. He held out his hand and she grabbed it, panting and blowing and shaking her head.

"It's not working!" she moaned as the contraction began to build.

"But it is working," he answered, looking at the confusing machine. "See?"

"I mean the damn breathing!" she yelled.

Startled, he glanced at the nurse, who shrugged and said, "You'd better help her. You're her coach, aren't you?"

"Her coach?"

"You really are rattled, huh?" the nurse asked with a grin,

as though she wasn't the least bit concerned with Suzanne's pain. "Go on, get in there and breathe with her."

"Oh, breathe. Coach her breathing." Damn it, he never felt more inept in his life. Deciding somebody in the room had to take charge, Charles said in a firm voice, "Now look at me, Suzanne. Let's breathe together. Come on, in," he said, drawing in a breath that puffed out his chest. "Now, out," he exhaled. "In . . . and out."

"No, like this," the nurse interrupted. "Heeee. Heeee. Hoooowwww."

"What?"

"Didn't they teach you anything in those classes? Do it. Heeee. Heeee. Long breath . . . Hooooowwww."

As insane as it all seemed, he started breathing as he was instructed and soon Suzanne was breathing along with him. He glanced at the machine. "It's going down now."

Suzanne nodded and sank back against the pillow, releasing his mangled hand.

"Okay, I'm going to examine you again, Suzanne," the nurse said when the contraction was over. She lifted the sheet and within moments peeked over Suzanne's knees. "Looks like we're progressing quickly. You're dilated to eight centimeters. It'll be any time now."

"What about my doctor?" Suzanne gasped, her face suddenly deathly white.

"Don't worry, I've delivered several babies without a doctor, but I'll call for a resident right now," she said, snapping off her strange rubbery-looking gloves and disposing of them in a basket by the door. "You two keep it up and do your part. We'll do ours."

The door gently closed behind her and Charles turned his head to look at Suzanne. Now, if possible, she looked even more scared.

"This baby's coming too quickly. I'm two weeks early. What if something's wrong?"

"Nothing is wrong, lass," he answered, stroking back the hair from her forehead. "The nurse didn't seem concerned at all."

"She didn't, did she?" Suzanne asked hopefully. "And I'm hardly a lass, but thanks for the sentiment."

He tried to smile. "The nurse just said you're progressing quickly. Isn't that a good thing?"

"I suppose it is," she mumbled. "I never knew it was going to be like this. Nobody really prepares you."

"I'm sure you're going to be just fine," he answered, glancing back at the machine. "Say, do you want a boy or a girl?" he asked, hoping to distract her.

"I'm having a boy. We found out months ago."

"What?" he looked back at her. "How could you know?"

"Tests. Ever hear of a sonogram?"

"No. Honestly, Suzanne, I haven't heard or seen anything that makes much sense to me today. Nothing. Not this . . . this place. These people. None of this."

"Look, Charlie . . . I already told you, neither of us is allowed a nervous breakdown, remember? Tomorrow we can both have one, just not right now," she insisted. "Do you have any children?"

"No. I'm not married."

She issued a sarcastic noise with her mouth. "Smart man. Truthfully, I don't know if I believe in it anymore. The whole family unit thing. I mean, what a joke. It was like I was hypnotized into believing that love and honor and marriage and family were the pot of gold at the end of a woman's rainbow. Just look at the statistics and you can see what a lie that is . . . and now I'm just another statistic. No husband. No love. No honor. No marriage. Just me and my baby. But we'll find our happiness together. We don't need a man for that!"

"You're angry," he whispered, knowing all too well the bitterness that can enter one's heart when one's been betrayed. He wished he could find the words that might soothe them both.

"You're right, I am angry. I have a right to be royally pissed off. I was duped."

He had known a few flappers in his time, women who flaunted society's standards, but Suzanne just didn't seem the type. Even though he'd only met her a few hours earlier, he'd detected her softer side. "I think you're hurt, lassie, and the way you're feeling is natural."

She stared at him and the wet film of tears appeared at her eyes again. "You know, if I really think about it, I might just lose my mind."

"Right now, I can definitely understand that, Suzanne. So don't think about it. Think about your son, who's going to be born today. Soon, you'll hold him in your arms. Surely, that will be your pot of gold."

"You're right. I don't know where you came from, Charles Garrity, but you're an answer to my prayers," she moaned.

He turned his head and watched the small window on the machine. "You're about to have another contraction," he advised in what he hoped was a calm voice.

"Brilliant deduction, Sherlock!" she muttered as she grabbed his hand again. "Like I need you and the damn machine to tell me that!"

It was obvious Suzanne didn't need to be soft now. Strength, however it manifested, would serve her better. Deciding it best not to be offended, Charles commanded, "Look at my face and breathe with me! Heeee. Heeee. Hoooowwww."

She stared into his eyes with such focus and determination that Charles felt like she was entering his mind and taking control. He even felt his body begin to tense, the muscles of his abdomen tightening along with hers. He kept breathing and staring and breathing. He was sure his face was as red as hers as together they rode out the crest of pain.

Suzanne collapsed once more against the pillows and sobbed. "I can't do this anymore," she cried. "It's like two steel claws are ripping me apart. Somebody help me. I want it all to go away. I want my normal life back. I want . . . I want *drugs*! Just knock me out and tell me when it's over!"

"Drugs? Like opium?"

"If you've got it, hand it over."

He couldn't help chuckling. "You can do this, Suzanne. You aren't alone. I promise I won't leave you."

She sniffled and opened her eyes. "When I was standing at the creek and feeling so alone, I asked for help and along you came. Thanks, Charles. Guess you never figured on this, huh? Standing in a labor room with a crazy woman?"

"Suzanne, you're right about one thing. I had no idea any of this was possible."

Neither of them said a word until Suzanne muttered, "Oh, God, here comes another one!"

He stroked back her hair once more and whispered, "C'mon, you can do it." This woman had saved his life and now, for some odd reason, it was of the utmost importance to him that he not let her down. "Let's ride this one out together."

And they did, over and over again, like two warriors united in battle, intent on victory, and the victory was life, a brand-new life.

3

She closed her eyes and inhaled deeply the sweet, soft innocent scent of him. There was such peace, such joy, and she knew it was all worth it to feel him outside her body, healthy, beautiful, precious. His head was nestled under her jaw and she turned slightly to kiss his tiny forehead.

"I love you, Matty," she whispered with a heart that was near bursting. "I made you a promise. Somehow . . . you and I . . . we'll make it."

She ran her hand over his small back and felt his breath going in and out of his little body as he slept on her chest. Even though he was almost two weeks early, the doctors had declared him healthy. How she was filled with love for him, all six pounds, seven ounces. A little over three hours ago, she would have done anything to get him out of her and she almost giggled when she thought of the comedy of his birth.

Poor Charlie . . . what she had put him through, and he'd taken it. He had gotten her to the hospital and had stayed with her until they'd wheeled her into the delivery room. Even she didn't have the nerve to ask a stranger to go with her and witness that. Her doctor had arrived as she was pushing on the delivery table and Suzanne swore the whole thing was like some bizarre TV drama. If she hadn't gone through it, she wouldn't have believed it herself. But Charles had been her lifeline, forcing her to concentrate and not lose her mind with pain. She wondered where he was and how she could possibly thank him for everything he'd done. How did you thank someone for saving your life and the life of your son? She'd asked for help and she'd certainly received it.

He truly was her hero, at a time when a hero was mighty welcomed in her life.

As though her thoughts made him appear, the door slowly opened and he walked into the room. She smiled at him and he smiled back, almost shyly, as he came closer to the bed.

"He's so tiny," Charles whispered in awe.

Suzanne swore she saw a film of tears in his eyes as he continued to stare at her son. Maybe it was just exhaustion. He still wore the green hospital shirt with his dark pants and brown boots. The man certainly had been through the proverbial wringer. "But he's strong. The doctor said I can take him home with me tomorrow. Isn't that wonderful?"

Charles nodded. "I'm happy for you, Suzanne."

"Thank you. So where have you been?"

"I've been sitting in the waiting room. A nurse came up to me and said I could visit. It's all right, isn't it? Would you rather I leave? I just . . . well, wanted to see him and make sure you were all right."

She reached out her hand for his and he looked at her with expectation.

"Thank you, Charles. You saved my life and my son's. I don't know if I can ever repay you."

He appeared embarrassed and waved off her hand. "Don't be ridiculous. You're the one who saved my life."

"Well, then we're even on that score, but I still owe you for his. How can I repay you? What can I do for you?"

"You don't have to do anything." He quickly squeezed her hand and then shoved his own into his pants pockets, jingling coins inside. "I would have bought you flowers, or something, but they wouldn't take my money in the shop here."

"That's okay," she said with a soft smile, touched that someone wanted to give her flowers to commemorate the birth of her son. She didn't feel quite so alone on this monumental occasion. "You don't have to do that."

"Well, I couldn't. I tried to argue with the woman, but she wouldn't listen and threatened to call security. I'm sorry, Suzanne. Every other mother here looks like they have flowers. You deserve them too."

Blinking rapidly, she felt a burning at her eyes and in her nostrils. "That's sweet of you, Charles." Determined not to get too emotional, she whispered, "Would you like to hold him?"

He looked down to the small bundle lying on her chest, and whispered back, "I've never held a baby. I don't want to hurt him."

Smiling, Suzanne gently lifted her son and said, "You won't. Just cradle him in your arms."

She watched as Charles stared down at the sleeping baby and slowly accepted him. Her throat began to close as she viewed the man holding the child. It should have been her husband. This should have been a time of bonding as a new family. Immediately, she shook that notion out of her head. She simply could not allow such thoughts right now. She had been thrust into a bizarre situation and would do what she must to survive. What she needed was to stay strong for her son and for whatever the uncertain future held for them. She may not know much about her life any longer, but she knew that much.

"What's his name?"

Clearing her throat, Suzanne said, "Matthew. Matthew Charles McDermott."

He glanced up from the baby with surprise. "Was that planned?"

She shook her head. "Seems fitting, though, since you came to our rescue, that he should carry your name too. I don't know how I can ever thank you for what you did in that labor room with me. You saved my sanity when I thought I was losing it. I don't know that I would have made it without you."

He smiled. "You would have. Little Matthew here was determined to come into this world, and I don't think he was too particular where that event took place."

Suzanne smiled back, realizing he was uncomfortable being complimented. "So why wouldn't they take your money?" she asked to change the subject.

Shrugging as he stared down to Matthew, he answered, "The woman said it wasn't real. I mean it's gold. How more real can you get?"

"Gold? You carry gold on you?" she asked, noticing that Charles looked very natural holding her tiny son in his arms. Even though it certainly wasn't the time or place, she had to admit that dry and cleaned up, Charles Garitty was one handsome man. His auburn hair was pushed back off his tanned face and the green of the hospital shirt brought out that extraordinary color in his eyes. He looked very . . . masculine, much more handsome than Kevin . . . and when she realized her thoughts she quickly shook them out of her head as she concentrated on his words. Really! What was wrong with her? She'd just had a baby, for crying out loud!

"I have some paper money, but she wouldn't accept that either."

Suddenly, the hairs on the back of her neck rose again in warning, but the words tripped off her tongue anyway. "Can I see it?" she asked, holding out her arms for her son.

Charles deposited Matty back into her arms and then reached into his pockets. Suzanne snuggled her child to her chest and then pressed the button to raise the bed so she could sit up more.

Looking at the bed, Charles's jaw dropped. "How does that happen?There's no crank, or anything."

"You act as though you've never been in a hospital before."

"Well, I have. But not one like this. This place is beyond anything I've ever seen. It's just one more confirmation," his voice trailed off. "Here . . ."

Suzanne looked at his palm and saw several thick gold coins. She picked up one and stared at it.

"It's a perfectly legit Indian Head gold piece," Charles declared.

Suzanne read the date. 1922. Her head started pounding, and her heartbeat raced. "May I see more?"

"Sure." He placed another gold coin in her hand, displaying the head of Lady Liberty surrounded by a cluster of thirteen stars. It was dated 1901. It wasn't like anything she'd ever seen before. "What is this one worth?" she asked, afraid of his answer.

"Ten dollars. I couldn't understand that store lady's reaction. In fact, I was the one who was shocked. Why, a small bouquet of flowers cost twenty-four dollars! You know, that's nearly the price of a whole acre of flowers!"

"And you said you had paper money," she whispered, ignoring his last statement.

He reached into his pocket and brought out a few bills and handed them to her. At first glance they looked normal, until she realized there was red ink on them. One stated Series of 1917 and the other 1923. The earlier one even had a Federal Reserve Note printed on it. When she turned them over, the bills were totally unrecognizable as modern currency. "Charles, where on earth did you get these?"

"Get them?" He again shrugged, as though her question didn't make sense. "I got them doing business . . . legal transactions. Like anyone gets money. There's nothing wrong with them."

"But modern money doesn't look like this. There are no five and ten dollar coins in gold now. And the paper money is completely different." Matthew started squirming, and Suzanne handed the currency back. "Charles, what's going on?"

Shoving everything back into his pants pocket, his expression became serious. "Well, I was hoping you might be able to tell me, Suzanne," he said as he sat in a chair by the bed. "Because I really need to know . . . about what's been happening here."

She nodded, while praying for some semblance of sanity, for what was going through her head was crazy. "Well, I'll try. Tell me what you're thinking."

He took a deep breath and she could see that he was trying to keep it together. Unconsciously, she held her son tighter to her body. She didn't know if she was protecting the baby, or Matty was grounding her, for suddenly, something, some deep instinct, was telling her that she wasn't going to like what followed.

"First of all, I don't think you hit me with your ring."

"You don't? How . . . I mean your head was bleeding and—"

He held up his hand to stop her words. "I was shot."

"*What?* By whom? Why?"

Before he could answer, the door was opened and a young nurse came into the room. "It's time to return the baby to the nursery."

Ordinarily, Suzanne might have fought for more time with her son, but considering the current conversation she gladly handed over the baby. Somehow she knew this man was decent and honorable. He was no criminal, for he'd certainly had more than enough time and opportunity to take advantage of her if he'd wanted. Waiting until the door was closed again, she turned to the man sitting in the chair and saw the exhaustion on his face. "Charles, you can tell me. Are you in some kind of trouble? Why was someone shooting at you?"

He told his story about the property he had just registered with the land office, about how he and Mitch had been walking home, discussing their partnership, and about how, on the bridge over the creek, his best friend had tried to kill him.

"Charles, that's not a toughie," Suzanne said. "Go to the police. What your friend Mitch did is a serious crime. Just have him arrested."

Sighing deeply, Charles closed his eyes for a moment. When he opened them, he stared at her and whispered, "I wish it were that easy. You see, something's happened to me, Suzanne. I know you're not going to believe me when I tell you this, and I wouldn't blame you if you didn't, but I've had time to think about it, and it's all I can figure."

"What is it?" Staring into his green eyes, she clutched the metal railing of the bed and waited for his answer.

"I'm not from this time."

"What do you mean, *from this time?*"

Leaning forward, he rested his arms on his knees, ran his fingers through his hair, and when he looked up his gaze was intense. "I knew my only hope of escape was to jump from that bridge and pray I didn't break my neck. When I was falling, all I could see was the sunlight reflecting off the water. It blinded me. I don't know, I felt something . . . as though something strange passed through my body, and then I . . . it all went black. The next thing I knew, you were kissing me."

"I wasn't kissing you," she protested again, embarrassed by the thought. "It happens to be a medical technique to blow air into your lungs and—"

"I know, I know." He held up his hand to placate her. "Suzanne, you've got to believe me when I say I'm surrounded by things I've never even dreamed of before. Your streets and automobiles. Your machinery here at the hospital. Doors that open by themselves. I don't recognize anything around me. *Everything* has changed. All I can guess is that I jumped off a bridge in nineteen twenty-six and landed in the year two thousand one."

She was rubbing her temples, as if the act might help her understand what he was saying. "Charles, what you're talking about is impossible," she said as calmly as she could, though she remembered when she had nearly been blinded by light reflecting off the water too. It was that moment when she had thrown the ring. "People just don't . . . leap into . . . time travel!"

"Then explain *me*. Explain my money. Explain to me why I don't know anything about what's going on here. I'm not stupid or insane. Suzanne, I know how crazy this sounds, but I'm telling you the truth. This isn't my time!"

"Okay, just hold on a minute. I'm really trying to absorb all this." She looked back at his anguished face. On top of everything else she'd gone through this day, she couldn't believe that she was actually considering what he was saying might be plausible. For her sanity and his, she wanted to convince the poor man that he must have hit his head and probably had amnesia. "Look, Charles—"

"I have no reason to lie to you," he interrupted in a calmer tone. "And I don't want anything from you but an ear to listen. Right now, you're the only person I can talk to about this and I need to talk to someone." He paused and stared at her, as though requesting her permission to continue. Suzanne simply didn't know what to say. His frustration was evident to her and she hoped her eyes might relay her sentiment of deep empathy for the man.

Tilting his head with a look of apprehension he began again. "Before you've concluded that I'm an absolute madman, let me finish."

She nodded.

"Okay, I've rationalized this as much as I can. I've considered that I might be having a really vivid dream or hallucinating, but this is all too real. And no dream I've ever had lasted this long anyway." Again he paused, running his fingers through his hair. "I know *who* I am, I just don't know *where* I am. Fine. I may be unfamiliar with my surroundings, but I'm not crazy enough to think I can just walk into the nearest precinct and announce what I've just told you. I know they'd lock me up and throw away the key."

"I'd have to agree with you there, Charlie." The remark slipped from her lips so quickly, she hoped he wouldn't think she'd meant it sarcastically.

"Why would anyone make up such an incredible story? Damn it. I'd give anything to walk out of this hospital and find myself back in my own time. I have a life there . . . waiting for me . . . land I just bought, a woman I was about to marry, and a debt I have to settle. I don't belong here. I don't *want* to be here."

For some odd reason hearing him talk about a woman suddenly made her heart tighten, and it really surprised her. She certainly wasn't about to entertain any romantic notions about him. In fact, she doubted if she could ever feel that way again with anyone after what romance had done to her. She was a mother now and that was all that mattered.

"So, if what you're saying is true, then what do you plan on doing?" she asked, hardly believing she was buying into his fantastic story.

"That's just it. I don't know. But I have to get back there."

"Back *where,* Charles?"

"Back to my life. My time. Nineteen twenty-six."

The silent moment falling between them might as well have been a locomotive crashing through a wall. "I . . . I just don't know what to say," Suzanne mumbled, wishing that her brain would start working to come up with reasonable explanations as to why none of this could be true. She looked into his eyes and saw he was desperately pleading with her to believe him. But to believe in the possibility of time travel was just plain nuts.

She had believed in marriage, in friendship, in honor, and

look where that had gotten her. What did she know anymore? Everything was turned upside down. All she really knew was that Charles Garitty had come into her life when she really needed help and he'd stayed by her side—which was more than she could say about those she'd trusted in the past. She knew she was a fairly intelligent woman and although she'd never considered such fantastic ideas as time travel, she couldn't deny what she felt so deeply inside of her.

As ridiculous as it seemed, she trusted him. After all they'd been through this day, it wouldn't hurt to show a little more compassion and she didn't need to dig too far to know she had enough to spare. In fact, she realized their situations were really quite parallel in a way. Right here and now, they both had no one but each other.

"Look, Charles, I don't think you're crazy, but I do think you might need some time to rest . . . you've been through a lot. You need time to think about what's happened and plan what you're going to do. I know you won't hurt me or my son. And since I'm kind of alone, I need some help right now so—"

"I would never hurt you, Suzanne. I owe you my life!" he interrupted, appearing shocked by her implication.

"No, no. I didn't mean that. I believe you. Listen, do you think you could drive to my house, if I gave you directions?"

He stared at her. "Your house?"

Nodding, she continued, "I don't have my purse and I need some things for tomorrow. And, as I mentioned, earlier today I told my husband to pack his things and get out of our house. He's probably staying with my . . . well, someone who used to be my friend, and I really don't want help from either one of them now. I'm not kidding myself. This isn't going to be easy for me when I return to an empty house with Matty. If you want, you can stay with me for a few days . . . at least until you figure out what you're going to do. There's plenty of room, that is, if you don't mind staying with a new-born baby."

He appeared to be biting the inside corner of his cheek to keep his emotions under control. "I surely appreciate all your kindness, Suzanne," he whispered.

"I'm glad I can do it," she replied, feeling that burning at her eyes again. "And don't get too soft on me now, Charles. I'm holding on by a thread myself. One of us has to be strong." Impulsively, she extended her hand. "Friends?"

In spite of everything, he slowly grinned and shook her hand. "Friends."

"Then it's a deal. We'll help each other not go crazy while we figure out our lives."

Still holding her hand, he looked deeply into her eyes and said, "Your husband must be the crazy one, or the biggest fool on the face of this earth. If I may say so without offending you . . . you're one hell of a woman, Suzanne McDermott."

It was too much and the tears spilled over her lids as she felt her facial muscles crumbling into a childish sob. "Thank you," she managed to spit out in between gulps of air. "You have no idea how much I needed to hear that!"

Still holding her hand, he patted hers with his other. "Come on, I didn't mean to make you cry even more."

Realizing how pathetic she must appear, Suzanne inhaled deeply, pulled her hand away and wiped at her cheeks. "Don't mind me. It's just my whores moaning."

"Excuse me?"

She couldn't suppress the near hysterical giggle. "I was trying to make a joke. Hormones, whores moaning?" Feeling even more stupid, she muttered, "Never mind. Don't ask me to explain body chemistry right now."

Any remaining tension between them was broken when he smiled knowingly at her and she saw relief in his eyes.

"You're going to be all right, Suzanne McDermott."

"You think?" she asked and sniffled the remaining tears. "I'm just so scared."

"You're not alone now, lass," he whispered, still smiling at her with tenderness as he shoved his hands back into his pockets.

Something small cracked inside of her, some wall she had been building, and she started nodding. "Right. I've got a friend now."

"That's right. We'll figure this out somehow."

She didn't know if he was saying that for her benefit or his. It really didn't matter any longer. Pulling her act together, she took a deep breath to steady herself and said, "Hey, check in that drawer behind you and see if you can find a paper and a pen. I'll draw you a map so you can get out of here. Get some rest, Charles. You look exhausted. Just come back tomorrow morning, okay?"

"I'll be here," he said, opening the metal drawer of the night table.

She merely smiled. She knew he would. Something deep and instinctive told her Charles Garrity was a man who could be trusted. Refusing to give power to that part of her that said she'd been wrong before, Suzanne took the sheet of paper and the pen and began drawing him a detailed map.

Driving at night was even more harrowing than in the daytime. It had taken him more than fifteen minutes to discover the switch for the headlights, and only after he had found an instruction manual for the fantastic automobile in the glove box. Once on the road, the glaring lights of oncoming cars unnerved him, and he purposefully stayed far to the right, allowing every car also going in his direction to pass him. Amidst honking horns and yells from those who drove by, he did his best to stay calm and follow Suzanne's directions. When he finally turned into the long drive in front of the large farmhouse, just as she'd described it, Charles felt his shoulders fall with relief.

He'd made it.

Putting the gearshift into park and pushing the headlight switch in, he turned off the engine with the key at the ignition and closed his eyes. He thought he might just get the hang of this machine, and could begin to enjoy its comforts if he could only relax when he was behind the wheel. No sense in getting comfortable with anything here, he reprimanded himself. There's nothing like this where you come from, Charles Garrity, and won't be in your lifetime. His lifetime . . . right now, he knew he couldn't engage that thought again.

He heard the rustle of leaves from the grand old tree in the center of the circular drive and felt a soft breeze cross his stubbled face. Allowing his tired head to drop back against the seat rest behind him, he listened as the chirping crickets began their lull. Exhaling deeply, he thought it was quite nice to hear that at least one thing hadn't changed. He opened his eyes to peer up at the bright, full moon. It still looked the same, even if it was seventy-five years older. Wincing from the stiffness in his neck, he realized there was one other thing that was certain . . . every muscle in his body felt as if it had aged three-quarters of a century. Yes, he was exhausted and needed to get some rest.

Opening the car door, he stepped out onto shaky legs. He needed to get some food in him too. Making his way across the gray gravel drive, he looked up at the old farmhouse that was silhouetted against the dark velvet sky. From the light of the moon he could see a wide porch with several hanging baskets of flowers. Squinting through the distance, he took a quick survey of the properties beyond the few rows of apple trees in the back of the place. The newer houses surrounding him appeared stark, without any mature landscaping. Just houses on rolling hills. They looked grand, yet cold somehow. Suzanne's house looked warm and inviting. It looked like a home.

The sound of his heavy bootheels thumped across the porch as he walked to the dark wooden and oval etched-glass door. He fumbled with the key ring in the darkness, until he found the one Suzanne said would let him in. Taking a deep breath, he inserted the key and turned the lock. As he eased the thick door open, Charles hesitated for a moment, as though he was somehow invading her privacy, and thought it would have been much better if she was there with him. It was a very odd feeling to walk into someone's home un-escorted. He was grateful for her hospitality, but even with her permission he couldn't help feeling that he was somehow intruding in Suzanne's life.

With an air of reverence he entered and quietly shut the door behind him. The place was dark and he ran his hand over the wall, hoping to find an electrical line. Instead of a large knob and wires tacked to a wall, he found a toggle switch and simply flipped it. Warm lights instantly shined throughout the most inviting room he had ever seen. In awe, he stood in the foyer just to take it all in for a minute.

The exposed timber framing and rafters across the cathe-dral ceiling revealed a strong skeleton in this old home. Gray stone pavers evoked a rugged and well-trod floor beneath his feet and welcomed him in further. The spacious area was light and airy, with a woman's soft touch in the tasteful mix of comfortable upholstered chairs and sofa. Opening one of the three sets of French doors on the far wall of the room he stepped out onto the porch, and realized it wrapped around the entire home. Turning back inside, he was drawn to the massive fieldstone fireplace that had to be at least eight feet wide at the hearth. His eyes traced the chimney that loomed far above to the crown of the gable. This was truly a magnif-icent home.

Walking into the kitchen, he made his way around the huge centerpiece, and opened what he hoped was an icebox. His shoulders sagged in relief when he saw the wide array of food inside. Suzanne had told him to help himself to what-ever he wanted, and he was starved.

Taking out a large, soft bottle of what he guessed to be or-ange juice, he uncapped it and reached for a glass on one of the open shelves. After filling the tall tumbler, he leaned against the marble counter and drank it all in a continuous series of gulps. Taking a deep breath and refilling it, he looked around the house and appreciated the warmth of the place. This home was much more to his liking than anything he'd seen so far in this modern world. This felt comforting to him. He couldn't imagine any man wanting to leave it—or the woman who had obviously created it.

He suddenly thought of his betrothed, Grace, and a dull ache yanked at his heart. In this time, she would have to be almost ninety years old, or was more likely dead. Small regrets began to fill his mind. He could admit he wasn't desperately in love with her, but it had been the time and years he'd spent nearly fulfilling all his dreams of a home and family that he felt were lost to him now. He might have spent a little less time pursuing his goals, instead of his happiness, and settled down sooner, but when he finally asked her, Grace lived up to her name and welcomed his proposal. He remembered her adoring eyes and open heart. *Dear Grace . . . what did she do when I disappeared from her life?* he wondered. *Did she marry another?* A part of him almost hoped she had, and wished she'd led a happy life. At least, since they'd never married, she wasn't left a widow. Still, if by some miracle he ever did get back, he would go forth with all his plans and never tell another about this fantastic trip to the future. Who would believe him anyway?

Deciding to take care of Suzanne's requests before eating, Charles left the kitchen and walked toward the expansive staircase. He flipped on the overhead lights in the hallway upstairs and passed by a bedroom, then another, then a large bath, and finally, at the end of the hall, he found Suzanne's room. Everything was exactly where she'd said it would be.

It was all in different shades of white, with touches of green and big watercolor paintings of flowers and the largest bed he had ever seen. He paused as he was about to open her closet door. On the night table was a framed colored picture of Suzanne and a man, and curiosity got the better of him. Knowing it must be her husband and wanting to see what such a fool looked like, he picked up the frame and studied the picture.

They looked happy, standing before a waterfall, smiling for the photograph.

Suzanne appeared radiant, as she grinned into the lens of the camera. The man . . . Charles looked closer, narrowing his vision to see better. The man was slightly taller than Suzanne, with brown hair and eyes that seemed oddly familiar. He shook off the thought and headed to her closet. He didn't want to look too closely, for what Suzanne's husband had done to her made him furious.

She had described exactly what she wanted and he flipped through the rack of Suzanne's clothing to find her desired dress. He wasn't looking forward to the rest of her request. The shoes he could handle. Searching through a woman's undergarment drawer was quite another thing, yet he had to admit that the two of them had established a certain intimacy that was unusual for him. Most of the time it took him a while to open up to anyone, much less a woman. Not many got past his defenses, yet he and Suzanne seemed to bypass all else and were more or less forced to rely upon each other. It was probably that reason he felt a great protectiveness toward her, and now her child, which was completely out of character for him . . .

Suddenly, he turned his head and stared at the photograph again.

Those eyes reminded him of that bastard, Mitch Davies.

He nearly jumped when the strange telephone on the bedside table began to ring, an odd ring, and he froze, just staring at it. It wasn't his place to answer. When it stopped, he turned back to the closet, then couldn't stop the grunt of sudden alarm that escaped his lips when he heard the male voice behind him.

"Suzanne, pick up the phone." There was a pause. "Look, I'm really sorry about today, but we didn't see the point in waiting. You deserved to know and . . . well, I'm here. At Ingrid's. Call me, okay?"

Charles stared at the small machine next to the telephone and slowly shook his head in wonder. He'd just realized another thing he and Suzanne had in common.

They each had trusted scoundrels.

4

He didn't even know *why* he was running. It was just an instinctive compulsion, but now he felt his legs weakening. He knew he couldn't keep this pace much longer, yet it was beyond his reason why he couldn't seem to get away from this area. Every path he took led him right back to the same damn bridge. It didn't make sense. None of it made sense.

Near exhaustion, he began to cross the bridge once again as the night air chilled the droplets of sweat on his temples. Gasping for another breath, the tightness in his chest forced him to stop and lean on the thick, aged trellis beam for support. The cry of an owl repeated, "Who? Who-who?" over the pounding of his heart and he closed his eyes. Rest. That was all he wanted, but when would it come?

Suddenly, the sound of bootheels on the boards behind him broke his trance. There was no time to turn before the shot rang out and hot pain entered his skull. It was at that moment he felt as though he'd been yanked out of himself and was now viewing the scene like a cinema flicker.

He saw the limp body crumple and tumble over the side of the bridge. He watched helplessly as it hurled toward the moonlit water. His mind raced with surreal theories and caught on one. *That can't be me,* he exhaled in denial. *I can't die. No, no, no,* his mind repeated in echoes. "Heaven have mercy, I'm dead!" Charles gasped.

Feeling as though the last breath had been punched out of him, his body stiffened, and he winced against the brightness. There was such intense light around him, he nearly feared blindness should he open his eyes fully to see. His heart continued to pound rapidly and his palms dripped of perspiration. Then he felt something soft and cool beneath his fingertips. It was cloth. Smooth and clean, he discerned, and then he sensed the same comfort around his bare skin. He inhaled slowly and deliberately.

Where am I? he wondered as he gathered the courage to open one eye. Blinking a few more times, he began to focus on the white coverlet draped over him. His gaze followed it down to the humps of his feet in front of the dark, polished walnut footboard of the bed. He wiggled his toes beneath the fabric.

"A dream. It was just a dream," he breathed out with relief. Swallowing the dryness in his throat, he looked around the room to gather his senses. He saw his familiar shirt hanging on one of the bedposts in front of him. His trousers were folded neatly and placed on a chair cushion with his boots tucked under it on the floor. "Where the hell am I?" he repeated aloud.

Charles rubbed his eyes in an effort to gain some more clarity. Leaning back on his hands, he allowed the morning to unfold around him. A fresh breeze came in through the open window and the songs of morning birds filled his ears. He shook his head for the thought that was playing in his brain. This was no kind of heaven he'd ever been told about.

He reached for his shirt and, in a flash, he recalled having washed it the night before. Pulling it down, he looked for the stains of blood he remembered scrubbing. Not a trace remained. Pausing for a second to consider another possibility, he reached for his temple. "Ow," he flinched. The wound was real. That's when it began to sink in rapidly.

Memories rushed through his head so quickly; Mitch and the bridge—the gun—the deed—jumping and nearly drowning—being pulled from the river by a woman—driving a fantastic automobile—going to a hospital—a baby being born—

"Oh, damn!" he exclaimed aloud, while throwing the covers back. "Suzanne!" His eyes darted around the room for a timepiece. Leaping off the bed while pulling his arm through a sleeve, he continued to search for a clock. "Damn it, what's the time?" he rasped.

It had all come back to him. He was supposed to pick up Suzanne at the hospital. Grabbing up his trousers, he shook them out of habit and then thrust a foot through a pant leg. Snatching up his socks, he began mumbling while pulling them on.

"None of this makes any sense. How does something like this happen?" he asked half to himself, half to the empty room. He shook his head in disbelief before adding, "Time travel?"

Yanking on his boots, he stood up and stamped one heel on the floor to fit it snugly against the leather hardened from a soaking in the creek. Then, after cinching his belt, he pondered his own question. *Don't think about it now, Charlie. It will all, somehow, make sense later.*

I doubt it, he mentally quipped.

"I'm losing my mind," he snapped after realizing he was actually conversing with himself. As he began to leave the room, he caught his reflection in a wardrobe mirror. He stopped and stepped back to view himself more thoroughly. In a vain attempt to tame the cowlick on the back of his head, he spoke aloud again. "You certainly *look* as crazy as a coot, Charles Garrity."

About twenty minutes later he was walking toward the

hospital doors. He felt proud of himself for, even as a man on the brink of insanity, he'd remembered how to operate the automobile and find his way back to the hospital. His confidence lessened very slightly as he looked around at the busy place. Now to navigate once more through this madness.

Just do this and get back home, he reassured himself. Funny how that word replayed itself in his mind. *Home.* Surely Suzanne's large farmhouse wasn't his home, and yet it was the only place that offered sanctuary right now, for his own was seventy-five years away and so far as he knew no longer existed. He realized how much he owed the remarkable woman who had saved his life. If this is where he found himself, no matter how he got here, then he was determined to make the best of his situation. Fit in. *Don't draw attention to yourself. Do whatever it takes until you can find your way back . . .* The words kept repeating inside his head.

Pushing the button for the maternity floor, he smiled at the older woman who got into the elevator with him and clutched the flowers he had gathered quickly from Suzanne's front garden. He thought it only right that she leave this hospital with flowers in her hands.

"I see we're going to the same floor," the older woman announced.

Charles smiled again, shifting the small bag of clothing for Suzanne.

Obviously wanting to make conversation, the woman added, "So tell me, what did you have?"

"I beg your pardon?"

"A boy or a girl?" the gray-haired woman asked with a chuckle, as though amused by his confusion.

"Oh, a boy," Charles answered, not feeling he needed to explain to this woman all the details.

"My daughter just had her fourth. Another boy. They certainly are a handful," she said in good-natured voice. "Are you prepared?"

"Prepared? He's just a wee babe," Charles replied, glancing up to the blinking numbers and once more marveling at the difference in elevators from his time.

"Oh, this must be your first," she announced with a knowing grin. "I guess you're never really prepared."

Charles was grateful when the door opened to their floor. As they walked out of the elevator and he was about to say good-bye to the woman, she reached out her hand and gently touched his sleeve.

"Be patient," she advised with another smile. "Both with your son and your wife. Don't be surprised if your wife suddenly gets the blues. Lord knows, I wasn't prepared for that myself. Patience is the best way to handle it."

"The blues?"

"Postpartum blues. Why, I thought all you young people knew everything."

Charles mumbled, "Yes, of course. Postpartum blues." What the hell was *that*?

"Well, congratulations on your son's birth. I wish you and your family a lifetime of happiness."

Startled by the woman's words, Charles simply nodded and said, "Thank you. And congratulations on your new grandson."

The woman smiled once more and turned in the opposite direction. Charles slowly turned toward Suzanne's room and straightened his shoulders. The way that woman just assumed he was the father of this new family really rattled him. It wasn't his role to play. In fact, he'd barely gotten a handle on how to be the man he'd always wanted to become when he'd been snatched away from his life and thrust into this one.

Walking down the hallway, he bit the inside of his cheek as things he'd done in his past flashed through his mind. Making a small fortune in bootleg whiskey was one of them. He shook the thought out of his head. All he had to do today was get Suzanne and Matty to their home. He'd figure out the rest later.

When he opened the door to her room, Charles stood for a moment and his breath caught in his throat. Suzanne was sitting in bed, nursing her son. Rays of sunshine fell across them, and he thought she looked almost angelic as she smiled down at Matty.

Glancing up, her grin widened. "I just knew you'd come back," she declared in a whisper.

He cleared his throat and walked farther into the room, allowing the door to close quietly behind him. "Of course I would," he whispered back. "Didn't I tell you I would be here this morning?"

She nodded and gently used the back of her fingers to stroke the infant's cheek. "I wasn't even worried, Charlie. Did you find everything?"

"I think so," he answered, putting the bag onto a nearby chair. He stood for a few moments, just staring, until Suzanne looked up at him. "These are for you," he announced, and thrust his hand out in her direction. Although he could barely even see any bare skin with a cloth diaper resting on Suzanne's shoulder and draped over her chest, still he was embarrassed.

"Aww," she murmured, holding out her hand to him as he stepped closer to the bed.

Averting his eyes from the intimate scene before him, he focused on her hand as he placed the flowers in them. "They're from your garden."

"How perfect," she whispered, sniffing a yellow blossom.

As she looked up to him again, she handed the flowers back and asked, "Does this embarrass you?"

"Embarrass me?"

"Yes. Breast-feeding Matty."

She just stared at him with those big blue eyes, waiting for his answer, and Charles was even more confounded when his gaze seemed drawn to Matty's tiny mouth tugging on Suzanne's breast. "No, it doesn't embarrass me," he lied in a rough voice, for his throat was tight with a surge of emotion. None of it made sense to him. Why was he so moved to see her nursing her son?

"Good," she proclaimed, slowly shifting the baby to her shoulder and adjusting the yellow hospital gown to cover herself. Gently patting Matty's back, she added, " 'Cause if we're going to be living together for a few days, you'll have to get used to it."

He just nodded stupidly and looked to the bag on the chair. "I found that car seat in the nursery, the one you told me about last night, but for the life of me I don't know how it works. I just left it on the backseat of the automobile."

Suzanne swayed slightly as she continued to pat her son's back. "That's all right, I'll figure it out. Now, do you want to hold Matty while I get dressed?"

He could actually feel his body tense. "You want me to hold him?"

She giggled slightly, as though his reaction was amusing. "Of course. We're a team here, aren't we?" Her brows suddenly narrowed. "Unless you want me to call a nurse to take him? Charlie, are you afraid of the baby?"

Charles shook his head, as though the thought were ridiculous. "Afraid . . . of a baby? Of course not. I'll take the wee lad." He'd held the child last night, so he could certainly do it now.

Suzanne seemed pleased by his answer as he held out his hands.

She gave him the diaper. "Here, put this over your shoulder first and then you can burp him while I get dressed."

Charles placed the cloth on his shoulder and Suzanne carefully handed over Matty. The baby made soft mewling sounds and curled his little body tightly at the disruption, making tiny fists with his hands and drawing up his knees. Placing the infant to his shoulder, Charles noticed that Matty soon relaxed as tiny breaths sounded close to his ear. He felt a little silly as a rush of pleasure surged through his body and he immediately began patting Matty's back while Suzanne tried to rise from the bed.

He reminded himself that he was indebted to Suzanne and would do whatever she asked in return for her kindness. He couldn't even imagine what might have happened to him had she not come along and taken him into her life.

"Ouch . . ."

His attention was drawn to Suzanne as she clutched the metal railing of the bed.

"Are you all right?" he asked, wanting to hold out his hand to her, yet afraid to let go of the baby.

She nodded as she slowly, carefully, made her way past him to the chair. "Just a little sore. I had a baby yesterday, remember?"

"How could I forget?" he asked in return, and was pleased when she glanced up at him, for she was smiling.

"You know, Charlie," she began, as she picked up the bag of clothing, "in spite of everything that's happened to me, I am probably one of the happiest women alive right now. I can't wait to bring Matty home."

Charles simply nodded as Suzanne took tiny steps toward a small bathroom. "Take your time," he spoke softly out to her back. "Matthew and I are doin' just fine here."

She turned around at the doorway and stared at him for a few intense moments. It looked to him as though tears were gathering at her eyes as the tip of her nose suddenly got red.

"I can see," she murmured, and then took a deep breath and closed the door behind her.

He patted the baby's back and thought he heard a tiny burp, but not being positive he continued. "You sure lucked out when it came to picking a mother, young fella," he whispered to the infant while still staring at the closed door.

Thirty minutes later they were all in the elevator. He was holding the bag and flowers and Suzanne, clothed in a cornflower blue dress, was seated in a wheelchair holding her son as a young nurse stood behind her. No one spoke during the short ride down. When they came to the admitting desk, the nurse stopped wheeling Suzanne and turned to them.

"If you bring your car around to the front, Mr. McDermott, we'll wait here."

Charles merely blinked at the woman.

"Charlie?" Suzanne called out. "Can you get the car for us?"

He simply nodded once before walking toward the exit.

Suzanne let out her breath as she followed him with her gaze. Clearly, he was upset being called her husband's name, yet why try and explain anything when they were minutes away from making their escape? She felt a twinge of guilt for allowing everyone to think otherwise, but now was not the time to examine how she had deceived the hospital staff. Charlie had brought her purse along with clothes for her and the baby, so they were prepared for anything, plus she'd taken care of all the insurance red tape when she'd done the preadmission forms last week. Funny how it all was working out. She didn't need Kevin at all.

Just thinking of her husband made Suzanne hold her son tighter to her heart. She would have to notify him of Matty's birth, but she just didn't want to see him yet. All she could think about was taking the baby home and getting settled in peace and quiet. Bless Charlie's heart for everything he'd done for her.

"He seems like a really good baby," the nurse murmured, looking down at her sleeping son. "What's his name?"

"Matthew. Matthew Charles," Suzanne answered, smiling at her precious child dressed in the white designer outfit she'd bought for him months ago. She'd known it was extravagant to pay so much for something he would soon grow out of, but her heart had melted at the detailed white-on-white stitching at the collar and the almost tissue-fine cotton of the gown and hat. The soft white receiving blanket that came with the set was wrapped around him and Suzanne touched his tiny fingers, watching as they curled around her own. She was in love. So deeply in love. "Am I prejudiced, or is this baby just beautiful?"

The young nurse laughed. "Yes, you're prejudiced . . . and yes, he's beautiful. With a husband as handsome as yours, you'd have to have beautiful children."

Suzanne froze, trying to banish Kevin's image from her mind. The young woman wasn't talking about Kevin. She thought Charlie was her husband. Again, guilt assaulted her as she thought of her many lies of omission. Her mind told her Kevin was the liar. He had lied to her for over a year . . . maybe more than that. What she was doing was to protect herself. And she had even greater reason now, she affirmed with a loving glance at Matty.

"And speaking of your husband . . . here he is."

Startled, Suzanne's head jerked up, half expecting to see Kevin storming in the front door of the hospital. Instead, she saw Charlie walking calmly toward them.

The nurse came behind the chair again and began pushing her and Matty to the door.

"The automobile is waiting," he announced to the nurse.

Suzanne almost grinned at his serious tone. Just a few more minutes and they would be away from this place and she could relax. As they left through the doors, the sun shone directly on Matty and he started sneezing.

"Oh my," Suzanne murmured, holding her hand up to cover his face.

"It's not unusual," the nurse counseled as they stopped in front of the car.

"He's not allergic to sunshine, is he?" Suzanne asked.

The young woman laughed. "Actually, it is an allergic reaction, but it will stop soon. Don't look so worried. It's nothing to be concerned about. Now, let me have him while you get into the car."

The nurse held the baby while Charlie helped her stand.

Taking a deep breath of clean air, Suzanne looked into the back and saw the car seat. "Oh, I have to fix that," she announced, and Charlie immediately opened the door.

"Just tell me what to do," he said, reaching in and holding the seat.

"You have to turn it backward and fasten it with the safety belts."

He turned it backward, then grabbed a belt and pulled on it. Holding it in his hand, he started to weave it through the seat and then looked up to her. "Now what?"

"You hook it, buckle it to that side."

"Buckle it?"

"New fathers," the nurse said with a chuckle.

"Here, allow me," Suzanne suggested, seeing that Charlie had absolutely no idea how to buckle a seat belt. He moved away from the door opening and she reached in and fastened the car seat. "Now, we're ready to take him home."

The nurse handed her the baby and Suzanne carefully placed Matty in the seat. She made sure he was secure and then sighed deeply as she faced the young woman. "Thank you for all your help," she said sincerely.

"You're very welcome." The nurse stood back and smiled at them as Suzanne slid gently onto the front seat. "You make a wonderful family. Good luck."

"Thanks again," Suzanne murmured, not daring to look at Charlie as he shut the door and walked around the front of the car. She waved at the nurse and then watched as Charlie opened the door and got inside. "I'm sorry," she whispered.

"It's all right, Suzanne," he muttered, inserting the key and starting the car.

Obviously, he knew why she was apologizing. It must be terribly awkward for him when everyone assumed he was not only her husband but also Matty's father. She watched as he shifted into drive and then turned her head and saw the nurse wheel the chair back into the hospital. As they left the building, Suzanne glanced once more at the man next to her. "You certainly seem much more comfortable driving today."

He smiled slightly. "I've had a bit of practice."

"Really, Charlie, I can't thank you enough for everything. I don't know what I would have done without you."

Shrugging, he said, "You don't have to keep thanking me. It's the least I can do. You saved my life, remember?"

"God, that seems like a lifetime ago. Was it just yesterday?"

"You're right," he answered, applying the brakes as they approached a stop sign. "For me, it was a lifetime ago."

Hearing the tone of his voice, she wanted to reach out and touch his arm, yet held back. "I've been thinking about what you told me last night . . . about . . . time traveling."

"And?"

She marveled at his ease as he pulled out into the traffic. It was like a totally confident man was now behind the wheel of her car. "Well, it's not something I ever thought was possible, but I will admit you do make an interesting case for it. I don't know what is possible anymore. I never thought I would be bringing my child home from the hospital without his father even knowing he's been born. I never thought my best friend would betray me. I believed in so many things and they proved false . . . so, I've decided to keep an open mind. Like I said last night, we'll help each other figure out our lives . . . okay?"

He nodded. "Okay, but I will make myself useful. I'm no freeloader. Whatever you want done, Suzanne, I'm your man. I don't mind hard work."

I'm your man.

The words repeated inside her brain and she shook them out as Matty made a noise behind them. Turning her head, she realized she couldn't see him. "I hope he's all right back there."

"It's not far to your house. He'll be fine."

As if in protest to that announcement, the baby began to cry and Suzanne fidgeted in her seat. "I wish I could hold him, but it's the law to keep babies in car seats."

"A law?"

"Yes. You could get a ticket if the police see you holding him, plus it's really unsafe to carry a baby in the front seat."

"I've never heard of such a thing as a mother not being allowed by law to hold her own child." He shook his head.

"A lot of things have changed in the last seventy-five years, Charlie."

"I should say so. I saw a store with a big sign that sells liquor. Obviously, there is no longer a prohibition on alcohol. And this morning I saw a woman with green hair running on the side of the road in pretty scandalous attire."

In spite of Matty's crying, Suzanne chuckled. "That was a jogger and I'm sure the green hair was . . . well, a fashion statement of some kind. Despite all our laws, there is still freedom of expression."

"That was some expression," he answered, concentrating on the road.

Suzanne smiled at his serious mood. She had no idea where he came from, if his story was fact or fiction, but she knew that she could trust him, and trust was something very precious in her life right now. Suddenly, listening to Matty's cry, she felt an odd tingling at her breasts and was shocked to discover that the front of her dress was beginning to stain a darker blue.

"Oh no," she muttered as she stared in shock at the ever widening circles.

"What's wrong?" he asked, darting a quick glance in her direction.

She watched his eyes widen as his gaze connected with her dress and she immediately crossed her arms over the front of it. "Nothing," she muttered in embarrassment. It was one thing to nurse her son calmly in front of him, but to have her breasts leak whenever Matty cried was quite another! "Can you step on it?" she pleaded, looking at the speedometer. "You can go five miles faster."

"I'm trying to be careful," he said, pushing down on the accelerator. "But I can see we have a bit of an emergency here."

"Right," she mumbled as tears came into her eyes. She tried reaching back behind her seat to touch Matty, yet his cries became even louder. How could she have been so happy only a short while ago in the hospital and now it seemed that everything was falling apart?

When they pulled into her driveway, she gulped down her tears and breathed a sigh of relief. Matty hadn't stopped crying the entire way home. She wondered if he was all right. What if it wasn't just hunger? What if something was really wrong with him? What did she know? She'd gone to all the classes, but they'd stopped at delivering the baby. No one told her what to do when she got him home. Maybe she should have stayed the extra day at the hospital instead of insisting that she be released as quickly as possible. They would know, the nurses would know. She was on her own and she hadn't any idea of what to do, except feed him and clean him and love him and— She stopped the mental anguish when she realized that Charlie was out of the car.

She opened the door by herself, not waiting as Charlie came around the front. Easing her way out, she hissed with a sudden burning pain at standing upright.

"Suzanne, let me help you."

Aware of how she must appear, she shook her head. "Don't look at me. Just open the back door so I can get Matty."

"What do you mean, don't look at you?"

"I mean don't look at me," she reiterated, trying to shield herself as she passed in front of him. Unlocking the straps, she lifted her son to her chest and soothed him while his cries were interrupted by a quick sneeze as the sunlight hit him full force. She shielded his face with her hand and berated herself for not being a more attentive mother.

"Suzanne, it's all right," he said as he closed the door.

She swallowed down fresh tears and nodded as she looked up at her home. It seemed like such a long time ago that she'd run out of it in sheer terror. "Let's go in."

He held her elbow as she slowly walked up the steps. When they were on the porch, she waited as Charlie unlocked the door and held it open for her. Once inside, she sat down on a rocker by the French doors and unbuttoned the front of her dress. "I'm going to feed him," she announced, praying that Charlie would go away.

He did. "I'll empty the automobile. I should leave Matty's seat there?"

"Yes. Leave it," she called out to his retreating back. As her son latched onto her breast, she felt such a strong surge of emotion rush through her body that she simply couldn't stop the tears. She had a son, but no husband. Her best friend had slept with him. Her life was out of control. Her body was out of control, and her only friend at the moment was a man who claimed he had time traveled! How much more insane could it get?

She sniffled and whispered, "I'm sorry, Matty. I wanted so much more for you."

Matty didn't seem to care as he nursed contentedly.

Suzanne felt like a failure. She hadn't even minded at the hospital that she had to wear a maternity dress home. Her belly was still swollen and soft, but now she didn't know if she would ever get her figure back. Her breasts were also swollen, bigger than they had ever been in her pregnancy, and she felt like a cow that needed milking!

"What else can I do, Suzanne?"

She turned her head and saw Charlie standing there in the foyer with her flowers and her bag, and she burst into fresh tears. Unable to stop them, she covered her mouth with her hand and just sobbed.

"Suzanne! What's wrong?" He put the flowers on the hall table, dropped the bag to the floor, and rushed to her.

She couldn't speak. Her throat was closing so she just shook her head.

"Tell me. I can help."

"You can't," she managed to say, and turned her face to the French doors as sobs racked her body. Matty pulled away from her breast and she hurried to cover it with the damp material of the dress. "Here," she said, thrusting her son out to the man. "Take him . . . please."

Charles immediately took Matty away from Suzanne and just held him out between them. "What's wrong?"

Suzanne merely shook her head and pushed herself up off the rocker. She kept shaking her head and her hand, as though she couldn't stop crying. "I'll be all right," she sobbed. "I . . . I just need to change, to pull my act together."

"What can I do?" Charles demanded, holding Matty to his chest, as the infant seemed to pick up the emotions of his mother and joined her in crying.

"Nothing. No one can do anything," she wailed over the noise and walked out of the room toward the stairs.

Charles simply stared at Suzanne's back as she slowly climbed each step away from them. He shifted Matty to his shoulder and started patting his back. "We're on our own here, lad," he murmured, still shocked by Suzanne's actions.

Didn't she say in the hospital that today she was one of the happiest women alive? What had happened? And then he remembered that older woman in the elevator and her advice.

"I guess this is post-something blues, my boy. Patience. All we need is patience."

Matty answered with a quiet satisfied burp and immediately stopped crying.

Hey, was it possible he was getting the hang of this?

5

She stood in front of the mirror in her bathroom and stared at her body. Even in familiar surroundings, she simply couldn't recognize the reflection. She looked like she'd been through a war, and she bit her bottom lip to stem the on-slaught of fresh tears. It was as if she now possessed a stranger's body! Her breasts were so huge, she thought she could use them as life preservers if the need ever arose. Her once smooth stomach resembled a large balloon that had sud-denly been deflated. Her hips and thighs were wider. Only her face looked familiar, yet those eyes that stared back at her were near frightening, for she appeared like a woman on the edge.

She touched her cheek, wanting to connect with some-thing vaguely resembling her old self, but couldn't seem to stop the torrent of emotions rushing through her. "Oh, God," she whispered through her tears. "What have I done?"

No wonder Kevin didn't desire her any longer. What

member of the male species could desire something that looked like the Pillsbury Doughgirl in dire need of Prozac?

Wait a minute, her mind commanded, stunning her out of her misery. She had been in pretty decent shape when she'd become pregnant, and Kevin had said he had been having the affair with Ingrid for over a year, so . . . that meant he'd been sleeping with both of them at the same time!

Suddenly, her being was suffused with righteous indignation. That bastard didn't have the right to make her feel like this. Of course she was out of shape! She'd just given birth to a human being who had inhabited her body for almost nine months, gaining every life-sustaining nutrient from her. No wonder her skin wasn't radiant and her hair looked lifeless. Less than twenty-four hours ago she had delivered a baby through natural childbirth, though she knew if anyone had seriously offered her drugs she would have taken them. Still, here she was being critical of a body that really had been through a war, a war of life.

She shook her head and, turning away from the mirror, picked up the nursing bra she had purchased months ago, and hooked herself into it. The thing was too small and reminded her of something her mother would have worn. Forget Victoria's Secret for a while. Deciding that any further thoughts about what had happened to her body would cause a mini breakdown, she picked up the white cotton nightgown and slipped it over her head. Mindlessly, she began buttoning it down the front and, when finished, she smoothed her fingers over the eyelet lace on the collar. It was soft and comforting and familiar. And so matronly. She walked into her bedroom and opened her closet door to find the matching robe. She just needed a little rest and then she would feel better . . . about her body, about her life, about everything. Now was the time to pamper herself, since there was no one else to do it. She would get Matty and bring him upstairs and then get into bed.

Noticing the blinking red light on her answering machine, Suzanne fluffed out her hair as she walked to the night table. Without thought, she pushed the button and listened as the machine rewound the tape.

She felt her body stiffen as Kevin's voice filled her bedroom. So he was staying with Ingrid? And he thought she would call him there? What arrogance! Deciding she didn't have to do anything right now, she turned toward Kevin's closet and threw open the door to see what he'd left behind.

How he had loved to spend money on clothes, as if expensive material could cover what was in his heart. He was selfish and dishonest and . . . not all that great looking, either. Picturing Charlie in his rumpled clothes, she reached out and tore a blue and white tattersall shirt from a hanger. She rummaged through a line of perfectly pressed trousers and grabbed a dark blue pair and added it to the shirt.

Now that the idea of dressing Charlie had materialized, she felt much better as she slowly bent down and picked up a pair of soft leather Docksiders. Maybe they would fit. She turned to the built-in drawers and was relieved to find that when Kevin had hurriedly packed, he'd left a few pair of boxers. Picking up one, she opened the next drawer and grabbed up a sleeveless undershirt.

Somebody far more deserving was waiting downstairs.

She came upon them in the living room. Charlie was lying back on the sofa with Matty cradled to his chest. It appeared both of them were napping. She stood for a moment and just stared at the serene picture they presented and again felt that tightness in her throat. What would she have ever done without him? She didn't even want to consider how badly it might have turned out and she was grateful he was in her life. She also was human enough to admit that Charles Garrity, time traveler, was one attractive man. Even though he'd benefit from a bath, his cheeks sported a day's growth of stubble, and his hair could use a good brushing . . . there was something very tenderly handsome about him. Even the nurse at the hospital thought so.

She sighed deeply and pushed such ridiculous thoughts out of her head. Now was not the time to be entertaining crazy notions about another man, especially a man who claimed to be from the 1920s. Better to busy herself with useful things—like making lunch. She was starved. Placing the clothing on the edge of the sofa, Suzanne walked into her kitchen and filled the teapot with water. How she loved this big homey room. It was here that she had entertained, here she had dreamed of a future with . . . When she felt that heaviness pushing down on her again, she immediately deleted thoughts of a future. *Don't think. Work,* she admonished herself. She opened the refrigerator and began pulling out leftover chicken. Within minutes, she was making chicken salad when she suddenly got tired. She dragged the wooden stool over to the island and sat on the edge, for she was still so sore.

"You're overdoing it, Suzie," she murmured to herself, and was startled when she saw Charlie standing at the doorway with Matty still against his chest.

"I agree," he whispered with a smile. "Why don't we trade? I'll take over the cooking."

Pleased to see him, Suzanne nodded and pushed away from the food preparation. "I want to apologize to you for my . . . my little breakdown earlier. I guess it was just postpartum blues," she said, as she reached for her son.

Charlie handed the baby over to her and nodded. "That's what I thought too."

She couldn't help chuckling. "You did, huh? So you've been around new mothers a lot, have you?"

"Actually, you're my first, but a grandmother in the hospital told me about it, and it looks like she was right on target."

"Hmm . . . well, I'm sorry. I didn't mean to make such a scene."

"Look, Suzanne, you've been through a lot, just since I've met you. You deserve to have a good cry if it helps."

Inhaling the clean scent of her son, Suzanne grinned. "It's hormones, mood swings, but I'm much better now. Just a little tired."

"Why don't you go lie down? I'll bring you a tray."

"Oh, before you do anything, I brought you some clothes, so you can take a shower and change."

Standing with his hands on his hips, he surveyed the ingredients before him and shrugged his shoulders. "You can wait?"

"I can wait," she answered, secretly wondering how Charlie would look all cleaned up. Again realizing how ridiculous her thought patterns were, she turned and said, "We'll be right down here. Turn off the water. We'll have tea later."

"Are they your husband's clothes?" he asked, doing as she'd asked.

She turned at the doorway. "Yes. Don't let that bother you, okay? Soon we can go to the store and get you something new. That's all I have to offer right now."

"Well, I thank you, Suzanne. I wouldn't mind cleaning myself up a bit."

"Do you know how to use the shower?" As soon as the words came out of her mouth, she thought how odd they were.

"Shower?"

"Yes." She was right when she thought she'd have to explain. "Use the hall bathroom. In the tub you will see a large knob. Pull it out and adjust the temperature. There are clean towels in there. Oh, and could you bring the bassinet downstairs for me? It's in the nursery."

He ran his fingers through his hair and grinned sheepishly. "And that's for a baby, right?"

She grinned. "It's like a portable crib. You can't miss it. It's right in the middle of the floor with long white skirt and—"

"I remember seeing it last night," he interrupted as he passed her. "I'll be right back."

Suzanne watched him hurry toward the stairs and she found herself really smiling. "We've got some help here, Matty. We're going to make it."

When she placed Matty in the bassinet, he stirred and made tiny whimpering noises as she lifted his gown and checked his diaper. He was wet. She went over to the bag Charlie had dropped in the foyer and found a clean one and some wipes. With each footstep, she could feel how sore she was and knew she had to get off her feet soon. No point in overdoing now when she had so much of her life to figure out. As she changed her son, she wondered when she should call Kevin. The question weighed on her conscience, for she knew it wouldn't be an easy conversation. He would want to come over and see Matty, and that wasn't what she needed today. All she wanted was some peace and quiet to rest. She deserved that after the hell she'd been through in the last day.

After she changed the baby, she picked him up and walked over to the sofa. Propping him up with a pillow under her elbow, Suzanne unbuttoned her nightgown and thought she would try and nurse Matty again. No one had prepared her for all this and she realized she was going to have to learn how to be a mother on her own.

She curled her legs up onto the sofa and relaxed as the baby latched onto her and began suckling. Allowing all the tension to drain out of her, she marveled at the miracle of her body to sustain life.

Yeah . . . it was all worth it, she thought, as she heard the water turn on upstairs. She didn't even care what her body looked like right now. So what if she never again looked like a siren. It was obvious she'd never made a good one anyway. This was a new season in her life. Now she was a mother, and that is where she would focus her attention . . . on the tiny miracle in her arms.

Surely it was a miracle, Charles thought as the hot water

cascaded down his naked body. There was no heater that he could see, and yet steaming water came right out of the wall like a hard rain. He found the soap in a dish on the side of the tub and began lathering himself. He lifted his face to the water and let the soap rinse off, while wishing that he could shave the dark growth of his beard. Still, he was grateful to Suzanne for offering her home and all its many wonders. It appeared that electricity fueled most of the conveniences, even the stove, which was like a flat piece of glass with rings painted upon it. All one had to do was turn a switch and it became hot. He admitted that he missed his home. He missed Grace, and he most assuredly missed the opportunity to even the score with Mitch, but he couldn't deny his pleasure in the future. And he had to acknowledge that since he'd met Suzanne his life had taken on new meaning.

Never before had he been interested in babies, though he knew at some point in the future he wanted children of his own. Yet Matty was quickly working his way into his heart and none of it made sense. He supposed he would feel that way about any helpless creature, but being there with Suzanne as that tiny being was working so hard to come into this world had changed him. He felt a part of Matty's life.

Wanting to erase such thoughts from his head, he lathered it and scrubbed his scalp. It wouldn't do to become attached to anyone now. He would figure out his situation and then he would be leaving Suzanne and her child. Maybe he wouldn't get back to his own time, but he knew he couldn't depend on Suzanne for long. He would help her until she was back on her feet and then he knew he had to move on. He'd done it before when he'd left Ireland, and he could do it again.

He knew about taking chances . . . but time traveling into the future?

Realizing how long he'd been bathing and not wanting to use up all Suzanne's hot water, he turned off the shower, as she called it, and reached beyond the curtain for a towel. He spied the clothes she had given him and had to admit that the thought of wearing her husband's belongings didn't sit well with him.

What was the old saying?

Beggars can't be choosers.

He was that, all right, not having anything of his own save the clothes that had been on his back. So he would stifle any pride he had left and wear what she had given him while he cleaned his own clothes. Drying himself off, he began to dress quickly. He had promised Suzanne lunch and had every intention of taking care of her until she could take care of herself. It was the very least he could do for her. He wouldn't betray her trust, for she'd had enough betrayal in her life, and he vowed to put Suzanne's and Matty's welfare before his own . . . at least for now.

When he came downstairs he found Suzanne in the kitchen, busily cutting a tomato.

"What are you doing? I said I would make lunch."

"I know," she nodded. "But I had my heart set on chicken salad and Matty fell back asleep and so—"

"And so," he interrupted, "you couldn't sit still. May I remind *you* that you just had a baby?"

She glanced up from the cutting board and seemed startled for just a moment as she took in his appearance before grinning. "Throwing my words back at me, huh?"

"If it will make you rest, then yes."

She held out the handle of the knife to him. "You may take over. I surrender."

He nodded and took it from her. "Now, sit down and relax. I'll take care of this."

She sat on the edge of the stool and watched as he sliced the tomato and divided it between two plates. "By the way, you clean up very well, Mr. Garrity. No one could ever tell you just time traveled seventy-five years into the future."

He looked at her from the corner of his eye. "Why, thank you, madam. And may I say that you're looking better yourself?"

She shrugged. "Oh, Charlie, you should have seen me before . . . well, before yesterday. Let's just say, I'm not myself."

He stopped what he was doing and stared at her. "Who else would you be, if not yourself?"

"What I meant was you didn't meet me at my best."

"Suzanne, from what I've seen in the last day, you were at your best. You saved my life. You gave life to your son. How could that not be your best?"

She appeared embarrassed. "I was talking about the way I look."

"Oh. Well, I think you look just fine. Now, sit at the table and allow me to serve you," he said, spooning chicken salad onto the plates.

Suzanne did as he requested and folded her hands at the edge of the table as she waited.

"Napkins?"

"In the drawer to your left," she answered.

He pulled out two cloth napkins and opened the drawer where he'd found the knives and forks. Taking the proper utensils, he then came to the table and set it for the two of them.

When he placed the plate in front of her, he asked, "What would you like to drink?"

"There's tea brewing in the pot."

Taking down two cups, he poured the tea and brought them to the table. "Now what do you take in it? Sugar? Lemon? Cream?"

"Just sugar," she murmured, as he picked up the bowl. "I'm impressed," she added when he sat down next to her.

He brought the napkin to his lap and turned to her. "Why? I acquainted myself last night with your remarkable kitchen and I should know how you take your tea, since I intend to serve you in bed. You really should be there, you know."

Her lips seemed to tremble slightly and she took a deep breath before nodding. "I know," she said with a weary sigh.

"As soon as lunch is over I'm going upstairs with the baby. I will admit I'm tired."

"Then let's begin, shall we?"

Nodding, she smiled as she placed the napkin on her lap and picked up her fork. "A joint effort. We've done well so far, Charlie, don't you think?"

"Yes, Suzanne, we have. Considering where we both were yesterday, I think we've done remarkably well. There's even a new addition asleep in the next room. May I say how much I admire you?"

She appeared embarrassed again as she shook her head. "Thank you, but I just did what nature demanded. You seem to forget how I lied to everyone at the hospital. Not much to admire in that," she muttered, putting the fork into her mouth.

Charles swallowed. "You did what you thought was necessary. I don't judge you, Suzanne. Besides, I'm too grateful to be here, clean, rested, eating this wonderful lunch you've prepared. My statement stands. You are a woman to be admired."

"Don't make me cry, Charlie," she said with a self-conscious laugh. "You know how easily I can do it now."

Shaking his head, he grinned at her. "Suzanne McDermott, allow the Irish in me to make a prediction. Sooner than you think, you will be just fine. Maybe better than fine. You're a strong woman."

She continued to eat, repeating his words in her head. She was a strong woman. The last twenty-four hours should certainly have proved that. All she had to do was—

Her thoughts immediately ceased when the door bell rang. She and Charlie just stared at each other until it rang again. Afraid it would wake Matty, she started to push herself away from the table, when Charlie reached out and grasped her wrist.

"Stay seated. I'll answer it."

"It may be Kevin."

"I said I'll get it." He wiped his mouth with the napkin before placing it calmly on the table.

Suzanne's heart started thumping in her chest as she watched him walk out of the room. She heard the front door open and when she heard Kevin's voice, she closed her eyes and tried to mine some reserve of strength for the inevitable confrontation.

"Where's Suzanne? Who are you?"

Standing up slowly, she walked into the living room and saw her husband at the door staring at Charlie as though he wanted to thrash him. "It's all right, Charlie," Suzanne called out as she stood next to the bassinet. "You can let him in."

Charlie waved his hand toward the living room and Kevin strode over to her. He was dressed in tan slacks and a pale yellow cardigan. He was probably on his way to play golf at the club. She noticed that his face looked red and his expression was sour. At one time it might have affected her, but not today. "I was going to contact you," she began, clutching the edge of the bassinet.

"Who *is* that man?" Kevin demanded, glaring back at Charlie, who was standing on the edge of the foyer watching them. "What is he doing here?"

"He works for me now," Suzanne answered and was amazed at how easily it came to her. "I need help around the farm since . . ." She took a deep breath. "Since yesterday I went into labor." Looking down into the bassinet, she murmured, "Matty was born at six-fourteen last evening."

"*What?*"

She didn't even bother to look up as Kevin slowly approached. Instead, she smiled down at her sleeping son. "He's perfectly healthy, though I don't think he cares for sunshine just yet."

"So that's why you didn't answer the phone," Kevin whispered. "I thought you might have . . . have . . ."

His words trailed off and Suzanne glanced up. "Don't flatter yourself, Kevin. I wouldn't harm myself or my son over you."

"May I hold him?" Kevin asked, ignoring her last statement.

She debated the question. Matty was sleeping, yet she knew if she didn't allow it Kevin would hound her. Bending down, she picked up Matty and held him out to his father.

Kevin accepted the baby and just stared down at him, a look of wonder on his face. "My son," he whispered.

A surge of anger rushed through her body. How she had pictured this scene in her mind so many times—her husband cradling their newborn. She just never imagined that he would be living with her best friend at the time and planning a divorce. Wanting to tear Matty away from him, Suzanne took a deep breath and said to Charlie, "Let's finish our lunch." If she didn't get away from Kevin, she couldn't be held responsible for her actions.

Charlie closed the front door and they met at the kitchen. "Are you sure about this, Suzanne? You want to leave him alone out there?"

"What is he going to do?" she asked with a shrug. "He certainly can't take Matty to Ingrid's. The woman couldn't even take care of a kitten when she was a teenager. He is the father. I'll let him have a few minutes with Matty."

She sat back at the kitchen table, yet didn't touch her food. Instead, she picked up her cup of tea and sipped. "No matter what he says or does, Charlie, don't listen to him."

He lightly touched her arm. "Suzanne, I'm not worried about him. I'm worried about you."

She could feel it happening again—that tightness in her throat, the burning at her eyes.

"Your nose is getting red," he said with a teasing grin.

"I told you not to be nice to me, or it will start again. And I need to stay in control. Finish your lunch."

"Finish yours."

"I can't eat right now."

Charlie picked up his cup of tea and sat back in his chair. "Then we'll both wait until he leaves."

They sat in silence for at least a minute, until Suzanne couldn't stand it anymore. "I'd better get back out there. He's had enough time."

"Do you want me to come with you?"

"No, you stay here, okay?"

"If you need me . . ."

"Thanks, Charlie, but I'll be fine," she said as she left the room.

She walked into the living room and inhaled deeply as she saw Kevin holding their son in his arms. "He needs to sleep," she said, coming farther into the room. That too was another fabrication, but she wanted Kevin out of the house. Just his presence was throwing off everything, especially her hard-won peace of mind. "I'll take him now," she stated, holding out her arms.

Kevin gently transferred Matty and whispered, "He's perfect, isn't he?"

"Yes, he is," she answered, kissing her son's forehead before placing him in the bassinet. When she straightened, she rubbed the small of her back and looked at her husband. In less than a day he seemed like a stranger. The man she had loved and dreamed of a future with was gone. In his place was this . . . this person whose genes made up half of her son's, but she couldn't even dredge up an ounce of love, and every dream they'd once shared had been crushed yesterday.

"We need to talk, Suzanne," he stated, running a hand through his sandy brown hair.

"Really, Kevin?" she replied, walking away from their sleeping son and toward the door. "I think you said enough yesterday, don't you?"

"I have some rights here," he answered, his voice rising slightly. "Why didn't you call me to tell me you were having the baby? It's early. Something could have been wrong, and I wouldn't have known. I'm left out of the loop? I am still the father."

It was enough to raise the hair on the back of her neck in retaliation. "You have whatever rights I give you. May I remind you that you walked out of here yesterday—"

"You told me to leave," he interrupted.

"Ah, yes, after you told me that you were in love with my best friend and had been sleeping with her during our marriage and that you wanted a divorce to marry her. I got all that right, didn't I? Of course, I was too shaken at the time to figure it all out. You were sleeping with both of us at the same time. That's adultery, Kevin, grounds for divorce in this state." She was at the front door and opened it for him before continuing. "I went into labor yesterday after you left and calling you wasn't even a consideration since I didn't have my cell phone with me. I needed help, not more betrayal." She paused and took a deep breath. "I will contact a lawyer and we can arrange for visitation, but until then please do not come here unannounced again."

"This is my home, my family's home. That is my son." His gaze narrowed. "Don't make this ugly."

She almost burst into laughter. "Ugly? *Ugly?* You've already done that, Kevin. It's hideously ugly. My husband and my best friend? We should all go on *Jerry Springer.*"

"That'd be something," he retaliated sarcastically. "Bring along *your* new friend. Who is that guy, anyway? Where did you find him?"

"I've already told you I hired him, for help and for protection."

"Protection?"

"Yes. You may have felt just fine about leaving me here alone, but I felt otherwise. He's here for me."

"You don't even know him, do you?"

"I know he is honorable and trustworthy, which is more than I can say for you and Ingrid—and I thought I knew both of you. What more do I need to know?"

"Is he wearing my clothes?"

She did laugh. With everything they had to discuss, he was more concerned with his damned clothes!"Yes, Kevin, he is. I let him borrow them. Don't worry, they'll be cleaned and returned to you. His were soiled and the rest of his things aren't arriving until later in the week. Now, I've had quite a time of it in the last twenty-four hours. I suggest you leave, and don't return until I've recovered. I'll notify you when that is." At that moment Matty began crying and her breasts started to tingle in response.

"You can't just leave it like this, Suzanne. I have rights and I don't feel comfortable with a stranger in *my* house with *my* son."

Suzanne gritted her teeth, in an attempt to suppress the scream that was pushing up from her gut. "Look, you may be Matty's biological father, but when you betrayed me, you betrayed him too. Didn't that ever occur to you?" She scowled at him and continued before he could. "As far as I'm concerned, you forfeited your *rights*, Kevin. Matty and I were one and the same. Just because he's out of my body now doesn't mean you can waltz in here whenever you want and disrupt our lives." She took another deep breath. "I'll have all your precious clothes packed and sent over to Ingrid's by the end of the week. That should make you feel better. As far as our son is concerned, we'll deal with that in court. And believe me, Kevin, it's already ugly. You have only yourself to thank for that."

"Suzanne?"

She and Kevin both turned to see Charlie standing not ten feet away. He was holding Matty to his chest. "I think he's hungry."

Suzanne watched as the two men stared at one another, each with a hard, penetrating glare. "It's time for you to leave, Kevin," she stated firmly.

"This isn't over," Kevin muttered, walking through the door and slamming it behind him.

Matty jerked in Charlie's arms, throwing his own arms out in fright, and began to cry even louder. Rushing to take him, Suzanne bit her bottom lip to keep her own tears in check. All she wanted was some peace . . . somewhere.

As she held her son against her chest, she lowered her chin and kissed his temple. "I'm so sorry, Matty," she whispered. "You won't ever have to be a part of this again."

"C'mon, Suzanne, let me take you upstairs. It's time for you to rest."

"Yes," she whispered in exhaustion and defeat. "It's time."

He placed his strong arm around her shoulders and used the other to hold her elbow as all three of them took it a step at a time. She could feel her legs shaking until the tremors started working their way through her entire body. "Take him," she instructed, putting Matty into Charlie's arms.

She sank to the stair and held on to the railing for support. "I just need to rest."

"Stay right there," Charlie instructed, walking back down the steps with Matty.

When he returned, Matty was in the bassinet and Charlie lifted it over her to take it upstairs.

"Would you put it in my room?" she requested, trying to stop the shaking of her body. Whatever was wrong with her?

He came back and looked down to her with a concerned expression. "That's it, Suzanne," he stated in a firm voice. "I'm taking over now. You are getting into bed and staying there, do you understand?"

"Yes, sir. I just need a few minutes to get my strength back and—"

Her words were interrupted when Charlie reached down and scooped his arm under her knees. "Hold on," he instructed as he started to lift her.

"I can walk," she protested, grabbing onto his neck.

"Oh hush up, Suzanne. The last time I did this we almost fell. Work with me here."

In spite of everything, she almost laughed while remembering the last time he had carried her by the creek. "What a pair we make, Charlie."

He reached the top step and turned his head while walking into her bedroom. Looking into her eyes, he said, "I think we make a fine pair, Suzie. As long as you start listening to me and get off your feet."

All she could think about when he gently placed her on her bed was that he'd called her Suzie. It had been years since anyone had used her nickname, and the tears she had been holding back started to stream down her cheeks. He released her and allowed her to rest back against the pillows.

"I'll get Matty," he said, and moved to the bassinet.

As she accepted her son, she looked into Charlie's eyes and whispered, "I think you were sent to me because I needed a friend so much."

He seemed startled for just a moment and then smiled tenderly. "Don't worry anymore, all right? I heard what you told him. I am here to help you, and I will protect you. Just rest now. I'll take care of everything."

Nodding, she brought Matty to her chest and began unbuttoning her robe.

"I'll leave you now. Your nose is getting red again. And I know what that means."

"Chicken," she whispered with a sniffle and a grin.

He chuckled and walked toward the door. "I'll be back later to bring you a fresh cup of tea."

Alone with Matty, Suzanne settled back to nurse her son. What a day, and it wasn't even half over. Well, at least she'd dealt with Kevin, so that part was finished. She could just imagine him running back to Ingrid to tell her everything. *Don't think about it,* she silently advised. Better to think about the way Kevin had been decidedly intimidated by Charlie's presence. Time traveler or not, he was certainly becoming invaluable to her in ways she couldn't have even imagined.

Allowing the tears to run, she touched her son's perfect little nose and whispered, "He called me Suzie."

She couldn't be this sappy, this sentimental.

It must be postpartum blues!

6

It was dark when she awakened, and the first thing she heard was a baby's cry, a plaintive wailing that resonated beyond her ears and into her heart. Somebody should help that child. Turning her head slightly, she was confused for just a moment as everything immediately crashed and fell into place—dragging Charlie out of the water, the delivery, the confrontation with Kevin. It was *her* baby! What had happened to her peaceful life? Still exhausted, as if in a sleepwalking state, she dragged herself closer to the edge of the bed. Turning on the lamp, she saw Matty in the bassinet and immediately guilt assailed her. He must need to be changed and fed and she had passed out! What kind of a mother was she?

"Okay, honey, I'm coming," she called out, pulling herself off the mattress and wincing as her sore muscles rebelled at the movement. She did her best to dismiss the aches, for her focus was on reaching her child.

He was tangled in his blanket and she felt even more

guilty for not being more attentive. Picking him up, she could feel his soggy diaper and tears came into her eyes. What a lousy parent she was making, she thought as she tried to ignore the sensation of having to relieve herself. She couldn't use the bathroom holding Matty, and yet she couldn't put him down when he was screaming and wet. Just as she bit the side of her cheek to stop the frustration building, Charlie came into the room with a tray.

"I heard him crying and thought you would be hungry."

"Charlie, can you hold him for a minute? I . . . I need to use the bathroom." To heck with modesty. She was desperate.

"Sure," he answered, placing the tray at the foot of the king-size bed.

"He's wet," she said, gently handing Matty over. "I'll change him as soon as I come out."

Nodding, Charlie cradled the baby to his shoulder and patted his back. "It's all right, lad," he whispered, trying to placate the crying infant.

Suzanne rushed into the bathroom and took care of business, feeling overwhelmed by the responsibility of a single parent that was now placed solidly upon her shoulders. It was like her life was no longer her own. Everything revolved around the baby, even something so elementary as sitting on the toilet. Rushing as she heard Matty's continued exasperated screams, she washed her hands and came back into the bedroom.

"There's no stopping him, Suzanne," Charlie said, looking worried.

"He's probably just wet and hungry." She took the baby and walked into the nursery as Charlie followed. Placing Matty in the crib, she said over the crying that was beginning to make her cry, "Could you get me a diaper from the top drawer?"

Turning her attention to Matty, she began undressing him. "It's okay, sweetie, we'll just change you and then I'll feed you and you'll feel much better. Please be patient with me."

She'd thought she had been so prepared. She had even imagined this Hallmark Card kind of homecoming, not bedlam every time Matty was wet or hungry. Frustrated with her inability to soothe her child, Suzanne could feel those damn tears gathering at her eyes as she struggled to remove Matty's clothing.

"It doesn't look like he cares for being naked," Charlie whispered over her shoulder.

"Maybe he's just cold," she answered with a sniffle, cleaning her child's tiny bottom with the disposable wipes. "I guess I have to be faster."

"Here, why don't you show me how to do it and then I can change him for you."

She glanced over her shoulder. "Really? Are you sure?"

He straightened and grinned. "I don't mind, and I said I was going to be of help to you. This way you won't have to get out of bed every time he needs to be changed."

They switched places and Suzanne directed him. "First you clean him with these wipes. You have to be very gentle, especially . . ." Now how was she supposed to say this? "You, ah . . . have to pull back the foreskin. The nurse showed me in the hospital." Inwardly, she cringed at speaking to Charlie like that, but if he was going to help with the changing, he would have to know everything. "That's right," she added, relieved to see Charlie was doing just fine, though Matty simply wouldn't stop crying. Still, her heart seemed to expand toward this man who had appeared in her life and now didn't flinch at such an awkward situation.

"Hold his legs up with one hand, like this," she said, reaching down and putting a finger between Matty's ankles to keep them separate. "Then you slide the diaper under him."

"Now what?"

"Bring the diaper up in between his legs and—*oh my!*"

Both she and Charlie automatically backed up, but not before Charlie's shirt sleeve was christened. Suzanne brought her hand up to her mouth to try and hide the laughter that threatened to explode. "I'm so sorry," she managed to mumble.

Charlie let out a laugh and shook his head. "The lad's got good aim, I'll say that for him."

They both laughed, even though Matty's face was deep red with indignation and his tiny fingers were closed into fists as he continued to cry and flail his arms and legs. "I'll get another diaper," Suzanne announced. Soon they were again attempting to diaper Matty and Suzanne instructed Charlie to roll the front of the diaper down so the umbilical cord wouldn't be covered.

"You say it dries up and falls off?"

Again, Suzanne laughed. "Yes. That's how you got your belly button, Charlie."

He sighed as he fastened the diaper. "There's so much I've never thought about before, especially about babies."

"I know what you mean," she said with her own sigh. "I thought I was so prepared, but nothing could have prepared me for this. I feel overwhelmed."

"You'll be a fine mother, Suzanne."

She appreciated his words. "Okay, you seem to have everything under control here. I have to change before I feed him. Do you think you could put this gown on him?" She placed a pale yellow one on the crib mattress.

"Now, that seems easy," Charlie remarked, holding it up for inspection.

Without thinking, Suzanne touched his shoulder. "You're a good man, Mr. Garrity. Thanks for coming into my life."

"I didn't really have a choice, Suzanne," he said, gifting her with a big smile. "Just glad I can help."

There was a moment that passed between them, a timeless moment when even Matty's wails seemed to be drowned out as Suzanne felt a rush of something pleasurable and familiar pass through her body. It was like when she just *knew* something good was going to happen, that she was in the right place at the right time, with the right person. It was, however, embarrassing for it to be happening now, with leaky breasts and a baby that wouldn't stop crying. "I'll be quick," she answered, and rushed away. It just wouldn't do to give those thoughts any more room to grow. Charles Garrity was her friend, and she wasn't going to mess up anything with misplaced feelings.

Grabbing a clean nightgown from her closet and a new nursing bra, she hurried to the bathroom and prayed for the strength to get through this first night with her new son. Maybe she could take a really quick shower? What a blessing that would be, even for a couple of minutes, to feel clean again. Forget shaving her legs. It would have to be a quickie. She actually felt guilty as she turned on the shower and stripped off her nightgown.

So this was motherhood?

An hour later Matty was asleep in the bassinet and Suzanne was resting back against the pillows of her bed, having finished two cold fried eggs, hard toast, and a barely warm cup of tea. Never would she admit that it was anything less than delicious as Charlie sat on the edge of the mattress and talked to her.

"And so I looked up to the sky and there it was, like nothing I've ever seen. I mean, I have seen biplanes, but this was . . . was huge and had single wings. I wanted to ask you about it, but you and Matty were asleep. What have I missed, Suzanne, in the last seventy-five years?"

She exhaled, wondering how to answer him. "Charlie, civilization has undergone the biggest leap in technology . . . machinery," she added when she saw his look of confusion. It was so hard for her to remember that she was talking to someone who didn't know these things. "That was an airplane carrying around a hundred or more people either into Philadelphia or away from it. It's a common form of transportation now."

"How I would like to travel in one," he mused, scratching the growth of beard at his jaw line.

"Perhaps you will one day," she answered. "You've already mastered driving." Seeing him absently continue to scratch, a thought suddenly came to her. "Do you want to shave that beard?"

He stopped scratching. "Yes," he answered with more than a tinge of gratitude in his voice. "You can't imagine how annoying this is."

"I can see," she said with a smile as she flipped back the comforter and attempted to rise. "I'll get you a razor."

Immediately, Charlie got up and offered his assistance. "You don't have to do it right now."

She was becoming used to his touch, his strength, and whispered, "Hey, Matty's sleeping. I'm coming to the conclusion that if I want to get anything accomplished at all, I have to do it while he's asleep. C'mon . . . let's go into my bathroom."

It was very intimate to be in a bathroom with a man that was not her husband. Suzanne realized how long it had been since she had even thought about any man except Kevin. Unlike him, she had really felt married . . . though a nagging thought came to her as she opened the glass door of her shower and pulled out her razor. She really hadn't been all that happy for some time in her marriage. Not really happy. It had happened so slowly . . . that sense of comfort, of settling into each other and their lives. There hadn't been any real passion for quite a while, passion where you couldn't wait to be in someone's presence, to feel their skin, taste their kisses. In six years she and Kevin had fallen into a routine, but she had believed the love was intact. She had thought it was the way most marriages unfolded, but it was obvious that Kevin had felt differently. It was as if a sledgehammer hit her between the eyes when she recognized the gradual evaporation of passion over the years.

Not wanting to deal with that revelation at the moment, she pulled herself together and closed the shower door. "Here we are. Let me change the blade for you."

She walked over to the row of drawers in the six-foot-wide vanity and pulled out the second one. "I'm afraid Kevin took his shaving cream. You'll have to use soap and water," she said as she picked up the disposable blades and began switching the one on her razor.

"Do you mind if I remove this shirt?" he asked. "It is a bit soiled."

"Sure, I have some things that need washing, along with Matty's clothes. I'll show you how to use the washing machine in the laundry room."

"You have a machine that washes clothes?"

Laughing at his look of wonder, she nodded. "Yes. As I said, you will be surprised at all the mechanical advancements today. And a machine that washes clothes is just one of them." She watched him unbutton his shirt and pull it down his arms. Looking away, she tried to concentrate on switching the blade and not on the definition of muscles in his upper arms. No wonder he's so strong, she thought, not unaffected by the sight of Charles Garrity in a sleeveless undershirt. "Sorry about the shaving cream," she whispered, feeling like she should say something to break the silence and the mental vision of this handsome man who stood before her.

"Soap and water is just fine," Charlie answered, picking up the bar in the glass dish.

Suzanne turned on the water for him and stood for a moment, watching as he lathered his hands and brought them up to his face. "Do you know how to use it?"

"I did use a straight-edge razor, but this looks fairly simple. At least some things haven't changed all that much." Once his face was fully lathered, he rinsed his hands and Suzanne handed him the razor.

"There you go," she said. "Try it out."

He brought the razor up to his cheek and shaved downward. "I don't think anything's happening."

"Here, let me try. You have to apply more pressure."

"But it's a razor."

She laughed. "I know, but it's a safety razor. Come sit down on the edge of the Jacuzzi so I can reach you."

"What's a . . . a Jacuzzi?"

"That tub. It has valves on it to make bubbles under the water. It's very soothing," she added, not even wanting to allow her mind to go where it was heading.

"Amazing," he said, staring down at the white porcelain.

Pulling a towel from the brass bar on the wall, Suzanne wrapped it around his shoulders and directed him to the saltillo tile platform around the huge tub.

"You've done this before?" he asked with a worried expression, sitting down and spreading his knees.

Chuckling, Suzanne stood between his legs and brought up the razor. "I've shaved my legs for more years than I care to remember. I think I can handle your face."

Charlie took a deep steadying breath and murmured, "Your legs, huh? I won't even question that. I am in your capable hands, madam."

"Oh, don't look so worried. I'm not about to slit your throat. Now, if you were Kevin . . ."

His hand shot up to capture her wrist. "Please do not compare me to that man, nor even think about him while you have a razor in your hand!"

She laughed. "Relax, Charlie. You can trust me."

He looked directly into her eyes and his expression suddenly softened. "Yes, I know I can, Suzanne. And you can trust me."

She was shocked by the wave of sexual recognition that raced through her body as he slowly released her wrist. It was uncalled for, misplaced, nearly insane considering she had delivered a baby twenty-four hours ago! It simply had to be fluctuating hormones. Steadying her hand, she tried to control her voice as she said, "Of course we can trust each other. We're friends. Now keep still, and don't talk."

"Yes, ma'am," he muttered.

She could see the laughter in his eyes and tried to ignore it as she brought the razor to his cheek. "Short strokes," she whispered, reaching back to the sink and turning the water on to rinse the blade.

She felt his breath on her chest as he exhaled and realized again what an intimate position she was in. *Concentrate on the job at hand,* she mentally commanded, not on the fact that you are standing between the legs of an extremely handsome man, a man who claims to have time traveled into your life!

She felt her hand tremble and stood frozen for a moment. She willed her fingers to steady themselves and began shaving him. She gazed at the lines of laughter around his startling green eyes. Close up, she saw the fine threads of gray mingled into his thick dark hair. Yes, Charles Garrity was one very handsome man. Combine that with his Irish charm, and it was no wonder he was wreaking havoc with her mind. *Stop thinking about it and focus,* her brain reprimanded. When she had half his face shaved, she finally said, "I think you can do it now. Just remember to press down gently and use short strokes." She handed him the razor and backed away as he slowly rose.

"You don't trust yourself?" he asked with a grin.

Knowing he couldn't possibly have read her thoughts, she smiled back. "I don't want to be responsible for any bloodletting. At least with you."

"Ah, Suzie . . ." he called out with a slight Irish accent as he stood in front of the mirror and rinsed the razor. "You're too gentle a lass ever to be responsible for bloodletting. I was never worried."

"I'm glad *you* weren't," she murmured, picking up his shirt and walking toward the doorway. "When you're finished in here, I'll show you how to use the washing machine."

She grabbed up her robe and put it on, as if the act would present a barrier between her and the man who would be coming out of her bathroom. How *could* she be so rattled by him when she had just delivered a baby? No one told her about these raging hormones, or what they could do to a libido that had been put on hold for the last four months.

She gazed down to her beautiful sleeping son and sighed with wonder. He had come out of her. By some miracle of nature she and Kevin had created this gift to the world. When she looked at him like this it didn't matter that her entire life was turned upside down, that she was exhausted and every muscle in her body ached. What did matter was that despite everything crazy that was happening in her life, she was going to make sure Matty was protected. She would do whatever it took, for she was now a mother.

A surge of appreciation rushed through her body for her own mother and everything she had taken for granted. A lump formed in her throat when she thought of her mother's death. How she wished her mother could be here now to see her grandson. Somehow, she felt her mother knew and would always watch out for her.

"I need some help, Mom," she whispered while continuing to stare at her son. Not only had her marriage fallen apart. She didn't know how "together" life was around her. She had an infant to care for and a time traveler shaving in her bathroom. Shaking her head, Suzanne grinned and slipped her feet into her slippers. Well, she certainly couldn't complain that her life was boring!

She walked across the room, opened Kevin's closet, and stared at the remaining clothes. She'd have to pack all this up once she got her strength back. She'd hire a messenger service to take it to Ingrid's, for she couldn't see herself doing it and she wouldn't ask Charlie. Remembering why she had come into the closet, Suzanne grabbed a long-sleeved cotton shirt and flicked off the light as she closed the door on a problem she couldn't immediately solve.

"Here's a clean shirt," she said, watching as Charlie bent over the sink and rinsed his face with water. He reached for the towel and smiled at her in the mirror.

"Thanks. When you get a chance you can show me how to use this machine that washes clothes."

"I can show you now. I have some things I should wash and, as I've said, if I don't do it while Matty's sleeping I don't know when I'll have the chance." She couldn't suppress the tired sigh.

He dried his face and hands and chuckled. "He sure does demand attention when he's awake, doesn't he? I didn't know babies were so . . . demanding is the only word I can think of right now. He has his needs and he wants them met *now*."

Smiling, she nodded. "I didn't really know either. I read so many books while I was pregnant and I thought I was prepared, but boy, did I underestimate a tiny baby."

He folded the towel and left it on the counter.

She was a bit startled when he turned his head to her and held out his hand for the shirt. He looked so clean and handsome and . . . and manly, that Suzanne swallowed deeply as she placed the shirt in his fingers. "I . . . I'll . . . ah, get those things that need to be washed. You can gather up your clothes and we'll do them together."

He nodded as he slipped his arms into the shirtsleeves and Suzanne quickly looked away as she left him. Yes, being in a bathroom with a man who was not her husband was far too intimate, yet she couldn't completely erase the vision of him in that sleeveless undershirt. Washing. Clothes. Action. She needed to shake any other thoughts out of her mind. She was a mother now, she reminded herself again. A woman of some dignity, though she would be hard pressed to find any in the last twenty-four hours. As she picked up her soiled clothes, she left the bedroom and walked into the nursery.

Gathering up Matty's things, she inwardly shuddered as the memory of what she had put Charlie through during labor flashed through her mind. *Dignity?* She'd certainly lost that in front of the man, and yet, it didn't seem to have affected the way he treated her. He'd seen her at her worst, knew the truth about her and her failed marriage, and still treated her with respect.

"Ready?"

Startled, she clutched the laundry to her chest and jumped as she heard him speak. Nodding, she walked into the hallway and headed for the stairs.

"Here, allow me," he said, taking the soiled clothes from her arms and adding them to his own. "You hold on to the railing and to me."

"I'm fine," she protested, not wanting to feel the muscles in his arms again.

"I insist," he stated, holding out the crook of his arm. "You weren't too steady coming up these stairs and the last thing we need is for anything to happen to you. You have to take care of yourself, Suzanne, and I'm going to make sure you do."

She couldn't help the smile from forming at her lips. "You're such a gentleman, Charles Garrity."

"I was brought up correctly, madam."

"Your family . . . your mother and father . . . are they still alive?" she asked as they slowly descended the stairs.

There was silence.

Immediately she saw what a stupid question that was and apologized. "I'm so sorry. That was ridiculous to ask. I keep forgetting that you're . . . well, from another time."

"It's all right, Suzanne. None of this is normal, not for either one of us. My father died while I was attending university in Dublin. I came home to find my mother distraught. It seemed my father had left us penniless and in debt."

"I'm sorry," she murmured, as they reached the bottom step.

"Thank you, but there's no need for your sorrow. It happened a long time ago." He shrugged as he looked about the house. "It appears now a very long time ago."

"C'mon, I'll show you the washing machine," she whispered with a smile. She could tell he really didn't want to talk about his past and she had to respect that after everything he'd been through. "And the real miracle, Mr. Garrity, is that there is also a machine that dries the wet clothes."

"No more hanging clothes on the line?"

She shook her head as they walked through the kitchen. "Nope. It's all done by machines now, though I sometimes miss the scent of laundry dried in fresh air." She noticed that he had washed the frying pan he had used for her eggs and her heart softened even more. Kevin never washed anything, not a dish or a piece of clothing. It dawned on her that she had really allowed her husband to get away with a lot, not the least was an affair with her best friend.

If she ever again got time to think, then she had a lot to go over in her mind about her marriage. Like why wasn't she grieving over its ending? Wasn't it just yesterday that she'd thought she couldn't get through the betrayal? What had happened to her, she wondered as they entered the laundry room. It wasn't just having Matty in her life now or the appearance of a very attractive, attentive man who claimed to be from 1926. Somehow, as crazy as it might seem . . . she really didn't want to try and salvage her marriage to Kevin. Somewhere in the recesses of her frazzled mind yesterday at the creek, she had envisioned him realizing his mistake and begging her to forgive him and take him back. That possibility, as distant as it might be, wasn't even an option. Not any longer. Something had changed within her after her son's birth. It was as if a surge of strength seemed to cradle her soul, gently reminding her that she didn't really need Kevin and could make it without him . . . and she might even be happier. How odd to have that insight in front of the washing machine.

Yes, she had a lot to think about. Decisions had to be made.

She sighed deeply when she realized the first one was finding a divorce lawyer.

"Okay, Charlie," she said with a quick smile as she slapped her hand down on the white metal. "Meet my Whirlpool."

7

"**Y**ou say this is called tell-o-vision?"

He heard the awe in his own voice, yet his mind simply could not grasp that he was seated inside Suzanne's house, watching what she said were people in a studio across the Delaware River. And they were talking to him!

"Yes, well actually it's pronounced tel-*eh*-vision and it's being broadcast from Philadelphia."

He turned and stared at her seated beside him on the sofa. Holding Matty, she looked so calm, as if this wasn't some kind of miracle. "How can this be? How can they be in Philadelphia and in your house at the same time?" He quickly turned back when he heard the man behind the glass asking if he was concerned about the quality of the air he breathed. "No," he answered, and heard Suzanne's chuckle.

"Charlie, he can't hear you. Only you can hear him. Television isn't interactive. It only goes one way . . . out to whomever is watching."

"But how does it work?"

"It's sent on radio waves and . . . and is picked up by an aerial and . . . oh, I don't know. Wait, okay. I've got it. Would you go over to that book shelf with the encyclopedias and bring me the one marked *T*?"

Reluctant to leave the amazing glass pictures, he got up and did as she asked. He searched the long row of leather bound books until he found the one she'd requested. Handing the book to her, he sat back down and watched as the picture changed once again to men with measuring equipment. They were measuring the air? How? Why?

"Okay, here," Suzanne said after a few moments, placing the book on the sofa beside her. "It says when you switch on your television set, the picture you see is created from a pattern of light formed by electrical signals. The television camera converts the picture it takes into electrical signals, and they are broadcast on radio waves at the speed of light. Look, here's a picture and a diagram."

He glanced down to the book and saw a confusing picture of something called electron beams. Turning his attention back to the glass, he asked, "Why are they measuring the air? What do they hope to find?"

"Well, they measure to find pollution, and we all hope the lack of it," she answered. "See, Charlie, all these marvelous inventions . . . well, a lot of them make the air we breathe less clean than what you're used to. The biggest culprit is the modern combustion engine. The car."

"Really? There are so many of them now."

"I know. Most of us want to keep the cars we have so I guess the answer is in technology again—coming up with a cleaner engine."

He watched the glass change again to a picture of a scandalously clad woman walking in the surf of the ocean. She was near naked! When she kicked her foot and sent the water spraying toward the glass, he involuntarily jerked sideways away from it.

"That's not live, happening right now," Suzanne said with

a giggle. "That's a commercial. There's a difference between what's happening right now, as in the live news reports, and what's been taped or filmed some time ago and is shown over and over again."

"A com-mercial?" How would he ever learn all this?

"See? It's an advertisement for Ballys, a fitness gym where people work out. This particular advertisement is saying that summer is coming and there's still time to get in shape."

He cleared his throat. "Well, excuse me for saying this, but that young woman certainly appears to have a . . . ah, *shape*. Is it accepted to show so much of one's body in this time?"

Watching her smile, he could tell that she didn't mind all his questions.

"Yes, Charlie, it's acceptable . . . even preferable, if you look like her. We're not quite as puritanical in this time about our bodies."

"But you don't dress like that."

She laughed good-naturedly as she glanced down to her yellow and white robe. "I don't look like that," she answered as she eased herself up from the sofa. Placing Matty into the bassinet Charlie had brought downstairs, Suzanne added, "Even before I got pregnant I guess I was never one to prance about in a bikini. Now, I'll be lucky to get into a one-piece this summer."

"A one piece?" *Bikini? What the hell is that?*

"Bathing suit," she said, rubbing the small of her back. "Right now, I'd just like to get back into the jeans I wore a year ago. Here," she added, picking up a thin black contraption and holding it out to him. "Press this button and watch what happens."

He did.

"Point it at the television."

This time he was astonished as the glass picture changed

right before his eyes to people yelling and pushing back chairs as they appeared ready to fight.

"Jerry Springer," Suzanne muttered. "Push it again."

The next picture showed a huge yellow bird talking to children.

"Sesame Street. Try it again."

He did and saw men galloping on horses through desert mountains. He pointed at the picture. "I've been there," he whispered with awe as he leaned closer.

"You have?"

Nodding, he said, "I don't know if it's the exact same place, but it certainly looks like a ranch I worked on in Texas."

"Really? You worked on a ranch? Like a cowboy?"

"For two years. Mitch and . . . well, someone I knew, and I, we did it together," he corrected, not wanting even to think about that sonofabitch Mitch Davies. The picture changed to what appeared to be a bunkhouse and he sat, fascinated, as he listened to a conversation between two men discussing how they were planning to steal part of the herd of horses. He glanced up to Suzanne who was still smiling at him. "Should we inform someone of this?"

Her shoulders dropped and her head tilted to the side as her smile widened. "Ah, Charlie, what a sweetie you are. This isn't real. It's a show, a movie. Didn't they have movies in your time?"

"We had black and white moving pictures, but no sound. You could read words on a huge screen, and a small orchestra in a pit up front would play music in the larger theaters. It was nothing like this, Suzanne. How will I ever catch up?" A part of him wondered if he really wanted to. It was as though the future was chasing him and he didn't know how long he could keep running from it. Raking his fingers through his hair in frustration, he sighed.

"Well, you could use the encyclopedia to look up things you don't understand, or . . ." she paused.

"Or?" he asked hopefully, as he glanced up at her.

"Or, we could rent videos . . . err . . . movies to watch here at home on the TV."

"The TV?"

"TV is short for television. See, what I was thinking was, we go to Blockbuster and you could get a sort of crash course pictorial history starting with . . ." She hesitated ". . . like *For Whom the Bell Tolls.* Ernest Hemingway's novel was made into a movie and it was about World War One. That was around your time period, right?"

"World War *One*? There was another?"

Nodding, she replied with a tone of sadness, "Since then we've had World War Two, the Korean War, the Vietnam War, the Persian Gulf War—"

"But the war I fought in was supposed to be the war to end all wars. They said it would never happen again . . ." His stunned words trailed off.

"I'm sorry, Charlie," she murmured. "A lot has happened since . . . wait. You were in the first world war?"

Staring at her, he sat in silence for a moment that spanned over seventy-five years. "That was a long time ago, Suzanne," he said with a sigh, then added, "a time I'd rather not recall." He looked up above the huge fireplace to the wreath hanging on the wall and beyond it to the ceiling. How he wished his mind would go as blank as the white above him, yet it would not rest. Peace, it seemed, had not come as easily to the world, either.

"I understand, Charlie."

The sound of her voice gathered him back again. "Are we at war now?"

"Thankfully, no."

That, he was relieved to hear. Although he had a strong sense of patriotism since he'd come to this great country, for a brief moment he thought he might have to volunteer his life again . . . and he was honest enough to admit that was not something he wanted to repeat. To him it was a plain and simple fact that war was ugly, no matter what age it took place in, and he had the scars to prove it. Looking back to Suzanne, he breathed deeply and attempted a confident smile. "So, you say I may take a pictorial history course of what I've missed then?"

"Sure." She grinned, then her eyes suddenly narrowed. "Well, in a sense. Much of it is embellished by Hollywood, but some of it is dead-on accurate. You'll get the basic idea."

His mind vainly tried to make sense of all the foreign words she was using. "Holly-wood." He repeated the word slowly as though saying it might give him a better understanding of it. Had he heard it before?

"You know, Hollywood, California. It's where they make most of the movies."

"Ah," he said with a nod, although he knew he wasn't completely clear on the subject. "Well then, how many blocks must we bust to get these vid-ee-os you speak of?"

Her sympathetic laugh was enough to expose his innocence. "Oh, Charlie, you are so precious," she said with affection as she sat down beside him. "Please don't be offended but, sometimes, talking to you is like trying to have a conversation with someone from another planet." She paused and appeared to reflect before adding, "And yet, it amazes me how much *I* take for granted."

He barely heard her comparison. He was too busy hoping the blush around his ears wouldn't be noticed. Damn. He felt completely ignorant. "Forgive me, Su—"

Startled, he watched as she leaned over to touch his lips gently with her fingertip. In an instant, a part of him felt compelled to repel her advance, but he swallowed his pride and accepted her offering. Another part of him was forced to acknowledge something even more troubling. It was the first time she'd touched him in such an intimate fashion and he was shocked by the turmoil of emotions that ran through his body. She was, after all, a married woman and he was promised to another.

"Shh, Charles Garrity," she said with a soft smile, interrupting his chaotic thoughts. "I'm the one who should apologize. I should be more sensitive to your . . . well, your incredible situation."

"But that's just the thing, you see," he responded, as she pulled back. "I'm not exactly sure what my *situation* is." He felt the pent-up frustration inside him mounting to a tremble in his hands, and he tightened his fists. "There are times I almost hope I'm suddenly going to wake up to find this has all been some wild, fantastic dream, and yet . . ." He gazed at her, hoping to find any semblance of reason and saw compassion in her eyes. "And yet, I'm still here."

Her eyes changed to an expression of concern. "Are you terribly unhappy here, Charlie?"

He'd only considered his own happiness in the private moments before he fell asleep at night. Keeping himself occupied by helping Suzanne during the past three days had kept his mind from wandering into the images of the past—his life. "Well, no . . . I'm not *terribly* unhappy. Sure, there are people and things I miss. But I had a real life . . . at least, I thought it was real." He closed his eyes for a moment. "I don't know what's real any longer. I try not to think about it, for none of it makes sense and, if I dwell on it too much, I fear I may lose my mind entirely." He looked back at her. "It's . . . it's indescribable, Suzanne. I just can't explain it."

"I can only imagine," she said in a near whisper as she stood up. "And I can partially relate. I've certainly had plenty of moments in my life when I've wished the absolute insanity of a situation was a dream, especially this last week." He watched her spin around and push a button on the box with the glass screen. The pictures instantly disappeared and silence enveloped the room. She looked back at him. "But this is no dream, Charlie. It seems we both have quite a dose of reality to deal with and, as incredible as your story is, I be-

lieve you. I promised to help you in any way I can. As I've
said, it's the least I can do for you—to repay all you've done
for me."

"Thank you, Suzanne." He glanced over to the resting
child and added, "We'll get through this together. Hell, I
guess I've been in tougher spots in my time." Reaching out,
he tenderly placed his finger under a tiny, curled hand. Although still sleeping, instinctively, the infant clasped his
fingertip. Just the sight of this real and fragile life gave him
the courage to accept that he truly had a lot of blessings—
regardless of the situation.

Over the last three days he had helped Suzanne regain her
strength by preparing meals for her and changing Matthew,
which he'd discovered was nearly a twenty-four-hour-a-day
job. He'd learned how to use the washing machine and had
done all the laundry. He'd even pressed his shirts and trousers
with an electric iron. He'd swept floors, used an incredible
contraption she called a vacuum, and acquainted himself
with an appliance that cleaned and dried dishes in a matter of
three-quarters of an hour. One thing was sure to him. The in-
dustrial age had made way to an age of automation, and he
had to confess he found it convenient. Though, to be honest,
he wasn't quite comfortable doing what he'd always considered women's tasks. He'd cooked and cleaned for himself
over the years, but now there was an endless list of chores.
No sooner would he feel a sense of triumph that all the laundry was completed, when Matty would soil something else.
How did women do it? There were times he felt frustrated,
fed up, wanting to run from the house and gulp in fresh air. It
dawned on him that it took a great deal of energy and patience to run a home and not feel like a prisoner inside of it.
But he'd found a way to escape.

During the afternoons while Suzanne and Matty napped,
he'd busied himself outside in the gardens around the porch
by tilling earthen beds and pulling weeds. He'd even had a
chance to explore the farm a bit and discovered a small barn

that housed a miniature tractor. At first glance he thought it might be a child's toy, but upon further inspection, he saw it had an exposed engine that was nothing like the steam-driven ones he knew. He meant to ask her about that.

Realizing several moments had gone by as he was lost in thought, he turned back to Suzanne. She had remained still and witnessed the scene. Slightly embarrassed, Charles gently withdrew his finger from the infant's grasp and broke the silence. "What do you do with the small tractor in the barn?"

She looked puzzled. "I don't have a . . . Oh!" she said knowingly. "You mean the riding lawn mower."

Now it was his turn to look puzzled.

"I'm glad you asked that, Charlie." She made her way back to the sofa and began gathering up the burping towel and other baby paraphernalia. He could tell she was aware of his uneasiness and was going along with his change of subject. "That's something you might enjoy doing a lot more than all the domestic chores you've handled around the house."

"Really, Suzanne. It's been no trouble at all," he lied. Had his thoughts been that transparent?

She smiled at him. "Oh, I'm not complaining, believe me. I'm grateful you've done all that you have, but perhaps you need a guy thing to . . . well, something more masculine."

He tilted his head in disbelief. Was she implying that his manhood was threatened or had diminished in some way? He looked down at his once calloused hands. They had begun to soften since he'd arrived here and had started helping her.

"What I mean to say is, I'm feeling much stronger now. I can begin to take over the responsibility of keeping up the house and still take care of Matty. You could be a huge help with some of the heavier work outside now that spring is here. Mowing the lawn is one of them."

"Ah, *strumming* the grass," he commented. He was beginning to get the picture.

When she looked puzzled again, he felt somewhat vindicated that he'd assimilated something without her having to explain it as though to a child.

"As you say, mow-ing the lawn." He grinned then and continued explaining, "When I was in Ireland, we called it 'strumming' to cut the grass, although we don't use such a fine machine. We do it manually, with a long-handled sickle."

"Oh. It sounded rather musical," she whispered, bending over to pick up Matty.

"Never let it be said that an Irishman can't keep rhythm with the earth."

"Well, I'd say the earth around this place certainly needs an orchestration, maestro. Have at it," she murmured with a grin as she gently cradled the child to her shoulder.

He rose from the sofa and smiled at her. Suzanne had a good sense of humor and he liked that. "I'm sure it's no more difficult than driving a car. Shall I get started?"

"No, it's too late in the day for that now," she said, and began to leave the room. "Tomorrow morning I'll show you how to start it and then you can strum to your heart's content. Right now you're going to drive the car." With one hand on the banister, she looked back at him and smiled. "I'll get Matty changed and wrapped up, then I'll dress and we're gettin' outta here, mister. Enough of this wallowing around, feeling sorry for myself. We'll all go to the video store. Our first outing. It's a beautiful afternoon and we've been cooped up in this house for days now. I think the drive and fresh air would do us all a world of good. Besides, I need to pick up a few things at the grocery too."

"That's a grand idea, Suzanne. I'll bring the car round."

"Okay, just give us a bit to get ready," she said, climbing the stairs.

"Of course." He watched as the new mother whispered sweetly to the child nestled against her neck and a sense of awe pulled at his gut again. He'd felt it once or twice before when he had handed Matty to her for feeding. In spite of his situation, he was definitely becoming attached to the two of them. Just then her question repeated in his mind. *Are you terribly unhappy here, Charlie?* When she'd asked him, he'd thought he had answered truthfully. But as her voice echoed through his head again, he wasn't sure if he had been entirely honest.

He mentally began conjuring images of the life he was sure of—a time when he was truly happy. He closed his eyes. There was his betrothed Grace, with their baby in her arms, standing before him and smiling as he showed her the deed to the property where they planned to spend the rest of their lives. He was so proud at that moment. Another memory flashed—his partner Mitch arguing with Suzanne at the door. How he wanted to flog the damnable scoundrel.

Wait! His eyes opened wide. That wasn't right. He and Grace had never had children. In fact, they hadn't even shared a moment of union, as propriety required they wait until they were married. Hell, Mitch and Suzanne had never met. How could he be confusing so many details?

He raised his fingers to his temples and began slowly to massage them. *Think rationally,* he admonished himself. It was obvious to him that somehow his mind was mixing his yesterdays with today and, his whole life was becoming more faint with each day he spent here. Damn, what was happening to him? Was he really beginning to lose his mind? His memories?

The sound of a door closing jarred him out of his self-examination.

"Almost ready, Charlie!" came the shout from upstairs.

"Right," he called back. Spying the automobile keys on the kitchen counter by the new-fangled telephone, he practically leaped across the room to grab them. Looking down at the flat, shiny metal pieces, he thought again how remarkable the inventions of this future were. He clutched them tightly in his palm and gazed around the house in which he had to admit he was becoming more comfortable with each passing day.

Yet these were places and things and images of a life that wasn't his. These were the things and lives of others who were not from his time—his life. He had a life. And he knew that was real. Wasn't it? But then so was this—more real than any dream could possibly be. And if both were real, were there two places that are *alive*, existing at the same time? Could he find a way to get back to *his* time? And if he couldn't, how would he survive and what would he do for the rest of his life in this time? Heaven help him, his head hurt just trying to think about all the possibilities.

Walking toward the door, it was as though his conscience spoke to him, and he recalled he'd heard it said before: *Only heaven knows what the future will bring.* He nearly laughed out loud at the irony. *If the person who said that only knew,* he mused.

But Suzanne's question still nagged at him. Was he unhappy? He reached for the knob and twisted it. As he pulled the door open, sunshine washed warmly over him and illuminated the entire room.

Looking out into the bright day he realized he didn't know where his happiness lay—was it in a past that was fading from his memory? Or was it in a future which was his present reality? He turned back to the stairs and cast his gaze to the second floor landing.

"Oh, how lovely!" Suzanne remarked as she stood at the top, ready to descend. She was staring out into the sunlit day.

"Yes," he answered softly, seeing her wearing a short yellow dress and white sweater. Her face almost seemed to beam, radiating happiness. "Yes," he repeated. "Quite lovely." Heaven help him . . . he wasn't just referring to the day.

"C'mon," she urged, almost giggling at the expression of awe on his face. She was carrying Matty in his infant seat—thank goodness he was sleeping soundly—and they'd just entered Blockbuster. Charlie was standing with his mouth open, staring at the rows upon rows of videos, the laser light display in the corner and the monitors showing the latest hi-tech sci-fi adventure available for renting. She figured it was an assault on the senses after all, and tugged on his shirtsleeve. "It's okay, Charlie," she whispered. "Let's go to the desk and ask for some help."

"Suzanne, this is . . ." he didn't finish his sentence.

"I know," she answered reassuringly. "C'mon."

After giving the clerk her list of rentals, they waited for a few minutes as the efficient young man came back to the desk with a stack of seven videos. "We're going to have a video marathon." She felt pretty good about herself and her idea of an outing. It wasn't much, but she was dressed, had pulled her short hair back with a headband, and was wearing makeup for the first time in almost a week.

"You'll have five days to view these," the man said, placing their choices on the counter. "Lucky they were all in."

"Yes," Charlie murmured. "Lucky." Turning, he asked her, "We're going to see all of these in five days? *The Great Gatsby, For Whom the Bell Tolls, The Way We Were, The Guns of Navarone, Bridge Over the River Kwa—*"

"Kwai," she offered. "*American Graffiti* and *Coming Home*. And, yes, we're going to see all these in five days. Heck, we haven't even touched on JFK, Nixon, the Beatles, Woodstock, MTV, the space shuttle . . . wow, Charlie, you really do have a lot to assimilate." Seeing that he was overwhelmed, she grinned and spoke more softly. "Look, we'll start slow with these movies and work our way up to the present. And when we go next door to the grocery store, we can stock up on all sorts of goodies and just veg out for the next five days. We'll shut out the world and have our own little holiday."

"Shut out the world," he repeated, as a group of teenagers came into the store with spiked hair and piercings in their eyebrows, nostrils, and tongues. "Sounds grand," he muttered as he blinked in disbelief.

Handing Matty's seat to Charlie, she couldn't help laughing, knowing how strange those kids must seem to him. Heck, they made her feel old, since the only thing pierced on her body was her ears. She handed the clerk her video card and her bank card, while smiling with anticipation. Spending the next five days ensconced with Charles Garrity seemed downright decadent. Maybe it was time to pamper herself a bit and—

"I'm sorry, ma'am, your card's been declined."

Startled, she stared at the man. "I beg your pardon?"

"Your card. It's been declined."

"But that's impossible," she stated, knowing that last week there had been over two thousand dollars in the checking account.

"That's what it says," the young man announced, glancing once more to his monitor.

"Try it again, please," Suzanne insisted.

She waited as he ran her card through the machine. She could feel her cheeks begin to heat up with annoyance. Really. She'd never had her card declined before. Maybe it was a problem with the magnetic strip or—

"I'm sorry, it's been declined again. Do you have another form of payment?"

Annoyance immediately turned into embarrassment. "I . . . I don't know what's wrong," she stammered.

"Maybe you should call your bank."

"Yes, I will," she said, fumbling in her wallet for her regular Visa card. "Can you try this one?"

The man took her card and she held her breath while she waited for the response. When she heard the machine processing and a receipt being printed, she released her breath and wanted to cry with relief. What in the world could have happened to her bank card? Figuring she'd call her bank as soon as she got home, Suzanne signed the receipt and picked up the two bags. "Sorry for that," she murmured, as they stood outside.

"What are you sorry for?" he asked, still holding the infant seat and instinctively pulling the white blanket around Matty's head.

For just a moment Suzanne was very still as she watched the action. It was obvious to her that Charlie was becoming attached to her son, and she couldn't deny that it pleased her.

"Suzanne?"

She blinked and looked up at him. Did he also have to be so handsome?

"What are you sorry for?"

"Oh, for what took place inside," she answered, nodding toward the video store. "I can't imagine what happened with my card."

"What is that card? Why don't you use money? Currency."

"We use money," she said, leading him toward the entrance to the supermarket. "We also use what's called credit cards. The one I was trying to use was a bank card, drawn directly out of my checking account. I don't know what could have happened . . ." Her words trailed off as a bizarre thought entered her mind. How she wished she hadn't left her cell phone on the night table by her bed. "I'm going to call my bank when we get inside the grocery store. Just to make sure."

She got a cart and positioned Matty's seat in the front, then pushed him toward the entrance, grateful he was sleeping like an angel.

"I'll never get used to that," Charlie said, staring as the automatic doors opened. "They had these at the hospital too."

Grinning, in spite of the turmoil racing through her head, Suzanne pointed to the top of the door. "Look, there's a sensor, that little box up there. When it senses motion, the doors open."

"Remarkable."

"Uh-huh, now let's find a telephone." She started toward the service desk to ask for directions when she realized Charlie wasn't beside her any longer. Stopping, she turned around and almost burst into laughter.

He was standing with his arms hanging at his sides. His mouth was open and his jaw had dropped in what appeared to be shock. She steered the cart back to him.

"What's wrong?"

"I . . . I have never seen so much food in one place in my entire life!"

She did laugh. "Welcome to the twenty-first century, Mr. Garrity, home of the mega superstores," she said while waving her arms out to the well stocked aisles of fresh produce and canned goods.

"Such an abundance, Suzanne!" he whispered, obviously still in shock.

"Yes, it is, isn't it?"

"How far do people come to shop at such a place?"

"How far?" Shrugging, she said, "I don't know, maybe five or ten miles. There's one, sometimes two or three of these in almost every town in the country, Charlie."

"No!"

"Yes, there is."

"America must surely be the richest country in the world now!"

Nodding, she murmured, "I suppose we are." And then she looked, really looked around . . . not like every other week, when she came to the store and took it all for granted. There really was such an abundance and she experienced a moment of guilt. She'd been taking it for granted that the shelves were always fully stocked and healthy vegetables were precisely stacked. She knew there were countries around the world where such a sight would surely be regarded as manna from heaven. "Yes, we are fortunate," she concluded, then forced her mind back to her situation. "I have to find the telephone."

She was directed to the front of the store and spied two pay phones attached to the wall. "All right," she whispered to her sleeping baby while picking up the receiver. "Let's get this all settled." She took out her wallet and flipped to the customer service number of her bank. Punching in the numbers, she smiled at an elderly woman who stopped to coo over Matty.

"Yes, hello, this is Suzanne McDermott. I believe there's a problem with my bank card. I just tried to use it and it was denied. The account number? Yes, of course," she responded, then read off the required information. As she was put on hold, she waited and mouthed a "thank you" to the sweet grandmotherly woman who pronounced Matty as "absolutely precious" before walking away. It was actually nice to be a mother now, like she was part of a group. She had labored to bring this precious child into the world and was now regarded as paying her dues and— All thoughts of being initiated into the sacred circle of motherhood vanished as the bank clerk came back on the line.

"Would you please repeat that?" she asked as a cold feeling of dread washed over her.

She heard the woman once more declare that the account balance was practically nil. "There must be a mistake. How can there only be ten dollars left? When was the money withdrawn?"

She found out that the checking account had been wiped out the day before. "Would you check our 401K please?" Stay calm, she told herself. Do not panic . . . *yet!* "No, I don't know the account number. I'm in a *grocery store,*" she nearly yelled, causing Matty to jerk in fright and begin squalling with annoyance at being awakened so rudely.

She tried to pat his leg to quiet him, but it wasn't working. Slowly, she looked up to see several women, checkers and customers, staring at her with with disgusted expressions, as though she had no business at all being a mother. Shame mixed with her own terror and she took a deep breath. "Fine. Thank you. I'll call back later," she muttered, and hung up the phone.

She attempted to recapture a shred of dignity as she nearly raced back to find Charlie. Where had he gone? He wasn't where she'd left him. Desperate, she scanned the store all the while trying to placate her son, who seemed to be having a royal fit as he yelled and kicked the blanket that bound his legs. "Please, Matty . . . work with me here," she pleaded, determined to save some sanity.

And then she spied him, in the bakery department, standing in front of the shelves of doughnuts. Shaking her head, she pushed the cart in that direction, and the closer she got the more she could see that he wasn't alone. It appeared he was in heated conversation with a worker who was clad in a white coat.

"Save me," she muttered, blowing a strand of hair away from her eyes that had escaped the headband. It was like she had two children! What kind of trouble was he in now? Even before she reached him, Charlie turned around. It must be the piercing siren of her son's vocal chords that tipped him off they were approaching.

"What's wrong?" she asked and then saw a dusting of confectioner's sugar around his upper lip.

"Well, I ate a crea—"

"He can't eat the doughnuts without paying for them first," the man pronounced with almost a snarl as he interrupted Charlie's explanation. He obviously worked in the bakery and was now acting as though he'd just caught D. B. Cooper.

"I said I have money and I'll pay for them," Charlie proclaimed, while shaking his head and giving Suzanne a look of embarrassment. "I will handle this," he insisted.

Seeing how they were attracting a good deal of attention with Matty's shrill, insistent cries and the baker's indignation, Suzanne took another deep breath. Right, as though anything was going to help now. "Look," she said in a voice loud enough to be heard above the din, "I will pay—"

"But your husband has to know you can't just walk up and

eat these without paying first," the man interrupted in a still angry voice. "I should call security!"

"He's not my husband and I *said* I will pay for the damn doughnut, all right?" It was only a doughnut, after all, yet she would later remember it as being the proverbial straw that broke her once strong back. "As a matter of fact," she declared in a huff, leaving her crying baby and walking past the man to the shelves of doughnuts, "I think I'll pay for a whole damn dozen of 'em!" Grabbing up waxy white paper bag, she picked up tongs and threw open the clear plastic doors.

"Let's see . . ." she muttered, gazing over the array of goodies. "You liked the cream, right, Charlie?"

"Suzanne. I said I will handle this."

She almost laughed. She didn't even like doughnuts, but she sure as hell wasn't stopping now. In fact, she felt like she was on a mission for these doughnuts. Plucking two cream doughnuts off the shelf, she plopped them into the bag. "Okay, what's next? Oh, how about glazed? Apple cinnamon? Crullers. They'll be good for breakfast. And blueberry muffins for the next morning. Technically, they're not doughnuts, but at least it's something I can eat and by damn, Charlie, we're gonna have one hell of a marathon, aren't we?"

A part of her realized that she was on the verge of losing it, and yet a stronger part was thrilled that for once in her life she was actually standing up for something, not taking the safe, polite way out. And it felt good. It felt *real* good.

"Here," she said, thrusting the filled bag toward the baker. "I believe there are eleven in there. Add the one already eaten and charge me for a dozen."

She walked back to Matty and unbuckled him from his seat. Pulling him up into her arms, she glanced around to those who had stopped to gawk and said, "There's really nothing left to see, folks. I'm finished." She didn't care that some looked at her with rolled eyes or clucked their oh-so-superior tongues. How many of them had just bailed out a time traveler *and* had their checking account nearly closed?

Feeling righteous, Suzanne accepted the marked bag from the baker and said "thank you" before looking at Charlie and motioning with her head for him to follow her. She rocked Matty against her chest and cooed to him, yet she knew nothing was going to satisfy him except her breast. Realizing she had little time, she asked Charlie to push the cart as they walked away.

"Why did you make that scene?" he demanded, following her down the aisle. "Didn't you hear me? I *said* I would handle it."

Evidently he was peeved, but his annoyance was no match for the indignation that was bubbling inside of her. Wait until she got her hands on Kevin! "Look, Kev—" she began, stopping herself before saying the entire name out of confrontational habit. Taking a deep, calming breath while slowing her pace to walk beside him, she continued. "Charlie, it was easier for me to—"

"You didn't make anything *easier*," he interrupted, then lowered his voice. "You made a spectacle of yourself and embarrassed me and that poor fellow back there." Stopping the cart, he turned and looked directly into her eyes. "I may not understand everything in this day and age, but I'm certain that treating people with a bit of respect hasn't changed. I can do that. Remember, I'm not a child, Suzanne. I could have worked it out. And I wouldn't have made a scene, I can tell you that."

"There already was a scene when I arrived."

"I was trying to reason with the man when you came up. Men use reason to settle differences, not hysterics. Please don't ever do that again."

She took a deep breath, feeling thoroughly admonished. She *had* treated him like a child. Hearing his words made her realize she had flown off the handle and an apology was due.

"I'm very sorry, Charlie." Now she was embarrassed. Looking back in the direction of the baker, she wondered if she should go and apologize to him too, but he was no longer in sight.

"Apology accepted. Let's drop it."

Hearing the clipped tone of Charlie's voice, she turned her gaze back to him and she knew the blush on her cheeks was quite evident. Damn, she hated how her hormones were betraying her usual self-control. Yeah, sure. When was the last time she had *any* control?

"Are you all right, Suzanne?" he suddenly asked with a concerned expression. "Is it that postpartum thing again?"

Pulling her shoulders up straighter at the very mention of postpartum blues, she set her jaw and replied, "No, it is not." She didn't have time to explain that her bastard of a husband was at the root of the entire mess. "It's a lot of things, but let's not discuss it right now. Help me fill this cart with food. And we have to do it in record time."

"But we have food," he protested as she threw two loaves of bread into the cart.

"Right, we have it now, but I don't know how long we'll continue to have it without any money to pay for it, so we're going to stock up on everything. I'm going to use this credit card while it still works, and most importantly, we're going to buy a *pacifier!*"

Okay, so she'd never win the Mother of the Year award.

At the moment, all she cared about was getting out of the grocery store with enough food to last until she figured out her next move. Well, not her *next* move. She knew that one. Her body almost tingled with a powerful energy when she thought of confronting Kevin at Ingrid's. All right, so the tingling might just be her breasts leaking again. But she *was* going to have it out with Kevin McDermott and find out just what the hell he thought he was doing.

First things first. A pacifier. Food. Feed Matty in the car and then track down that sonofabitch husband of hers and let him have it. What kind of man would do that? Especially with an infant at home? She almost laughed. The same man who cheated on her and then left her while she was pregnant. She felt as if someone had rung a bell in her head and her brain was still reverberating from the shock. It was almost as though she was waking up from a hazy dream.

She had thought herself safe and secure. Comfortable. It was becoming more clear to her that she'd just been sleep-walking through life, but now . . . now she was wide awake. And life, at the moment, wasn't pretty. How *dare* Kevin wipe out their account without speaking to her first? Just how much had she allowed that man to control her life?

She'd get that question answered before the day was done.

8

"You stay here in the car, Charlie," she said, looking at the house where she had spent so much time talking, laughing, sharing with her best friend. Now, it felt like the camp of her enemy. "Matty is sleeping. He's been fed and changed and should be just fine until we get home."

"You're sure you'll be all right, Suzanne? If you want, I'll come with you."

She shook her head, as she opened the car door. "No. You stay with the baby. I'll be fine."

"I'm here, if you need me," he said with a smile of sympathy.

She could only nod, for Charlie's expression of support almost threatened her resolve. She couldn't allow any weakness now. *Now is a time for strength*, she thought as she walked up the driveway and past Kevin's black Porsche convertible. She understood the rage some women felt toward a man, and was glad she didn't have keys in her hand or Kevin's precious car top might just have a few punctures in it. In truth, she wanted to shoot him, but she knew violence wasn't in her nature. But she sure understood the need to even the score. It was a sense of unfairness, of justice being way out of balance.

She felt like everything in her life was out of place, as she passed Ingrid's plantings of daffodils and crocuses. They were withering, as their time of blossom was almost over, and she sorely identified with them. She, too, felt like a death was occurring—the death of her marriage, her dreams, even a friendship that had lasted since junior high school.

Remembering that she must remain strong, she walked up to the front door while reminding herself that the flowers really weren't dying. At their root they were strong and alive and, given a new season, they would push themselves out from all the dirt that surrounded them and thrive again. Just like her.

For some reason the thought gave her comfort—that there was a season to life, just like in nature. Important things in her life might be withering right before her eyes, but if she remained strong at her root, at her core, then she could rest, gather her strength through this tough time, and one day lift her face once more to the sun and blossom. Okay, so it was a scattered analogy, but right now it made a great deal of sense to her.

She took a deep breath and rang the doorbell.

The first thing she thought when she saw Ingrid was that her once best friend looked tired, even though she was smartly dressed in tan slacks and a white short-sleeved cashmere sweater, a sweater she had given Ingrid two years ago for Christmas. Shocked, Ingrid could only stare at her with wide brown eyes.

Suzanne wanted to take back the sweater. Actually, she wanted to rip it off, but cleared her mind and stated, "I want to see Kevin."

Ingrid brushed back her long brown hair, which Suzanne noticed had been highlighted with streaks of dark blond in the last two weeks, and took a deep breath. "Look, Suzanne, I've wanted to talk to you. To explain every—"

"You can't explain anything, Ingrid," Suzanne interrupted before she lost her temper. She wanted to save that for Kevin. "Now, please get my husband."

Ingrid's face became rigid and her body seem to turn to stone. "Just a minute. Do you want to come in?"

"No, thank you," Suzanne replied, dismissing her as she cast her attention to the brick exterior of the expensive house.

She heard Ingrid walking away and bit the inside of her cheek to stop the flood of emotions that threatened to ruin her composure. How many times had she walked through that door, ready to share her life, eager to hear Ingrid's latest accomplishment or comfort her over the last boyfriend who had turned into a loser? Why, she'd even been the one who'd helped Ingrid find this house when her friend had made her first profits in e-trading. She'd assisted in the decorating, and her housewarming present was right there in the foyer . . . an original watercolor by Ingrid's favorite local artist.

She wasn't just losing her marriage. She was losing her best friend at the same time and the weight of that grief almost overwhelmed her.

"Suzanne."

Startled back into the present, she took a shuddering deep breath and faced him.

"I want to know just what the hell you think you're doing, wiping out the checking account without even talking to me." There. That was the question, now what was his answer?

"I tried to call you, but you don't pick up. You just let the answering machine take the calls."

"I let the answering machine take *your* calls," she retorted, noticing that he looked very relaxed in a pair of jeans and a cream cashmere sweater. Damn, if she didn't buy *that* one too! "I never thought you would stoop low enough to pull such an unconscionable act such as this—leaving me and your son without any money. Oh wait, I suppose I should have been prepared since you left us both the day he was born!"

"You can't make me feel any more guilty, Suzanne."

"I'm not trying to make you feel guilty, Kevin. You have to have a conscience for that, and you've certainly proved you don't. What I do want to know is what the hell you think you're doing by closing the account. Matty and I have to *live*, damn it."

"I didn't close it."

"You left ten dollars!"

"I did it for protection," he answered, putting his hands into his pockets as he looked over her shoulder to the car at the curb.

"Protection? From whom? You think I'm going to wipe you out?" she demanded, incredulously.

He almost smirked. Almost. And the slight movement of his lips was enough to make Suzanne curl her fingers into her palms to avoid hitting him.

"I don't know you anymore. You're acting irrationally, Suzanne."

"Excuse me? *I'm* acting irrationally?"

"You give birth to our son and don't even tell me about it. Then I come to find a stranger living in my home. I know how naive you can be, Suzanne, and I don't intend for some *handyman* to take advantage of you or to—"

"*Naive?*" she interrupted in a louder voice. "Oh, I guess I was, Kevin. Never would I have thought that my husband and my *best friend*," she directed over his shoulder, knowing that Ingrid was lurking somewhere within earshot, "would both betray me. That was a rude awakening, but make no mistake, Kevin McDermott—I am awake now. Wide awake! And I will not be treated like a child who can't make responsible decisions. I demand you reinstate the money in that checking account immediately so I can be free to—"

"I intend to give you an allowance," he interrupted.

A wave of disbelief seemed to wash over her body, making her legs weak, but she held on, for this was too important. "An allowance?" she nearly choked. "You've got to be kidding me. Haven't you insulted me enough without this?" She simply couldn't believe he was being this condescending. Did he really consider her to be this simple-minded?

"You've got that man out there living with you and with my son. How do I know he's not going to use you? You appear to have given him the car, not to mention my clothes. What else will he get? I'm just being practical, Suzanne, something you don't seem to be able to comprehend lately."

She wondered if homicide would be justified in this situation. Reminding herself to stay strong, she willed her limbs to stop shaking and said, "I'm getting an attorney."

Kevin nodded. "I think you should, and make sure you give him a copy of the prenup. It's iron clad. I intend to give you child support and alimony until you get back on your feet, but I am not supporting that man . . . whoever he is."

"That man," she nearly hissed, "has more integrity than you could ever hope to possess if you lived to be a thousand. He happens to drive the car *for me*, because you see I'm not supposed to drive, something you would have known if you'd taken any interest in my pregnancy. I'm all alone and he's helping me. Don't you dare malign someone you don't even know. It isn't really him, and down deep you know it. It's just you. You've always been selfish, spoiled, and scared that you'd never fit in with those you considered to be important. Rich people, Kevin. You always wanted to be more than you really were. Maybe I should feel sorry for you, since you're so insecure about being *you* that you'll use anyone or anything to secure this false image. You're just a scared little farmer's boy with an inferiority complex, and all your millions won't make you a man. But I won't allow you to use me any longer to boost your ego. You may have fooled your parents into spoiling you and maybe I just picked up where they left off, but be prepared, Kevin McDermott—the woman you left isn't the one who will see you in court. I've changed in

the last week, and this time you're going to have to grow up and accept responsibility for your actions."

She was shaking so badly that she just turned around and walked toward the driveway. Tears were streaming down her cheeks and her eyes were blurring, but she saw Charlie getting out of the car and walking around it to open her door.

"Aye, you deserve so much better than that . . . that *fellow*, Suzanne." The tone in Charlie's voice was filled with contempt. "I'd be happy to rough him up for you. You just say the word and I'll take care of him but good," he muttered, holding open the door.

Shaking her head, she tried to smile as she climbed up into the front seat. Thank heavens Matty was still sleeping soundly. There were small blessings, even amid ugliness. She wiped her eyes as she watched Charlie walking around the car to the driver's side. When he was seated next to her, she reached over, touched his shoulder, and whispered, "Thanks for the offer, but he'd only sue you and you'd be in court along with me. No," she said with a sigh, "I'm going to have to come up with something besides violence to balance the scales."

"Such as?" he asked, turning over the engine and putting the car into gear.

"I don't know," she answered with a sniffle. "But I've got to contact an attorney tomorrow and see what my options are."

"It's not right, what he's done. And I don't like seeing you upset like that, Suzanne. That bas"—he stopped the obvious obscenity that was about to leave his lips and corrected his word—"*man* needs to be taught a lesson."

She glanced over to him and almost smiled as she observed him grinding his back teeth. "I agree, but violence isn't going to solve anything. It's his arrogance that gets to me. He treats me as though . . ." She paused as the thought came into her head and exploded with clarity. "As though he has no respect for me. I guess he never did. I never wanted to create a problem, to rock the boat, so I tried to stay calm while he would rant and rave if things didn't go his way. Everyone around him gave in to him, myself included. Why, I *allowed* him to treat me like that!"

"You did? I can't imagine you allowing—"

"No, wait," she interrupted. "I always thought his parents spoiled him and I was stuck with what they did, but I spoiled him too. I just took over where they left off. I allowed him to manipulate me so he always got everything he wanted. How can I blame him entirely when I allowed it to happen?" She felt as though a stillness was enveloping her. Something important was trying to come to the surface. She couldn't figure it all out right now, but she knew she had been correct when she'd told Kevin that she had changed. "If he thinks I'm about to roll over and allow him to walk all over me, he's in for a rude awakening."

"There you go," Charlie stated with a grin. "Now that's my Suzie."

"Really?" she asked, grinning in spite of everything that was happening around her. Why did she get this sudden jolt of happiness hearing him call her *his* Suzie? It was endearing, yet totally uncalled for, considering that she was technically a married woman and a brand-new mother. But she liked it.

"Sure. I remember you at the water when you went into labor. You certainly didn't allow me to walk all over you."

"I think you had to carry me," she said with a laugh and a sniffle.

"I'm not talking about that. You took charge. You knew what had to be done and you did it."

"I did, didn't I?"

"You certainly did," he said with a smile and a nod. "You were quite . . . spectacular. Why, I'm not known to cower before any man and . . . well, you had me marching, even when I didn't know how or where I was going."

Giggling at the memory of them trying to get to the hospital, she reached out and patted his upper arm. "Thanks for reminding me of that. Maybe that's who I really am, under all those years of trying to please everyone. A woman of conviction."

"Suzanne, you're going to be just fine."

"Well, Kevin did say that he would pay alimony and child support. I don't know how long the alimony will last, but I can't see myself going back to work with Matty just arriving." They entered the highway and headed back toward her house. "Besides, he's rich; he's just selfish."

"You worked?"

"Of course. I was a buyer for a major department store based in Philadelphia. I was pretty good, too, but then it's shopping and I love shopping. But it's also gambling on what's going to hit the next season. I quit when the morning sickness became too draining. I was either sick, or falling asleep. We didn't need my income, so Kevin and I agreed I should just quit working and prepare for Matty's birth."

"Did you like working?" he asked, as he turned off the highway and drove toward home.

"I did," she answered, and then she really thought about it. "Well, I guess I liked the marketing end of it, too, since that was my major in college." But it really wasn't all that satisfying in the end, for her conscience had begun to bother her. She'd started to question her motives and the whole business of brainwashing women that their wardrobe choices one year wouldn't be suitable the next. Why, she'd been as bad as Kevin, contributing to the lie that consumerism would somehow make one a better person, more acceptable by society. Where were these thoughts coming from, she wondered, seeing her whole life flash before her as some sort of illusion.

"You went to college, to a university?" Charlie asked, interrupting her mental meanderings.

"University of Pennsylvania. That's where I met Kevin."

"I'm impressed."

"Surely you're referring to the college."

He laughed as he turned the car into her driveway. "Most definitely not to Kevin. That man . . . I can't explain it, and it doesn't just have to deal with his actions toward you, but there's something about him. Something that makes me suspicious."

She nodded. "He doesn't have many male friends. Lots of acquaintances, mostly for business, but not many friends. Obviously, he prefers women. He took my best friend."

Charlie shut off the car and turned to look at her in the fading sunlight. "That must have hurt you a great deal. I know what it's like to lose a good friend, when they disappoint you and make you realize you never really knew them at all."

She tried to smile and keep her emotions in check. "It hurts like hell, Charlie. And you sound as if you really do know."

"Perhaps someday I'll tell you my story. And I grant you, it isn't any nicer than yours."

She knew there was something troubling him, something that had nothing to do with his incredible leap through time. This was more personal, deeper, more painful. Respecting his privacy, she put her hand on the door release. "C'mon, we have frozen food in those bags in the back. Let's get this stuff in the house before Matty wakes up. Hopefully, we can even put it away before the little tyrant starts demanding attention."

Standing outside the car, Suzanne glanced into the backseat and once more her heart melted at the sight of her precious son. Filled with love, she gently closed her door, as Charlie opened the back one to get Matty. "I think all babies are demanding," she whispered. "I just didn't anticipate how completely they take over your life. I guess that's why they're so adorable that they capture your heart. Why else would any sane person go through all this?"

Carefully lifting the infant seat and holding Matty, Charlie looked down to him and whispered back, "Because you love him, Suzie. He's a part of you."

Her heart seemed to heat up within her chest when she heard his words. How blessed was she that Charlie Garrity had appeared in her life. She couldn't even imagine what she would be like without him now. Probably shut up alone with the baby and quietly having a nervous breakdown. Instead, she had help and friendship and . . . nope, she would not allow her mind to wander any farther than that. They were friends. Period.

"Here," she said, holding out her hands. "I'll take him."

Shaking his head, Charlie motioned to the steps. "You go and unlock the door and get off your feet. You've done enough today."

"Really, I'm okay," she insisted.

"Suzanne, I must insist. You look tired, especially after that confrontation with Kevin. Look, I'll bring Matty in and then unload the car. You should rest a bit because you know this little fella is going to wake up soon enough, so I suggest you take advantage of it now."

Shrugging, she walked toward the steps and when she was on the porch and approaching the door she couldn't help patting her hair into place. Did she look that frazzled? When she opened the door and walked into the foyer, she went to the small table with an oval mirror above it and dropped her keys. She also took a peek to check herself.

Her mascara had run black half circles under her eyes. No wonder she looked dreadful! Rubbing at the stains, she hurried to finish before Charlie came in the door. She turned on a lamp in the family room and whispered for Charlie to set Matty on the sofa.

"I'm almost afraid to pick him up to put him in his bassinet for fear he'll wake up," she added, while looking at her peaceful child.

"Why don't we put him on the floor then?" Charlie

asked, gently placing the infant seat on the rug. "That way we don't have to disturb him, but we'll hear him when he does wake up."

"Good idea," she whispered back, carefully loosening the blanket around Matty. They both stiffened when Matty made a tiny noise and moved his fist closer to his mouth. A few moments later, she mouthed, "Let's retreat while we can."

They actually tiptoed into the kitchen and were giggling like two fools who had barely made an escape. "I hope that pacifier works," Suzanne mumbled.

"What *is* a pacifier?"

"Hmm . . . how do I answer that? Well, from everything I've read, babies don't always cry because they're hungry. They're programmed . . . ah, instinct demands that they suck . . . le," she finished lamely, trying to keep a blush from creeping onto her cheeks. "So, I can't always have a baby on my . . . suckling," she quickly inserted, now definitely feeling the blush on her face. "Anyway, they make an artificial . . . you know."

He glanced down at her breasts and then quickly back at her face. They stared at each other, as though what she was describing was painting a vivid picture. How crazy that a rush of pleasure surged through her body at his mere glance? Damn, she was trying to make it as clinical as possible. God, what must he be thinking?

"I've got a good idea," he finally whispered, and then broke the eye contact by looking around the kitchen.

"You do?" she muttered, wondering if he was talking about the pacifier or her breasts. The look in his eye hadn't been too clinical when they'd just caught his attention.

"All right then . . ." he said, clearing his throat to end whatever was taking place between them. "I should bring in those bags now. Why don't you sit in the family room with Matty? I think I can manage to put everything away."

"Oh, nonsense, Charlie," she proclaimed, relieved that *whatever* just happened was over. "I am a little tired, but I certainly have enough energy to help put away groceries. Besides, after dinner we're going to be sitting for a while, watching our videos." She shooed him off with her hand. "Now, let's get this show on the road."

"You do look better, Suzanne, since you're home."

Grinning, she said, "I'm hungry. Are you?" No need to tell him about makeup running and her attempt at salvaging some vanity.

"Actually, I am."

"Then get the bags, Charlie, and I'll start dinner."

"You're sure you're up to preparing a meal?"

Her eyes widened. *"Go,"* she commanded, and pointed toward the front door.

He performed a perfect salute and grinned back at her, as though he was glad their relationship was back to normal. "Yes, ma'am," he answered crisply, and then pivoted in the direction of the door.

She was about to turn on the kitchen faucet when she heard him say, "See, I told you, it works when you're assertive."

She couldn't stop the small laugh. As she was washing her hands she marveled that two men could be so totally opposite. Kevin had broken her heart and had made her cry. And Charlie seemed to wrap himself softly around her heart, like a warm clean bandage, enabling her to heal. And he made her laugh.

She'd forgotten how much she had loved to laugh.

What else had she forgotten?

Oh, yeah—that she was still a married woman who had no right, whatsoever, to allow her heart to heal with Charlie. Anyway, if she ever entertained the thoughts of another man intimately in her life, she didn't want a bandage.

She wanted the only thing that could heal her without scars—real love.

Obviously, considering the man she had married, it was something she had yet to experience.

9

"This does look pretty tight, Suzanne. He may be right," Laura Silverman muttered, slowly shaking her head as she flipped through the prenuptial. "Unless you weren't in your right mind when you signed this thing."

Suzanne clasped her hands together and tried to keep her cool. She wasn't really comfortable dealing with lawyers. Kevin always took charge of those things. Right—and just see where that got her. She looked across the wide desk to the woman who once went to high school with her. Laura was short and petite, with large brown eyes and a cap of dark curly hair that framed her attractive face. Out of habit, Suzanne tried to guess the maker of Laura's tailored suit. Probably Ellen Tracy. She hadn't seen Laura in many years, but she had to admit that the young, serious girl in high school had blossomed into a striking woman. She really looked wonderful. Without having any referrals, Suzanne figured she would have to trust someone to be her lawyer.

"You know, Laura, I don't think I've been in my right mind for some time. Why else would I have married such a man, and believed it would last forever? Why would I think I needed protection?"

"Look, prenup be damned, considering his actions and his assets, I'm going to demand full property disclosure. We'll get him to pay alimony through the nose, and we should start child support right now since he's out of the home. You understand, unless you can prove that he's negligible as a father, he'll have visiting rights to your son."

Suzanne couldn't suppress a sarcastic laugh. "Would the court consider leaving me for my best friend the day of his child's birth negligible?"

Laura smiled at her sympathetically, having heard the whole ugly story minutes ago. "You said you went into labor early, so he wouldn't have known. It looks like you'll have to grant him visiting rights—at least until we get into court."

"How long will all this take?"

"Depends on the judge and when it can get onto the court docket. The sooner we begin processing all the papers, the sooner you can be divorced."

"Well, let's do this as quickly as possible."

"So you want to divorce him? He's not going to file?"

"Well, after my confrontation with him, knowing the wimp Kevin is, I'm sure he's going to get the most expensive divorce lawyer his money can buy. I don't want to take a chance he may try and drag this out. I want to file immediately. Besides, what am I supposed to do for money? Wait until he pays me an *allowance*? No, now is the time to be proactive and protect myself and my son."

"Okay," Laura said, and pulled the large yellow legal pad back in front of her. "What shall we ask for alimony?" she said with a mischievous smile.

Suzanne shrugged. "I haven't thought that through. I mean, I don't know when I'll be going back to work, or if I even want to go back to my old career. Everything seems to be happening at once and I'm just trying to take it one day at a time."

"Let's think of this, Suzanne, as a new beginning for you. Right now you don't have to concern yourself about going to work. Since he sold that land, Kevin's assets can easily provide you with the means to stay home and take care of your son. Is that what you want?"

She nodded. "I don't want to leave Matty with strangers if I don't have to."

Laura agreed. "Who's taking care of him now, while you're here?"

"I . . . ah, I've hired someone to help me and—"

"So you'd also need to pay this person's salary," Laura said while writing on her pad. "What are you paying them?"

Startled by the question and how fast everything was proceeding, Suzanne tried to make her brain work. "Well, we've sort of discussed coming up with a salary, but . . . I guess three hundred dollars a week would be good, plus room and board."

"This person's living with you?"

"Yes. He's really very good with Matty and he's a tremendous help around the house and—"

"No need to explain it to me," Laura again interrupted. "How does five thousand a month sound to you?"

"A month?" Suzanne repeated, a bit shocked by the figure. "Well, the house is paid for—I mean, we don't have house payments, just real estate taxes and insurance. Quite frankly, I really don't have that many expenses. Are you sure that isn't too much?"

Laura put down her pen and stared across the desk. "What I was really thinking was six thousand. Now listen, Suzanne, this is the time for you to put yourself first. Kevin is a multi-millionaire, and paying sixty thousand dollars a year to you isn't going to break him. You have a right to continue living in the manner to which you've been accustomed for six years. Don't sell yourself short. You have the overhead of the operating expenses of the house and farm until you have to find a new place to live. You said he's going to fight for the entire property?"

"Yes. I know he wants it."

"You also have a salary to pay. That's twelve hundred a month. Speaking of salaries, you worked until you became pregnant, right?"

She nodded.

"And did you put any of that money away for yourself?"

"No, I . . . I just deposited it into our joint account."

Laura shook her head as she wrote a note on her legal pad, and Suzanne wanted to tell her that she never thought she would be in a position to protect herself from her husband. That she had bought into the whole marriage thing. Till death do us part. Somebody should have added *or until the husband decides he's tired of you and takes another.*

"We're asking for seven thousand. You'll start a 401K of your own, invest some of it, and start thinking about *your* future, Suzanne."

"Won't Kevin fight that?"

"I hope he does," Laura pronounced. "Then we can bring up the prenup and tie him and his assets up in court for years. I'll go for seven thousand a month and, if necessary, we'll negotiate down to five. Now what about child support?"

"That doesn't include child support?"

Laura leaned her elbows onto her desk. "We're playing hardball in the major leagues here, Suzanne. Now is not the time for weakness. We'll negotiate from our strength. A good upstanding woman contributed for six years to the family income, was deserted by her filthy-rich husband who had been committing adultery with her best friend while the wife was pregnant with their first child. With any luck we'll get a female judge."

"I really don't want to be the angry, bitter, jilted wife, Laura."

"Okay, let me ask you this. Are you not angry, a bit bitter, and have you not been jilted by a man without a conscience?"

She took a moment to think about it. "I guess I am. What a cliché."

"Suzanne, you're not a cliché. You're a decent woman who's going through something sordid. You know how many women react exactly like you? They want to play fair, even when their partner didn't. The shame of all this is you're being asked to make decisions about your future when you're still in the grieving stage."

"I think I'm transitioning into the anger stage at this point."

"You haven't even hit it yet. Wait until Kevin and his lawyers start their game plan. Don't be surprised if they try to smear your name somehow. Was there any time during the marriage when you were not faithful?"

"Never," she answered with conviction.

"Good, now let's talk about child support."

An hour later she was sitting in the car, staring at her house as her past came crashing in on her. Everything she had dreamed was over. Would she have to fight Kevin to live here? It was his family's home. Her name wasn't even on the deed. How much she had trusted, and how much of a fool had she been to believe in love. What *was* love? She was afraid she really didn't know. She loved Matty with all her heart, yet he was a child born through her. Was romantic love a myth, something people are led into believing is true?Does it really exist? She thought back to her own mother and father. They had rarely shown affection for each other in her presence. She'd thought it was just their generation, but maybe they too had been deceived. Maybe everybody has been deceived.

Her attention was drawn to the porch as the front door opened and Charlie appeared with Matty at his chest. He looked frantic and Suzanne quickly opened the car door. "I'm so sorry," she called out, realizing that she had wanted to prolong that moment of silence and contemplation. However, silence was not to be hers as she heard her son's wailing.

She rushed up to Charlie and shook her head. "It took longer than I thought with the lawyer and I . . . I guess I was just lost in thought sitting in the car."

She took off her jacket as Charlie said, "There's no satisfying him, Suzanne. He's been crying for the last fifteen minutes."

"I'm so sorry," she repeated as she walked behind him into the house and closed the door. She threw her jacket onto the brass clothes tree and held out her arms for her son.

"He slept most of the time. When he woke I changed him. I tried that pacifier, but after about ten minutes he spit it out and started crying and he hasn't stopped."

"It's all right, Charlie. You did real well, and I thank you for watching him. This meeting was very important," she said as she unbuttoned her blouse. Poor Matty had started rooting for her breast right through the material. Sitting in the rocker by the window, she positioned her son and sat back as he latched onto her and began suckling. Exhausted, she closed her eyes and sighed deeply.

"Maybe I should have driven you," he said from behind her.

She shook her head and rocked gently while stroking Matty's forehead to soothe his frayed nerves. "The doctor said not to drive for a week. It's been a week. I was all right. It's just been a long day."

"Have you eaten anything since breakfast? I've prepared a can of tuna fish just like you showed me and I've been waiting for you to get home so we could have lunch."

"Thanks, that would be great," she murmured, her mind still whirling with everything that was happening. For one solid week, ever since Kevin had told her he was leaving, her life seemed to be one crisis after another. It was exhausting! There had been those wonderful two days when she and Charlie and Matty had shut out the world and watched videos, but even that was draining as she had to explain so much to Charlie about history. Tonight they were watching *Forrest Gump*, so maybe that movie might be easier.

An image of Charlie being shocked at the love scene in *The Way We Were* made her smile at the memory. Although he had enjoyed the movie, he really had been embarrassed watching that particular scene. She tried to remember if there was anything that might embarrass him tonight, but figured they'd deal with it the same way . . . by avoidance. Really, the last thing she wanted was to explain modern sexual freedom to Charles Garrity.

"Here's your sandwich."

She opened her eyes to see Charlie placing the dish on the small table next to her. He moved the vase of flowers and positioned her sandwich so she could easily reach it. Grateful for his presence, she smiled. "Thanks, Charlie."

"Hey, I'm just glad the lad finally stopped crying. It's really . . . I don't know . . . heart tugging to have him go on and on and not be able to do anything to help him."

She smiled down at her son as she picked up half of the sandwich. "I know," she murmured. "He is a handful."She tasted her lunch and moaned in appreciation as she swallowed. "Oh, this is delicious! You really were watching."

"I'm trainable," he replied, obviously pleased by her words. "What will you be drinking, then? I've got some water on to boil."

"I'd love some decaf tea," she answered with a grateful smile.

"Right away," he said, turning quickly to fulfill her request.

What an extraordinary man, Suzanne thought as she watched him walking back into the kitchen. In all the time Charles Garrity had been with her, he'd never asked a thing for himself. He seemed entirely unselfish, so unlike her husband. Trying to envision Kevin even making his own lunch, let alone offering to make hers, she shook her head at the ludicrous thought. What would it be like if Kevin was still with her? Considering that thought, she shuddered so hard, Matty flinched from her movement.

"I'm sorry, sweetie," she whispered. Looking down to the child still nestled to her breast, she felt a lump growing in her throat. She was sorry. Sorry for herself, sorry for her son, sorry she had chosen such a jerk for a husband, and sorry she'd trusted her best friend. As her eyes uncontrollably welled up with tears, one trickled down her face and fell on Matty's cheek. Tenderly, Suzanne wiped it away and swallowed hard. At that moment she vowed her bad choices wouldn't penalize this innocent child. If nothing else in life was fair, she would do her best to be free from self-interest, self-pity, bias, and deception. She would be honest with her son and raise him to be the man his father wasn't.

"Here you are, madam," Charles said in an officious tone as he walked over to the table and set down her tea. "Will there be anything else?"

She could tell he was teasing. "No, this is more than enough. Thank you, Charlie."

"Perhaps a tissue?"

He knew she'd been crying. "I'm fine." She sniffed.

"Right then," he said as he began to turn away.

"Hey, where's your lunch?"

"In the kitchen."

"Why don't you bring it in here and eat with me."

"All right, I'll get it," he said, walking toward the kitchen.

She took another bite of her sandwich and looked around the living room she had worked so hard to renovate and then decorate. Would Kevin bring Ingrid here to live? Where would she and Matty go? Should she start searching for a place? It was all too much to think about right now. She would just take it day by day. Today, she had acquired the services of a pretty aggressive lawyer. That was a good start. She had a roof over her head at the moment. The fridge was stocked. Her son was healthy and content. Seeing Charlie walking toward her again, this time with his lunch, she smiled. She also had a wonderful, miraculous time traveler for a friend—a strong, caring, and trainable man. In this moment she had a pretty decent life.

Now, if she could just stay in the moment and keep her mind from wandering into the scary unknown future.

"Oh, here," she said, handing him the box of tissues. "You might as well blow your nose too."

He took them and just stared at the white feather dancing in the wind, away from Forrest and into the sky. "Thanks," he muttered in a husky voice. As the credits rolled up the TV screen, he sniffled once and then cleared his throat.

"Blow your nose," she whispered, dabbing at the tears rolling down her own cheeks. "It's okay to express your emotions, you know. It doesn't make you any less masculine. In fact, it makes you more whole."

Pulling out a tissue, he blew his nose and sighed deeply. "Whole? You think I'm somehow broken if I don't cry?"

She glanced at him and could see a slight smile on his face. "Not broken, just incomplete. I've always thought it was a sad thing that men feel it's not . . . well, manly to cry if something affects them deeply. I can't imagine what it must be like to keep everything you're feeling so tightly bottled up inside of you. Anyway, I was talking about a whole human being. Having both masculine and feminine sides."

Chuckling, he said in disbelief, "*I* have a feminine side?"

She clicked off the VCR and looked at him. "Yes, Charles Garrity, *you* have a feminine side. That's how you began life."

"Why, because I help you take care of Matty and have cooked a few meals? You think I'm . . . feminine?"

She could see that he was becoming defensive, and grinned to diffuse any tension. "And washed clothes and vacuumed the rugs too, for which I am eternally grateful. I don't think you're becoming feminine. I think you, like most men, have been denying what is innately a part of you."

"I am not feminine, Suzanne," he stated firmly.

She couldn't help it. She laughed. "Oh, Charlie. You have to get over your macho programming. I wasn't insulting you. I was actually paying you a compliment."

"It doesn't quite sound like a compliment," he muttered, putting the box of tissues on the coffee table, away from him, as though holding them was an admittance of weakness. "And what's macho programming?"

"Well, it's how you have been taught—programmed or brainwashed by society, ever since you were born, with instructions or dictates on how a male should act."

"That doesn't feel like a compliment, either," he retorted, looking away from her.

"The same thing's been done to women, dictating how one should act or behave." She carefully tried to weigh her words. "Listen, remember when you said I should take charge? That I should be more assertive, more commanding. Those are considered male traits. You suggested that I should use them more often. As a woman, I wasn't insulted by that. I'm telling you, Charlie, everyone—you, me, every single human being—starts out as a female."

"I should know what I am. You call Matty your son. He's obviously a male."

He really appeared to be getting upset. She realized that women had only gotten the right to vote six years before he'd time traveled, so he still might consider feminine as being weak, but she was right about this one and she could prove it. "Wait," she said, getting up from the sofa and pulling her robe together. She walked over to the built-in shelves and searched for the book she felt might help. "When I became pregnant, I did a lot of reading about human physiology. I must have bought every book I could find about conception and babies and how they grow. Here it is," she pronounced, grabbing the volume she was seeking. *The Course of Prenatal Development.*

She came back to the sofa and sat next to him. Paging through the book, she stopped on the pictures of growth from a zygote to a full-term baby. "Okay, now look at these," she urged, pointing to the first. "This is right after conception, when the egg and the sperm unite into a one-cell organism called a zygote. Everything, all the other cells in your body, develop and grow from this one cell, as that cell multiples over and over."

She pointed to the next pictures. "Then it becomes an embryo at two weeks and a fetus at two months and there's no male definition at all. See? It looks female. It's somewhere around the third month, the *third* month, that sexual organs develop and, at that point, if the Y chromosome is present, indicating a male . . ." How was she ever going to say this, and to this man in particular? Figuring she'd might as well keep it clinical, she took a deep breath and continued, ". . . If the Y chromosome is present, the ovaries drop into testicles and the clitoris extends into . . . well, into a penis." She exhaled.

There was silence after she finished and Suzanne bit her bottom lip in apprehension, wondering if she had upset him even more. But how was she to explain her point without the correct terms?

"I'm confused," he said finally. "What are cells and chromo . . ."

"Chromosomes," she completed the word, grateful he was at least asking questions. "Okay, this will take a bit more explaining. A cell begins when the male fertilizes the egg and, see, in the diagram, how it multiplies? That is what you are made of—cells. Your heart is a group of cells, making an organ. And chromosomes are at the center of every cell. They are threadlike strands of . . . of DNA. This is going to sound complicated, but everything builds on another and inside of the chromosomes are genes which carry the details of your hereditary blueprint from your father *and* your mother. You are both. Male and female. To deny one part is to deny half of yourself."

Charlie didn't say anything for a long time and Suzanne remained silent, allowing him to look at the book and digest her words. Finally, after about two minutes, she whispered, "Well, what do you think?"

He closed the book and handed it to her. "I am *not* a woman," he stated, as he got up from the sofa.

She laughed. "I never said you were a woman! I said that all human beings have a masculine and a feminine side and to deny it is to deny a part of yourself. It's been programming, socialization, that has made women swallow down their rage because it isn't seen as feminine. No wonder women get ulcers. And men have been taught to suppress all tender emotions because that isn't seen as masculine. Talk about heart disease. Let me ask you this. How do you feel when Matty closes his tiny hand around your finger? Do you feel a rush of affection, like a melting around your heart?"

"Maybe."

"Does it sort of break down all your defenses?"

He shrugged his shoulders. "I guess," he reluctantly mumbled.

"Hard to be tough and assertive around him when he's like that, huh?" He didn't answer, so she just continued. "To be soft, warm, receiving those feelings is the feminine side of you. It's as equally important to receive, Charlie, as it is to give. I guess that's one lesson most of us need to learn."

He looked around the room. "It appears I have a whole lot to learn."

She stood up and faced him, wishing she had the courage to take him into her arms and hug him. "I think you've learned a great deal since you've been here. I am so proud of you, Charlie. You really listen and, even though some of it goes against everything you've been taught to believe is true, you're still trying to keep an open mind. I admire that, and you."

"Thank you. I'll accept *that* compliment," he said, looking slightly embarrassed.

"No, thank you for everything you've done since we met. I know how hard this has been, faced with all that this time presents. I know it's confusing and sometimes even painful. And I know you left a life that you want to get back to . . . yet you've stayed with me and done more for me than any man ever has, including my husband. I might have truly lost it, if you hadn't come into my life."

"I've told you, there's no need for you to keep thanking me. It's been mutual."

She looked deep into his striking green eyes and whispered, "Learn to receive. I'm still complimenting you."

He chuckled and his grin was so appealing, so inviting, so downright sexy that Suzanne felt her body tensing to fight the growing attraction.

"Won't make me a woman, will it?"

She grinned back. "No, it won't. I never doubted your masculinity, Charles Garrity."

She was standing close enough to hear his breath exhale after listening to her words. Knowing she was treading on thin ice here, she added, "Now, I'm going to go upstairs and see how much sleep I can get before Matty wakes up." Bending down to pick the book up off the sofa, she realized that Charlie was quicker and their hands brushed as they both tried to reach for it.

"I'll do it, Suzanne. You go on up to bed." He took the book and walked over to the shelf. "I'll turn off all the lights and close down the house."

"Okay," she murmured, still tingling from their skin contact. She would think about it later. Just not right now while her mind was in an uproar of emotions. "Well, good night then. I enjoyed our evening."

He turned around from the shelf and smiled at her. "Yes, so did I. The video was very good and the conversation was . . . well, informative to say the least. Sleep well."

"You, too," she whispered and turned toward the hall stairs. Sleep well. She fully intended to do just that.

Somehow, toward the end of it, she knew it was a dream and yet nothing in the world could have stopped her from continuing. For Charlie was on top of her, staring down into her eyes with such love, such tenderness, as the rhythm of his body brought her closer and closer to the edge. She *felt it*, in every cell of her body as it built and built, driving her near madness until it exploded in a great, glorious, exquisite orgasm. She awoke fully as the aftershocks pulsed through her body in waves and she was filled with an odd mixture of shame and intense gratification. It must be true that the brain was the most powerful sexual organ, for her hands were tightly clasping the sheet.

Dear God, it had been *so* long since she'd had an orgasm!

And then it started, a pain, so deep and piercing, that she was not only still clutching the sheet but gasping for breath. It felt like . . . like labor, like what she had experienced after Matty had been delivered. Oh, no . . . her uterus was *really* contracting now!

She rolled over to her side and pulled her legs up to lessen the pain, but nothing was helping. She gasped again, this time louder. Soon, she couldn't stop the moans from escaping from her lips. She tried Lamaze breathing. It didn't work.

"Suzanne? Are you all right?"

No. No! Do not let this happen, she cried out to the universe. Grant her *some* dignity to ride out this humiliation. "I'm fine," she huffed, as another contraction pulled her under its firm grip.

"No, you're not," Charlie stated, coming to the side of the bed and sitting on the edge.

"I'm all right. I'm telling you I'm all right," she blurted out in a rush of breath.

He placed his hand on her forehead, as though checking for a fever, and then gently stroked back her hair. "What's wrong? You're in pain."

"No, I'm not," she gasped, now pleading with her body, with God, with anyone, to take away this pain and indignity.

"Suzanne, I am not blind. You are in pain. Where? What's happening?"

She kept shaking her head, as if the movement would take her mind away from the reality of the situation. "Please, Charlie, leave me alone. I'll get through it."

"I am not leaving you like this. Tell me. Maybe I can help."

She took a deep breath and just spit it out. "My uterus is contracting, all right? Are you satisfied? What can you possibly do to help me?" She didn't care any longer about humiliation. All she wanted was for the pain to go away. No orgasm was worth this, especially one that had only started in her head!

"Here, try to relax. Let's do the breathing like we did in the hospital."

"I did try that. It doesn't work."

"And this is normal? This pain after having a baby?"

She opened one eye and nearly glared at him. "If you had something in your body blown up to the size of a watermelon, it might take a little while for it to contract back to the size of a pear—ya think?"

He nodded and began to soothe her back in long gentle strokes. When she concentrated on his touch, the pain actually began to lessen. She tried breathing with each stroke and soon there was only an occasional cramping. After about five minutes, she relaxed the muscles in her body and just allowed him to soothe her. "This feels heavenly," she whispered.

"Good. Just relax, and see if you can go back to sleep."

She opened her eyes and turned her head to see him better. From the light in the hallway, she could see he was wearing a sleeveless undershirt and a pair of boxer shorts. It was more than she could handle at the moment, as his touch was bringing back memories of that dream and nothing, but nothing, was going to make her have a repeat performance of *that!* "I feel much better now. Thanks." Why wouldn't he just leave?

He smiled down at her. "Shh . . . go back to sleep." Sleep? She was terrified of sleep now! "I'm sorry I woke you."

"You didn't. I was reading," he said, while continuing to run his hand so gently, almost tenderly, over her shoulder and her back.

Oh, he simply has to stop this, she thought, and yet a part of her was almost melting under his touch. It had been so long since anyone had been tender with her. Certainly Kevin hadn't touched her for months and her body seemed to crave the tenderness, soaking up each stroke as he— She immediately stopped that train of thought. This was dangerous territory she was treading, which could produce some painful results.

"What were you reading?" she asked, to change her desperate thinking.

"The Course of Prenatal Development."

She opened her eyes and stared at him. "Really?"

"Really," he said with a laugh. "I am simply amazed at how far science has developed since my time. It's fascinating, and I'm looking at Matty like the greatest miracle on the planet."

She smiled. Matty. There was a safe subject.

"Matty! What time is it?" she asked with sudden alarm.

He looked at the clock on her night table. "Three twenty-five."

She immediately pushed herself up from the bed. "My God, why hasn't he awakened for a feeding?" In seconds her brain ran frightening thoughts about sudden infant death syndrome.

Charlie attempted to stand up, but not before Suzanne

nearly pushed him out of the way as she threw her legs to the floor and bounded up and out of the room. Her heart was pounding in her chest and in her ears as she raced across the hallway and into the nursery. She stood, for just a moment, and stared at her still son. Hearing Charlie coming into the room to stand behind her, she bravely put her hand on Matty's chest and almost cried out in relief as she felt his tiny rib cage expanding with precious breath.

"He's okay," she whispered, near weak with relief.

Charlie put his hand to her shoulder and whispered, "You're a good mother, Suzanne. He's just sleeping, like you should be doing."

She sank her back into his chest as the fear left her body shaky. "He's missed a feeding."

"I think he'll survive the night. He does have a healthy appetite when he's awake. He must be satisfied."

"He does look peaceful," she whispered back, trying to ignore the shivering sensations of his breath at the back of her ears.

"Come along, and get rest while you can."

She turned to leave the nursery, but Charlie didn't move back. She stood facing him. Stunned by the close proximity, she merely stared into his eyes. It was a moment too long, when propriety demanded that one of them step back. Instead, Charlie reached out and put his hand firmly around her waist as he turned to the lighted hallway.

"Your body is shaking from fright. Let me help you back to bed."

She simply nodded, sure that no words would be appropriate. She was only certain of one thing. She probably would not be taking advantage of Matty sleeping through the night. Instead she intended to remain awake, mentally chaste, and try not to think about how breathtakingly right it felt to be embraced by Charlie Garrity's arm.

10

She held the receiver to her ear as she stood at the kitchen window over the sink and watched Charlie mowing the back lawn. In seconds her mind ran facts she couldn't deny. He looked so . . . so manly, sitting on that mower, concentrating so hard, making sure that the mowed lines were exact. He was wearing a pair of jeans, his boots, and a denim shirt with the sleeves rolled up. She had to admit he looked good—really *good*—and no one would guess that he had traveled seventy-five years into her life. She watched the sunlight hit his auburn hair and sighed deeply in appreciation as he turned to start a new line. The lawn was as manicured as a putting green at a country club. He certainly did everything with precise care, whether it was folding laundry or painting the small barn at the corner of the property. A tiny part of her wondered what it might be like to make love with such a man. She bet he would be an exquisite lover, paying meticulous attention to—

"Suzanne, are you listening? This is really important."

Shocked by her thoughts, she blinked and brought her attention back to the phone conversation. "I'm sorry, Laura," she said, walking away from the window. "I didn't hear that last part." Damn, she simply had to get her mind on reality.

"Okay, I did a little creative accounting and began negotiations at seven thousand."

"Seven? I thought we decided on six."

"We decided on seven. They settled for six, with the stipulation that within three months you surrender the house to Kevin. That's six thousand a month, and that doesn't include child support, which will add another two thousand for the next eighteen years. We can always go back and renegotiate."

"I have to move in three months?" She looked out to the family room as a sinking feeling grabbed hold of her stomach. Kevin must really want this house to pay her ninety-six thousand dollars a year to get her out.

"Suzanne, this is an opportunity to move on with your life, without any memories that must be attached to that place. He doesn't want to fight you in court for the house. It's in his name, but you are entitled to a portion of the marital home, regardless of the prenup. And I haven't even told you the best part. His lawyer brought it up."

"What's that?" she asked, as the sinking feeling started to cause panic. As if there could be a best part to any of this. Where was she going to move?

"Kevin would like the divorce to proceed as quickly as possible."

"Well, so do I."

"He asks that the charge of adultery and naming Ingrid as correspondent be dropped."

"What?"

"He asks that you file for irreconcilable differences."

"Excuse me?" she asked in disbelief, as the panic dissolved into anger. "He wants *me* to protect *Ingrid*?"

"I know it's shitty, Suzanne, but listen and consider this carefully. This is your future we're discussing and he's willing to compensate you with an offer in compromise of one point four million dollars to file for irreconcilable differences. Of course, all of this—the alimony and child support and the offer of one point four million—is before we've received full financial disclosure, so any of it might increase. We'd just go back to court. I think they're dragging their feet on that until you agree to drop the adultery charge."

She didn't say anything. She couldn't make her mouth form words. Her mind was reeling that Kevin would do this to her, and think he was granting her a *favor* by trying to buy her off! "Wait a minute," she finally asserted. Yes, now was definitely the time to be assertive. She had never cared about money. It wasn't why she had married Kevin and it wasn't why she had wanted her marriage to work, but this was now hardball, like Laura had said, and Kevin McDermott was about to find out that his once pliable wife was moving up into the major leagues. "I happen to know that Kevin received thirty-three million for the land six years ago. Since then, Ingrid's been advising him on investments, especially in e-trading, and by now he's got to have at least doubled that. And he's only offering me one point four million dollars to last the rest of my life and my son's? What a greedy little bastard."

"Wow, why didn't you tell me this last week when you were in my office?" Laura sounded shocked. "This changes everything."

Suzanne's jaw was clenched and she forced herself to relax the muscles in order to speak. "I guess I was still grieving, like you said, and wasn't thinking clearly. Now I've definitely segued into the anger stage."

"Well, stay there, until this settlement is completed. If there's anything else you think of, pick up the phone right away, *please*. You have my private line and my beeper number. Damn, Suzanne, this is going to be one hell of a package we're going to put together."

"It won't make up for six years of my life," she muttered.

Laura's voice softened. "I know, Suzanne. No amount of money can take away the pain you've been through, the deception, but you have to start thinking about the rest of your life. You tell me how much you want me to ask for as a settlement and for dropping the adultery charges."

Kevin must be desperate to protect his and Ingrid's names, and the thought that her husband cared more about Ingrid than he did about her and her son almost made her nauseous. Gripping the edge of the marble counter, she said, "Ask for ten million, and don't settle for less than six. He sold that land right after we were married. Screw the prenup. Let's just see how much he loves Ingrid."

"Oh, I like the way your mind works," Laura said, and Suzanne imagined the grin of anticipation on her lawyer's face.

"Now isn't the time to be sentimental," she answered in a serious voice. "Now is the time to allow my mind to work logically. I have a pretty good idea of Kevin's worth. I know Ingrid is financially set for life with her own investments. Between the two of them six million will cause them to wobble, but it won't break either of them." Suddenly, she was reminded of her detailed conversation with Charlie last week after they had watched *Forrest Gump*. So this was her masculine side? What the hell, she was going with it.

"Okay, Suzanne, I've got some phone calls to make and I'll keep you informed every step of the way. Looks like we're on a roller-coaster ride for a while. Glad you've got the stomach for it, 'cause this might get really bumpy."

Thinking about the last few weeks, she almost grinned. "I can take a roller-coaster ride, Laura. For me, this feels more like a high-wire act."

"Well, keep your balance then, and you'll make it to the other side."

"Right," Suzanne answered, picturing herself venturing out onto a thin wire. On the other side was safety, a new beginning. Laura was right. The only thing that was going to get her there was balance. "I'll wait for your call."

Hanging up the phone, Suzanne stared at it for the longest time. She could just imagine Kevin's reaction when his lawyer conveyed her demands. He would hit the roof and Ingrid would calm him down and be the practical one, going over their joint finances and coming up with a counteroffer. No matter what happened, she was going to be a wealthy woman on her own. She would take care of Matty and be careful with the money she received. She would make sure that Matty was protected.

She walked away from the counter and went into the family room, where her son was sleeping in the bassinet. Staring down at him as the sun's rays bathed him in warmth, she thought of her own upbringing. Her parents had never been wealthy. They had lived sometimes paycheck to paycheck, saving for her college education as though it was the most important thing in the world. She had taken out a student loan in her junior year at Penn when she'd realized that paying for college meant her parents would have nothing for their retirement. It had taken her years to pay off that loan, but she had come into her marriage debt free.

And then her mind brought up images of Kevin and Ingrid. She and Ingrid had met Kevin at Penn, never realizing that the three of them had grown up fifteen miles from each other. They had become fast friends and Suzanne remembered being immediately charmed by Kevin's spontaneous nature. He was so unlike her, who always seemed to weigh every consequence before making a move. She had been overjoyed he fit in so well with her best friend, so she didn't have to make a choice between them. The three of them went everywhere together, starting with a Bruce Springsteen concert in '84.

She went to the bookshelves, grabbed an album, and allowed it to open randomly. Her heart seemed to flutter with pain as she gazed at a picture of them huddled in the student union, watching the TV replaying the shuttle *Challenger*'s explosion. It had been taken for the college newspaper. She forced herself to travel down memory lane as she viewed other pictures. They had studied together, eaten together, volunteered at Live Aid at JFK Stadium, where they actually met Madonna and Dire Straits and swore they were going to save the hungry of the world.

She sighed deeply, wondering where all their youthful enthusiasm had gone, and why making money seemed to have replaced their once altruistic natures. They had become everything they had protested against in college—capitalists. And now she was going to become a wealthy one. A part of her felt guilty about the money she would be getting, no matter what the size of it, and another part of her was relieved that she would never have to worry about money again. Maybe she could take a chunk of it and start a foundation, like Second Harvest or Habitat for Humanity. That would be one way to contribute to society and she would still feel productive if she oversaw the running of it. Realizing she didn't have to make a decision today, she closed the album and held it to her chest, wishing she didn't have so many good memories of people who had turned into strangers. Maybe that was the part that sliced so deeply into her heart. Well, she would move and she'd make a new life somehow, somewhere, and she would heal. At least she and Matty would be financially secure, despite having signed that prenup.

Suddenly, she saw a possible future that wasn't quite bleak. She would be free to become whoever she wanted. But who was she, besides a mother now? Maybe it was time to find out.

Freedom. It was a startling thought, and a little frightening.

Charlie walked in the back door and she stared at the album cover. So much for tripping down memory lane. She was putting it back onto the shelf when he came into the room.

"I've left my shoes by the washing machine," he announced, "just as you asked."

She returned his smile and nodded as she followed him into the kitchen. "The lawn looks great. You could start a landscaping business."

"Do you think?" he asked, opening the refrigerator door and taking out a container of filtered water.

She could tell he was pleased by her words and she automatically turned to the cabinet above the dishwasher and brought out a tall glass. Handing it to him, she said, "Now I'm not making that suggestion, mind you. You still work for me, remember. And speaking of that, I'm going to raise your salary."

He stopped pouring his water and looked up at her. "Why? Already I'm making more in one week than I thought possible—and I'm not really doing much of anything."

"Well, three hundred dollars isn't a terrific wage in this day, even with room and board. Once I start getting money from Kevin, I was thinking about raising it to five hundred, and then when the divorce is final I'll have enough money to make sure you're taken care of. You won't have to worry, Charlie."

Putting the container of water back into the refrigerator, he shook his head. "That's *far* too much, Suzanne." He closed the door and turned back to her. "And I don't need to be taken care of. I can do that myself. Always have, always will. What brought all this up?"

She watched as he gulped the water and how his Adam's apple moved as he swallowed. A rush of attraction started low in her belly and began to cluster. She simply had to get control of her thoughts. It wasn't fair—to either of them. "Kevin wants this house and is willing to negotiate for it. I will have to move, and I don't know yet where I'll be going.

I mean, you're welcome to come with me. I'd even appreciate it, but I don't know what your plans are, and you need to start thinking about putting together some money for your future—wherever that will be." There. She said it, but she didn't mean it. She didn't want him to leave.

"You're moving away?" His voice sounded surprised, almost shocked.

Shrugging, Suzanne held on to the edge of the counter. "I suppose I am. I haven't wanted to think about it, but it looks like I will be relocating somewhere."

"But you love this house," he protested, wiping his forehead on his sleeve.

"It doesn't look like I will have much of a choice. This is Kevin's family home. It's been in his family for generations. His grandfather built the main house. His parents added on to it and then we did. His name is on the deed, not mine."

"What kind of man would put out his wife and child?"

"Kevin McDermott, that's who. But don't feel too sorry for me. I intend to be compensated, well compensated. It appears I took your advice to heart about being more assertive."

"What did you do?" he asked, trying not to smile.

"I asked for ten million dollars to change my petition for divorce to irreconcilable differences, a hazy term that can be interpreted as anything. That means I don't have to name Kevin as an adulterer and Ingrid as correspondent."

"Ten million!"

She actually giggled. "I know it's outrageous! I just blurted it to Laura when she called about this. I said I would settle for six million. I didn't even recognize my voice as my own. I sounded so sure of myself and now . . . now I don't know. I guess I was angry that Kevin wants to protect Ingrid so much that he's willing to buy me off. Anyway, we'll see what happens. This is now a game for the lawyers."

"Kevin has that much money?"

"Yes. He made a fortune when he sold off his family's land to developers and then he invested very well. I told

Laura that I think his worth is around seventy million. It may even be more."

Charlie truly looked shocked. "Why, you were rich, Suzanne. Beyond rich."

"Well, first of all, a million dollars in the twenty-first century isn't what it was in 1926, but it's still a great deal of money. Funny, I never felt rich. Money wasn't important to me. I knew there was more than enough to cover our needs and anything else was Kevin's business. At least I *used* to think that. Now I'm making it mine. I just want to make sure that there's some balance here. He tried to buy me off with one point four million." She shook her head and found herself grinning, yet she could hear the sadness in her own voice. "Even talking about figures that high seems ridiculous, unless you look at the big picture. That's approximately one seventieth of his worth. That's what he thinks of me. It's time I stopped concentrating on being hurt and sentimental and started to think with both sides of my brain about this divorce."

"You're using your masculine side now?" he asked with a wider grin.

"You betcha!" She chuckled. "There's a time and a place for it, and now's the time." She opened the freezer and said, "Enough of my problems. What would you like for dinner?" She simply had to change the subject, for the weight of it was too heavy to carry right now. She would need some quiet time to integrate it all.

"Well, I'd like to bathe. Do I have time?"

"You have time. I'll have to defrost something. How does beef sound? Steak? I haven't had a steak in almost a year."

"You don't eat beef? It was so plentiful in the grocery store."

"I stick mostly with chicken and fish, but I stopped eating it entirely while I was pregnant. I bought the steaks for you, but for some reason I really have a taste for it tonight."

"A thick steak sounds grand." He finished his glass of water and put it in the dishwasher. "I'll be back down in a bit to help."

"Take your time, Charlie," she called after him. "There's no rush."

She stared at the dishwasher. How could something so simple have such a profound effect on her? Charlie was considerate. He never left things sitting around. He was organized and yet not anal about it. It was like when he had loaded the back of the car after they'd gone shopping. At the time she'd been too upset about confronting Kevin to really take it in fully. After all their bags were in the car and Charlie had asked her what to do with the cart, she'd showed him where they were returned, and he had walked to the receptacle. He didn't leave it at the front of the car, like Kevin did, as though walking twenty feet to be considerate of someone else was too much to ask of him.

She knew if she ever entertained the idea of marrying again, she wanted someone who walked the cart back. It was important to her. Maybe she should begin a list of attributes she wanted to find in a male one day.

At the top would be integrity. Most important.
Considerate.
Respectful.
Honest, but that would fall under integrity.
Giving.
Good with children.
Self-assured.
A sense of humor would be mandatory.
Sexy would be a definite plus.

As she stood at the freezer with cold air blowing on her, she realized she had just described Charles Garrity. Grabbing the steaks, she slammed the door and headed for the microwave. Stop these incredibly stupid mental wanderings, she warned herself as she punched in the defrost numbers.

She had a life to straighten out before she allowed such thoughts even to begin. But down deep, in a place she wasn't quite ready to admit existed, she knew it was too late.

Charlie was mirroring for her everything she had wanted in a man, and the reflection of what had been missing in her marriage. Could it be possible that this divorce wasn't such a terrible thing after all? She looked out the kitchen window to the back lawn and envisioned Charlie as she'd seen him earlier. Kevin had bought that riding mower three years ago as a lark, and then lost interest in it a month later. Just like he did with the sailboat that was in dry dock down at the harbor. Suddenly she felt like she was being saved from spending the rest of her life tied to a man she couldn't respect.

She felt a surge of something within her, as though she'd broken through some barrier that was revealing an important issue. What she had once wanted was some romantic dream, of a knight in shining armor riding in as the perfect husband and father. Kevin's armor was sorely tarnished and all those years she had just been making excuses for him as she kept on polishing—but it was never enough, and she couldn't polish fast enough, either. In truth, she didn't want to polish anyone's armor anymore.

She thought about her list again, ticking off each item in her head.

Could it be possible? Was *she* her own knight in shining armor? She could be strong and considerate and respectful. She had integrity. In reality, all the attributes she had wanted in a husband, she had herself. Maybe she really didn't need a man.

Then she heard the shower water running upstairs, thought of the man she now shared space with, and honestly admitted it to herself. She might not need a man, but she sure would like a partner in life someday—someone like Charlie, someone like—why, someone like herself!

She laughed at her silly thought as the microwave beeped. She and Charlie were alike. They certainly were compatible. She almost groaned when she realized that again her mind was taking her down a path that was better left untraveled. Checking on the steaks, she decided they needed more time and gave them another three minutes to defrost. Beef—she really was getting back in touch with her masculine side today.

And it felt pretty darn good.

They were falling into a routine. One of them would make dinner, the other would clean up the dishes. If she started the laundry, he would fold it. She didn't even mind that he dealt with her underwear. They were friends. He'd seen her at her worst and accepted her. He didn't seem to mind vacuuming, dusting, or any of the other "womanly" chores that kept a house running. He appeared to enjoy spending time with Matty when he wasn't crying, and didn't immediately hand the baby over when he did. He recognized when Matty needed to be changed and didn't ask her to do it. Now that the baby's umbilical cord had fallen off, they both gave him his baths and laughed at how much Matty enjoyed being surrounded by water.

Somehow, Suzanne felt that she had the best part of being with a man, a friendship, a partnership—that they were in it together, and would support each other no matter what.

Two days later, it shouldn't have surprised her when, as she was putting Matty down for the night, Charlie appeared at the nursery door with a worried look on his face.

"What's wrong?" she whispered, as she led him into the hallway.

"Someone is here to see you."

"Now? Who is it?"

"A woman. She said her name is Ingrid. She's the one who used to be your friend, isn't she?"

Suzanne felt a wash of anger and dread. "Tell her I'm busy. I don't want to see her."

"I told her you were with the baby and she said she would wait. She's in the house."

"I don't care. Tell her to leave." Really, what nerve, to barge in here without calling.

"Don't get upset. I'll handle it." He turned to leave.

She watched him descend the stairs when all of a sudden she called out, "Wait!"

Charlie turned around on the stairway.

"Tell her I'll be down in a few minutes."

"You're up to this?"

"Might as well get it over with. I can't postpone talking to her forever."

"Right," he said with a nod and a smile of encouragement while turning to go down the rest of the stairs.

Suzanne took a deep breath and then nearly ran into her bedroom. She threw open her closet and surveyed her wardrobe. She still couldn't wear most of her clothes, but she was determined to look the best she could when she had this confrontation. And she knew it was going to be one hell of a confrontation too. If Ingrid wanted this, then she intended to get some answers. The truth might be nice for a change.

Flipping through a row of blouses, she picked one that she'd worn in the beginning of her pregnancy. It was pale yellow silk and would go well with her jeans. She could leave it out to hide the small belly that she still had. No time to change pants. She pulled off the cotton sweater she'd worn all day, dropped it to the floor, and then quickly put on the blouse as she hurried into the bathroom. Looking at herself in the mirror, she was grateful she had washed her hair that very morning and she only needed to fluff the short curly wisps around her face. She opened a drawer and grabbed concealer, mascara, blush, and lipstick. Within minutes she finished and then took a deep breath as she surveyed her reflection.

She looked fairly put together and was presentable. Maybe too much lipstick. She was at home, after all, and didn't want Ingrid to think she'd gone through all this for her, which of course she had. Grabbing some toilet paper, she wiped off her lipstick. There. That was better.

Suzanne squared her shoulders, nodded back to her reflection, and left the bathroom figuring she was as prepared as she was going to get. She kept her chin held high as she walked down the steps. Ingrid was sitting in the family room. Her back was to Suzanne but she could tell Ingrid was sitting stiffly. It was obvious she was uncomfortable being in the house. A flash of all the evenings Ingrid had thrown her feet up onto the sofa and shared a glass of wine and an evening of companionship played out in seconds, but Suzanne wiped those memories away. That was the past. She had to learn, and remember, that the past was over.

"Ingrid." She said her name as she walked around the front of the sofa and sat in a wing chair by the fireplace. She said no more, not wanting to encourage any degree of friendship. That had definitely ended.

"I know why Kevin is intimidated by this man who's living with you now. He seems very protective of you."

"I don't think that's what you came here to discuss. Or are you now spying for Kevin?"

Ingrid seemed to swallow hard. Her hands were tightly clasped together in her lap. "Thanks for seeing me, Suzanne," she said in a low voice, as she started over. "I need to talk to you, to tell you how sorry I am for everything. Neither one of us planned to hurt you like this, but—"

"Excuse me?" She really had no intention of interrupting, wanting to make this as difficult as possible for Ingrid, but that last statement just couldn't be ignored. "Neither of you planned on hurting me?" she asked in an incredulous voice. "Just what did you think sleeping together was going to do to me? Or didn't you think at all?"

"I don't know how to say this . . ."

"If you came here to make some statement, then just make it. But do try to keep to the truth. You can recognize truth, right?"

"Please, Suz—just hear me out. I know we've deceived

you and hurt you. I know I can never make this right, but the truth had to come out."

She refused to allow Ingrid to ingratiate herself by using her nickname or by the tears that were gathering at her dark eyes. Grinding her back teeth to remain in some semblance of control, Suzanne muttered, "The truth finally did come out. When Kevin told me he'd been screwing around with you for over a year . . . my God, who *are* you? I don't even know you anymore. I wonder if I ever did."

"You knew me, Suzanne," she said with a sniffle. "I loved you like a sister and—"

"Stop," Suzanne interrupted. "Do not say that. Remember, we're sticking to the truth now."

"Okay," Ingrid said with a deep shuddering sigh. She wiped her eyes, and looked directly across the space that separated them. "You just didn't know all of me, the part of me that has loved Kevin since our senior year of college."

Now that stopped her. "You loved Kevin for all these years?" Just when she thought nothing could surprise her . . . *this!*

Things started falling into place. All those nights together, the three of them, laughing and playing with each other. A few times she'd noticed that Kevin's hands would linger a fraction of a second too long on Ingrid, but she'd put it down to too much wine. Now she knew the flirtatious friendship had been more than that. No wonder every man Ingrid dated turned out to be the wrong one. "How long, Ingrid?" she demanded. "Tell me the truth. Kevin said it had only been a year. Now I want to know it all."

"It started in college when you two were dating," she muttered, glancing at Suzanne and then looking down to her knees. "Just one night when you had to come home for your aunt's funeral. We were drinking and . . . one thing led to another and we wound up in bed together. Suzanne, I'd never had a night like that before."

"I don't want the details," Suzanne spit out, wondering if Ingrid was talking about the same man. Kevin was never a hot lover. Kind of methodical and—

"Well, we both knew we never should have done it, but we just couldn't stop seeing each other. We were always thrown together because . . . well, because we both wanted to be with you too. It's like we had to fight the attraction."

"So this took place the entire time?" Suzanne asked in a weird fascination that was mixed with outrage and disbelief. It was like watching a shipwreck from outside her own body.

"Sometimes we could fight it for two or three years and then—"

"Wait. Are you telling me that you and Kevin have been having these . . . these sexual romps on and off for over *fifteen years?*"

Ingrid looked as if she had been hit as she slumped back on the sofa. She put her hand over her eyes and nodded as she tried to control her tears.

Suzanne couldn't have cared. She shot up out of her chair and stared at the woman, this stranger who sat on her sofa. "Why the hell did he ever marry me, then?"

Ingrid looked up at her. "I . . . wouldn't marry him."

Now Suzanne felt like some invisible fist had punched her in the gut. Immediately she wound her arms across her belly, as though to protect it. "What do you mean, Ingrid?" she demanded, though a part of her didn't want to hear the answer.

"You know me, Suzanne," she said, sniffling and wiping the moisture off her cheek. "I was on the fast track. I told myself I couldn't settle for a fruit farmer, even if his family owned the biggest orchard in the county. I wanted more."

"And you got more when Kevin sold the land, is that it? Then he was good enough for you?" My God, this was worse than a soap opera!

"I don't need his money. You know I've done very well for myself."

"Why did he marry me, Ingrid?"

The woman shook her head, as if she couldn't say it. "You never deserved all this, Suzanne," she muttered against a stream of fresh tears.

"Why did he marry me, Ingrid?" she nearly yelled.

When she saw that Ingrid wasn't capable of telling her, she found her own throat pushing air past her teeth, past her lips, forming words. "He married me to stay close to you, my best friend." She sank back onto the chair and stared at the rug under the coffee table. "He lied to me, used me, deceived me into thinking he loved me when he really loved you, but couldn't have you!"

Ingrid started crying small sobs, and shaking her head. "You . . . you never deserved this. I couldn't tell you. I started to once, but then I was afraid of losing our friendship."

"*What* friendship?" Suzanne demanded, still reeling from the shock. "It was one-sided. My God, the two of you . . . all these years . . . trusting you both . . . thinking how great it was that we were all so close. He married me to stay close to *you!*"

Ingrid didn't say anything and Suzanne's mind was spilling out thoughts one on top of the other. "This means the prenup is null and void. He married me under false pretenses."

Ingrid's face was ravaged as she looked up at her. "I'll never testify to what I've just told you, Suzanne. I . . . I just thought it was time you knew the truth. You never deserved this. And having your baby all alone like that. God, I'm so very sorry about all of it."

Ingrid's flow of tears couldn't penetrate what was wrapping around her heart. Where had she been all these years not to have known something like this was happening? She and Kevin had broken up after college while she started her career, but he'd kept pursuing her through the years, off and on they had dated, while she had dated others, until six years ago, when she honestly had thought Kevin McDermott must surely love her never to have given up on her. And all this time it had been about Ingrid, staying as close as possible to the one constant woman in her life, the woman who wouldn't marry him. She felt so foolish for trusting, for loving them both. She stared at her once best friend, who was shaking her head and crying.

"So now you'll finally marry him, after the two of you have played God with my life. You both used me." Just saying it made bile rise in her throat.

"It must seem that way to you, but I never wanted to hurt you. Especially like this. But yes, I want to be married now."

It was as though a bolt of lightning came right through the roof and slammed her smack in the head. Ingrid looked pretty bad, tired and worn, and it couldn't all be a result of her guilt. Suzanne whispered the insane thought that was flashing in her mind like a neon sign.

"You're pregnant, aren't you?"

11

Ingrid looked at her with an expression of desperation as fresh tears streamed down her face. Running her hands through her long, dark hair, she closed her eyes briefly and then nodded.

"How long?" Suzanne breathed through her fingers over her mouth.

"Four months. I never would have pushed him if . . . if I wasn't so scared."

Suzanne got up from the chair and started pacing in front of the fireplace. "That means when he stopped having sex with me because *I* was pregnant, he was impregnating you! Dear God, is there no end to that man's arrogance?" She paused for a moment, staring at the shrunken shell of a woman before her. "Oh, Ingrid, I feel sorry for you. I'm getting out of it, but you're jumping in headfirst. You don't have to marry a man because you're pregnant. You could raise the child on your own. Think about what you're doing!"

"I love him, Suzanne. I have since I was twenty-one years old."

And then she knew, no matter what she said, it would fall upon deaf ears. It wasn't her place to save Ingrid. She'd made a choice many years ago and was playing out the drama of her life.

But this was one soap opera she, herself, was exiting as quickly as possible.

"Now you know everything. I've talked Kevin into giving you eight million," Ingrid said as she stood up and picked up her car keys from the coffee table. "I know nothing can ever repay you for what we've done, but I hope someday you find happiness."

Suzanne couldn't hold back the tears any longer. She felt as if she'd explode if she tried. Ingrid was pregnant with Kevin's child! "So our children will be related. Great! I'll never be out of this mess!" Tears drenched her face and burned her cheeks.

Ingrid walked toward the front door and Suzanne followed her, too stunned to add anything else. They had both used her for years. Everything, all her memories, felt like a lie.

Ingrid opened the door, but didn't look back. "I know you may never forgive me, but I want you to know that you were the sister I never had. Thank you for all those years of being there for me. I didn't deserve you."

"You're right, Ingrid. You didn't," she whispered as the door closed behind the woman she too had thought of as her sister.

Firmly wiping the wet streams from her face, Suzanne stared at the closed door for the longest time, absorbing the shock, feeling it move into her body and take hold. Her marriage was a lie. Her friendship with Ingrid was a lie. All of it, everything in the last fifteen years, was an illusion. She suddenly felt a hand on her shoulder and jumped in fright.

"I couldn't help but overhear some of it," Charlie whispered, running his hand over her back in small circles of comfort. "Come sit down."

She allowed him to steer her back into the family room. "It was all a lie, Charlie," she muttered.

He put his arm around her shoulders and felt a slight tremble in her body. He'd tried not to listen, but when Suzanne had yelled, asking why Kevin had married her, he couldn't help but hear the answer. From that point on he was vigilant, waiting to see if Suzanne would need him, for he was prepared to remove Ingrid from the house if necessary.

He sat in the corner of the sofa and pulled her down with him. Without thought, he took her into his arms and she instinctively curled her upper body into his as she buried her face in his chest and began to cry, deep body-wracking sobs of anguish. Holding her tightly with one arm, he began to stroke her hair with the other. "It's all right, Suzie. Cry it out; get it out of you."

"All of it was a lie," she wailed in what sounded like a little girl's hurt voice.

"I know," he murmured, wondering what kind of people play with lives like that. A picture of Mitch Davies ran across his mind and he banished it quickly. There were people in the world who really didn't care what they did to others. People without conscience. The war should have taught him that. His heart opened to Suzanne, that she would have to go through this kind of pain. Hadn't she had enough?

He sat with her, holding her, stroking her, listening to her sorrow, and it was then he realized how natural it all felt. Perhaps it was because they were friends, but secretly he knew it was more than that. She just felt *right* in his arms. There was no other way of putting it. She belonged there. Immediately he realized how inappropriate his thoughts were and tried to banish the feeling, but it simply wouldn't go away. She fit. A fleeting image of holding Grace flashed and he knew it hadn't felt like this. In some distant part of his brain he now knew that marrying a woman he didn't really love would have been just as damaging as what Kevin had done to Suzanne. Grace had loved him, like Suzanne had loved Kevin . . . maybe they both thought if they loved enough they could make it work. He now realized that Grace would have been disappointed with him. For as he held Suzanne even tighter and rested his chin on the top of her blond curls, he knew he had never felt like this before—not with any other woman in his life. Was it possible, he wondered, had he come to this time to find—the emotion rushing through his body was demanding a definition—*love?*

He loved Suzanne?

His body became rigid with the thought. He stilled his hand for just a moment as he tried to think about it. It was so strange, so totally beyond him, that he tried to rationalize it away. He had never known any other woman like Suzanne. He had never become friends, real friends, with a woman before. They had bonded because he had been thrown into this time, into her life, at a time when she needed him and he needed her. There were so many reasons to believe that what he was feeling wasn't love. But how could he explain how he *felt*, holding her in his arms like this?

"Ingrid's pregnant," Suzanne muttered, sniffling as she hiccuped and wiped at her eyes.

He held the back of her head tighter and breathed in the floral scent of her hair. "I know. I heard it. I'm so sorry, Suzanne."

"That's why he wants to protect their names," she said. "That's all he cares about now. What a total shit he is! Getting Ingrid pregnant while I was pregnant! What kind of man does that?"

"I wish I could wipe away this pain for you, but I can't. I know it's hard for you right now, but the faster you get out of this situation the better." It was all he could think to say.

"I'll never be free of him!" she cried, as the tears resumed.

"He's Matty's father and now my son will have a brother or sister and . . . and I'll be tied to this ugliness for the rest of my life!"

"I promise you," he whispered, running his cheek over the silky strands of her hair, "that one day you will be happy again. I don't know how it happens, but everything always works out in the end. It always has, and it always will. Think back on your life," he added. "At the very worst times, when you thought you couldn't go on or get through it, you did. And it worked out somehow."

"But this is different," she protested. "My life has been a lie for the last fifteen years. How does that work out? How can I heal that wound, knowing the two people I trusted most in the world were going behind my back and deciding my life for me? How could I have misjudged them? What's wrong with me?"

"Shh . . . there's nothing wrong with you. I know what you're feeling. I, too, trusted someone who turned out to be a scoundrel. I don't think either of us is to blame. Were we fools? Maybe. But I'd rather be a fool than a scoundrel."

She sniffled. "Scoundrel. That's a good word for them." She raised her head and patted his chest. "I've ruined your shirt."

"Nonsense. It's just tears and will wash away." He grinned as she looked at him with red-rimmed, sorrowful eyes. "I'm getting very good at laundry, you know."

In spite of everything, she smiled. "Yes, you are, Charlie. Again, I don't know what I would have done if you weren't here with me. You really were sent to me. I believe that with my whole heart . . . because I needed you now."

"A man likes to be needed," he whispered, gently pushing a curl off her damp forehead. "I guess doing laundry qualifies."

She seemed to become very still as she raised her face and looked at him seriously. "I wasn't talking about laundry, and you know it. I can't even imagine being alone now to handle all this. You've saved my sanity, Charlie, and maybe even my life."

"Then we're even on that score, for you've done the same for me."

There was a moment when they just stared deeply into each other's eyes, going beyond the superficial and making a connection. His first inclination was to look away, but he held her gaze, knowing somehow that what was taking place was important.

"Tell me about your scoundrel, Charlie. Take my mind off this madness," she whispered in an exhausted voice.

"My scoundrel?" he asked with a short laugh, grateful that the intense moment was over. "He isn't quite so interesting as yours. Mine was just greedy. He wanted my life and tried to take it that afternoon you pulled me from the creek."

"He's the one who shot you?"

Nodding, he said, "I realized I could either jump off that bridge and take my chances, or be killed by Mitch."

"That was his name? You mentioned him before."

"Mitch Davies." Even saying it now had a profound effect on him and he tried to relax the muscles in his body. "We left Ireland at the same time and met on the ship. We banded together and went west, working on ranches, and then coming back east to run bootleg whiskey up and down the eastern coast."

She sniffled and then startled him by chuckling. "Bootleg whiskey? During Prohibition?"

He couldn't stop the grin. "I guess I'm a bit of a scoundrel myself."

"Well, obviously you know by now that Prohibition was repealed, so I wouldn't classify you as a *true* scoundrel."

"I was desperate to make money. I wanted to settle down."

"Yes, you told me you were engaged to a woman."

He nodded. "I'd seen the land I'd wanted shortly after coming to America. Funny that it's right here, where I am now, but I can't identify it anymore. Everything is so different. Even the railroad bridge is gone. New roads. New buildings. This was all farmland then. Every time we drive, I try to see something I can remember, but there are no landmarks. And even if I had the deed, it wouldn't do me any good today."

"I wonder whatever happened to it," she murmured, putting her head back onto his chest and sighing with a shuddering exhaustion.

He stroked her shoulder and said, "It doesn't matter anymore. That dream is gone. I don't believe I'm going back, Suzanne. I've been thinking about it and, if it was going to happen, I think it would have by now. It's been almost a month. I think I'm here to stay."

She clutched the front of his shirt and whispered against his chest, "Would you resent me for saying I'm glad?"

He shook his head and smiled. "No, I wouldn't. And honestly, I don't even think I'd want to go back if the opportunity presented itself. I can't imagine a life—" He almost said without her and Matty, and stopped himself just in time. "A life without all these modern conveniences. I'm starting to like it here."

"Good," she answered in a tired voice. "Then stay here. You know, you're right, Charlie. Everything always does work out in the end somehow. It may take years, but it does, doesn't it?"

"You're going to be okay, Suzanne. Believe that," he whispered, stroking her hair again. "Just be patient with yourself. You've been through a lot lately and I think you're one terrific lady for how you're handling it all."

"Thanks," she murmured, and sighed deeply.

He felt her breath against him and, within minutes, she was sleeping, yet he didn't stop stroking her hair. He wanted to touch her, to feel her warm body next to his, to take it all in while he could. What a woman she was. Strong. Intelligent. Funny. Warm. Charming. Resilient. Through all of her pain she was still beautiful and, sometimes, when he watched her with Matty, she took his breath away. She stirred something within him that was new. It went beyond being protective of the gentler sex. Hell, he didn't think of her as being weak at all. It was as though for the first time he felt he'd met his equal. He could trust her.

Deliberately, he paused his thoughts.

He should be scared.

He probably should make plans to leave her when she moved from this house. He should let her heal and live her own life with her son. But right now he knew he didn't have the strength to walk away. It wasn't that he was frightened of making his way in a strange world. He'd done it before and he knew he could do it again. He didn't want to leave her and Matty. It didn't matter to him that Matty was another man's son. He'd been there for the lad's birth. He'd diapered him. Rocked the child to sleep. Bathed him. He was even teaching the lad to smile just like him . . .

Maybe he was setting himself up for a big fall.

Someday Suzanne would want to get on with her life, maybe even remarry. Would his presence hold her back? She thought of him as a friend. That's all. And he didn't want her to come to him in order to fill a gaping wound left by her husband's betrayal. There really was no way out of this except for him to leave. But he couldn't do it right now. He'd make that decision after she found a place to move. She'd said she had three months to get out of the house. Three months. You could make a lot of memories in that time. Memories he'd take with him when he left her and Matty. He had time yet, before thinking about moving on.

That is, he thought, as he tenderly placed a kiss on the top of her head and pulled her closer to his body, if he could hold out that long.

"You heard me, Laura. Ingrid's pregnant. Four months. No wonder they want this over as quickly as possible. Tell them

I'll take the eight million for the last fifteen years of lies, and the alimony and the child support. I want to get out of this house as quickly as possible and protect myself and my son."

"I understand, Suzanne," her lawyer answered over the phone. "My God, this just keeps getting more and more . . . I don't even know what the word is anymore."

"Sordid," Suzanne supplied. "I'm telling you I would look at tabloid television and wonder what kind of people lived lives like that. Now I know. *Me!* Talk about learning never to judge!"

"Oh, Suzanne, you're the victim in all this. You're not sordid."

"Please do not refer to me as a victim, Laura. I can't stand the word. I can't stand feeling sorry for myself. I find myself crying for the most ridiculous reasons and I can't put it down to postpartum blues any longer. I just want this over as quickly as possible so I can move on with my life. I'll pay whatever it takes to get this moving."

"It is moving, Suzanne. Look how far we've come already. I can't get a judge to move you up on the docket, but I can harass the hell out of Kevin's lawyers to get the paperwork completed. Then I'll see what I can do. I know a few clerks in family court."

"Oh, there's one thing more," Suzanne said. "It's the primary reason I called you."

"What's that?"

"I want full custody of Matty. I can't imagine Kevin fighting me on it, since he'll have another child in five months."

"Okay, I'll tell them. What if he does put up a fight?"

"He won't. He doesn't even know Matty. He's only seen him once and only for about five minutes. Besides, he's too much of a coward, especially now, when his lawyer lets him know that Ingrid told me the whole ugly story."

"You know we could fight to put aside the prenup now. You could be entitled to half of all marital assets . . . might even be thirty million."

"As they tie us up in court and it takes years to free myself from that man? No thanks. I don't need that kind of money and I don't want to fight for anything, except full custody of my son."

"All right. I'll get on the phone as soon as we hang up. You've opened a checking account in your name?"

"Yes, two days ago."

"Give me the account number, so I can have Kevin's lawyers wire the first transition payment into it. Start concentrating on building a new life, Suzanne. At least it will help take your mind off the rest of it for a while."

"Yes, I think that's just what I'll do, Laura. Thanks."

After giving Laura her new account number, she hung up the phone and looked around at the farmhouse. Once she had loved it. Now it seemed like a place of lies. Even the decorations were planned with a future. What kind of future could she possibly have had with a man who only married her to stay in the life of her friend? Had she just imagined that Kevin loved her? Was it merely affection? Did she provide the perfect front? A naive woman who had loved both of them unconditionally? Who tried not to see their faults, and excused them when they were too blatant to be ignored? Who honestly believed they could be trusted? It didn't seem possible that something like this had happened to her, and yet it had. She'd admitted it to Charlie, how she felt like such a fool for being so easily deceived. And maybe that's what this anger was all about. Being a fool for fifteen years was hard to swallow.

She found him in the backyard, fixing a bird feeder that was attached to a graceful limb of an apple tree. "Hey, Charlie," she called out.

He turned around and smiled, something that she knew she would never tire of seeing—the way his green eyes lit up lately whenever he looked at her, the lines of laughter that surrounded them, the big grin, showing his perfect white teeth. She sighed as she walked closer. *Put it out of your mind,* she again reminded herself, even though she knew she would never forget being held in his arms the night Ingrid had dropped her bombshell. What comfort she had felt cradled against him. He'd thought she was sleeping, and she was—almost—yet she knew he'd kissed the top of her head and held her even closer. It was a display of sympathy for being wounded once again. The poor man was witness to her worst times and still he supported her through it all. What a good friend he was, and she wasn't about to mess it up with romance.

Hell, romance was definitely out, no matter how great-looking he was, how kind, honorable, and half a dozen other things she had always been searching for in a mate. Even though she had settled for less in her marriage, romance had almost ruined her life and she wasn't about to dive into it again any time soon, if ever. She was done with illusions and fantasies.

"Hey, Suz," he called out as she approached. "Almost finished with this. Soon we'll have the song of spring right outside the door."

"No we won't."

He held the hammer in his hand and turned his head. "We won't?"

"Forget fixing anything more here. We've got more important things to do."

"We do?"

Nodding, she said, "We've got to start packing. We're moving away from here as quickly as possible."

She noticed he set his jaw, as though accepting bad news. "Hey, this is it, Charlie. We're about to start a new adventure."

His smile was forced as he nodded. "You'll do fine, Suzanne. I know you will."

She saw a sadness in his eyes now. Funny, she didn't know he was so attached to the farm.

12

She looked down at her son, asleep at her breast, and smiled with the love that filled her heart. In spite of all the ugliness, she was blessed with this incredible being who was changing before her eyes. His hair was getting lighter, turning blond like hers; his eyes were blue, like hers. He even had that tiny thin line under his nose, just like hers. When he nursed, he now looked right up at her, staring into her eyes with such wonder that her whole body almost vibrated with love. His last visit to the pediatrician indicated he was in the upper twenty-fifth percentile in weight and length. The doctor thought her due date must have been off by two weeks as Matty appeared as healthy as any full-term baby.

Yes, she was definitely blessed.

That's what she was doing lately—counting her blessings instead of her woes. She was sick of woes, sick of the drama, the tears. She wanted to be happy again. She remembered happiness, that feeling of well-being, and wanted it back.

Right now she had her son. A wonderful, supportive friend. A good lawyer. And her health. There was more than enough to be happy about, and she wasn't waiting until the rest of her life fell into place. Maybe it would take years, but that was her focus now. The divorce was proceeding, as Kevin had agreed to her retaining full custody, and Laura's connection to a family law clerk had moved the case up on the docket. In less than two weeks, she would be single again.

She was getting her life in order. Piece by piece. She'd looked at a few rentals, but hadn't picked one out yet. She didn't want to leave the area, or rather to leave Matty's pediatrician yet. Maybe in a few months they would just pack up and leave for another state, but right now she didn't want a drastic move. Charlie had been helping with the packing, or more accurately, she'd been helping Charlie with the packing, as Matty took up so much of her time. She wasn't taking everything from the house. She'd leave the furniture, save for the nursery. There were too many memories attached to furnishings she had chosen with Kevin in mind. No, she would start fresh in a place free of memories and begin to heal her heart and mind.

She glanced at her wristwatch and realized she had just enough time to put Matty down for his nap, take a quick shower, and then make it to her appointment. She eased her breast away from Matty's mouth and, after adjusting herself, brought her son to her shoulder. Patting him on the back, she rose from the rocker and headed for the stairs. Before she hit the upstairs hallway, Matty burped and Suzanne grinned as she headed for his room. When she lay him gently in his crib, he murmured once, opening and closing his eyes sleepily, then sighed a tiny breath. Now he should sleep for at least three hours and she would have time to get to her appointment and be back before he awoke.

Thank heavens Matty had turned into such a good sleeper, she thought as she walked into her bedroom. She stood for just a moment and looked at the king-sized bed, the place where Matty had been conceived. It had been love, at least on her part. She would always be able to tell him that when he got older and started to ask questions. She walked into the bathroom and turned on the shower. She was dreading this appointment with her gynecologist. It was her six-week checkup, and she knew he would tell her it was fine to resume marital relations. Sex. Like she would even consider it now. And with whom?

Charlie's face crossed her mind, but she quickly dismissed it. Something was up with Charlie. He'd become . . . distant. Well, maybe not distant, but quiet. He didn't laugh as much and sometimes she caught him looking at Matty with the oddest expression of sadness. It was way too weird, and she had tried to speak to him about it, but he'd claimed he didn't know what she was talking about, so she'd dropped it. Maybe it was just the pressure of the move and the uncertainty of his future. She had assured him his future was with her and Matty for as long as he wanted. What more could she do?

Pulling off her jeans, she threw them on the platform around the Jacuzzi, followed by her blouse and her bra. She looked in the mirror briefly and sighed at her reflection. Her stomach was flatter now, but she didn't know if it would ever be firm again. She had no time for sit-ups or gyms, at least not now. Her breasts were still far bigger than they'd ever been in her life. She was a mother, with a definite motherly form. It was worth it, she thought, thinking of her son sleeping down the hall.

She giggled as she opened the glass shower door and spied her razor on the shelf next to her bath gel and sponge. Time to shave her legs. She'd do it for her doctor, but then that was it. She had more important things in her life right now to concern herself with—like getting out of this house and beginning her new life. That's what she liked to call it. Her new life. Hers and Matty's—and Charlie's too. She'd made another appointment with a property management company for five o'clock today. This time she'd plead with Charlie to come with her and Matty.

Standing under the spray of hot water, she picked up the tube of scented soap and squeezed a portion of it onto the sponge. She began washing herself as she thought of Charlie again. Something was really bothering him. It was as though he were slowly shutting her out, and she didn't know how to mend whatever it was that was causing it. Maybe getting him more involved with choosing a new place would make him feel better about the move.

As she was shaving her legs, she thought about the places she had already seen. Too small. Too modern and sterile. Too close to neighbors. She didn't want to buy a house, just rent one until she knew which direction she was heading. It was the first time in her life that she didn't know. It was like her life was a blank page, waiting to be filled. Kind of scary, but also kind of exciting.

Who was she now?

Besides being a mother, she really didn't know.

Two hours later, she walked into the house having been given a clean bill of health from her doctor. She felt uplifted, almost bubbly, as she greeted Charlie, who was packing away the books she had chosen to take with her. She glanced at Matty, who was asleep in his infant seat on the rug by Charlie's work area.

"He's still sleeping?" she whispered, bending down to check on her son.

"He woke up, but I gave him the pacifier and he went back to sleep."

"What a good baby," she murmured, gently stroking his fine blond hair.

"He is a good lad," Charlie agreed.

She straightened and said, "I have a five o'clock appointment today to look at some rentals. Won't you go with me?"

"I have work to do," he answered, packing more books into a box.

"We both have work to do, but I really want your input on this, Charlie. It's important to me."

"Suzanne, you'll do fine. I keep telling you that and—"

"Okay, what's going on?" she whispered, interrupting him as she walked away from Matty and came closer to him. "You've been acting weird for over a week now. Every time I try to talk to you about it, you put me off. Are you upset with me? Have I done something?"

He looked up at her and there was that sad smile again. "You've done nothing, Suzanne."

"Come on, Charlie. You've been downright miserable. Just tell me what's bothering you."

"Nothing is bothering me. Why won't you believe me?"

She shrugged. "I guess because you've changed. You're not happy any longer."

"I've a lot on my mind, Suzanne." He paused and threw the book into the box. "Do I *have* to be happy all the time? Do I have to smile while I'm cleaning the house or washing clothes or—"

"I help," she interrupted, a bit defensively. "I wash my own clothes and I've been cleaning the house too. Is that it? You can't stand doing housework?"

He laughed, just a little sarcastically. "Who likes it? I've done what you've asked of me."

"And I keep telling you how grateful I am. If it's bothering you so much, don't do it anymore. I can manage. I'd rather have you happy again than moping around and—"

"I am not moping around!" he answered before she could finish.

She glanced at Matty to make sure he was still sleeping, since Charlie had raised his voice and it was the first time she could remember him being so upset with her. "Look, I apologize if I've hit a nerve, but I just wanted to clear the air. Something isn't right, Charlie. I can feel it."

He sighed deeply. "If it's so important to you, I'll go with you today."

"Well, I don't want to force you," she answered, feeling like he had once more halted any kind of close communication. Where had that ease between them gone?

"Do you want me to go with you?"

"Yes. I would really appreciate it."

"Then I will." He looked at the clock on the wall and added, "Give me a few minutes to finish up here and get ready."

Nodding, she said, "I'm going to wake up Matty, feed him, and then change him. It will take about a half hour."

"I'll be ready," he said, reaching for another book, as though he'd dismissed her.

Feeling a little hurt, Suzanne picked up the infant seat and walked out of the room. Why was Charlie acting like this? Didn't he want to move with them? Where else would he go? He was just unnerved, she assured herself. This was the only place he knew. Together, they'd find a new home where they could figure out their lives and make plans for their futures. Only it couldn't be here. Even though she had months to leave the farm, she knew she couldn't remain in a place that felt like a house of lies. She *had* to make a fresh start as quickly as possible.

As soon as she saw it, she knew it was the right place. Situated on the bank of the Delaware, it was an old Victorian home with a wide porch overlooking the river. It wasn't large, more like a cottage, but it was adorable and had a nice yard with lots of trees and a garden.

"The owner is on a six-month consulting assignment on the west coast, so this is a short-term rental."

"That's fine," Suzanne answered the rental agent, a nice woman who seemed determined to find her the right place.

Turning to look at Charlie, the woman asked, "Shall we go inside?"

Suzanne had Matty strapped to her chest and she too looked at Charlie, who was standing with his hands in his pockets.

"Sure," he answered in a monotone voice.

Well, he could be a little more enthusiastic, Suzanne thought, as she held her hand under Matty's bottom, not yet trusting this new form of transporting her son.

The agent unlocked the front door and they walked into the home. Immediately, Suzanne could see them living here. It was decorated in comfortable contemporary furniture with pale creamy walls and off-white window treatments. It was bright and homey, and Suzanne wanted to move right in. "Three bedrooms?" she asked to verify what the woman had told her earlier.

"That's right. Oh, there's only two stipulations. No dogs and no smokers."

She smiled at Charlie, who still seemed to be lacking any interest. "We don't have any dogs and neither one of us smokes. May we see the rest of the house?"

The woman led them through the dining room, the bright kitchen, and a sun room that would receive the morning's rays. She could just picture sitting with Matty on one of the thick cushions of the wicker furniture, looking out to the back garden. It seemed perfect for them. "Let's see the bed-rooms."

A half hour later, as they left the house, the agent said, "Shall I leave you and your husband to discuss it?"

"Yes, thank you," Suzanne answered with a smile. Wher-ever they went publically, everyone assumed they were mar-ried and she was tired of explaining Charlie wasn't her husband. It was easier just to allow them to think what they wanted.

Turning to Charlie, she couldn't help grinning with happi-ness. "Well, what do you think? Isn't it just perfect?"

He smiled back. "Looks like you've already made your decision."

"But do *you* like it?"

"It's only important if you think you'll be happy here."

"C'mon, Charlie, give me a break. What do you think of the house?"

He looked back to the Victorian and nodded. "I think it's a fine place, Suzanne."

"Then this is it," she proclaimed. "At least for six months. And I won't have to buy furniture yet or window treatments or anything." She glanced back to the white trimmed porch. "I can figure out my life here."

"Then I'm happy for you. Tell the agent you'll take it."

She could hardly contain herself. "I will. Let's go back to her office and I'll sign the papers."

All the way home from the agent's office, she kept talking about the house, but Charlie was oddly silent. When they entered the farm house, she unbuckled Matty from her chest and placed him on the sofa as she took off his tiny hooded jacket. He was wide awake and fussing and she knew he would want to be fed soon.

"Why don't we just order out tonight, instead of cooking?" she asked, bringing Matty to her shoulder.

Charlie dropped the diaper bag in the foyer and muttered, "Order whatever you wish."

She was passing him, making her way to the stairs, when she stopped. "Would you please tell me what's wrong? I thought you'd be happy we found a place that's so perfect. What *is* it, Charlie?"

"I don't know what you're talking about. I *am* happy for you."

"You may say that, but it's not how you're acting. I just wish you would talk about it. I keep thinking I've done something and you're upset with me." She brought Matty closer to her face and kissed his soft cheek as he made noises of hunger.

"Suzanne, put your mind at ease. I told you before, you haven't done anything and I'm not upset with you."

Matty suddenly turned his face and began sucking on her chin. Surprised, she pulled back and he started to whimper. "I think he's really hungry."

Charlie grinned. "Looks like it."

She met his gaze and said, "I wish you could be happy again. I don't know what to do to help you."

"Don't worry yourself about me, Suzanne," he answered, picking up the diaper bag. "Feed the lad, and then we'll get something to eat."

She simply nodded and headed for the stairs. She would use the phone upstairs to order a pizza. That was something new Charlie hadn't yet tried. Maybe it would brighten his mood.

He really seemed to enjoy the pizza, eating five slices, and when Suzanne suggested they put their feet up and watch TV, he came with her into the family room almost reluctantly, muttering about having work to complete before the move in two weeks.

"Oh, Charlie, you've been working all day, and I'm exhausted from running around. Can't we just have a nice quiet evening? The packing will still be there tomorrow." She picked up the remote control and plopped herself down on the sofa. "Let's see what's on cable."

She watched as Charlie sat down at the opposite side of the sofa, as she flipped through the channels. He didn't look relaxed at all. "Oh, look," she said, pointing the remote at the screen. "This is just starting . . . *Ryan's Daughter.* I saw it years ago. It's about Ireland, around World War One. Want to watch it?"

"I suppose so," he murmured, concentrating on the movie.

She thought he could be a little more enthusiastic. Sheesh, she was going out of her way to try and lift his dark mood. Feeling a twinge of resentment for his behavior of late, she crossed her arms over her stomach and stared at the screen. Almost immediately she thought of all the wonderful things Charlie had done for her in the last six weeks and was immediately contrite. "From what I can remember, the British are occupying Ireland during the war and that girl, the one with the blond hair, falls in love with the schoolteacher and she marries him. Although he's a great guy, she's disappointed in the marriage, disillusioned. She knows there's something more, but doesn't know what it is. And there . . . that's the British officer who's suffering from shell shock from the war and he's just taken charge of the battalion that's occupying her town."

Charlie simply nodded and Suzanne shut up, allowing him to figure it out from there on his own. They watched in silence as the officer came into the pub, owned by the girl's father. She's alone with him when a noise suddenly starts a flashback to the war and she comforts him. There are no words, no music, just silence, as they stare into each other's eyes and begin kissing passionately. Finally, the girl knows what has been missing in her marriage.

Suzanne glanced at Charlie and could see his jaw set as he stared at the screen. She looked back to the movie as the officer and the girl make plans to meet the next day. The scene then changed to the two of them on horseback, riding through the woods until they come to a beautiful glen of purple flowers. She halts her horse at a pond and they both dismount. Again, no words . . . nothing but passion. It appears the girl doesn't care that she is married, that he is British, her enemy. They sink to the ground and quite a love scene begins.

Suzanne had forgotten how graphic the scene was. Actually, compared to more modern movies it was fairly tame. Oh dear, there's a glimpse of a bare breast, she thought, feeling the air between her and Charlie come alive with an uncomfortable silence. She couldn't even look across the sofa to him to see his reaction. Best just to say nothing. It would soon be over and . . . oh, geez . . . now the officer is on top of the girl, moving slowly, watching her face become animated as she finally experiences an orgasm and—

Charlie suddenly stood up. "I'm going out," he announced.

Startled, Suzanne looked up at him from the sofa. "What do you mean you're going out? Where?"

"I don't know," he stated, raking his fingers through his hair. "I just have to get out of this house."

"Charlie, if it's the movie, we can turn it off. I know seeing love scenes is pretty shocking to you and—"

"Why can't you understand I just want some time *alone*, away from this place?"

She sat up straighter and stared at his whole body language. He looked like he wanted to run. "Then go. Do what you want. I'm certainly not keeping you a prisoner here." Really, what the hell was wrong with him?

"Fine."

"Fine," she retorted, flicking off the TV and standing up. "You've had this . . . this attitude for over a week and I'm tired of trying to find a way to fix it."

"Fix it? Like you've tried to fix me?"

"I've never tried to fix you," she shot back, feeling a bit under attack now.

"Oh, really? It's like you're molding me into someone I'm not. I'm not female, no matter what the damn book says. I like when a woman takes care of the house and a man works outside it. And for your information, I do smoke. When life had some semblance of normalcy to it, I liked my occasional pipe!"

She just stared at him, not quite believing what she was hearing. "Well, I didn't know about the pipe thing," she muttered.

"It doesn't matter, I'm getting out where I can *breathe!*" And he walked away from her. He grabbed the keys, opened the front door, and left.

She didn't move. She stood perfectly still and listened as he gunned the motor and drove away. Shocked by the entire scene, she stared into the foyer. What the hell was that all about? He couldn't breathe around her? She wasn't trying to mold him . . . was she? She'd liked him just the way he was. All she'd been doing was trying to make him fit in better, to bring him up to par with the modern world. He was so part female, and she'd proved it to him! Why was that so damned threatening to a man? What an insult! She'd accepted that, through her father, she was part male. She didn't feel it diminished her in any way.

Men!

It didn't matter what century they came from, she would never understand them.

He pulled into the parking area of the establishment that advertised a red sign spelling out Guinness. It was just what he wanted. Without thinking, he walked up to the door and threw it open. Immediately, he was assaulted by the noise and the loud music, but that too would serve him. The very last thing he wanted to do was think about Suzanne and the argument they'd just had.

He found a stool at the bar and slid onto it, while reaching in his pocket for the money he carried, but had nowhere to spend. Suzanne always paid for everything, and that too galled him. She was utilizing a little too much of her masculine side lately. Pulling out one of the twenty-dollar bills she had paid him, he slid it toward the front of the bar.

A bartender walked in his direction. "What can I get you?"

"A pint of Guinness would be appreciated."

The older man scratched his eyebrow and grinned. "Well, I don't know about a pint, but I can give you a tall glass."

"That would be fine," he answered.

The man nodded and walked to the taps. Charles watched as the dark brew filled a glass and he unconsciously licked his lips in anticipation. It had been some time since he'd sat at a bar, a legal bar, and drank to his leisure. Funny how different it was now. He remembered walking into a "speak" after giving a password, and all for a drink. He shook his head with the memory of all those raids, all those people prosecuted . . . and for what?

He thought of Mitch, just getting out of jail for running bootleg, when he'd contacted him about the land he'd just purchased. Maybe the time in jail had turned Mitch. Or maybe he'd always been a bastard. Looking around the bar, he saw people of every age. They seemed perfectly normal to him, and he wondered how many of them would believe he came from a time when they would all be arrested for doing exactly what they were now. No one would believe him.

"Hey, stranger. I haven't seen you around here before."

He turned his head and looked into the eyes of a woman, he figured in her late twenties, who slid her slim body onto the stool next to him. In seconds he took in her appearance. Dark hair, pinned back with a clip, pretty blue eyes, a wide friendly smile. She wore a tight top that molded to her breasts, and black leather encased her long legs.

He smiled back. "Hello."

The bartender placed his mug of Guinness in front of him and said, "I'll run a tab. And, Jen, don't break his heart."

The woman threw back her head and laughed. "Oh, he'll probably break mine, Tommy." She looked to her side and smiled again before adding, "Should I be worried, stranger?"

Charlie shook his head. "Not at all, ma'am." He picked up his glass and drank deeply.

"A Guinness man, I see. Do I detect a trace of the ole sod in your voice?"

"Yes, ma'am. I was born in Ireland." Was she now going to make some remark about micks or paddys and drinking? He'd heard enough to last his lifetime, and hers too.

"Hey, I'm Irish. At least my grandfather was." She stuck out her hand. "McGee. Jennifer McGee."

He grinned at her friendly expression and accepted her handshake. "Charles Garrity. A pleasure to meet you, Jennifer McGee."

"Call me Jen. Everyone does."

Tommy, the bartender, put a drink in front of her and she just nodded her thanks. She must come in here often for the bartender to know what she drinks. He looked to the end of the building, beyond the tables, and saw a group of young men playing billiards. Taking a deep breath, he began to feel the muscles in his body finally relax. Yes, now he could breathe.

"So, are you from around here?"

He turned his attention back to the attractive woman. "Not really."

"Not real talkative, are you?" Her smile was meant to charm.

"I suppose not," he answered. "What about you?"

"What about me?" she asked, picking up her drink. "Am I from around here? God, yes. Trying to put together the cash to get myself out of Jersey."

"Where might you go?" He was mildly interested, and this woman's presence at least took his mind off the situation a few miles away from here.

"California. Definitely California. Maybe San Diego. No more rain and snow. You know the weather there is gorgeous and the people . . . well, they're not from Jersey, so that's a definite plus."

"You don't like people from New Jersey?" he asked, taking another sip of his Guinness.

She studied her drink, as she ran a painted red fingertip down the side of her glass. "Listen, Charlie . . . have you ever been in a place too long, where you know you've gotten everything you're gonna get from it, but you just can't get your act together long enough to get out?"

"Yes, Jen, I have."

"Well, that's where I am now. It's not the people. Most of them are real nice, but I was born here, educated here, married and divorced here. I'm sitting in the neighborhood bar where I had my first legal drink. It's like there's nothing left here for me, yet I can't get out."

"Why not just leave?"

"Money. It's always about money. Or the lack of it."

Money. He'd had enough talk about that lately. "How much would it take?"

She shrugged her shoulders. "Well, first I'd have to get my car out of the shop. A new clutch isn't cheap. Then, I'd need enough to get there, plus first and last month's rent, with a security deposit to put down on an apartment. And then enough to keep everything going until I found a job."

"What kind of work do you do?" If he kept her talking maybe he wouldn't think about another woman who was trying to move on with her life.

"I process loan applications for a mortgage company. Not exactly exciting."

He nodded. "And you want excitement?"

"Sure!" She laughed. "Who wouldn't?"

He didn't. He'd had enough excitement in his life. Now he wanted peace. "What's that?" he inquired, as someone asked in a loud voice when car-ee-oak something was going to start.

Shaking her head, she looked at him with a quizzical expression. "Karaoke. You've got to have heard of it!"

"No. Can't say as I have. What is it?"

"You're kidding! Where you been hiding yourself, Charlie?" She laughed, as though her comment was meant to make him feel comfortable about his ignorance. "Well, these locals are gonna try to sing, along with a tape. See that big screen over there?"

He nodded.

"The words to the song appear on that screen, and then your ears are assaulted by those with dreams they can actually sing." She sipped her drink. "Can you?"

"Sing?" Shaking his head, he added, "Not a lick of musical talent, I'm afraid."

"Well, that's the first thing you've told me about yourself."

He looked sideways to her and could see that she was smiling in a teasing way. "I'm not all that interesting."

"Now, there I differ with you. Tall, handsome, mysterious. I call that interesting."

He realized she was flirting with him. Immediately a vision of Suzanne appeared across his mind, and he quickly willed it away. He didn't want to think about her. He simply had to get it in his head that soon he would leave her and Matty. No point in prolonging the inevitable. He turned in his chair to face the pretty young woman and smiled, glad she was sitting beside him.

"I shall take that as a compliment, Jen McGee. May I buy you another drink?"

Her eyes widened with even more interest and she pushed her glass toward the front of the bar. Still keeping eye contact with him, she called out to the bartender, "Another round for us both, Tommy. Charlie's laying on the brogue pretty thick here. See, I told you he'd break my Irish heart."

Laughing, Charlie picked up his Guinness and finished it. It felt good to be himself again. Free. Free from women's chores and babies spitting. Tonight there would be no diapers needing to be changed. No clothes needing to be washed. No blond-headed woman who'd look at him with those big blue eyes and try to make him into someone he wasn't. He was a man. All man. Always was, always would be, and no amount of science was going to change that. Why, he'd just allowed himself to get soft. Even the callouses on his hands had disappeared, since he'd been domestic for six weeks!

He picked up his fresh mug of Guinness as Jen picked up her drink. Raising his up in a toast, he smiled into her eyes and said, "Here's to getting out of New Jersey."

Jen grinned and clinked her glass to his. "I'll drink to that. To a new life!"

"Yes," he murmured. "A new life."

He drank half the glass to that one.

It was the perfect toast.

13

"Charlie, are you sure you won't come in? I could make you some coffee. We could sit around and talk . . . and just let the night take us where it will."

"Ah, Jennifer McGee, you are a temptress. But I'm a proper gentleman and I've delivered you to your door, as I should. Off with you now, lass!"

Instead of getting out of the car, Jen raised her face and laughed at his words. Sighing deeply, she rested her head against the cushioned headrest and looked at him with those beckoning eyes. "You can stay the night, if you want. I mean, if you're too tired to drive home, or anything."

He grinned, flattered by her interest. "Are all women so accommodating? Coffee and a place to rest my head?"

"You know that isn't what I meant. I like you, Charlie, but I'm guessing the car seat in the back means you've got commitments, huh?"

He swung his head around to the back of the car and saw Matty's baby seat. Maybe a little too fast, for his head began to swim a few seconds. Steadying himself, he said, "Aye, that. Why, that belongs to a friend of mine. This isn't my automobile."

"Auto-mobile," she repeated and giggled. "You sure do talk funny sometimes, and you're so proper, but I'm glad that car seat isn't yours," she added, leaning closer to him and touching the arm of his shirt. As she ran her fingers lightly over the material, she sighed again. "C'mon, Charlie, let's go inside and we can talk. I know almost nothing about you."

He looked down at her hand on his shirtsleeve. She wore several silver rings on her thin fingers and her nails were creating a reaction. He almost shivered. Young Jen had been flirting with him for over three hours now, and a man could only be so strong. "Lass, you'd best be taking yourself up that walk and into your home. The last thing you'd be wanting to know is anything about me."

"Oh, you're wrong, Charlie," she whispered, coming even closer, so that he could feel her breath on his cheek. "I want to know everything about you."

"And I am most assuredly flattered, Jennifer McGee," he answered, trying not to look in her eyes. "But the truth of the matter is, you wouldn't believe me if I told you. It's best for us both that we not go down that path."

"You know when you drink your accent is more pronounced?"

"Aye, so I've been told," he answered with a grin.

"And Charlie?"

"Hmm?" Lord, but would she stop looking at him with those soulful eyes.

"I'd go down that path with you," she breathed.

He stared at her full lips and although a part of him wanted to kiss her, he suddenly found that he couldn't. And that annoyed him to no end! Straightening his upper body, he clutched the steering wheel. "No, you don't," he muttered, staring out to the night and the parked automobiles.

Jen also straightened. "You're not even going to kiss me?" she asked in a shocked voice.

"No, lass, I'm not. 'Tisn't my place."

"You *are* committed!" she accused.

"I am not. There'd be no committing to the impossible."

"Who is she?"

"She?"

"The one who's holding your heart, Charlie Garrity."

He sighed deeply and relaxed against the headrest. Closing his eyes, he murmured, "She's a lovely woman, Jennifer McGee. Aye, truly a woman to be treasured."

"So why aren't you with her now?"

"Because," he drew in a deep breath before continuing, "I stormed away from her earlier tonight."

"What did she do?"

"She didn't do anything. It was . . . well . . . I just couldn't be around her another moment. I couldn't breathe. I was fighting myself to keep away from her," he said with an exhale. "So, I just had to get out."

"So," she repeated, "this woman doesn't know how you feel?"

He opened his eyes and looked at her. "I could never tell her. She deserves more than me. I have nothing to offer."

Jen sighed, as though with annoyance. "Men. How the hell can you expect her to know if you don't tell her? Tell her, Charlie. If you love her, she deserves to know!"

"You don't understand the whole of it. This is a woman of . . . of substance. In a few weeks, I'll be nothing but a drifter. I've lost everything. It just isn't meant to be—her and me."

"I'll tell you what isn't meant to be. If you don't tell her, you're making her choice for her and then you're right. It will never be. But you aren't even giving her a chance. Shit, I can't believe I'm talking myself right out of this, but you're one of the good guys, Charlie. Any woman would be crazy to let you go."

He listened to her words and found himself grinning. "I think you're one of the good ones, too. 'Tis a shame you aren't living your dream."

"Looks like neither one of us is. Instead, we're sitting in someone else's car, talking about not having the courage to get on with our lives. Could you stand it, Charlie, if you never tried with her? Are you willing to walk away and never know what might have been?"

"That I don't know, lass," he whispered. "There's more to it. She's not yet divorced, and has been sorely used by those she trusted. I can't and don't want to take advantage of her situation."

"You don't want to be the rebound guy."

"Rebound guy?"

"Yeah, when someone is hurt and vulnerable and is looking to fill the void in their life they get involved with someone, instead of healing first. Believe me, I did it enough times until I realized that all I was doing was attracting losers, guys who were as damaged as I was. Now I don't get into relationships. I'm willing to wait for the right one."

"You deserve the right one, Jen," he said with a smile of friendship. "Thanks for understanding about tonight. It certainly seems to me you're a very wise young woman."

"Hey, it's taken me years to get this way," she said with a laugh. "Okay, so I was coming on to you, but I wasn't looking for a relationship, or anything serious. I've learned my lesson and I've yet to finish getting my own act together. But don't think I wouldn't have shown you a hell of a good time, Charlie."

He laughed. "You're a true gem, Jennifer McGee."

"Oh, and there's the blarney if I've ever heard it. Listen to me. Go to her, Charlie. Tell her. Don't leave without giving it a chance. You know you'd always regret it."

He looked out the window again, thinking about Suzanne. "You may be right."

"Of course I'm right!" she answered with a chuckle. "I know women. And I'm starting to understand men."

He turned his attention back to her. "May I ask you a question, Jen? It may sound ridiculous to you."

"Go for it. Might as well impart some of my vast expertise," she said with another laugh.

"Well, what I'm wanting to know is this. Do you think men, males, have a part of them that's female?"

"Ahh, you talking bisexual here?" Her voice was cautious.

"Bi-what?"

"Bisexual. Uhmmm, are you attracted to guys too?"

His body stiffened. "No. Certainly not. *No*, that's not what I'm saying."

She patted his arm. "Calm down, Charlie. It was just a question."

"Well, the answer is no. Just forget it," he said, embarrassed for even bringing it up. "I was talking about something else."

"Okay." There was a prolonged moment of silence, until Jen perked back up. "Oh, you're asking about a man being in touch with his feminine side?"

Relieved that she had heard of it, he breathed, "Yes. That. You think it's true?"

"Is that why you took her car and wound up at a bar? You had a fight about it?"

"How did you know that?"

Smiling, she answered, "I told you I'm almost an expert now."

"Well, yes. Partly about that. I mean, I read a book about it, but I don't feel this female side in me and I can't make myself do it."

"Who said you have to feel female? Who said you have to feel anything but who you are? All that means is that you aren't afraid to express how you *do* feel, that you aren't cut off from your emotions, even ones that are traditionally thought of as feminine. I know men are wired different than females, and I'm not expecting them to cry at the drop of a hat, but I won't ever again get involved with a man who avoids his feelings, or is intimidated by mine. I've had enough macho men. I used to think they made me feel more secure, but I was just avoiding my own strength."

"She said that word. *Macho.*"

Jen laughed. "Yeah, well it takes some time to figure out the difference between macho and manly. At least it did for me." She turned in her seat to see him better. "See, Charlie, I want a partner, an equal partner. Not one in a position of strength and the other submission. There's no superior sex in an equal partnership. You work together for the partnership. That's what's important. Not individual egos. Maybe that's what she was trying to tell you."

"Where did you learn all this?" She certainly was a smart young woman.

"Hey, I've watched Oprah. Seriously, I've read a lot and experienced enough drama in my life to now know what I want."

"Well, you deserve it. And I hope you find it."

"Thanks, Charlie. You deserve it too." She leaned over and kissed his cheek. "Now, go back and talk to her. She should know how you feel."

"Thank you, Jen. I'm glad you sat down next to me tonight."

"Hey, it was meant to be, bucko. Nice meeting you, too," she said as she opened the car door. Closing it, she blew him a kiss and said, "Thanks for the ride home. Be happy, Charlie Garrity."

"You, as well, Jennifer McGee," he called out. "You as well." Now he felt sober enough to drive to the farm. Maybe Jen was right. Maybe their meeting and their discussion was meant to be. Aye, what did he know? Only that he couldn't wait to get back and see Suzanne. If he'd learned only one thing tonight it was that he didn't want just any woman.

Heaven help him. He wanted Suzanne.

* * *

"Where have you *been?*"

"Now, now, Suzie, no need to be gettin' your dander up," he said as he walked in the front door and dropped the keys onto the hall table. "A man sometimes needs some space to figure out life's problems and—"

"Don't you *'Suzie'* me!" she interrupted, the edges of her robe flapping as she marched up to him in a fine lather. "Do you have any idea what I've been through tonight?"

Now why was she shrieking like a harridan when he wanted to talk sweet to her? "I just stepped out for a pint, though it really wasn't a pint. A tall glass of Guinness, it was. No harm done at all. Just some Guinness and good conversation. All's fine."

She looked horrified. "You've been *drinking!*" she accused.

He tried to smile, but she really did look like a harridan after all, with her curls sticking up in all directions. "I just said I was. Guinness." What was wrong with her now?

"This is unbelievable," she continued to rant, as she waved her arms around her like she was about ready to take flight. "Here I am, at my wit's end, ready to call nine-one-one to find out what's wrong, and you . . . you're in some bar drinking!"

"Now calm down, lass, and tell me what's happened," he said in a soothing voice. He was about to give her a sweet smile, but was not prepared for her to curl her fingers into fists and place them firmly on her hips.

"It was Matty."

"The lad?" He looked toward the stairs. If anything had happened to him, he'd never forgive—

"Yes. The *lad*," she mimicked. "He was screaming in pain and . . . and I had no idea how to help him. I didn't have the car or I would have taken him to the emergency room at the hospital. So I called instead."

"Suzanne, *is* the child all right?" He couldn't stand the suspense while she told him every detail.

"Well, he is now, thank heavens. When the nurse asked if I was nursing him, she then asked what I had eaten for dinner. I didn't know pizza would cause such gas for him. I'm telling you he was in excruciating pain. I couldn't calm him and I can't nurse him until tomorrow. He finally passed the gas and then fell asleep from exhaustion. I just put him down."

"Suzanne, it was gas. He's all right. There's no need for this excitement now." She was such a conscientious mother. He smiled at her and added, "The crisis has passed."

"Oh, *then*, on top of everything, I'm worried about *you!*" Shaking her head, as if she didn't even hear his last words, she gathered the edges of her robe and tied the belt tightly. "How dare you storm out of here with no explanation and then come home drunk and—"

"I am not drunk," he interrupted, straining not to lose his good mood.

"You are so. You're slurring your words and pouring on the Irish accent, like that's supposed to charm me or something."

"Suzanne, don't speak to me as if I am a child." She really was pushing it.

"Don't act like one, and I won't. You don't even have a license to drive a damn car, let alone drive it after you've been drinking! It's against the law! You could have been arrested for that and I wouldn't be able to get you out of jail. How would I even explain who you are?"

He smiled at her and closed the few feet separating them. "All your worrying and I'm fine. Now, calm yourself down, and I'll make us both a cup of tea and we can talk this out like adults and—"

"Adults? Do you think your behavior tonight was responsible?"

"I have been very responsible, more than you can ever

know," he said, walking toward the kitchen. "And I am not slurring my words," he added, making sure he enunciated each one perfectly.

"Well, you're not now, but you were when you first came in," she said from behind as she followed him into the kitchen. "Honestly, Charlie, you can't drink and then get behind the wheel of a car. It's not just irresponsible, it's breaking the law."

"I've heard you, Suzanne." He put the kettle on to boil and then turned to the cabinet. "Do you want some tea then?"

She shook her head.

He merely sighed as be brought out a tea bag. So much for talking to her tonight. The way she was staring at him, with her arms folded across her stomach, told him to back off as far as possible. And then young Jennifer's words ran through his head. *Tell her.*

"And another thing," she began, as she leaned against the refrigerator. "I know that you've been cooped up with me and Matty for six weeks now. I understand you need a break. Sometimes I feel like I need one too. I'm not keeping you prisoner. I'm not stifling you. At least that's not my intention. If you can't breathe, then . . ."

"Enough of this talking." It was time for some action. He cut off her words as he came to stand directly in front of her and stared into her wide blue eyes. He'd had enough words tonight. "Then?"

She was startled by his close proximity, and yet he didn't back off. "Then . . ." she barely mumbled, still staring into his eyes, as though she couldn't look away.

"Aye, Suzie . . . haven't we had enough words for tonight?" He could feel her breath on his chin as she stared at his mouth. He could sense her breasts, mere inches from his chest, moving up and down with each shortened breath.

"I was . . . was just going to say that if you can't breathe around me, maybe it's . . . it's because . . ."

"Save your breath," he murmured, right before he lowered

his mouth to hers and pressed her body back against the refrigerator with his. He grabbed her hands and curled his own around them. He felt her body stiffen with surprise and then slowly, sweetly, she melted into him as she clasped her fingers deeply into his own.

It was everything he had imagined and more. Her lips . . . so tender and yet now responding, matching his passion with her own. Magnets fell to the floor, along with the rental agreement, and neither of them cared as the astonishing kiss deepened with intensity.

Dear God in heaven, she tasted so sweet and, when he heard a moan low in her throat, he pressed his mouth even more firmly against hers, exploring her, grinding his body into hers, feeling her luscious breasts crushing against his chest, her heartbeat pounding with his own need to melt with her, until there was no longer any separation between them.

She slowly broke the kiss and gasped for breath, as he began to kiss her temple softly, running his mouth ever so gently over her throbbing pulse. "Ah, Suzie . . . sweet, sweet woman," he murmured against her warm skin. "I've waited so long."

"I . . ." Her breath at his neck was ragged.

He broke the embrace and leaned back to see her face. She was flushed. Her eyes were almost glazed. Her lips appeared full and sensuous. She looked like a woman well kissed.

"You what?" he whispered with a soft smile.

"I . . . I don't know what to say." She extricated her hands from his and pushed her hair away from her forehead. It too was glistening with a sudden sheen.

Hearing her words, he backed up a bit to give her more room. "Have I offended you?"

She shook her head. "No . . . not at all. I . . . ah. You startled me, that's all. Save my breath, huh? Well, I would if you hadn't just plundered it." She giggled with nervousness.

Now he really backed up. What was that supposed to

mean? She was making fun of him? "It appears I have offended you, Suzanne. My apologies. Blame it on the drink."

"Wait a minute," she called out as the kettle whistled and
he walked toward the stove. "I wasn't offended, Charlie, but
you have been drinking. It's just that this . . . this isn't like
you."

"You may very well be right," he stated, feeling a cold
dread wrapping around his heart. How could he have misjudged her and the situation? He had no right to plunder her,
as she put it. "Please accept my apologies," he said as he
poured the water into the cup. "I had no right to accost you."

"Charlie, you didn't accost me. In fact, I enjoyed it very
much." She ran her fingers nervously through her hair. "It's
just that it came out of nowhere. I wasn't prepared."

"I understand, Suzanne. Please, let's just forget it happened."

"But I don't want to—"

"Let's forget it," he interrupted, looking her directly in the
eye. "It was a mistake and I apologize. Why don't you get
some sleep? You look exhausted."

She seemed to pull herself together, straightening her
body and her robe. "You think it was a mistake?"

It took him a few seconds before he could force the word
past his lips.

"Yes. I do."

She simply nodded and slowly walked away from him. He
stared down at his cup of tea and wished he could just disappear. Soon. As soon as he had her and Matty moved into the
new home, he would leave. Tonight had taught him it was the
right decision.

She fell into bed, not even checking on Matty. God in heaven,
please let him sleep, she prayed. Curling her body around a
pillow, she could still feel Charlie's lips upon her own. She'd
been rattled. More than rattled. She was unprepared for it, the
way he took her mouth, the intensity of that kiss. And then

when it ended, she'd ruined it by trying to make a joke. But how was she supposed to have reacted when her body was still vibrating? God, it was like nothing she'd ever experienced before! She didn't know if it had been because of the kiss, or if she'd been feeling the motor vibration of the refrigerator!

Damn it, she had been rattled!

Just thinking about that brief encounter in front of the refrigerator was enough to make a moan slip from her lips again. She was as bad as *Ryan's Daughter* . . . she'd never known it could be that passionate, making her mindless. And now, Charlie wasn't even comfortable in her presence. How was she going to fix this one? Okay, so she was beginning to exercise more assertiveness and command in her life, but she couldn't exactly walk up to him, throw him down on the sofa and tell him she'd finish what he'd started. And, oh . . . how her body was pleading with her to do just that.

It was shameful. She was shameful. But that kiss had unlocked something within her she hadn't even known existed. She wanted mindless passion, and she wanted it with Charles Garrity.

Somehow, she had to fix this.

14

He was leaving. She knew it. She could tell by the way he was avoiding her. Every attempt she had made to gloss over that kiss had been politely rejected. It was as though he'd made up his mind and no matter what she did, it wasn't enough. Suzanne blamed herself and her stupid reaction, making a joke, instead of being real. She had wondered who she was now, besides being a mother. Obviously, a comedienne wasn't high on the list.

Finally, after three days of awkwardness, she couldn't take it anymore and she asked Charlie if she could speak to him after they'd had dinner and she put Matty to bed for the night. Now it was here, the moment she had been waiting for, and she prayed she would have the right words this time.

He had lit a fire earlier as the evening had turned cool, and Suzanne was glad, since the fire definitely made it more intimate. Dressed in jeans and a pale blue cotton sweater, she sat on the sofa, pulling her legs up under her and staring into the low flames as she waited for him to join her. He came into the room, bringing with him a cup of tea. Placing it on the other side of the coffee table, he bent over and picked up another piece of wood, then added it to the fire. Suzanne watched as the dark cooling embers flashed with brilliance and several trails of ash scattered up the sooted chimney like shooting stars.

"You're leaving, aren't you?" she whispered to his back.

He became very still for a few prolonged moments, and then stoked the fire. "Yes, Suzanne. I am. After you move into the new place. It's time I took off on my own."

"Why?" she pleaded. "We were doing so well together until that other night in the kitchen. I messed everything up, Charlie. I'm sorry."

He turned around and she was again reminded of how much she was attracted to him. Dressed in jeans and a long-sleeved white shirt, he smiled at her with such affection that she had to bite the inside of her cheek not to moan with a mixture of sadness and regret.

"You didn't mess up anything. I had been thinking about this for some time now. I can't depend on your kindness any longer. I have to strike out on my own and try to make my way in this strange new world I find myself in."

"Why, Charlie? Why can't you stay with us?" she asked, placing her feet on the floor and leaning forward to him. "I'll pay you a decent salary, more than you could—"

"For what?" he interrupted softly. "Doing housework? Minding a baby?" He joined her on the edge of sofa and smiled. Looking down to his cup of tea, he added, "I never knew how hard it all was. Trying to find the time to wash clothes, or a dozen other things, and take care of a little one at the same time. And I don't even have to feed him. I have a new respect for women, but I don't want to do it anymore, Suzanne. It's not *me*. I need to be out there, in the world, finding my place. It isn't here." He raised the cup to his lips and sipped.

"Okay," she said, yet not willing to give up. "I can understand that. But why do you have to go away? Can't you find your place and still live close to us?"

He looked at her then, and she could see the pain in his eyes. "Suzanne, there's nothing here for me. The land is gone. Everything I knew no longer exists. My life . . ." he paused, as though stifling a thought, then finished, "It's all gone."

"I'm here," she blurted out. "And Matty. We . . . we care about you."

His face softened. "And I'm very grateful for that. I, too, care about you both. Probably more than I should. And, well . . . that's another reason why I have to go."

She would not cry, even though it felt like her heart was breaking. In that moment, she realized, as crazy as it was, she had been falling in love with an incredible man, a man who had time-traveled into her life and had captured her heart. Taking a deep breath, she whispered, "I've lost everyone, Charlie, please don't let me lose you too. I promise I won't ask you to do any more housework. I'll take care of Matty. You can go and find some *manly* job if that's what you want. Just don't go, *please*."

He looked into her eyes and held out his arm. "Come here, woman," he whispered, in a rough voice.

She couldn't hold back the tears any longer as she closed the space between them. Enveloped in his warm embrace, she clung to him and cried, "Don't go, Charlie. I'm sorry for making a joke after you kissed me. I . . . I was so rattled and—"

"Shh," he whispered above her head as he stroked her back and shoulders. "Don't ever think you've done anything wrong. It isn't about that. It's about me, Suzie."

"What? What is it?" she begged, looking up at him.

He reached down and gently placed a piece of hair behind her ear. "I have nothing to offer you, Suzanne. Nothing. A man doesn't come to a woman like that."

"*That* is what this is all about? Charlie, it doesn't matter. I'll have more than enough for both of us for two lifetimes! You can't be serious." Relief swept through her and she changed position, pulling her legs up onto the sofa and laying across his chest so she could face him. God, it all felt so natural, so right.

"I'm very serious," he said, adjusting to her changed position. He now held her in his arms and looked into her eyes with a grave expression. "I don't want your money. I don't want to live like that. Can't you understand I have to do this my way? I have to get out there and see what I can make of myself."

"This is about pride?"

"This is about what's right."

What she felt was right at that moment was for her to remedy the blunder she'd made in the kitchen the other night. "Kiss me, Charlie." It was bold, but she was desperate not to lose him, for she could feel how serious he was about this. And it was the only way she could think how to fix it.

He smiled into her eyes with tenderness. "That's not going to change anything. Things are the way they are, and we must play our cards as they've been dealt."

"Kiss me," she whispered, leaning even closer to him. "I'm asking."

She heard his quick intake of breath, as he lifted his face to meet hers. When his lips barely grazed hers, he breathed, "This won't solve anything," into her mouth and hesitated less than an inch from her face, not pulling away.

"Don't talk," she whispered back. "We've already said enough." She smiled teasingly at him, hoping he'd know she was giving him back his own words.

The sly smirk on his face let her know he knew what had just happened and he pulled slightly away. "Sweet Jesus, Suzanne, you're not making this easy."

"Good. I don't want it to be easy," she murmured, just as

she closed the space between them and pressed her lips firmly to his. She felt him equal her insistence and their kiss deepened.

He pulled her into his body and she wrapped her arms around his shoulders, clinging to him, willing him to know how much she wanted him with her. After so long, she finally had the freedom to touch him, to feel the strength of his muscles, the silkiness of his hair as she ran her fingers through it . . . nearly desperate for the contact; to caress as much of him as she could. She opened her mouth to accept his exploration, while feeling his hand skimming over her breast then sliding down her sides to her waist. She felt the reverberation of his moan deep in her throat when he clutched her hips and pulled her completely against him.

He wanted her. She knew it. She felt it in every inch of her body.

It only lasted seconds more.

Breaking away from her, he quickly moved his hands to hold her shoulders, and she opened her eyes to see a pleading expression upon his face. "This isn't going to change anything, Suz," he muttered in a hoarse voice. "I must still leave."

She was breathing heavily, staring into his deep green eyes, knowing that he was feeling the same as she. He had to be! "But . . ."

"It will only make it more difficult." He kissed her temple and added, "for both of us."

"How can you leave, Charlie?" she demanded, still reeling from their kiss. Her body was throbbing and she could feel his arousal against her. Now was not the time to be coy. Now was the time for honesty. "I want you. I want you to stay. I—"

"And I want you, love," he whispered tenderly. "But not like this. I need to go make my own way. When I come to you, I will come as your equal. I've lost everything and have nothing to offer you now. I would only weigh you down when you need to get on with your life. We've both been through so much—"

"You *are* my equal!" she protested. "Look, I've lost almost everything too! We're in the same boat."

He was shaking his head.

"If it's the money, then just forget about it. It doesn't make a difference to me. I'm not like that."

He gathered her once more into his arms and held her close to his chest. Cradling her head in the palm of his hand, he whispered into her ear. "It makes a difference to me, Suzanne."

She stared at the fabric of his shirt, realizing no matter what she did, or what she said, he really was going to leave her. A deep ache in her chest began, as though she were losing a part of her heart. "I can't make you stay," she murmured, trying to keep the tears from forming at her eyes.

"No, my love, you can't."

Be brave, she told herself. *Do not plead or make this any harder.* He was determined. He had to prove something to himself and she had to respect him and his wishes, as crazy as they seemed to her. "Money will not buy happiness, Charlie. I should know."

"This isn't just about money," he whispered, stroking her hair, trying to calm her. "It's about something much more important."

"Self-esteem?"

He nodded. "Worth. It has to do with more than money. I have to feel honorable about my life. I don't feel that now. It's like I'm without direction. I knew it once, before I was taken away from everything, but I don't know that anymore. I have to see if I can find it again. And staying here with you . . . bless your pure heart, you'd make it so easy I could put it off forever. But I'd never feel good about it. It would wear away whatever is good between us, until one day what we had was ruined." He held her closer. "I could never do that to you, Suzanne. You've been through so much already.

And I don't want to do it to myself. I couldn't have you and then lose you. Trust me, this is for the best."

"Is this forever? I'll never see you after you leave?" She didn't care that her voice sounded like a child's. She had to know.

"I don't know the future. I just know it's the right thing to do now."

Cradled against his chest, she listened to his heartbeat and ran her hand up and down his arm in a slow motion. She would not cry, she told herself, as the burning in her eyes increased. She would wait until he was gone, and then she might just have that nervous breakdown she'd been putting off for almost two months. "Just so you know you don't have to prove anything to me, I already think you're the most honorable man I've ever known."

"Coming from you, that is a high compliment."

They sat in silence for a few precious minutes, neither of them wanting to break the embrace.

"Charlie, what was your childhood like?" she whispered, wanting to prolong the intimacy and needing to change the subject.

She listened to his soft breathing as he hesitated for a moment. "You want to know about me starting that far back?" She heard the playful tone in his voice.

"I want to know everything about you, Charlie," she replied seriously, then added, "I think you're a remarkable man, and I'm sure your parents must have been wonderful to have instilled in you such integrity. Why don't you start by telling me about them?"

He sighed deeply, while continuing to stroke her hair. "My mother," he exhaled, with a thoughtful pause. "Well, let's just say, if she'd been Catholic, she probably would have been a nun. She was a fine woman."

"Irish, and you weren't Catholic?" She was surprised.

"No, I was born an only child into a Protestant family, and had a privileged upbringing. My father was a gentleman, although, quite frankly, he did a bit of gambling . . . none of us understood just how seriously he was involved in it until after he died."

"How old were you?"

"I was attending Trinity College in Dublin when I received word, so I suppose I was around twenty."

"That's still a young age to lose a parent. I'm sorry, Charlie."

"Thank you," he said, wrapping his arms more snugly around her.

After a moment of silence, she encouraged him. "Please continue."

"Indeed, his death was sudden—taking us all by surprise, but I learned more about him after he was gone than I'd ever known while he was living. You see, when I came home for his funeral, just the day after he was laid to rest, my mother and I were confronted by my father's . . . let's say, for lack of a better term, *dubious creditors*, if you know what I mean."

"Yes, I understand. Go on."

"Well, they took everything, as my father's debts exceeded our estate assets. There had already been a lien placed on the property, which my father had kept secret for quite some time. In the end, even the house furnishings had to be sold to satisfy the creditors. It all happened so suddenly. My mother was forced to go live with her sister in Westport and, after I saw her settled, I couldn't afford to continue my schooling, so I headed for the coast and took the first ship to America I could get."

She was fascinated, as this was the first time he'd opened up about his life, and she wanted to know everything about him, to put together all the pieces, for one day she would tell Matty about this incredible man who came into their lives just when they needed him most. "Wow," she breathed. "I'm so sorry," she repeated.

"Actually, I'm not," he answered, squeezing her and planting a kiss on the top on her head. "I've had quite an adventure, you know. I think had I gone on in the lifestyle to which I'd become accustomed, I would have eventually become an unsufferable bore."

"Oh no. Not you," she protested. "I can't imagine you being like that."

He laughed. "Oh, you should have seen me then, Suzie. I was quite the dandy. I'm not sure you would have even liked me. I started out with the attitude that only the best would do. Yet before I even stepped foot on this continent, I learned what it was like to be without."

"Was it a rough journey?"

"Well, not so much the journey itself. You see, I was suddenly cast into a class distinction I hadn't really been exposed to before. As far as anyone on board was concerned, I was nothing more than a poor emigrant, looking for a new start in America."

"Were there a lot of people coming here then?" Her own question made her realize she was getting a first-hand history lesson from a person who lived through actual events. It was a fascinating thought, even if a bit daunting; for to know this incredible man and his story was far beyond anything she'd ever been taught or had experienced. And she wanted to know all of him.

"The ship was full, or nearly, to the best of my knowledge, yet how many were emigrating, I'm not sure. I'd say most of the passengers aboard in first class were probably made up of tourists and those who had business affairs to conduct in America. I could only afford a single bunk in a steerage cabin, which I shared with five other men."

"Ah," she interjected knowingly. "That's where you met Mitch."

"Yes. He was younger, more green than myself, and I sort of took him under my wing. Not that I was much better, mind you, but if I put on my best manners, I could talk to the stewards, and finagle an extra ration of dried beef on the occasion. You can't imagine what steerage was like. Dreadful.

But we decided we would make our fortune in this grand new land and filled ourselves with fairy tales of wealth. Such were the stories bandied about of America's opportunities. And we believed them, every one of us. When we landed in New York, we thought for certain we could attain good positions and better ourselves. There were signs everywhere: 'No Negroes or Irish need apply.' I found out what it meant to be Irish in America. And an Irishman without money was even worse."

Listening, Suzanne could almost see it in her head. Steerage. Hope. Disillusionment. Slums. Prejudice. She had never really paid attention to what her ancestors, everyone's ancestors, went through to come to this country and make a new life. What courage it must have taken just to leave everyone and everything familiar, to cross an ocean and venture into the unknown. She was uncertain about leaving the state!

"We heard there was work in the coal mines for the Irish, but neither Mitch nor I could see ourselves digging in the ground to stay alive. It took some time, but I eventually got us associated with a group of fellows who were moving on west, for the slums of New York were horrendous. Some of the boys were worse off than the Irish at home. But I remembered everything I had learned while I was in New York. I could see where there was money to be made. A day out of New York and I saw land, so fertile and rich with potential. I actually could see, in my mind's eye, the acres of apple and peach trees. I wanted it. I wanted to make it happen. It's what drove me as Mitch and I made our way west, working at ranches, being drovers for cattle drives. But there was no real money in it unless you owned the herd, so we came back east. Then Prohibition hit. I saved every bit that I could running bootleg whiskey and I invested in the stock market—in the Edison Light Company, Bell Telephone, railroads, and the oil fields of Pennsylvania and Texas. Regular Western Union dispatches kept me informed of my earnings."

"Your scoundrel days," she said with a smile.

"Yes, lass, my scoundrel days," he said, patting her back in agreement. "I'm not too proud of that time, but I did what I did, and I'll not apologize for it now."

She shrugged. "I don't think you have to, since the law was repealed. You weren't a gangster, like Al Capone, were you?"

He laughed. "A gangster? I drove a truck."

"And Mitch was with you?"

"We were living in Jersey City. Whereas I was saving everything I could, Mitch was living the high life—spending it as fast as he made it, and there was plenty of money to be made. I was driving a truck of whiskey across the Canadian border when word came to me that Mitch had been arrested. It was only when I arrived back in New York that I found out what had happened. He was always the fool when it came to drink, and had been bragging about the small fortune he was making. It wasn't long before he was being followed and when he was making a delivery, he was arrested. After a quick trial, he was sentenced to two years, and there wasn't anything I could do about it. But I felt guilty, for I had gotten him into it, filling his head with my own dreams."

"Charlie, it's not your fault he was caught."

"I know that now, but by the time he was released I had already purchased the land here in Mount Laural, and I wrote to him, asking him to be my partner, just like we'd always planned."

"Then what happened? Why did he shoot you?"

"I don't know. Greed, perhaps. Spending those two years in jail had hardened him. I could see it when he finally showed up. He was a changed man and he'd lost everything. I bought him a new suit. Grace even cut his hair. We did what we could . . ."

"Grace? That was the woman you were going to marry?"

He didn't speak for a few moments, and Suzanne patiently waited.

Finally he said, "Yes. I had asked her to be my wife."

"Can you tell me about her? It's all right if you don't want to. I'll understand."

Sighing deeply, he said, "She was a good woman. She had a heart of gold and would take in a stray cat or an injured bird. I guess that's why she tried so hard with Mitch. She could see he was injured inside. She had the gentlest hands. That day, the morning all this happened, she had given me and Mitch a haircut, and again I was reminded of how gentle and sweet she was."

"You must have loved her very much." It was okay to say it, to admit to herself that Charlie had loved another.

His hand stopped stroking her hair. "It was time for me to dig in roots and settle down, to become the man I knew I was capable of becoming. I wanted a family. I wanted stability . . . and Grace loved me. It's hard for me to admit this, but I don't think I loved her. I know I didn't love her the way she loved me, but I was sure that given time I would grow into it as we made our home and family together. She was a good woman. And I'm sorry I must have hurt her by disappearing from her life."

He didn't think he had loved Grace. That admission stirred threads of excitement and gratitude. She allowed him his moment of reflection, stroking his arm and shoulder with compassion. She knew what it was like to lose and how hard it can be to let go. They sat in silence, listening to the crackle of the burning wood as memories came alive and then faded.

"So when did Mitch shoot you?" she asked gently.

"The third day after he came. I took him to the land I had recently bought, telling him all my plans for this grand or-chard. Informing him of the contacts I had already made for distribution. I sketched out everything. Within five years I knew I could make a profit." He paused, as though willing himself to relive a painful experience. "We were walking across the railroad trestle when he suddenly pulled out a gun and demanded the deed to the land. I couldn't believe he was serious, but when he shoved that gun into my chest I knew he wanted everything. He wanted my life. So I jumped, figuring I'd rather take my chances in the water. I heard a shot. I felt a burning at my temple. I guess the bullet grazed me. I saw this light as I fell and the next thing I knew I was looking into your eyes."

He sounded so sad, she raised her face and smiled. "And then you came into my life. I'm so sorry you lost everything and Mitch betrayed you, but I'm so grateful, Charlie, for you being here now."

"Yes," he whispered with a smile. "Here and now. Wherever I find myself. That's where my life is . . . in this twenty-first century, with all these marvelous inventions and—"

"With me?" she asked hopefully, unable to stop the big grin from appearing on her face.

He shook his head and laughed. "You never give up, do you?"

"Not when it's something this important," she answered.

"I'm still going to leave, Suzanne. I've made up my mind."

"I understand that. I think you should go out there into the world and see if you can find what you're seeking. I know now I can't keep you here and you'd be unhappy if you remained. Just promise me you'll stay in touch. Call me. Write to me." She took a deep breath and added what was in her heart. "Come back to me, if you can."

"I won't ask you to wait."

"So you're not asking."

"I want you to get on with your life."

"Do you think I have any other choice, with Matty in it now? I have to keep going."

"I'll miss the lad," he whispered, looking at the dying flames of the fire.

"We're going to take pictures tomorrow," she pronounced. "I want Matty to remember you. And I guess I'm selfish too. I want them for myself."

"Whatever you want, love. Now let me throw another log onto the fire."

She moved, allowing him to get up and tend the flames. Watching him, she smiled, in spite of the seriousness of the situation. He called her his love again. She didn't want to make a big deal of it. It could be just an endearment, but it sounded heavenly to her ears.

So he was leaving. The thought settled into her mind as she rose from the sofa and walked up behind him. No longer did she feel she had to hold back, for she didn't know when or if she would ever see him again. Slipping her arms around his waist as he looked into the fire, she leaned her head against his back and whispered, "It's okay to say I'm going to miss you, isn't it?"

He turned around and took her into his arms. Looking deep into her eyes, he smiled sadly. "I'm going to miss you, too. More than I can ever express. You've been my savior, my teacher, my mentor . . . my friend. Perhaps the best friend I've ever had."

"I don't want to be your teacher or your friend right now," she said, lowering her body and pulling on his hand for him to follow her. "I want you to hold me tonight. I want to be as close to you as you'll allow. Give me tonight, Charlie. Give me this memory."

He came to her and gathered her into his arms as they laid in front of the fire. She could feel the heat from the flames on her back and the length of his body as he pulled her into him. Leaning up on his elbow, he stroked her hair and looked down to her. "I'll not make love to you, lass," he murmured. "For to do so would break my heart when I left."

"Then just stay here with me like this. It's enough . . . for now."

They spent the night in each other's arms, talking, sharing stories, sharing a lifetime of memories. She fell asleep and awoke when she felt a slight draft at her back. Turning her head she saw that the fire was out. Slowly she turned in the other direction and saw him sleeping—so soundly, so peacefully. The light from the kitchen illuminated his face, and she gazed at his features. He was the most handsome man that had ever been in her life. But it wasn't his great looks that had attracted her. It was his soul. He wasn't perfect. He was a good, decent man, who knew how to be a scoundrel when he had to be. She knew, somehow, that he would be all right when he left. After listening to his stories, she was confident that he would make it. She only hoped that he found whatever it was he was seeking and came back to her one day.

For she now knew she loved him.

He must be chilled, she thought, and realized how protective she was of him. Even if she had to let him go in less than two weeks, she was going to spoil him until then. Easing out of his embrace, she crawled away and forced herself into a standing position. Her muscles ached from sleeping on the rug, and she stretched them as she quietly walked toward the stairs. She would check on Matty and then bring the down comforter from her bed. Grinning as she walked upstairs, she thought she hadn't made out and cuddled with a man like that since college. Somehow it was even better than making love, for the closeness they had achieved was remarkable, surpassing any other relationship, male or female, in her life. They were friends who loved each other.

Although he hadn't said the words, and neither did she, it was love they had shared last night. She would cherish the memory and fold it in along with others they had made.

Matty was fine and, as she tiptoed from the nursery, she thought back again to Charlie's story. What an exceptional man, and she knew now why he understood her loss and the pain of betrayal. He had lost a friend and left a woman. Grace. It was a common enough name, yet as she was about ready to pull the comforter from the bed, she turned instead to her closet. In the bottom of it, in the corner, was Kevin's grandmother's chest. It was a tad small, so Suzanne never really used it. The sweet old woman had given it to her, filled with the most beautifully embroidered pillowcases. She had always meant to use them, but wanted to save them for a special occasion . . . and then she had forgotten about them.

Realizing she wanted to pack it to take with her, for it was Matty's great-grandmother's, Suzanne picked it up and brought it to the bed. She wrapped the big comforter around it and took it all downstairs with her into the kitchen.

She set the oak chest on the kitchen table so she would remember to have Charlie pack it and took the comforter into the living room. Spreading it over him, he shifted his position and murmured, "Where did you go?"

"I just wanted to check on Matty," she whispered back, crawling in next to him and snuggling into the warmth of his chest as she pulled the comforter around them both.

Held in his arms, listening to his breathing and the sure beat of his heart, Suzanne closed her eyes and knew, no matter what happened, right here, right now, she was happy. It was with that thought she fell back into a dreamless sleep— sure of the love within her heart.

"Suzanne!"

Startled, she jerked awake, her heart pounding, trying to figure out where she was. The fireplace was dark and cold. The light was coming in through the windows.

"Suzanne!"

"What?" she demanded, recognizing Charlie's voice. "Is it Matty?" she asked, throwing off the comforter and trying to get up. God, she must be out of shape for her muscles to be rebelling so much.

"Where did you get this?"

She attempted to focus on him and what he was holding. It was the chest she had put on the table last night. "I've had it for years. I wanted to have it packed. Is Matty all right?"

He was staring at the box as though he couldn't believe what he was holding.

"What's wrong?" she asked, trying to wake up completely

and coming closer to him when she saw his hands were shaking. "Charlie, *what is wrong?*"

He looked up to her and his eyes were wide with amazement. "I made this," he whispered in a shocked voice. "For Grace."

15

"What do you *mean*, you made it?" She wasn't sure if she was awake or dreaming. God, she needed a cup of coffee! And to hell with decaf! "How could you have made it? It was Kevin's grandmother's . . ." Her words trailed off as everything started to crash into place. It came so fast, so shockingly, all she could do was whisper the old woman's name. *"Grace!"*

They stared at each other in disbelief. It couldn't be! Charlie's Grace had married Kevin's grandfather? Shaking her head, she said, "What we're thinking is too unbelievable. Stuff like this just doesn't happen in people's lives!"

"What about me being brought to this time? That's unbelievable, but we both know it happened," he muttered, staring at the box as though he still couldn't believe it was before him. "There's one way I can prove it."

"How?"

"Here, let me show you." He walked into the kitchen and

reverently placed the chest down on the table. He lifted the front edge slightly and looked beneath it.

"What are you going to do?" she asked, brushing her hair back from her face as she watched him put his hand under the chest, as though he was feeling for something.

"Shh, wait," he murmured, concentrating on his actions.

She heard a click and then, to her utter amazement, she watched a drawer slide out from the back of the chest. "My God, how did you know that?"

"I told you," he breathed, "I made it, with a false bottom, but I never told her about it."

She peeked into the drawer. "What is all that?" she whispered, seeing an envelope and pieces of paper that were obviously yellowed with age. She watched as he picked up the envelope. Underneath it was an old black and white photograph with a white scalloped border.

"This is Grace," he said in a low voice, holding the picture out to her. "And Mitch."

Suzanne looked down to his hand and saw the couple standing before an apple tree in full glorious bloom. "That's Kevin's grandparents. That can't be Mitch, Charlie. It can't. His name is Michael. Grace and Mike McDermott. Kevin's grandparents," she repeated.

"That's Grace and *Mitch Davies*. I ought to know the bastard that tried to kill me." He sank onto a chair and just stared at the picture, as the implications of it all seemed to descend upon him. Suddenly, he threw the picture and the envelope on the table and picked up an old, yellowed piece of paper.

She watched as he stared at it, an expression of awe upon his face. "What is it?" she asked, just as she heard Matty's awakening cries of hunger.

"The deed," he muttered. "To my land."

"Wait! Wait . . . this is all getting too complicated," she said holding up her hand. "I have to get Matty. Don't move until I return!" She sprang up the steps, taking them two at a time. She picked up her son, quickly changed him, and had

him at her breast as she hurried back downstairs. It couldn't
have taken her more than ten minutes to attend her son and
yet, when she came into the kitchen, Charlie was gone. She
called out his name, but there was no answer and her gaze
took in the opened envelope and the pieces of paper laying on
the table.

Sliding into the seat that was still warm from his body
heat, she picked up the first piece of paper as Matty suckled
at her breast. It was in a woman's beautiful script, a little
shaky from old age, but Suzanne recognized it as Matty's
great-grandmother's.

*I don't know who will find this, if anyone, ever. It took
me almost twenty years to discover the hidden drawer
Charles had ingeniously created. Inside is the deed to
his property. I know now that he never would have
walked away and left it, or me, and I fear something
terrible has happened to him. I have feared this for so
many years since his sudden withdrawal from our lives
in 1926. I never really believed Mike when he told me
Charles disappeared that day they went to see the first
orchard. He said he had left him there and had come
back by himself. I fear I shall never know the truth.*

*Why am I writing all this now? Is it the shadow of
death that seems to hang over me in all my waking
hours? Perhaps. Having an inoperable brain tumor
makes me shun sleep. I want to stay awake and live
whatever time I am granted. I don't fear death, for I
have lived a full, long life. I have been given a son,
though Sean has shown more and more of his father's
grasping ways. Even my young grandson Kevin, who
has just taken a wife, seems to have inherited that trait,
and at times I question my role in all of this. Why do I
not see more of myself in them? Have I been left closed
off from it all, even in my bloodline? I don't regret the
marriage I have made, though I will admit here, on this*

paper that will remain hidden, my heart has always be-
longed to my first love.
    Charles Garrity.
    Mike, who came to me first as Mitch, Charles's
friend, knows of this love I have carried. He told me his
real name was Michael McDermott, and as he immi-
grated from Ireland, there are no records to dispute
him. Perhaps it was the grief, after losing my Charles,
but I allowed Mike to comfort me, to help mend my
heart. I so wanted to see Charles's dream come true
that I married Mike and worked at his side to bring it
into fruition. And we succeeded. I have tried to be a
good wife, a supporter of my husband, but I must have
failed. Was it that my heart was not large enough to
fully include another? These questions haunt me, as
does what really happened to Charles.
    When I found this drawer many years ago I was
shocked to see the original deed for the land and
Charles's bill of sale for it. How could Mike have come
back, a week after Charles disappeared, with a new
deed telling me he had bought the land with the money
he had saved before going to jail? How could I have
believed him? For all these years I have looked at my
husband, the man who shares my bed, and I wonder
what darkness he carries within his heart. I have kept
quiet, knowing by now that Charles, dear Charles, will
not come back to reclaim his land, nor me. And I have
made my life by my choices and must see them through.
    I am an old woman now. The doctors give me five
years to live, perhaps less. They say I will most likely
go to sleep and never awake. What a blessing that is,
but I cannot leave this world without clearing my con-
science. I may not have had the courage to confront my
husband, but I will leave this chest, made by the hands
of my love, to someone who, I am certain, will one day
discover the truth.

May someone right this wrong I fear has been done.
With a fervent prayer that God may forgive us all, I
remain a quiet witness.

Most sincerely,
Grace Stinson McDermott

"Oh my God," she murmured, dropping the last piece of paper onto the table. She was stunned, beyond stunned, as she took Matty from her breast and placed him at her shoulder. Where was Charlie? Dear God, how he must be feeling!

"Charlie!" she called out again.

Nothing.

Rising, she looked out the kitchen window, but didn't see him. She hurried to the back door and flung it open. And that's when she saw him standing at the corner of the property, looking out to the acres of houses that had been built on his land. She wanted to run to him, to take him in her arms, and her heart ached with what he must be going through.

Rushing into the first-floor bathroom, she grabbed a towel and wrapped it around Matty before hurrying from the house.

He was standing with his hands dropped at his sides, as though all the strength had been knocked out of him.

"Oh, Charlie," she whispered, coming up to him and placing her hand on his arm. "I am so sorry. I read the letter and . . ." She didn't know what more to say. It was so incredible, the whole story.

"Is that sonofabitch alive?" he muttered. "That's all I want to know."

She didn't say anything, having never heard that coldness in his voice before.

He turned and stared hard into her eyes. "Is he?"

She simply nodded, as a fear began low in her belly.

"Where is he?"

She couldn't seem to find her breath.

"Where is he?"

Startled, she clutched Matty tighter and muttered, "He's . . . he's in a nursing home. He's old, Charlie, barely kept alive by machines."

"That's good enough." He turned and headed back for the house.

Suzanne followed him. "Charlie, wait! Think about what you're about to do!"

Stopping, he held out his hand. In the palm of it was a small square of glass, edged in silver. She leaned down to look and saw it contained a lock of hair and was etched with the words *Charles Patrick Garrity 1926*.

"She must have had it made."

"She cut your hair," Suzanne whispered, remembering his story from the night before.

"That man has stolen my land, my woman, my dreams, my entire life. All this time, Suzanne, and I've been right on the land . . . but I couldn't recognize it."

"Of course you couldn't. Look at it. Kevin sold it off and they cut down the orchards and put up these houses."

"But it's my land! *Mine!* No one had a right to sell it. I'm going to take care of that bastard Mitch Davies." Clutching the glass keepsake in his fist, he turned to the house.

Scared, she followed him until they were inside. Shutting the door behind her, she held her son protectively closer to her chest, for she had no idea what was about to happen. She had never seen rage in anyone's eyes that could match what she saw in Charlie's. Looking around for Matty's infant seat, she spied it in the corner of the family room. Hurrying, she brought it into the kitchen and put it on the table next to the antique chest. She placed the baby in his seat and buckled him in, while saying to Charlie, who was gathering up the papers, "Let me make some coffee and we'll discuss this rationally. Too much has happened and there has to be a way to handle all this without resorting to violence."

"I want justice, Suzanne. And if Mitch is still alive, I intend to get it."

Nodding, she hurried to make coffee, busying her hands while her mind seemed to crash around her. "Will you just wait until we can discuss this? You can get justice. Why—" She turned around to him as the coffee maker began to drip. "Kevin sold off land that wasn't even his to sell!"

They both looked at each other and Suzanne's brain really started to kick in. "Bless Grace's heart for saving your hair. Charlie, do you know what this means?"

He just shook his head.

"Let me see that keepsake again."

Handing it over, he asked, "What are you talking about?"

"Wait a minute," she muttered, examining the silver edging. She took it to the kitchen window and exclaimed, "Here, c'mere . . . look."

He stood at her side as she held the keepsake in the rays of the morning sun. "Look at what?"

"This," she said, pointing to the silver edge. "There's a marking here, from the silversmith who made this. All we have to do is have this marking traced to that person and we can verify its age."

"So what does any of that mean?"

"Okay, let's sit down and I'll try and explain this crazy plan that's running through my head." She handed the glass keepsake back to him and poured them both a cup of coffee. "Could you give Matty his pacifier? I'm really shortchanging him this morning, but he'll forgive me."

A few moments later she put both cups of coffee on the table and kissed her son's forehead in gratitude for his accommodating nature. "Now this is what I'm thinking," she began, sliding onto a chair. "If we can verify that keepsake actually was made around nineteen twenty-six, since it had to have been put together with glue first and then sealed in the silver, we've got proof . . . undisputable proof that you are who you say you are."

He was shaking his head. "How does that prove anything?"

She smiled. "It's the hair, Charlie."

"I don't understand. What does my hair have to do with proof? It could be anyone's hair."

Shaking her head, she said, "Be patient with me. Science has advanced so far that it can do a DNA test on that hair and the hair on your head and when they match . . . voilà! Proof. Together with your deed, the bill of sale, and Grace's letter. It was your land, and Kevin's grandfather stole it from you; then, Kevin sold it for thirty-three million dollars seventy years later."

"I don't understand. What is this DNA?"

"Oh, don't ask me to explain it completely, because I don't understand it all, but I can tell you what I know. Trust me. Remember when we had that talk about cells and chromosomes?"

"When you said I was part female," he muttered, picking up his coffee.

"Well, you are, whether you like it or not, but this is about a . . . a blueprint of you. Uniquely *you*. Contained in your hair, in every cell, every flake of skin, is the whole blueprint showing there never was or ever will be another exactly like you. You *are* unique, one of a kind. We all are. That's what DNA proves. Match the DNA of that hair in the keepsake with the DNA of the hair on your head now and we've got proof, viable proof, you are who you say you are."

"Suzanne, who is going to believe I'm . . ." He did the math in his head. "One hundred and eleven years old?"

She stared at him, so young, so vibrant. "You're right," she whispered with disappointment. "No one will believe that." In seconds her mind put together scenarios of the government using Charlie as a guinea pig. Then she thought about Grace's letter. "But we can't just let them get away with this."

"Tell me where Mitch is, and he won't get away with it."

"Does it mean that much to you, that you would commit murder? Be put away in jail for the rest of your life? You've got to calm down and think this through. Kevin had to have had a deed to sell that land. They had to have done a title search. Everything must have checked out."

"Mitch didn't have the money to buy that land, especially a week later. How could he have bought the land without me selling it? My deed was on record."

She slapped the table. "Then that's where we go! To search the county records."

"Suzanne, just tell me where Mitch is."

"I'll tell you *after* we search the records. He's a very old man, in his late nineties, and kept alive by machines. I'm sure he'll still be there tomorrow. I want to investigate this first, 'cause you know, Charlie, if we can find some proof of an illegal transaction, then you are a very wealthy man."

"Wealthy?"

"Sure. If the McDermott family never legally owned that land, they had no right to sell it. And I happen to know that Kevin sold it for thirty-three million dollars. Look out there," she said, pointing toward the kitchen window. "Look at all those expensive houses. Can you just imagine what a legal mess we will create if this is made public? Kevin would have to make good, not just to the developers, but to all those people in all those houses who think they have legally bought land. His name would be ruined, his precious fortune gone, because he'd have to pay *you* what has always been yours."

He just stared at her. "And you think we can do this?"

"I don't know," she answered honestly. "But we can try. Beginning with doing our own title search today. Listen, Charlie, I can understand why you want to wring what little life is left in Mike's—er, Mitch's—neck. But that isn't the way to get justice. Let's try my way first."

He sat for a few moments, staring into his cup of coffee. "All right," he finally consented. "We'll try your way first."

She let out her breath in relief. She actually had no idea if her plan would work, but it would take Charlie's mind off a murderous act and, for that, she was willing to do just about anything.

Two hours later they were sitting in front of a microfiche machine, tracing back county records. Charlie had Matty strapped to his chest and Suzanne was working the machine. "We're almost there. How's he doing?"

Charlie looked down to the infant snuggled against him. "He's busy sucking on the pacifier. He's still awake."

"Thank heavens for that pacifier," she muttered, turning the forward knob to bring up the records. "Okay, here's some from nineteen twenty-six. What month did you buy the land?"

"May."

"Gimme a few seconds here, and *oh my God . . .*"

"What?"

"It's here," she whispered staring at the black and white film. "Along with a copy of your bill of sale."

Charlie leaned down and when his face was even with hers, he said, "How do we get a copy of this?"

"We print it out," she said with a nervous giggle, stunned that they had succeeded. "Now let me see where Mitch's deed appears. There! A week later, just like Grace wrote. But wait a minute." She moved the film forward and then brought it back to Mitch/Michael's deed. "There's no bill of sale. How could they record a deed without it?"

"Of course there's none."

"But it had to come from somewhere. He had to produce something to prove he bought the land. There's your deed and bill of sale, and then there's Mitch's, recorded under the name Michael McDermott. There's something strange here."

"You know it and I know it, but what can we prove?"

"I don't know," she answered, printing out Mitch's deed. "I'm going to call up my lawyer and see what she thinks."

"You're going to tell her about all this?"

She looked up to him, holding his firm hand against her son's back, and smiled. "When you're dealing with this level of dishonesty, it's best to stick to the truth. We have the truth on our side, Charlie."

Shaking his head, he said, "I don't know what good it's going to do us now. Who's going to believe I'm Charles Patrick Garrity, even with the testing of my hair?"

"I think we should talk to a lawyer, present her with all our documentation, and see what she thinks. Something will come out of this, Charlie. Grace gave me that chest when she was a very old woman. She gave it to *me*. She wanted me to find those papers. I didn't, but then you came into my life. That's more than a coincidence. It was all meant to happen, and I'm not going to let Grace down without trying to right the wrongs. Are you?"

She got up and picked up the printouts of the deeds and the bill of sale. "Come on. Let's go home and get some lunch. I'll call Laura and ask her to come to the house. We can tell her our story and see what she thinks."

"And you're going to tell her everything?" he asked, following her from the small room.

"I think we should."

"Everything?"

Chuckling as they left the county building, Suzanne held open the door for Charlie and Matty. "Yep. Everything. Your cover is about to be blown, Mr. Garrity."

Suzanne and Charlie stared at each other as the doorbell rang. Slowly, Suzanne started walking toward the door. Right before she opened it, she looked at Charlie and held up her hand with her fingers crossed for good luck.

"Hi, Laura," she said, holding open the door. "Thanks for coming over."

"Well, you made it sound so important. Are you okay? Has Kevin tried to contact you and renegotiate the property settlement?"

Smiling at the smaller woman dressed in her perfectly tailored suit, Suzanne waved her inside. "No, nothing like that.

Come in and we'll discuss it. Would you care for a glass of wine?"

Laura was staring at Charlie standing by the fireplace in the family room. "Ah, no thanks."

Suzanne led Laura into the room. "Laura, may I present Charles Garrity. Charles, this is my attorney, Laura Silverman."

Always the professional, Laura put out her hand in greeting. "How do you do?"

Charles shook it and said, "Fine, thank you. It's a pleasure to meet you, Miss Silverman."

Laura smiled in return and then looked at Suzanne. "How can I help you?"

"Please, have a seat, Laura. This might take a while to explain. Are you sure I can't get you a glass of wine?"

Smiling again as she sat down on the sofa, Laura said, "Are you trying to ply me with wine to prepare me for something? Now I'm really curious."

Suzanne could only return the smile as she sat down at the opposite end of the sofa and Charlie took the chair by the fireplace. "Well, you might want it later."

"You've whetted my curiosity. Now tell me what's going on."

She took a deep breath for courage. "First of all, everything will be protected under lawyer-client privilege, right? Confidential."

"Completely."

"Okay. What I'm about to say is going to challenge everything you've been taught to believe is possible, but I promise you I'm telling you the truth. I could take a lie detector test, a dozen of them, and pass every single one. And so could Charlie."

"What *is* it?"

Suzanne looked at Charlie and smiled. She inhaled deeply.

"Allow me to start at the beginning, when Kevin told me

he was leaving me for Ingrid. I ran out of the house and drove to Rancocas Creek to try to calm down. It wasn't working. I don't know if anything could have that day. I was staring at the water and I took off my wedding ring and threw it into the water, and then I saw this body floating by me. I could tell it was a man and he was alive, so I waded in and pulled him out and that's when I went into labor. That man was Charles."

She watched as Laura looked at Charlie and then back at her.

"Okay, so why was he in the water?"

"He'd been shot."

"Shot?" Again, she looked at Charlie. "Who shot you?"

"Mitch Davies," he answered. "Who now goes by the name Michael McDermott."

After a few moments, Laura said, "Now I'm lost. Who is Michael McDermott?"

"Kevin's grandfather," Suzanne answered. "I know this is confusing, but bear with me. Charlie had just purchased a large tract of land and was offering Mitch Davies a partnership when Mitch pulled out a gun and demanded the deed to the property. Charlie refused and decided to take his chances jumping from the old railroad bridge and into the creek, rather than wrestling with Mitch and his gun."

"And then you pulled him out?" Laura finished, looking at Charlie. "Kevin's grandfather tried to kill you?" she asked in disbelief.

"Yes. Every word Suzanne is telling you is the absolute truth."

"But, Laura . . ."

Laura turned back to Suzanne. "The shooting happened in nineteen twenty-six."

The lawyer didn't say anything, just continued to stare at Suzanne.

"I'm telling the truth, Laura."

Shifting her position on the sofa, Laura turned fully to Suzanne. "I don't understand. How could Kevin's grandfather have tried to kill Charles, but you pulled him out of the water—in *nineteen twenty-six?*"

Nodding, Suzanne answered, "Charles jumped into the water in nineteen twenty-six. I pulled him out in two thousand one."

Laura waved her hands, as though it might clear the air and also her head. "Wait a minute. What are you talking about?"

"I'm telling you the truth," Suzanne stated. "I know it sounds crazy. I know nothing like this has ever happened before in my life, or in anyone else's that I know of, but I do know it happened, exactly as I told it. Now look, you don't have to take our word for it. We have some interesting items—evidence that will verify all of this story."

She looked at Charlie and nodded to the antique chest that was now sitting on the coffee table. He rose from his chair and began to open the hidden drawer as Suzanne continued. "Grace Stinson had been engaged to marry Charlie. He made this chest for her and stashed the deed to his property in that hidden bottom compartment. As you'll soon read, in her own writing, Grace questioned Charles's disappearance. She'd found the hidden drawer some twenty years after she married Mitch, who had changed his name to Michael. But she put some interesting things in it, along with Charlie's deed. A year before she died, Grace Stinson McDermott, Kevin's grandmother, gave me this chest. It was filled with embroidered pillowcases and I never used them, or it. In fact, it remained in the bottom of my closet until early this morning when I realized I had it and wanted to pack it for the move to the new house."

"I'm throughly confused," Laura muttered, looking at the opened drawer.

"I'm doing a terrible job explaining it all. Why don't you read Grace's letter, then we'll continue."

Charlie handed the thick envelope to Laura and then sat back in his chair. He looked at Suzanne and she raised her eyebrows and shrugged her shoulders, trying silently to convey to him that they were flying by the seat of their pants now.

No one said anything until Laura finished the last page.

"What does all this mean?" she muttered, holding the pages in her lap and staring at them.

"It means that Mitch Davies stole my life," Charlie said.

Laura looked up at him. "You can't be Charles Garrity. You'd have to be . . ."

"One hundred and eleven years old," he finished. "I know."

"But he is!" Suzanne protested. "And we have proof."

"What kind of proof can there be for something that . . . that incredible?"

"Charlie, show her the keepsake."

He picked up the small glass and handed it to Laura.

She held it in her hands and stared at it. After a few moments, she looked back up at Charles. "This is your hair? How did Grace get this lock of it?"

"She cut my hair the morning before all this happened. She cut Mitch's too."

"Look, Laura," Suzanne directed, pointing to the silver around the glass. "Hold it up to the light. You can see the silversmith's marking. If we can trace that, we can verify its age. The person who made it probably died a long time ago. And once we get that, we can open it and do—"

"DNA tests," Laura interrupted, shaking her head. "This is just too unbelievable. You want me to believe that this man is a hundred and eleven years old?"

"I'm thirty-six," Charlie stated. "I left nineteen twenty-six at thirty-six years old and I still am that age. I've been here for a little over six weeks."

Laura ran her fingers through her short hair and stared out the window before turning back to them. "Look, people just don't . . . travel through time!"

Suzanne shrugged. "Obviously, he has. DNA will prove it." She said to Charlie, "Show her the deeds, and your bill of sale."

They waited as Laura reviewed them.

"See, Charlie's deed is registered, along with his bill of sale. A week later, just as Grace wrote, Mitch somehow had a deed made up and registered for the same land in his new name of Michael McDermott . . . but there's no bill of sale. How could he do that, Laura?"

"He could have paid off the county clerk," Laura murmured. "They didn't keep great records back then, and when they were transferred to microfilm, nobody was checking accuracy, just filing everything."

"Makes perfect sense," Charlie muttered. "Mitch had just come out of jail and wouldn't hesitate to bribe someone."

"But you'll never prove that," Laura said. "The county clerk must be dead by now."

"But Mitch isn't," Suzanne stated. "He's an old man, but he's very much alive."

After a few moments, Laura said to Suzanne, "Okay. Now I'll have that glass of wine."

Laughing nervously, Suzanne got up and hurried into the kitchen.

"Not that I'm buying this time-travel thing, but say the DNA shows what you say. We have the letter. We have the deed. What do you want to do with all this? What do you hope to gain?" she asked Charlie.

"I want my life back. That man took everything from me."

Nodding in agreement, Laura accepted the wine glass from Suzanne and said, "You want the money for the land?"

"He's entitled," Suzanne answered, sitting back down. "It never belonged to the McDermott family. Kevin sold land that wasn't his to sell. He made thirty-three million. Charles deserves some of that. Imagine, Laura, if all this were made public. Kevin would have to make restitution to Charlie, to the developers, even to those people living in those big houses out there."

"It would break him," Laura murmured. "You realize your own settlement with him would be in jeopardy?"

"I don't care," Suzanne pronounced. "It's time for justice. Besides, we couldn't touch his investments, right?"

"No. Just the original profit from selling the land. But still, you'd have to prove Mitch, Michael, whoever he is, obtained that land illegally. And there's only one person who can tell the truth about what really happened."

Both Suzanne and Charlie said the name at the same time.

"Mitch."

16

Amid the chaos of moving to the new house, Laura arranged for them to have Charlie's hair tested at a DNA lab. The lawyer had already taken all the evidence and was having the age of the glass keepsake verified. There were calls back and forth between Laura and a real estate attorney as to the best way to proceed. Laura still couldn't believe the time-travel aspect of the case and said until the DNA tests came in, she was going to be an ostrich with her head buried in the sand—denial by avoidance.

Looking around the living room of her new house, Suzanne appreciated how well her own things blended with the furnishings that came with the rental. Hearing Charlie upstairs, she smiled. He had removed the bedroom furniture in one room and was installing Matty's crib and dresser. It was a fairly easy move, since they mostly brought boxes and clothes, and she was glad to be out of the farm house with all its memories. It felt as if a huge weight had been removed from her soul. Here was a place to make a fresh start, she thought, walking into the kitchen.

Testing the iron to make sure it was hot enough, she once more reassured herself that she had made the right decision. The move had taken their minds off the incredible circumstances of finding the contents of that hidden drawer. They just kept working and Suzanne was sure Charlie needed the distraction more than she did, for he was once again solemn, withdrawing from her and his mind seemed to take over his personality.

It was understandable, she thought, picking up a clean pillowcase and laying it on the ironing board. She ran her hands over it, smoothing out the wrinkles, and thought of the woman who had made them. Spraying starch over the white cloth, she wondered how Grace had lived with Mitch all those years, knowing in her heart that her husband was somehow involved with Charlie's disappearance. Maybe it was because she shared something with Matty's great-grandmother, loving the same wonderful man, that she found she couldn't judge the woman for her silence.

She looked up from her ironing and gazed at her son in the sun room, sleeping in his infant seat. He was such a good baby, now taking water from a bottle, and Suzanne once more thought about his lineage. Matty was also Mitch's great-grandson. Grace had been right about the grasping ways of the men in the family. She remembered Mitch, who she could no longer think of as Michael McDermott. Many years ago, while still in college, she had begun visiting the family, and she remembered Mitch as a cranky, manipulative old man, more concerned with the orchard than with his family. Was it any wonder that Kevin and his father had turned out to be selfish when each in turn never experienced any love from the male figure in their lives?

Returning her attention to the pillowcase in front of her, she vowed that she would bring Matty up differently. Kevin wouldn't have any influence on him, if she could help it. She took a deep breath and continued her ironing, carefully applying pressure to the delicate, intricate embroidery at the hem of the pillowcases. *What a work of art,* she thought, and then she remembered seeing Grace at holidays seated in a corner of the living room, her hands always busy, crocheting or reading her prayers. No one seemed to pay much attention to her. She was an old woman, forgotten. Suzanne had spent some time with her, listening to her stories about how the orchards began, but she now realized it wasn't enough.

Folding the first pillowcase, she once more had to admire the beautiful work. It must have taken days, maybe even weeks, to complete. Was this how Grace kept herself sane? Keeping her hands busy, while her mind prayed for her family? She would never know the answers, but she would honor the memory of the woman and use these pillowcases.

"I'm finished," Charlie announced, coming into the kitchen and holding the small toolbox they had taken from the farm house.

She glanced up and smiled. "I'll put away Matty's clothes as soon as I'm finished here."

"What are you doing?" he asked, looking down to the folded pillowcase on the table.

She grabbed up another from her ironing pile and answered, "I'm going to honor Grace by using these. It seems right somehow that the first night we spend here, we'll be putting our heads on her pillowcases."

Charlie just stared at them, and she could tell memories were running through his mind. "Is that okay with you?"

He took a deep breath and reached out his hand, as though to touch the pillowcase, and then slowly drew back as if he had changed his mind. "Where is she buried?"

"Not too far from here," Suzanne whispered. She looked at him, sensing his anguish, and added, "Would you like to visit her grave?"

"Tomorrow?"

"Well, I'm getting divorced tomorrow," she reminded him, even though she had been trying to push it from her mind. "I have to be at the courthouse at eleven in the morning. We could do it later in the afternoon."

"Do you want me to come with you tomorrow morning?"

She wanted to say yes, come with me, hold my hand, make it all better, but she knew she had to do this one alone. "If it's all right with you, I'd like you to stay here with Matty. I don't want to bring him into that courtroom as his parents' marriage is dissolved. Laura will be with me and, since I'm filing and Kevin isn't contesting the divorce, he probably won't even be there. At least that's what Laura said."

"Whatever you want, Suzanne. Are you okay with all this happening at once? We really haven't talked much about it."

She shrugged, knowing he had been the one who'd been distancing himself. "We've been pretty busy with the move," she said, beginning to iron the next pillowcase. "What's there to talk about? Now, more than ever, I want to divorce myself from Kevin and his family. The one good thing is that having the divorce take place so quickly, my settlement with him will be a court judgment. The money will be deposited into my account before he's hit with . . . well, with whatever happens next."

"I'm glad you will be protected," Charlie said, walking toward the door that led into the garage.

And that was it, the extent of their conversation. She knew all the reasons men were different than women. When they had something on their minds they liked to hibernate in their caves, where women wanted to talk it out. She acknowledged Charlie was doing his best to hibernate, but it wasn't easy to be around him. Neither one of them mentioned the night they had spent in each other's arms. Suzanne looked back on it as if it had been a dream, for the very next morning all hell had started to break loose around them and it seemed since then he was putting out mental fires right and left.

She also knew that Charlie was frustrated by waiting for

the results of all the testing. He wanted to go to Evergreen Nursing Home and strangle Mitch Davies. She couldn't blame him, but knew it would serve no purpose. The best thing they could do was wait.

Patience. It was a hard lesson to learn.

The next morning she dressed with care. She wore her gray Armani suit with the longer jacket. The waistband of the skirt was a little tight, so she didn't button it, sure the zipper would hold it up. She applied full makeup, perfume, even jewelry. Gold earrings and a gold omega necklace. It had been quite a while since she'd worn panty hose, and she couldn't believe that she'd spent years doing this every morning. What a chore. That was another thing changing within her. Her sense of self was altering. Once it had been so very important to her what others thought of her looks, her clothes, her makeup, her hair, her weight, her job, her husband, her home. Now, she couldn't care. It was more than clear that right now, in this season of her life, she was more comfortable wearing jeans than Armani.

However, she thought, while looking at her reflection in the mirror, there was a time and place for Armani, and going to court to get divorced was one of them. Satisfied with what she saw, she took a deep breath and left her bedroom.

Charlie was feeding Matty his bottle of water when she came downstairs. "Well, I'm off," she said cheerily, though her stomach was in a tight knot.

Charlie looked up from her son and his expression was priceless.

"Well?" she asked, doing a neat pirouette in the foyer.

"You look so . . . different," he muttered.

"Ah, different good, or different bad?" Her self-confidence was starting to slide away.

"Different good, I guess. I've just never seen you looking so . . ." His voice trailed off as though he couldn't find the right word.

"Dressed." She supplied it with a grin.

"You just look so dignified, so proper."

"And you're used to me in jeans and T-shirts," she added, walking over to him. "I do have other clothes." She bent down and kissed Matty's forehead and then patted Charlie's arm. "I'll be back as soon as I can."

Nodding, Charlie said, "We'll be fine. And Suzanne?"

She turned around at the door. "Yes?"

"You look lovely."

Her heart melted and she smiled back at him. "Thanks."

"Good luck."

Luck. It seemed to be on her side, for a change.

Charlie looked down at the baby in his arms. He couldn't deny the surge of affection that ran through him when he looked into Matty's soft blue eyes. Truth was, he was torn by the emotions running within him. This child he now held was the great-grandson of Mitch Davies, the son of Kevin Mc-Dermott, both of whom he considered unconscionable bastards, yet he couldn't hold the babe responsible for the actions of his ancestors.

He had been there for Matty's birth, brought him home from the hospital. Changed him, bathed him, fed him. He was more a father than his own. And despite what he felt, he knew he couldn't stay and raise him, for it would be a daily reminder of everything he had lost and how he had been betrayed. He loved Suzanne, and God help him, he loved Matty, but he had to be honest. Right now, Matty was a reminder of Mitch and he knew he couldn't stay.

He felt guilty for his feelings and knew he could never tell Suzanne the real reason he would be leaving now. Let her think it was because he wanted to get away and find himself, as she put it.

"I'm sorry, lad," he whispered down to Matty, who was staring up at him with what looked like adoration. He knew what it was like to want so desperately the approval and love of a father. His own had none to give him. He wouldn't do that to this innocent child. One day Suzanne would move on, and Matty was too young to remember him.

But still, his heart felt like it was breaking apart. One more loss.

Suzanne sat with Laura at the plaintiffs' table. She was so glad Kevin hadn't shown up, though why would he, when he always took the easy way out? So again she would be the adult and go to court to make sure the proceedings were final. Her mind traveled back as she recalled being the only one to call whenever anything needed to be done around the house. If there was an unpleasantness, she had always taken care of it, handled it so he wouldn't have to be bothered. That's what Kevin would say to her. Handle it. What he meant was, make it go away.

She blinked a few times, trying to stop the memories.

It wasn't a very impressive courtroom, and she'd answered yes to about five questions, dealing with her intent to petition for divorce. She answered yes to irreconcilable differences and her voice had been strong and emphatic. There was no reconciling the differences between herself and Kevin McDermott. Feeling she ought to pay more attention to the judge, she focused on him and what he was saying.

"This matter having been presented to the Court by Laura Silverman, Esquire, attorney for the plaintiff, Suzanne Marie McDermott, and the Court having heard and considered the complaint and it appearing that the parties were married, and the plaintiff having pleaded and proved a cause of action for divorce under the statute in such case made and provided, and the plaintiff having been a bona fide resident of the State for more than one year, it is by the Superior Court of New Jersey, Chancery Division, Family Part, ordered and adjudged, and such court by virtue of power and authority of this Court does hereby order and adjudge that the plaintiff, Suzanne Marie McDermott, and the defendant, Kevin

Michael McDermott, be divorced from the bonds of matrimony."

That was it? She was divorced? She looked at Laura, who
motioned with her head to wait. There was more.

"It is further ordered that the agreement entered into by
and between the parties regarding support, disposition of
property, and other collateral issues is hereby permitted by
this Court to be made part of this judgment. It is further ordered that pursuant to Paragraph one point one of the said
agreement, wife shall have full custody of the unemancipated
child of the marriage, Matthew Charles McDermott."

The judge banged his gavel and looked directly at
Suzanne. "Good luck in your life, madam."

"Thank you," she answered, startled by his consideration.

Laura touched her forearm. "We're done, Suzanne. Let's
go."

Nodding, feeling numb at the finality, she rose from her
chair and walked out of the courtroom. Funny, she wasn't
sure what to expect, but she thought it would have taken
more than five minutes to end a marriage. She was stunned
by how easy it was. Maybe she wanted something more final
so she would feel it really was over.

"That's it?" she asked Laura when they were in the hallway.

"That's it. Congratulations. You're a single woman again."

"Single. Hard to believe it's over, just like that."

"Oh, it was over a long time ago, Suzanne. This just
makes it all legal."

She glanced at Laura. "Doesn't all this make you cynical
about marriage? Is that why you're still single?"

"Oh, you wouldn't want to know my views of the institution of marriage."

"I would," Suzanne insisted, as they walked toward the
parking lot.

"Well, first of all, who the hell wants to be in an institution? I'd change the label of it and then I'd change the contract. I'd make it renewable every seven years."

"Renewable?"

"Sure. Think about it. Once the romance wears off, and it always does, if you really loved your spouse and you knew your contract was up for renewal, would you take that person for granted? Not if you wanted to continue the marriage. You'd try harder to communicate, and if it didn't work there would be a way out without everyone being put through this emotional wringer."

Suzanne thought about it and immediately liked the idea. "A renewable marriage contract. You're right, Laura, you wouldn't take the other person for granted. You'd really work on the relationship, instead of thinking it would always be there. People who were married would really want to be married, instead of . . ." Her words trailed off.

"Instead of being in an institution," Laura supplied.

"Exactly!" She laughed. "You should work on this, Laura. I think plenty of people would agree with you."

"What? And ruin a good career?" Chuckling, Laura shook her head. "Anyway, we were talking about you being single again. What are your plans?"

"How can I get back my maiden name?"

Walking with her through the huge parking lot, Laura asked, "Are you sure you want a different name than your son's? It might prove difficult as he gets older."

"I hadn't thought of that," she answered, putting on her sunglasses and looking toward her car.

"Well, think about it. We can do it later, if you still want."

They stopped at Suzanne's car. "Thank you, Laura. I never expected it to be this fast."

"We were lucky I could pull a few strings to get your case higher on the docket."

"Well, thank your contacts, whoever they are. I am indebted."

"Speaking of that, you might get the opportunity to thank him yourself."

"I will? How?"

"First of all, the results came back on the silversmith's marking. A man by the name of Abraham Rissen made it. He had a shop in Trenton. And here's the part I still can't believe: He died in nineteen twenty-nine."

Suzanne felt goose bumps rising on her arms. "So then if the hair in the keepsake is the same as Charlie's, then—"

"Then we all should be committed to Ancora State Hospital, because this is freakin' incredible!"

Suzanne laughed. "I know how you feel, Laura. But you'll see when the DNA tests come back. Now how and why am I going to meet this contact of yours?"

"Ah, here's the good part," she said with a mischievous grin. "Wait till you hear what Sam Knueson and I came up with."

He stood at the gravesite, staring at the headstone with Grace's name, the date of her birth, and the date of her death. There was a dash between the two dates, and Charlie kept staring at the dash. That was her life. A dash. He felt the emotion welling up inside of him, wishing that he could have loved her the way she had loved him. He felt like he had somehow failed her, though he knew he didn't ask to be taken away. Still, her life, through her letter and what Suzanne had told him, had sounded so sad. Whereas her capacity for love was great, she ended up being surrounded by those who couldn't love. He imagined her life with Mitch and he felt even worse.

He didn't seem to bring luck to those who loved him.

Feeling a deep ache within his chest, he blinked back the tears. What good would tears do now? It wouldn't bring back anything. It was all gone, lost by the greed of one man. He took a deep breath and set his jaw, determined not to lose control. Not now. Not yet. Suzanne had said it would be less than a week before he would see Mitch. He pictured in his mind strangling the very life force out of his body, making him pay for marrying Grace, for taking his land, for living his dreams.

"I'm so sorry, Grace," he whispered, his throat raw from unshed tears. Placing a bouquet of spring flowers at the headstone, he touched the marble briefly and then turned away.

Suzanne watched him walking back to the car. She straightened in the driver's seat and was thankful Matty was fed and asleep. She could tell by the grim set of his facial muscles that he was very upset, and it was understandable. Not knowing what to say to him, she prayed the right words would come out of her mouth. It was odd that she felt no jealousy toward his memories of Grace. Somehow, she felt honored that they loved the same man.

He opened the car door and slid onto the passenger seat.

"You okay?"

He nodded, staring out the front window.

"You want to talk about anything?"

He shook his head, yet she saw the muscles in his jaw working as though he was clenching his back teeth.

"All right," she said, starting the engine. "Let's go home."

"I don't have a home," he muttered.

She glanced at him as she shifted the car into drive. "Of course you do. Your home is with me and Matty, for as long as you want."

He didn't say anything as they left the cemetery and pulled out onto the main road. Reaching out her hand, she put it on top of his and squeezed. "Remember you told me that through the worst times in your life, somehow you make it through? That it all turns out? I don't know how, Charlie, but this will all work out. I know it."

When he didn't respond she figured the word gods hadn't heard her prayer.

Dinner that evening was solemn. Not even informing him

of Laura's plans for confronting Mitch and Kevin could perk him up. She didn't know what to do. She cleared the table and did the dishes while he sat on the front porch looking out at the river. She took care of Matty, playing with him in the sun room until he was hungry and, after feeding him and changing him, she put her son to bed.

And still, Charlie was out on the porch. It was dark and she didn't know if she should turn on a light. Figuring he wanted to be left alone, Suzanne walked into her bedroom. She now had a queen-sized bed, smaller, and yet it was okay. She didn't feel quite so alone in it.

A single woman.

Those words kept repeating in her head. She was free now. Maybe it would take time to feel it. A part of her would always be connected to Kevin through their son. And another part of her resented that fact. Somehow, she would raise Matty to respect his father. She wouldn't be one of those mothers that bad-mouthed the father, even though she could say some damaging things. Thankful the time when Matty would question her was far in the future, she unbuttoned her skirt and allowed it to fall to the carpet. She had a few years to instill in her son the virtues that she thought were important. Besides, it didn't appear that Kevin would want much contact with Matty. She was grateful in one way, but knew that could change with the years.

She had never thought she would be a single woman again, or a single mother. Picking up her skirt, she thought she might as well look at it like an adventure from here on out. She had no idea what her future was going to bring. By tomorrow Kevin will have transferred into her account millions of dollars. She shook her head at the ridiculous amount as she walked into the bathroom. Still, she had no idea what the rest of her life would bring. She guessed she was drifting along right now, waiting for the last pieces of the puzzle to fall into place. In a few days she would get more of the picture when they confronted Mitch. But she didn't want to think about Mitch now. She didn't want to think about any of it. She wanted to get clean, crawl into bed, and sleep.

The bathroom was much smaller than the one at the farm, but it did hold a large tub. How she would love to soak in hot water, allowing all the tension to leave her body. But in truth, she admitted she didn't have the energy to wash it afterward and so she headed for the stall shower. Within minutes she was clean and she wrapped the long bath sheet around her before walking back into the bedroom.

She stopped short when she saw Charlie sitting on the edge of her bed.

"Hi," she breathed, startled and wondering if she should get her nightgown and bring it back into the bathroom to change. "Are you feeling any better?"

He raised his face and she was shocked by his expression of sorrow. "I tried to stay away, tried not to burden you with this, but Suz . . . I feel like I'm breaking apart."

She hurried across the room, taking him into her arms, and allowing him to bury his face against her chest. "Oh, Charlie, it's all right. Let it out. Stop trying to fight the process. You're grieving, sweetie, for everything you've lost." Stroking his hair, she whispered, "It's okay to cry."

"This is my feminine side?" he muttered against the thick towel. "I don't want to feel like this."

Smiling, she kissed the top of his head. "And I'm telling you, you will feel like this until you let it out of your body. Think of it, Charlie, you have tear ducts for a reason. To cry. If you don't use them, you'll take this energy and bottle it up and it will come out another way. Get it out now. Don't make yourself sick. Let go, my love."

She felt the tension in his body.

"I can't."

"You can. Here, wait a minute." Pulling away slightly, she tightened the bath sheet and said, "Come with me," as she crawled on top of the bed. She put the pillows behind her back and spread her legs, glad that the large towel covered them. Patting the space in between, she said, "C'mere, Charlie."

He merely stared at her.

"Trust me," she whispered. "I won't bite you."

In spite of the turmoil raging inside of him, he smiled. "Suzanne . . ."

"I said trust me, Charlie," she repeated, taking another pillow and placing it against her chest. "Lie on your back and put your head here."

He hesitated.

"Don't you trust me, Charlie?"

"I don't know if I trust myself," he answered, shifting his body so that his head was on the pillow.

"Now," she said, "let go."

"What?"

She ran her fingers through his hair and then looked at the lamp on her night table. "Wait, let me turn this off." When she was resettled, she sighed deeply and said, "Okay, let's try it again. Let go."

"Let go of what?" he demanded, holding out his hands.

Smiling, she said, "Let go of the tension in your muscles. And don't tell me you aren't tense. I can feel it. Now, just relax."

"I am relaxed."

"You are not. I told you I can feel your tension." And she could as his shoulders and hips were against her legs. "Don't talk or interrupt me. Just let go."

He took a deep breath and exhaled into the darkened room.

"That's good. Deep breaths. Inhale." She waited a few seconds. "Exhale."

She breathed with him four more times and then began to speak slowly, soothingly. "Now, I want you to think of the muscles in your toes. Really think of them. Feel them. Feel them relax, like ropes becoming untwisted, free from any tension. Feel the soothing energy traveling to the arches of your feet, relaxing, unwinding, up over your heels . . . your ankles . . . each muscle relaxing, becoming heavier, one after the other. Just letting go. Feel it slowly traveling up your legs, around your calves, your knees, up your thighs, across your torso, relaxing the large muscles around your stomach, your chest . . . one after the other . . . just breathing in relaxation and breathing out all tension."

She paused, allowing him to feel it and smiling when she experienced the heaviness of his hips against her legs. He was doing it. Years ago, she'd gone to a hypnotherapist for stress reduction and had been surprised by how well it had worked. Not sure what else to do for him, she continued.

"Now I want you to feel your lower back and feel the tension leaving as you release those muscles, one after the other, working all the way up your spine, allowing each muscle to fall easily into place, one right next to the other . . . releasing all the tension you've been holding. Release those heavy muscles across your shoulders, feeling the soothing, peaceful energy moving up your neck and now into your scalp . . . releasing . . ."

His shoulders sagged against her upper thighs.

"Feel that soothing release pouring down over your head, over your ears, over your forehead, around your eyes, your nose, your mouth, releasing the stress in your jaw so that there isn't a place in your body that can contain any tension any longer.

"Breathe it in, Charlie. Feel the peace." She waited almost a minute, feeling him heavy against her. "Now, in this peaceful place, you are allowed to release all the pain, all the sorrow, all the loss. You can feel it drain out of your body. Allow it to come out naturally, through your eyes. Let it go . . . you don't have to be strong any more, not right now. Right now you're *safe*. I've got you, honey. Let it go."

And he did. Slowly at first, and then she could feel his shoulders moving as he freed himself of his sorrow. Suddenly, he turned to his side and hugged her leg, pulling it in closer to him and burying his face into the pillow.

"God, Suzanne," he muttered. "It hurts."

"I know," she soothed, allowing him to release it as she stroked his hair. "You're grieving, sweetie," she whispered as her own tears fell upon him. "I know what it's like."

And she did, all too well.

She continued to stroke his hair as she laid her head back on her pillow. They stayed like that, entwined, for the longest time. Neither one of them spoke as a deep peace seemed to envelope them. To her it felt beautiful, precious, almost sacred. She felt honored that he had come to her to release his sorrow. She also felt closer to him than any other human being in her life. He trusted her.

Suzanne finally felt his body once more go limp and she knew he had fallen asleep. Closing her eyes, she realized today was the first day of her single life. And she was in bed with the man she loved.

Funny the way things turn out.

Maybe she and Charlie weren't meant to make love.

17

She was dreaming. It had to be a dream, yet it felt so real.

His hands were stroking her back, her shoulders, and she moaned with the pleasure of it. She didn't care any longer, feeling him behind her, holding her, cradling her against his hard body. Instinctively arching her back, she felt his arousal meeting her thrust. His hand slipped around her waist and she felt him cup her bare breast. She sighed as she melted back into him.

She heard a deep, sexy moan by her ear and her eyes fluttered open.

Staring into the moonlit darkness, she realized within moments this was no dream.

Immediately her heart seemed to burst open with love as she felt his caresses. His touch was so gentle, almost reverent, as he pulled apart the towel to expose more of her naked body. She allowed him to roam freely, until he again captured her breast. Afraid to ruin the precious moment by words, she simply put her left hand tenderly over his at her breast and raised her right to encircle the back of his head, lifting her breasts, and again arching her back, telling him with her body she was accepting wherever he wanted to go, needing to be closer to him, wanting to prolong the contact. He seemed to curl around her, sliding his hand down her rib cage and grasping her hip to pull her back against him.

"Suzanne," he whispered into her ear in a ragged breath.

"Get undressed," she whispered back, her whole body tingling to feel his skin against her own.

"Don't move. Not a muscle."

She didn't care anymore what the future held. She only knew this moment, and in this moment she wanted to meld with him, to fuse her body with his, to know that joining. She loved him. In this moment, it no longer mattered that he would be leaving her. If she only had this night, she would take it. Feeling him shift away from behind her, she heard him stand by the bed. She experienced a deep sense of loss by his withdrawal, yet quicker than she thought possible, she felt the mattress again take his weight as he slid up against her, this time without the barrier of clothing.

"Oh, God," she murmured, sucking in her breath at the searing naked contact of his chest against her back, his arms around her, his hard arousal against her bottom. They started moving slowly, grinding against each other as his hands again roamed over her body, first her breast, then her stomach and then lower, ever so gently, touching her with featherlike strokes. It was everything she had imagined, and more, a sense of being, belonging, heightened awareness of every inch of skin, his and her own. Moaning as he continued to stroke her, explore her, bringing her closer to the edge, she allowed her head to fall back against him.

He cradled her in his arm, reaching across her shoulder to again cup her breast. He ground his mouth against her skin, kissing her temple, her cheekbone, her neck, breathing into her ear, sending shivers racing across her skin as his leg crossed over her hip and eased her own leg back over his own. She never felt so open, so vulnerable, and yet she trusted him completely.

Half lying on him, she felt him. The hard length of him. Probing the delicate folds of her. Gently gaining entrance into her. And still he continued to stroke the core of her, driving her near mad for him as he teased from beneath and above.

"Please," she begged, no longer able to take it. "I . . . I want you, Charlie!"

"You have me, love," he whispered, grasping her hip and entering her fully.

She threw back her head and inhaled deeply with exquisite pleasure as he filled her completely. "Oh, Charlie," she breathed. "I've waited so long to feel like this."

"No longer than I, my love," he breathed back into her ear. He began to move slowly, gliding back and forth, while his hand once more found the throbbing core of her and brought her back to the edge, closer and closer, mindlessly going further, knowing she would fall and not caring, as long as he was with her.

"Charlie?" She called out his name, feeling every nerve ending in her body come alive, focusing and clustering where they were joined together, begging for release.

"Charlie!" she called out again as the exquisite explosion came, thrusting her over the edge and into the night, seeping out through her pores, sending fragments of her beyond her physical body to soar and mingle with the heavens. Her muscles convulsed around the length of him, pulsing and urging him to join her.

Turning her onto her back, he reentered her quickly and she clung to his upper arms as she wrapped her legs around him, lifting herself to meet each thrust. He stared into her eyes with an expression of wonder and she knew, no matter what happened between them, in this moment he loved her. Filled with a sense of power, she stared back, willing him to come with her, hearing it in his breath, watching it on his face

as he came closer and closer and then, with a sense of amazement, she felt it all building again in her, only this time it was
deeper, more acute, demanding a more complete release.

White-hot with passion, they performed an ancient ritual,
melding bodies, minds, souls and when they soared, they did
so together . . . clinging to each other, crying out their joy,
making love come alive, making memories to last a lifetime.

They held each other, coming back into their bodies, as
their hearts pounded in perfect rhythm against each other.
The only sound in the room was their ragged breathing. She
felt him slide off her and collapse next to her. Turning her
head, she moved to her side so she could face him.

She reached out her hand and tenderly caressed his face,
feeling a rough stubble against her palm. It only further excited her, for she couldn't believe that her body still wanted
him. "Thank you," she whispered, meaning it with all her
heart.

"Oh, sweet precious one," he breathed, running his hand
over her hip. "Thank you. I tried, Suzanne, for so long, but
when I awoke with you next to me near naked . . . I simply
couldn't resist any longer. I'm not that strong and—"

"Shh . . . I'm glad. More than glad, Charlie. I'm glori-
ously happy." It was now her turn to touch him, to trace the
slope of his shoulder, the expanse of his chest. Her fingers
traced a ragged scar on his side, the curve of his hip, the hard
muscle of his thigh.

He pulled her against him, gathering her back into his embrace, and she was shocked to find him still hard. Following
instinct, she gently pushed his shoulders until he was lying
on his back and then she slid over him, sucking in her breath
as he once more entered her. Slowly, ever so slowly, she began to move.

"Sweet mother of god, Suzanne," he murmured, grasping
her hips to anchor her.

This time tenderness was replaced with something more
primal as man and woman came together, shedding all

boundaries, all inhibitions, all definitions, until they were one.

Dawn was slipping into the room as Charlie ran the water in the tub and Suzanne laid back against the pillows watching him. He'd already gone downstairs, naked as the day he'd been born, and brought them tall glasses of water. Her hands had been shaking as she'd tried to hold the glass, and she had to use both hands to steady herself. Never before in her life had she experienced such an exquisite union. It seemed almost like a reunion, as she felt so natural around him. She felt love, a love that was so intense yet so easy, as though she had come home to it finally, having only encountered shadow images of it before.

Hearing the water turn off, she watched as he walked into the bedroom and up to her. He was magnificent, without the least bit of shame at being naked. Men were like that. Holding out his hand, he said, "Come, love. Our bath awaits."

She grasped his hand as he helped her to stand. It didn't bother her that she was naked and her body wasn't perfect, she realized when he put his arm around her shoulder and led her into the bathroom. Here, within his embrace, for the first time in her life she had found total acceptance. And there was freedom in that, a freedom that had been missing in her life.

"Oh, Charlie," she whispered, seeing the filled tub. "How thoughtful."

He squeezed her shoulders. "After the night we've had, it was all I could think of to ease our aching muscles."

"I am a bit sore," she admitted, as he held her hand while she stepped into the tub.

"As am I," he said, smiling at her as she lowered herself into the water.

When she was settled against the back, he then entered. The water reached the very rim of the tub as he sat down, putting his legs at her sides and she resting her legs between his and on his hips. Suzanne said with a laugh, "I'm afraid to move, or we'll have a flood up here."

Grinning, Charlie reached behind him and began letting out some of the water. When he resettled and leaned back with his arms resting on the sides of the tub, he looked across the water at her and smiled.

"What was your name before you were married?"

"Lawrence," she answered, leaning her head back against the rim of the tub, while running her hands over his legs. "This is heavenly," she breathed, feeling the warmth of the water enter her pores and soak her aching muscles. It was as though they had been together forever, she thought, as he began to massage her foot.

"Well, Suzanne Lawrence, you are quite a woman."

She tilted her head to see him better and smiled back. "You are quite a man, Charles Patrick Garrity. I think we're evenly matched."

"Like equals?"

"Yes, like equals," she breathed, feeling a surge of gratitude for him, for the water, for life. She felt totally content.

"An equal partnership," he murmured. "I've heard of that."

"Where?"

"Just somewhere."

She giggled. "Probably when you were watching television. It must have been on *Oprah*."

"Perhaps," he answered, running his hands up her calf and massaging away the ache.

"May I ask you a question?"

"Of course. You know everything about me already. I have nothing to hide."

"Where did you get that scar on your side? Was it in the war?"

"Yes." His voice was a whisper.

"It's all right, Charlie. You don't have to revisit those memories."

"Thank you."

She smiled. "I prefer the memories we made earlier."

"As I just said, you are quite a woman, Suzanne."

"Why, thank you, sir, but I will admit it had been a long time since . . . well, since I was . . . involved."

He chuckled. "Well, it's been longer for me. Seventy-five years."

She laughed. "You're right. That explains it."

"Explains what?"

"How . . . how virile you are."

"Is that a polite way of saying I was randy?"

"There's an old-fashioned word. Randy. Yes, you were quite randy. And so was I." She looked deep into his eyes. "But it was the most beautiful night of my life, Charlie."

His smile was tender, and yet sad.

"You're still going to leave, aren't you? Even when you get paid the money for the land." It was the question that was burning in her brain.

"Yes, love. I have to."

She wanted to tell him to stay, that they did make an equal partnership, that she knew he loved her, but only silence filled the small room. And then, as though to put an end to that train of thought, she heard Matty's cry as he awoke. Shifting to sit up straighter, she said, "I should get him."

"No," Charlie answered, already rising and dripping water. "I'll get him and bring him in here with us."

"Really?" She'd never taken her baby into the tub with her and the thought was appealing. "Okay, thanks."

She waited a few minutes and then grinned as a naked Charlie held a naked Matty against his chest as he brought the baby into the bathroom. He handed him over and Suzanne cradled her son to her breast. "It's okay, sweetie," she whispered, helping Matty as he latched onto her. His legs and arms were moving in the water and she grinned up to Charlie. "Come join us."

When Charlie was back in the tub, Suzanne laughed at her son. "He likes it!"

"Why wouldn't he?"

"You're right. It must be like being back in the womb."

She looked up at Charlie and grinned. "Thanks for this. Thanks for everything since you came into my life."

He smiled at her with such tenderness, she felt tears suddenly welling up in her eyes.

"I will always remember you both like this," he whispered. She couldn't speak. She couldn't beg him not to leave. She knew that there was some ache within him that she couldn't help ease. Only he could do it. Rather than thinking of him leaving, she forced her mind to stay right where she was, with her son and the man she loved. Here and now was beauty, contentment, and such an incredible sense of love that she wouldn't ruin it with regrets.

They stayed in silence for the longest time, soaking in the peace.

The morning remained peaceful. Matty was down for his nap and Suzanne was cuddled next to Charlie in the sun room. They couldn't seem to get enough of each other, touching, kissing, making memories. Each knew it would end, but neither spoke of it again.

Suzanne felt married, more married than when it had been legal. And how strange was that, since this day was the first full day of her renewed single life. Yet she couldn't deny the closeness she felt with Charlie. They had begun as friends, needing each other when their lives had been turned upside down, and they had ended up lovers, beyond lovers. They were united in their hearts and souls. She knew that when he left, he would take a part of her with him and she was willing to allow it, for he was so firmly entrenched within her own heart now.

All she could do was give him freedom.

The phone rang and Suzanne reluctantly slipped away from Charlie and hurried to answer it.

"Hello."

"Suzanne, it's Laura."

"Hi, Laura. How are you?"

"I'll tell how I am. I think I should be seeing a shrink! The

DNA tests came back positive. I'm asking you again, how can this be possible?"

Grinning, Suzanne answered, "I don't know how it happened, it just did. Charlie is who he says he is, and I never doubted it."

"Well, I feel like I'm in the middle of a dream and I can't wake up."

"You're awake, Laura. Things happen that are unexplainable. This is one of them."

"What if someone gets hold of this information? I mean, I've done everything very quietly, but seriously, Suzanne—this is *news!*"

"Laura?" Suzanne began in a grave voice. "No one can ever hear of this. This must be kept confidential, except for those involved. I won't allow Charlie to be exposed. He's been through enough."

"I understand. I mean, I agree. I don't think I'll ever understand."

"I don't think any of us ever will, but think of all the so-called coincidences. All I can say is it was meant to happen. I don't know who or what is orchestrating this, but I've accepted my role in it and I'm playing it out. I suggest you do the same." She paused for a moment. "Just think of your fee. Twenty percent of thirty-three million. That will keep you centered."

"Right. Well, I wanted to call you immediately. Now I need to make the rest of the calls. We'll all meet at ten A.M. at Evergreen. I'm bringing Knueson, a court stenographer, and our friend from court. Also, I have contacted someone from the district attorney's office to meet us—not in an official capacity, but Kevin and his lawyer won't know that. I just want to make this as official looking as possible and cover all bases if we're going to pull this off."

"We'll do it, Laura. We haven't been led this far to fail now."

"I hope you're right."

"I know I'm right. We'll see you tomorrow morning."

She hung up the phone and came back to the sun room. "The DNA test came back positive," she said, sitting on a chair opposite Charlie. "We're all meeting at Evergreen Nursing Home tomorrow at ten."

"I heard your end of the conversation. So I'll see Mitch tomorrow."

"Yes. I'm glad you're seeking justice this way, Charlie. Anything else would just ruin what life you have now."

Nodding, he stared out the window in silence yet she could see that muscle moving in his jaw. She knew he still wanted to wring Mitch's neck. "If we can pull this off, you'll be a very wealthy man, Charlie. Have you thought what you'll do?"

"I can't think past tomorrow," he murmured. "Do you really think all this was meant to happen? That we are all being led?"

"I do," she said emphatically. "I don't know how, but think of everything—me being at the creek at the exact time when you needed to be pulled from the water; you being with me when I needed someone to support me during the birth; coming to live with me. Being there for me when the truth of my marriage came out. I honestly don't know what I would have done without you. Then finding Grace's chest with all the clues hidden all these years. It's like a puzzle and we're finding and fitting all the pieces back together."

He turned to look directly into her eyes. "Who would be doing this?"

"Someone who loves us, that much I know for sure."

"Grace? But how could that be? She was alive all those years . . ."

"Charlie, what do we really know about time? I thought I knew. I thought it was linear, from point A to point B. Now I realize it isn't. It can't be, because you're here right in front of me. It must be curved, bendable, able to be manipulated somehow."

"You think Grace is behind all this?"

"Maybe. I don't know what's behind it. My whole belief system, what I've been taught, has been shaken by the unexplainable. But something, some *force*, is moving all this forward. I think we just have to show up, follow our hearts, and play our roles. Can't you feel it, Charlie? That something is behind all this?"

He slowly nodded. "I can't explain it either."

She got up and came to sit next to him. Sliding her arm across the front of his chest, she buried her face in his shoulder and kissed his neck. "We don't have to explain it. We know the truth."

They were having lunch in the kitchen when the doorbell rang. Suzanne got up to answer it, yet nothing could have prepared her for who it was.

"Kevin," she said his name, as he stared at her with a murderous expression. "What do you want?"

"I want to know what the hell is going on! I wired you the settlement. It's in your account now."

"Well, thank you for that. I don't know what else you're talking about."

"My lawyer called after hearing from your lawyer, and I'm supposed to be at Evergreen Nursing Home tomorrow at ten? What is this about? What are you doing, involving my grandfather in all this?"

"Actually, your grandfather started all of it, but you'll find out tomorrow morning. I can't say more than that now."

She was holding the door and it suddenly opened wider. Charlie was standing beside her.

"What's going on here?" he demanded, staring at Kevin.

"That's what I want to know," Kevin shot back. "And what are *you* doing here? None of this is your business."

"He lives here," Suzanne answered.

"And you don't," Charlie stated. "Now leave."

"I'll leave when I'm good and ready, when I've got some answers."

Shaking his head, Charlie came out onto the porch. "I heard Suzanne tell you you'd get your answers tomorrow."

Kevin backed up. "I want to know what the hell is going on!"

Charlie swiftly grabbed his arm and twisted it behind him, turning Kevin toward the porch steps. "This isn't your home. You have no rights here," he said, shoving Kevin off the porch as he released his arm. "Just do what she said. Be there tomorrow."

"You'll pay for that," Kevin retorted as he stood on the walkway and glared back at them.

Charlie stared right back. "Anytime you want. Just you and me."

Kevin took a deep breath and straightened his shirt. He didn't say another word as he turned away. Charlie watched him until he got in his car and started the engine. He then turned back to Suzanne.

"Let's finish our lunch."

She simply nodded as they walked back into the house.

It appeared life was about to get even more interesting.

18

Her stomach was in knots as they walked down the corridor of the nursing home. She concentrated on her breathing as she glanced at the others. Charlie was there next to her, dressed in the charcoal gray suit they had bought yesterday. She had to admit he looked handsome, even with his somber mood. Ahead of them walked Laura and Sam Knueson, the real estate attorney. A court stenographer and Alina Mallon from the district attorney's office were behind them. Everyone was dressed in dark colors, as though for a funeral, and Suzanne again felt the muscles in her belly twist with apprehension. If they could just pull this off and get out of here . . . for Alina Mallon only clerked for the assistant district attorney. She wasn't *exactly* representing that office.

Suzanne had been to Evergreen Nursing Home three times before, each time with Kevin for an obligatory holiday visit. It was a nice place, but depressing just the same. This time her visit was different. This time they very well might destroy a man, and possibly his grandson. A small part of her felt almost sorry for Mitch and Kevin, and yet a stronger part of her felt justified. This was about justice, about balancing the scales without resorting to violence. It had to work. For Charlie. For Grace. And maybe even for herself.

They stopped outside Mitch's room. Laura turned to her and Charlie.

"Are you ready?" she asked.

Charlie simply nodded, and Suzanne took a deep breath and murmured yes.

"Then let's do it," Laura pronounced, placing her hand on the door and pushing it open.

Suzanne said a silent prayer, yet she wasn't really sure who she was praying for . . . maybe just that the truth would finally be revealed and Charlie might find his peace.

Charlie felt his heart beating in his chest, resonating in his ears, pulsing at his fingertips as the door to Mitch's room was opened. He had waited for this moment and now he wasn't sure how he would react. He first saw Kevin and a smaller man, standing at the bedside of an old, shriveled man, whose face resembled a cracked walnut.

Mitch?

Suddenly, all the hatred he had harbored for the man seemed to seep out of his body as he stared at the shrunken and skeletal frame that had once housed his best friend. His hair was nearly gone; his skin dotted with dark spots. Tubes were attached to him and he seemed to be surrounded by machinery.

"What is this about?" Kevin demanded, interrupting all his thoughts.

Laura came forward and said, "Please be patient. Everything will be explained shortly. First, I'd like to introduce Samuel Knueson, a real estate attorney, and Alina Mallon from the district attorney's office, along with a court-appointed stenographer who will be taking a deposition—"

"I wasn't informed of any deposition," Kevin's attorney stated. "Why *have* we been called here?"

"And what's *he* doing here?" Kevin asked, nodding his head toward Charlie.

Laura motioned to the stenographer to set up her equipment and then looked at Kevin's lawyer. "We're here to gain testimony that will confirm your client sold land four years ago that wasn't his to sell."

"What the hell are you talking about?" Kevin demanded, staring first at Laura, then glaring at Suzanne and finally at Charlie. "And who the hell *are* you?"

He stepped forward, facing Kevin. "My name is Charles Garrity. And you illegally sold my land."

"This is bullshit," Kevin stated to his lawyer. "She put him up to this. She thinks that she can get back at me and—"

"Charlie!"

They all turned toward the bed and the surprisingly distinct voice. It was raspy, yet loud enough for all of them to hear.

Charlie turned and stared at the man lying helplessly, just waiting to die. "Mitch." He walked past the group of people and stood at the side of the bed, seeing the ravages of time wreaking its revenge. "It's time to tell the truth, Mitch."

"What is he talking about?" Kevin demanded, coming to stand on the other side of the bed. "That's not even my grandfather's name." Pointing at Suzanne, he added, "She's putting all of you up to this to get back at me!"

"Kevin," Suzanne called out in a weary voice, "for once in your life, just shut up and listen."

"These are not random allegations," Laura stated, as she placed her briefcase on a side table and opened it. "We have proof. I suggest you and your lawyer examine these deeds. Mr. Knueson will explain the radical discrepancies."

Charlie watched as Kevin walked over to the table. Shifting his attention back to Mitch, he looked down and repeated, "It's time for the truth."

The old man stared back at him and the only thing Charlie

could recognize was his watery eyes. He would never forget those eyes . . .

"I'm dyin', Charlie," the man rasped out.

"I know," he answered, trying to keep all emotion out of his voice. "I want the truth, Mitch. Now is the time to tell it." From the corner of his eye, he noticed that Laura and the stenographer were now closer to the bed.

"This is my judgment day? I don't care anymore," he muttered, staring up at Charlie with a look of wonder. He raised a thin shaking hand and pointed. "You're so young . . . all those years ago . . . maybe it's time I cleared my soul, huh? Are you a ghost, Charlie? Is that why you've come? To take me?" His hand fell to his chest. "God, I'm sick of livin' . . . this ain't no life, not like this."

"Just tell the truth now, Mitch. That's all any of us wants."

"But I killed you. I saw you fall. You have to be a ghost."

"Shut up, old man!" Kevin shouted from across the room. "He's senile. He doesn't know what he's saying."

"Tell your client to be quiet, or I'll have him removed from this room," Alina stated, as she walked closer to the bed. She looked at Charlie and nodded. "Please continue."

Mitch almost laughed and then coughed. "Messed up really big, Charlie, huh? But I had it all you know, everything . . . the land, Grace . . . I was a respected man in my time."

"How did you get it, Mitch?" Charlie asked, trying to keep his temper under control.

"Money," Mitch answered, closing his eyes as though remembering. "It's always about money. It can buy you anything, even a doctored deed. Wasn't hard buying a county clerk." He coughed again and when he had his breath under control, he added, "The hard part was convincing Grace to marry me. She always loved you. Couldn't get her to love me like that. She knew, I think, about me getting rid of you. But I did it, Charlie, I lived your dream. I had to get rid of you, don't you see? It was my chance and I took it. And it worked. I was the most successful fruit grower in the county. I had respect and—"

"Shut up, you old fool!"

"That's it," Alina announced. "Get your client out of here."

Mitch watched as Kevin's lawyer led him out of the room. "I'm glad I said it. Got it off my conscience finally." He looked up to Charlie and spoke hesitantly, as though almost afraid of him. "You remember us in the war? How I got gut shot and you saved my life? I've had lots of time . . . lying here in bed . . . waitin' to die, thinkin' about old times. And I come to feel real bad about what I done to you. You gotta believe me. I'm sorry, Charlie . . . for everything. Maybe them preachers are right. I don't want to die with this on my soul. Tell me you forgive me."

He couldn't say anything. He could barely breathe, listening to Mitch, watching the sorrow come into those old eyes. He still wanted to strangle him, yet a part of him felt sorry for how he had ended up, with no one around him who cared whether he lived or died. Maybe that was the justice in it all.

"You gonna take me now, Charlie? I'm tired of this livin'. It ain't worth it no more. I want to rest."

He swallowed hard and whispered, "I'm not a ghost. I'm not the Angel of Death. I can't save your soul, Mitch. I just wanted the truth to come out."

"I told you the truth. Now you gotta end this! You don't know what I go through. Every day, wakin' up, bein' put through torture just to live another day. I want it over. I killed you. Now you take me, and we'll be even."

Charlie looked up to Laura. "Did you get everything you needed?"

She looked at the stenographer and then back up to him. Nodding, she said, "I can take it from here."

Charlie turned away while hearing Laura speak.

"Now, for the record, your real name is Mitch Davies, is that correct?"

"Yes, Mitch Davies. Charlie, where are you going? Take me with you! Don't leave me in hell!"

He looked at Suzanne, who was standing by the door. "Let's get out of here."

She simply nodded and followed him from the room as they heard Laura asking if he remembered the name of the court clerk he had bribed.

Kevin and his lawyer were standing in the hallway and Charlie took a deep breath, realizing it wasn't over yet.

"What do you think you're doing?" Kevin demanded. "How can you be Charles Garrity? This is impossible!"

"I am who I say I am. And you sold my property without my permission."

"The DNA proves it, Kevin," Suzanne said in a strong voice. "You either go into court and have all this become public record . . . Mitch's testimony, Grace's letter, the fake deed, and then you have to make restitution not only to the developers but to all those people who built houses on land that was never yours to sell." She took a deep breath, "Or you make restitution to the proven rightful owner and all this legal mess disappears."

Kevin looked like he might just explode. Turning to his lawyer, he muttered, "This can't be happening."

The smaller man sighed deeply. "Well, something *is* happening, Kevin. We'll need time to go over everything and come to a conclusion."

"We aren't about to take years to unravel this, Kevin," Suzanne said. "Mr. Garrity deserves to be paid for his land. Even your lawyer will agree to that, after hearing your grandfather's testimony. We could always hurry things up by going to the newspapers. It is quite a story about greed and lies, and you know how they'd love to investigate land fraud."

"Are you threatening me?"

"Not at all. I'm just telling you that it would be in your best interest to settle this matter as quickly and as quietly as possible."

Kevin looked at Suzanne with near hatred and then turned his attention to Charlie. "What do you want?"

"I want to be paid for my land," he answered, while admiring the way Suzanne was handling her ex-husband. "I'm sure we can come up with a compromise. I won't demand the entire thirty-three million."

Kevin's mouth dropped.

"Of course, Mr. Garrity, we'll be in touch with your lawyers," Kevin's lawyer piped up.

"You can't be serious?" Kevin demanded, not just of his lawyer but also of Charlie and Suzanne.

"The district attorney's office is involved, Kevin," his lawyer answered. "This is now public record. How public you want to make it is up to you."

"I'll expect to hear from you within the week," Charlie said and then held out his arm to Suzanne. "Shall we go?"

Nodding, Suzanne threaded her hand over his arm and took a deep breath. "Yes. I believe we're finished here."

They had walked no more than five feet away when Kevin called out, "You hate me this much?"

Suzanne stopped and Charlie watched as she turned around.

"I don't hate you, Kevin. Actually, I feel sorry for you, because this time you'll have to take responsibility and grow up. You really don't have any other choice. No one can bail you out of this one. In a weird, strange way, I'm grateful to you for the divorce because now I'm truly free to live my life with integrity." She turned back and took Charlie's arm.

As they walked down the hallway, Charlie wanted to take her into his arms and kiss her soundly. What a woman! She had been right about seeking justice, for as soon as he'd seen Mitch he'd known that what the man was suffering was far worse than anything he could physically do to him. She'd known that and had protected him from his male instinct to destroy. Instead, she'd used her mind . . . and he knew in that moment that he loved her more than he'd ever thought himself capable of loving. She was beautiful, tender, intelligent . . . graceful yet humorous, resilient, yet vulnerable and she made his body throb with desire. Plus she had more decency and goodness in her than anyone else he had ever met. How he wanted to sweep her into his arms and take her away from all this ugliness, but he knew he couldn't act on his fantasy. It wouldn't be fair to either of them, and nothing would be good or last between them until he got rid of this cold, hard stone in his heart. Although his body yearned to melt with hers again, he knew he had to distance himself from anything or anyone connected to Mitch Davies.

And, even though it ripped apart his soul, that included her son.

It was better to leave as he had planned. She would never forgive him if she knew . . .

"We did it, Charlie," she whispered, as he opened the front door for her. "We won."

He smiled sadly. "It appears we did."

"You're not happy," she said, standing in the sunlight and pulling back on his arm.

He looked down at her and squeezed her hand on his arm. "I am happy that it's over, Suzanne, and I'm grateful to you for your brilliant mind and for keeping me from following my first instincts. Once more, you have saved the day . . . and me."

"But I can hear a 'but' coming," she said with a smile.

How he wanted to take her in his arms, yet he knew it would only be selfish. "But I still must leave this place."

"I'll go with you," she said impulsively. "We could make a new beginning somewhere else."

His heart felt like it was breaking apart and he slowly shook his head. "I have to do this alone."

She stared into his eyes and he could tell she wanted to say more. Instead, she nodded and murmured, "We should get back to the house. This is the first time I've left Matty with a baby-sitter."

He started to put his arm around her and she pulled away. He was startled for just a moment and then he recognized her hurt expression. How could he tell her the truth?

In the car on the way back to her house, Charlie tried several times to speak with her, but she only muttered one-word answers and he was grateful when they pulled into the driveway. She immediately opened the door and he watched as she walked onto the porch and entered the house. He turned off the ignition and stared at the small place Suzanne now called home. What had he really won today? An admittance of betrayal? Why didn't it feel better? He would be a wealthy man, able to do whatever he wanted. But what he wanted was Suzanne, and he couldn't have Suzanne without Matty.

He ran his fingers over his face as he accepted his shame. He loved the lad, yet he couldn't stop thinking of him as being a part of Mitch Davies. Everything Suzanne had told him, everything he had read about chromosomes and DNA proved that Matty *was* related to Mitch. How could he hope to raise the child and not resent him? Matty didn't deserve that. He was the innocent in all this, yet the shame of what he was feeling washed over him. He didn't trust himself to be a good father to the child. What if as Matty grew and, like all children, misbehaved? In his heart, would he see Mitch or Kevin?

He knew it was unfair, even shameful, yet he couldn't deny the fear inside of him every time he thought about a future with Suzanne and Matty. He had to leave, to sort this out away from them.

Turning the key in the ignition, he shifted the car into reverse and backed out of the driveway. Maybe there was a way.

19

She knew their time together was coming to a close. She could feel it in the air, in the tension between them. She felt hurt that he seemed able to leave her so easily, and yet at the same time she was almost protective of Charlie. Where would he go? What would he do?

The days led into weeks as they waited for Laura and Kevin's lawyer to negotiate the settlement and Charlie frequently went out at night. He never told her where he was going, but he also never came home slurring his Irish accent either. She was dying to know what he was doing and even got so paranoid as to think he might be seeing another woman. She kept telling herself it was none of her business. That he was free to do as he wished, and yet she was honest enough, at least with herself, to admit that her heart was breaking. Then she would tell herself that she knew from the beginning that he would leave and she had risked it all to be with him. It had been her choice and she had to be responsible for her choices . . . even if it led to heartbreak.

"You're lost in thought."

She turned from the sink and smiled. "I guess I was," she whispered. Why did he have to melt her heart just by being there?

"Do you want to talk about it?"

"Not really." What was there to say? He was leaving.

Charlie leaned against the kitchen doorway and sighed. "You've been avoiding talking to me for almost two weeks now. What can I say to make you feel better?"

"You don't have to make me feel better, Charlie. That's not your job. I . . . I guess I just have to work this out by myself. I mean, I know you're leaving. I know there's nothing I can say to stop that. It's not like I'm asking for a commitment from you or anything." Here she said she didn't want to talk about it, and she was doing just that. Maybe it was time to put it out in the open, for she knew time now was of the essence.

"Suzanne, I don't know that I can be committed to anything right now, except myself. I know it must sound selfish to you, but something's happened to me. I don't know if I can explain it."

Putting water on to boil for tea, she said, "I'd appreciate it if you tried, Charlie. I don't know, maybe I was setting myself up by . . . by feeling the way I do about you." She glanced up at him. "I don't make a habit out of jumping into bed with every time traveler that comes into my life."

Grinning in spite of the serious conversation, he pushed away from the wall and came into the kitchen. "I never thought you did," he answered, taking out two cups and placing them on the counter. "You have to know the night we made love was magical to me, Suzanne. I will always treasure the memory."

"You didn't really want to," she murmured, placing the tea bags into the cups. "I guess I was the one who kept pushing it, even though I knew you might leave."

He placed his hand on her shoulder and it took every ounce of willpower not to lean back against his chest.

"Listen to me," he commanded. "You didn't have to push anything. I wanted you more than you can ever imagine. I tried to stay away from you, knowing it wasn't fair because I always knew I would be leaving. But I couldn't resist you, Suzanne. Don't ever think you had to push anything. I love you. You must know that."

She turned around and faced him. Trying desperately to keep the tears from her eyes, she whispered, "And I love you, Charlie. So why *can't* we make this work? Why do you have to leave?"

He tenderly pushed a curl behind her ear and smiled down to her. "You know how upset I was when I realized I lost everything, even my old life? Well, since then I've realized there's great freedom in that. There are no attachments, nothing holding me. I always thought I needed roots and that's what I was trying to do when I bought that land. Plant roots, dig in deep, and settle down. Then I would have the life I thought was my dream, but you know what I've found out since I've been here in this time?"

"What?" she whispered, staring into his eyes, at his mouth, wanting him to take her into his arms.

"Nothing is forever, Suzanne. Thinking there is anything that lasts forever is an illusion. Anything could happen, at any moment, to change it all. All that's real is *this* moment, right here, right now. I don't know about tomorrow. I only know that here and now I love you more than I thought possible. But I have to leave you and sort things out on my own. I can't make any promises to you about a future, and I don't want you living your life waiting for me. I don't know where I'm going or what I'll be doing. I just know, deep in my soul, I have to leave."

"You love me," she whispered, sniffling back tears.

"Of course I love you," he said, pulling her into his arms. He kissed the top of her head and added, "I think I started to fall in love with you the moment I laid eyes on you by the water. The moment I looked into those beautiful bright eyes."

She wound her arms around his waist and rested her head against his chest. "Love can last forever, Charlie."

He didn't say anything for a long time, just continued to hold her and stroke her back. Finally he whispered, "What *is* forever? I don't think I can answer that. But maybe you're right. Maybe love is the only thing that can last."

The tea kettle whistled and Suzanne reluctantly pulled out of his arms just as the phone rang at the same time. "If you pour the water, I'll get the phone," she said, resenting the intrusion. How she just wanted to stay within his embrace.

She picked up the receiver. "Hello?"

It was Laura, who said she had an offer for Charlie. Holding the phone out to him, she said, "It's for you. It's Laura."

They switched places and Suzanne continued preparing their tea. She tried not to listen and placed both their cups on the table, along with a plate of cookies. Sliding onto a chair, she wrapped her hands around the warm cup and waited.

Within minutes, Charlie hung up the phone and stared at her.

"What?"

He shook his head in disbelief. "Laura said tomorrow she will bring a cashier's check for sixteen million dollars!"

"Oh, Charlie . . . that's wonderful!"

"So much money," he muttered, dropping onto the opposite chair. "It's hard to imagine it."

"I know," Suzanne answered, reaching across the table to touch his hand. "But it was your land, Charlie. You deserve this."

"Sixteen million!" he repeated, still in shock.

Suzanne shook her head. "Well, here we are, both of us wealthy, and both of us depressed about what our futures hold. What a sorry lot we are."

He stared into her eyes. "You were the one who said money can't buy happiness."

"And it can't, Charlie. I know that. I just think we ought to do something to get us out of this mood."

"To celebrate?"

"Yes, to celebrate—that no matter what the future holds, here and now, in this moment, we've acknowledged we love each other. I say that's worth rejoicing over."

"Can we be friends again, Suzanne?" His expression was almost pleading. "These last two weeks have been torture. I couldn't stand it if I went away with you resenting me and—"

"I never resented you," she interrupted. "Maybe I resented the situation, whatever it is that's keeping us from not being together. I won't ask you to explain it further. It's your business. Just go and do whatever it is you have to do. Maybe it's just an act of faith on my part. Surrender to the unknown. I don't know if we'll always be lovers, but I do know we'll always be friends." She reached out her hand and he sighed as he placed his in hers.

Once more they shook to their friendship, and Charlie said, "How was I ever so blessed that you should come into my life?"

She laughed as she withdrew her hand. "Actually *you* came into *my* life, but I feel the same way." Suddenly she became serious. "You know, we are blessed, and I guess you're right. If we stay right here with love, health, friendship, we really are abundant and no amount of money can buy that."

"It's hard to remember that when you're struggling to make ends meet, though. I remember times when I didn't know where my next meal would come from, and now here I am, about to be handed a cashier's check for millions of dollars. I don't feel any different."

"Don't ever let it make a difference in who you are, Charlie. The man that came into my life without anything but the clothes on his back is a man worthy of being. Money won't make you a better person. In fact, it easily corrupts if you aren't careful."

"Mitch."

She nodded. "Kevin." After a few moments of silence, she

placed her elbows on the table and leaned forward. "So where are you going to take me to celebrate?"

"Anywhere you desire, my love."

Charlie gave her that killer smile and it was difficult not to groan. But she had learned her lesson. He wanted freedom. And she found that she valued their friendship as much as their love, so she would be brave. She had made a choice to open her heart and love him, so all she could do now was allow it to break when he left. Yet she knew she'd live through it. She just wasn't sure what was on the other side of it.

"Dinner and dancing? I haven't danced in years," she said, picking up her cup of tea and sipping.

"You? It's been longer for me. Are you sure I won't embarrass you on the dance floor?"

"You would never embarrass me, Charlie. And I can't think of anything I'd rather do than be in your arms while we danced." She watched as he quickly inhaled, as though she was making it more difficult for him. Quickly she added, "I'll have to call Mrs. Hailey to see when she's available to baby-sit Matty."

"Then call, Suzanne. Let's do this as soon as we can."

She didn't need for him to tell her that he would be leaving within days. A part of her thought she could postpone his departure by saying she couldn't get a baby-sitter until the end of the week, but she knew that was childish and she couldn't be deceptive with him. Whatever they had, whatever this relationship was, it was too precious to her not to respect it. She simply had to believe that she could do it, that she could let him go when the time came. "I'll call her now," she said, sliding off the chair and walking to the phone.

She made the call and was a bit disappointed when Mrs. Hailey said she could come the next night. When she hung up the phone, she turned to Charlie and said, "Well, dust off your dancing shoes, Mr. Garrity. We're on for tomorrow night."

"Wonderful." He picked up his cup of tea and held it up in a toast. "Let's make tomorrow a night to remember."

She had to bite the inside of her cheek not to burst out crying.

Standing in front of the mirror in her bedroom, Suzanne surveyed her appearance and was satisfied that she had done all she could. She was grateful that her little black dress had slid over her body, though her breasts certainly filled out the low-cut neckline far more than the last time she'd worn it. She couldn't help but wonder what Charlie was going to think when he saw her in it. The creamy strand of pearls and stud earrings set off her hair nicely and she was thankful the curls seemed to frame her face, instead of sticking out in all directions. Glancing down to her black high heels, she felt like she was going out on her first date.

Actually, it was her first date with Charlie. How odd that they had shared so much together, opened up about their lives and their disappointments, and this night was the first time they would be going out socially. First they became friends, true friends—and it was the friendship that mattered most to her. She didn't know if they would ever again be more than lovers and, even though her heart tightened to think of never being intimate with him again, she knew she cared more that he found whatever it was he was seeking. How else would he ever be happy? And it jolted her to know she wanted his happiness more than she wanted her own.

Maybe that was what unconditional love was about?

She felt that for Matty, a love without any conditions. Was it possible to feel that for an adult? To love without wanting anything in return? She'd have to think about it later. Right now she needed to get downstairs, she thought, as she dropped her lipstick into her purse and turned away from the mirror. Tonight was a time to celebrate.

Mrs. Hailey was talking to Charlie as she came into the

kitchen. He stopped speaking and stared at her with a surprised expression.

"Well, don't you look just lovely," Mrs. Hailey proclaimed, smiling broadly at her.

Suzanne could feel a blush starting at her cheeks as she smiled. "Thank you."

"I agree," Charlie quickly added with a grin of appreciation. "Suzanne, you're beautiful."

Now that blush was spreading all over her face. "And may I say you look quite handsome yourself." He really did look great, dressed in that tailored charcoal suit, white shirt and a burgundy striped tie. She quickly turned her attention to the baby-sitter. "Mrs. Hailey, there are two bottles of milk in the refrigerator. Matty will probably only drink the one, but I wanted to make sure you would be covered, just in case. He usually sleeps right through the night and I wrote the number of the restaurant on the wall calendar if you should need me, along with my cell phone number."

"Oh, we'll be fine," the older woman stated, as she walked them to the front of the house. "He's a little angel."

Suzanne really did like the woman, who had raised six children of her own, yet she suddenly felt nervous about leaving Matty at night and going out to kick up her heels. What if something happened? What if the baby got sick, or—

"Your coat, madam."

She smiled at Charlie, who was holding her black jacket open for her. "Thanks," she murmured, slipping her arms into it. Everything would be all right. She and Charlie deserved this night together. For all she knew it might just be their last.

Ferrini's was an elegant Italian restaurant in Philadelphia. She hadn't been there in years, yet she had remembered that it had great food, great atmosphere, and dancing. She'd made reservations in the morning, remembering that the place had reminded her of an old-fashioned nightclub.

"Are you worried about Matty? Is that why you're so quiet?" Charlie asked, as they drove toward Philadelphia.

She looked at him driving so confidently through the traffic and grinned. "Actually, I was thinking about the place we're going to tonight. I hope you like it."

"I'm with you. How could I not like it?"

Good answer, she thought, unable to stop a wide grin as she continued to look at him. "I can't help but think how comfortable you are driving now, Charlie. You've certainly become accustomed to this time in the last two months."

She watched as he smiled back at her.

"I will say I do like driving these newer machines. It's much easier, once I got over the speed difference." Shaking his head, he chuckled. "What you must have thought of me that first day!"

She joined his laughter. "Well, I found it hard to believe you didn't know how to drive, especially since I was in labor and needing to get to the hospital. But you know what?"

"Hmm?"

"You came through. You were my hero, Charlie."

Staring out the front window, he sighed deeply and held out his hand to her. She took it and he squeezed it tightly.

"Thank you for saying that, Suz. It means a lot to me."

She knew he was thinking about leaving and what she would think of him when he was gone. Deciding tonight they wouldn't dwell on *that* subject, she said, "There's a ramp coming up for the Betsy Ross Bridge. I'll get the toll."

She began to open her purse when his hand rested on top of hers.

"Tonight, Suzanne, *I* am paying for everything. Allow me this."

"All right," she answered, closing her purse. Laura had brought his check in the morning and together they had gone to the Social Security office and then the bank to establish an account. He really was all set now to take off on his own. Again, she stopped herself from going down that path, yet it seemed that's all she could think about.

Charlie paid the toll and pulled onto the bridge as though

he'd done it every day in rush-hour traffic. She thought about all he had been through in the last two months and secretly she was very proud of him and the way he had adapted. He was quite a man in any time, and once again realized she was blessed that he had come into her life. It wasn't a coincidence. She truly believed it all had been meant to happen.

They rode in silence, enjoying each other's company, and Suzanne relaxed as they entered the city. It was so nice to be with someone with whom you didn't have to make conversation. Just being in each other's presence was enough. She looked at the lighted skyline, the familiar buildings, and told herself to memorize this night. It would have to last a long time.

The valet parked the car and Charlie held out his arm to her. His smile was devastatingly sexy. His auburn hair was combed back from his forehead. His clothing was impeccable and he looked like he could pose for a Ralph Lauren ad. What a fortunate woman she was to walk in on his arm.

She looked up at him as they made their way to the entrance. "Thanks for tonight, Charlie."

Gazing down at her, he grinned. "No, thank you, Suzanne. You honor me tonight."

Yeah. She was going to miss him.

She watched as Charlie expertly handed the maître d' money and they were shown to a table by the window, not far from the dance floor. It was obvious in his own time Charlie had been comfortable in social situations, for he now seemed almost like a man of the world. He held out her chair for her and then seated himself. The maître d' unfolded their napkins for them and then handed them the menus. When they were finally alone, they looked at each other across the crisp white linen and the small crystal vase with cymbidium orchids and grinned like two kids who had finally been set free.

"I can't remember the last time I acted so grown-up," Suzanne said with a giggle. "It feels like I've been pregnant or cooped up in the house forever."

"You deserve this night, Suz. Let's order champagne."

"Oh, I don't know if I should." And then she thought about the previous day, when she had spent hours expressing breast milk for Matty. He wouldn't drink two bottles in one night. "Okay," she agreed, unable to hold back her smile. "Let's celebrate!"

Looking very pleased, Charlie held up his hand to signal a waiter and then ordered Dom Perignon. When the waiter left, she couldn't help her expression of surprise.

"I asked Laura what would be a good champagne in this time," he said in answer to her unspoken question.

She was touched that he too wanted this night to be special. A part of her was just sitting back, watching Charles Garrity come alive—not as a time traveler, someone she had to protect and instruct, but as a highly confident man, able to conduct himself with anyone. He was exactly what she wanted, a man who was honorable, kind, responsible, funny, and sexy—and he was soon going to leave her.

He looked out the window to the trees that were wrapped in tiny white lights and whispered, "You made a good choice tonight, Suzanne. I like this place."

"So do I," she murmured, just as the waiter came back with their champagne in a bucket of ice.

Charlie sampled the wine and nodded to the waiter, who then poured it into their glasses. He thanked the man and then picked up his glass as the waiter left their table.

"I would like to make a toast," he announced.

Grinning, Suzanne held up her own glass.

"To the loveliest woman I have ever known, in any time. Thank you for your kindness, your intelligence, your patience, your humor, and especially your love."

She felt tears entering her eyes. "That was beautiful, Charlie. Thank you." They touched glasses and sipped the delicious wine.

"I can never repay you for all you've done for me," he said, placing his glass on the table and reaching inside his suit jacket. He brought out a flat box and Suzanne immediately recognized it as being from Bailey, Banks and Biddle. "Please accept this with my gratitude, and my love."

Her hand was shaking as he placed the box in it. "Charlie, you didn't have to do this."

"Yes, I did. *I* needed to do it. Please accept it, Suzanne."

Biting her bottom lip, she held her breath as she opened the box. "Oh, Charlie," she breathed. Nestled against black velvet was an exquisite gold necklace with a diamond pendant in the shape of a star. The diamonds were perfect and sparkled brilliantly in the dim lights.

"I don't know why, but I was drawn to it. Perhaps because the diamonds reminded me of your eyes—bright, sparkling, the first thing I saw in this time."

"Oh, Charlie, it's absolutely beautiful!" she whispered, taking it out and holding it in her hand. "Thank you."

"You're very welcome. I'm glad you like it."

"I love it," she proclaimed. "As a matter of fact . . ." She placed the necklace back on the box and reached up to unfasten her pearls. "I think I'll wear it right now."

"Allow me." He rose from his chair and came to stand in back of her.

She handed him the necklace and inhaled deeply as his fingers brushed her skin. She felt the weight of the jewelry on her chest, his touch at the back of her neck, and she couldn't help but reach up to capture his hand when he finished fastening the necklace. She looked up to him as he stood beside her. "Thank you, Charlie . . . for everything."

He smiled tenderly at her and squeezed her hand before sitting back down. "It looks lovely against your skin, Suzanne."

"It's stunning, Charlie," she said, touching the diamond star and feeling it take on the warmth of her body. "I'll always treasure it."

The waiter came back and recited the specials and then gave them more time to look over the menus. Suzanne's

mind was reeling and she found it hard to concentrate, but finally settled on the salmon al forno. Closing the menu, she
leaned back in her chair and gazed at the man sitting across
from her.

After a few moments, he looked up from his menu and
smiled. "What?"

She shook her head. "I'm just looking—and appreciat-
ing."

His grin widened. "I think I'll have the chicken abruzzi.
Sounds a bit exotic."

She nodded her approval. "You'll be experiencing so
many new things now, Charlie. Are you prepared?"

"As much as I'll ever be," he answered.

She simply nodded as their waiter came back and they
gave their selections. *Better not to touch on that subject,* she
again reminded herself. Tonight she could pretend that they
had all the time in the world.

The band started to play music and she watched as the
dance floor began to fill. There were couples in their twenties
and couples in their sixties and all ages in between. As she
was watching them, Charlie asked, "May I have this dance?"

Grinning back at him, she nodded, and he came around
the table to pull out her chair. He followed her to the dance
floor and then they faced each other, that moment of indeci-
sion as to whether they actually could dance well together.
Charlie reached out to hold her waist and Suzanne placed her
hand upon his shoulder as he took her right hand in his left.

And then they moved—slowly, sensuously, gracefully, in
an old-fashioned waltz. It was a dance from his time and she
was grateful that she could follow as he led her around the
dance floor, easily maneuvering the space between the other
couples. She stared up into his eyes and he smiled. It was so
right, so natural. She sensed his movements and her body followed as they seemed almost to glide across the dance floor.

She felt very feminine, being held respectfully yet firmly
in his arms. Everything seemed to disappear around her, the

other couples, the band, even the tables. There was nothing but Charlie, the way his green eyes were smiling down to her, the way her breasts brushed his jacket, the clean scent of him, the almost tangible sexual tension between them.

"You're quite a dancer," she murmured, with a smile of happiness she couldn't deny.

"Why, thank you, madam. And may I say the same for you?" For the first time he looked around him to the others on the dance floor. "We are doing quite well, aren't we?"

She laughed. "Yes, we are," she agreed. "But then you're easy to follow."

"You're easy to lead," he whispered back with a sexy grin.

"We are talking about dancing now, aren't we?"

His eyes became a deeper green and he actually moaned as he looked up to the band and tightened his hold on her. "You could tempt a saint, Suzanne," he muttered, just as the music ended.

He held her in his arms and she looked up at him. "Neither one of us is a saint, Charlie. We're just two human beings who love each other in spite of everything."

The other couples were moving off the dance floor and still he held her. "Suzanne . . ."

She simply nodded. "I know. I feel the same way," she whispered.

He broke the embrace and held her hand as they walked back to the table. Neither of them said a word as the waiter brought them their salads. It was as though they didn't want to continue the conversation that had begun at the end of the dance. And yet, trying to avoid it they couldn't seem to hold any other conversation.

"How's your salad?"

"Delicious. Yours?"

"Wonderful." She watched Charlie nod as he continued to eat. Dear God, it was as though a wall was now erected between them. Desperate to find something to talk about, something neutral, she said, "Isn't it nice that couples of so many different ages come here? There's young people and older couples."

Charlie looked around the room and again nodded. "It's a very nice place."

"Oh, for God's sake, Charlie. Why is it so awkward between us?"

"You think it's awkward?"

She nearly groaned. "Of course it is. We keep avoiding the one conversation we should be having."

He was saved from answering as one waiter took away their salads and another placed their dinners in front of them. When they were once more alone, he looked across the table and smiled sadly. "Just for tonight, Suzanne, let's pretend I'm not leaving tomorrow. Let's have a good time."

Her heart felt like it had dropped six inches right into her stomach. "You're leaving tomorrow?"

"Yes, but we have tonight. Didn't we say we were going to celebrate?"

"Tomorrow," she repeated. She shouldn't be stunned. She had known this was coming. Maybe she thought she could put it off, if she put it out of her mind.

He reached across the table for her hand. When she felt his warm skin enclose her fingers, she experienced the burning of tears at her eyes.

"Don't go to tomorrow yet, Suzie. Stay here with me, right now. Let's eat and dance and enjoy ourselves. Let's make memories."

And so here it was, the moment when she could decide to remain miserable or accept his invitation to stay right here with him and enjoy their last night together. His fingers tightened on hers, as though to request an answer. Swallowing down her fears, her questions, even her tears, she forced a bright smile and asked, "What kind of memories are we talking about?"

He laughed and released her hand. "Well, we'll start off by eating this meal, which, by the way, smells delicious.

Then, if you can stand it, I would love to take you back onto the dance floor."

The decision was made. Tonight she would make memories with this man who had captured her heart. "Gimme your best shot, Mr. Garrity," she murmured. "I can stand it."

"What a woman," he said with a chuckle as he picked up his knife and fork.

"You've got that right," she said, following his suit. "Don't ever forget it."

He looked up from his dinner and stared at her. "I could never forget you."

With all her heart, she prayed that was the truth.

20

How she wished they didn't have separate seats. A sports utility vehicle was not exactly a romantic car, and she sure would have liked to sit next to Charlie as he drove them home. Maybe it was the champagne. Maybe it was the dancing, sometimes so slow and so sensual that she could feel his arousal against her belly. She sighed deeply, remembering how she had taught him to slow dance in a more modern style, closing up the space between them. He claimed he liked it, though he wasn't sure it was truly proper. She loved that about him, being so old-fashioned and worrying about her reputation, as though he always wanted her to appear at her best. He was protective of her, and she found she was old-fashioned enough to enjoy it.

They were listening to the radio, a soft jazz station, and Suzanne closed her eyes, wanting to memorize each moment, for this night had turned into the best date of her whole life. Again, she sighed deeply with contentment.

"You sound either sleepy or happy. I can't decide which."

She opened her eyes and looked at the most handsome man she had ever dated. "I'm happy," she whispered to him.

"I'm glad," he answered in a low voice.

"This is the very best date I have ever had," she pronounced. "In my whole and entire life," she added emphatically.

"It is?"

"Definitely," she proclaimed with a nod. "And you are the most handsome man I have ever dated in my whole and entire life."

"Well, thank you."

Her hand touched the jewelry at her neck. "And this is the best gift I ever received in my whole and entire life!"

He laughed. "In your whole and entire life?"

"Yep. My whole and entire life. Tonight was the best of everything."

"You don't think it might be the champagne talking?" he asked.

She shook her head vigorously and when she stopped she had to wait a moment for her vision to clear. "Okay, I might just have had a tad more champagne than I would usually, but I'm happy. I want to stay happy. Don't you want to stay happy, Charlie?" she demanded as he turned onto their street.

"Yes, love. I want to stay happy."

When he pulled into the driveway and turned off the engine, he turned to her. "You should get some rest."

"I don't want to rest," she retorted. "I don't want the best night of my life to end. C'mon, Charlie," she invited, opening her door and sliding off the seat. "Come down to the river with me. Let's not go in yet."

"Suzanne, wait," he called out as she closed her door and started walking down the driveway.

If he said anything else, she didn't hear him. She was already making her way across the street when he caught up with her. Threading her arm through his, she leaned on his shoulder and said, "Let's go down to the water."

"It's dark," he protested. "You're wearing those high heels and you could turn your ankle or—"

"I'll take them off," she interrupted. "Simple." Holding the straps of her heels in one hand, she nudged his arm with her shoulder. "C'mon, Charlie."

"I definitely think the champagne is talking now."

She giggled as they stepped onto the grass. "Oh, don't sound like a disapproving adult. I just want to walk by the river." Less than twenty feet farther they were standing at the edge of the embankment. The Delaware River was dark, with only the lights from the city and the stars in the sky adding to the moonlight. "It's peaceful here," she whispered, leaning her head against his upper arm.

"Yes, it is."

She stared out to the river. "Water is an important element between us."

"You're right," he said, after a few moments. "It's what brought us together."

Neither of them spoke for the longest time, until Suzanne could feel him, not just his body, but his energy, his thoughts. It was intangible, yet powerful, and she slowly turned to face him.

"Will you kiss me, Charlie?"

"Suzanne . . ."

"Please. This is our last night together. I know you're leaving tomorrow. I know all the reasons why you think it would be better if you didn't. But I'm asking that right here and now we forget all that. Don't you want to kiss me?"

He groaned and looked up to the stars for a moment. Gazing down at her, he whispered, "Woman, have you no mercy?"

"No. Not tonight. I love you, Charlie. I may never again be able to say that to you. I know you love me. Maybe it is the champagne talking right now, or maybe it's just loosened my tongue. It doesn't matter. What does is that we have the perfect setting to end a perfect night. And I so want a goodnight kiss."

She could see him smiling as he raised his hands to cradle the sides of her face. She dropped her shoes to the grass. He stared into her eyes for the longest time and then slowly, deliberately, he kissed her forehead. His touch was almost reverent, before raising her face and lowering his mouth to hers. His lips barely grazed hers in the softest kiss and then he pulled back slightly and inhaled her, before claiming her lips once again. This time the kiss deepened and passion entered into it. His hands slipped from her face and he held her shoulders, pulling her into him.

She gladly surrendered. It was what she wanted, what she had been wanting for over two weeks, and she clasped him tighter to her, running her hands over his back, his shoulders, through his hair. His tongue entered her mouth for a quick exploration and then he slowly, gently, pulled back.

"Lord above, Suzanne, what you can do to a man."

"Oh, Charlie," she breathed, resting her forehead on his chin as she tried to recover. "That kiss—"

"It was the best? In your whole and entire life?" he supplied with a chuckle.

She looked up at him and laughed along with him. "Why, yes it was. You're making fun of me."

"No, I'm not. I'm highly flattered. And I would agree with you."

"It was the best?"

Holding her in his arms, he nodded.

"In your whole and entire life?"

"In my whole and entire life," he repeated before again kissing her on the forehead. "Now, come along back to the house. It's late and Mrs. Hailey will want to go home."

She sighed deeply and snuggled against his chest as his arms encircled her. "I don't want this night to be over," she murmured, trying to keep the disappointment out of her voice. "Sometimes, I get so tired of being a grown-up. Doing the *right* thing. I wish I could just stay out here by the river with you like I would have done as a teenager."

"You would have?"

"Oh yes," she breathed against his chest. "I would have blown my curfew and remained here for as long as you wanted me."

"Sounds scandalous," he answered with a hint of laugh.

"Hmm . . . well, I am a grown-up now and I can make my own choices. I would be scandalous tonight, Charlie."

He tightened his arms around her. "I don't think I could take it, Suzanne. I can't love you again and then leave you in the morning. Don't you think my leaving is just as hard on me?"

She shook her head. "You seem to be able to do it so easily."

He pulled back on her shoulders and made her face him. "Listen to me carefully. Leaving you is the hardest thing I've ever had to do. Nothing compares to it."

"Then why? Please answer me. *Why* are you doing it?"

His face seemed to harden. "I've told you. I have to get away from here, from all these memories. I have to settle things in my mind, make sense of it all, find my place. I can't do that here with you."

"Then tell me: Will you come back?"

"I can't answer that. I don't know."

His face held a painful expression, yet she couldn't stop now. "Will you send for me?"

"Suzanne, please don't make this any harder on either of us. I don't want you waiting around for that. It isn't fair."

"Will you make love to me tonight?" She didn't care if it was the champagne, she needed answers. Now was the time to be bold.

"I can't. I told you I can't love you and then leave you tomorrow. I would feel like my heart is being ripped out from my chest." He grabbed her into his embrace again and whispered into her hair, "Believe me, it's better this way, for both of us."

"Then hold me tonight, Charlie. Let me fall asleep in your arms. Give me that."

"Come on, let's go home now," he said, picking up her heels from the grass and then sliding his arm around her waist.

"My magical night is over. It's time to be a grown-up," she murmured, staring across the street to her house.

"You're one of the best grown-ups I've ever met."

She glanced up at him as he added with a sly grin, "Yes, in my whole and entire life, Suzanne."

Leaning her head against his arm, she sighed deeply. "We've profoundly altered each other's lives, Charlie. Maybe this is what is meant by soulmates."

"I haven't heard that term—*soulmates*."

"Mates, like deep friends. Friends of the soul. That's what we are."

"I'll accept that," he said, leading her across the street. "Now, let's allow Mrs. Hailey to get home."

"I hope Matty was good for her," Suzanne muttered, still staring at the house. As much as she loved her son, she just wasn't ready to resume her motherly role.

"He's a good baby."

"Yes, he is. He's going to miss you."

She felt Charlie's arm stiffen with her words and she thought he was going to miss her son. How could he not? He had been present when Matty came into this world and had been a part of his life ever since. Of course Charlie was going to miss Matty, too.

They opened the front door and Mrs. Hailey rose from the sofa. "Did you have a good time?"

"A wonderful time," Suzanne pronounced, slipping her arms out of her jacket and draping it over a chair. "How was Matty?"

"An angel. Drank most of the bottle and he's been asleep ever since. You certainly were blessed with that child, Suzanne."

"I know. All the horror stories of children not sleeping through the night, and he started in less than a week."

"Oh, my," Mrs. Hailey said, as she walked over to where Charlie was holding out her sweater. "What a gentleman. Thank you," she added, putting her arms into the sweater and adjusting the edges over her chest.

"Yes, Charlie is quite a gentleman, isn't he?" Suzanne couldn't help grinning at him as she opened her purse and took out some money. She handed it to Mrs. Hailey. "Thank you for sitting on such short notice. I really appreciated the evening out."

"I'm glad you had a good time," the woman said, putting the money into her sweater pocket and picking up her purse.

"It was the best time," Suzanne couldn't help saying.

"In her entire life, Mrs. Hailey," Charlie added with a grin.

"Really?"

"Yes," Suzanne answered, impulsively reaching up to her neck. "I received this gift tonight." She was just so proud of the necklace Charlie had presented to her.

Mrs. Hailey came closer and inspected it. "My, my, what a lovely piece." She nodded her head toward Charlie and whispered, "I'd keep him, if I were you."

Suzanne stared into the woman's eyes and tried to smile. "Good idea," she whispered back. If it were only that simple.

Charlie opened the door for the woman, who took her car keys out of her purse. "Call anytime, dear. Your Matty is a pleasure to watch."

"Thank you," Suzanne answered, then as the door closed she threw her purse onto a chair. Her mood felt like it was plummeting. Even Mrs. Hailey recognized Charlie was a keeper. Shaking the thought out of her head, she said, "I'm going to check on the baby."

"I'll close up down here."

She simply nodded and headed for the stairs.

Matty was sleeping soundly and she left his room to go into her own. Staring at the bed, she closed her eyes for a moment and then shut the door. She undressed slowly, carefully hanging up her dress and dropping her underwear into the hamper in the closet. She reached for a nightgown and then stopped herself. She was about to pick a white satin gown, one she hadn't worn in almost a year. What did she think she was going to do? Seduce Charlie? One last round of lovemaking before he left her? Funny, she didn't even want it now. Obviously, she had sobered. Instead of the sexy white one, she chose a thin cotton one with straps. It wasn't sexy. It almost looked virginal.

She heard Charlie come up the stairs and enter his room. Walking into her bathroom, she washed her face, brushed her teeth and left the necklace in place. She didn't know when she would take it off, or how she could bring herself to do it. Right now, she wanted it against her skin. He had bought it for her and she lovingly touched the diamond star with her fingers.

It really had been a wonderful night. He'd made it so, going out of his way to show her a good time. Leaving the bathroom, she sat on the edge of her bed wondering what she should do. After about ten minutes, she walked to her door and opened it. Without further thought, she crossed the hallway and knocked on his door.

A few moments passed and she felt her heart thudding against her rib cage. He opened the door and stared into her eyes.

"I . . . I wanted to thank you again," she whispered. "For tonight, for my necklace. For everything."

He smiled at her with tenderness. "You're very welcome. And thank you. I had a great time."

A few tense moments passed and then she simply nodded. "Well, good night then. I'll see you in the morning."

"Of course."

"Okay. Sleep well," she said, turning back to her own bed-room.

"You too."

Before he could close the door, she spun around. "Char-lie!"

"What?"

She held out her hand. "Sleep with me? Please? Nothing more. Just hold me tonight." It took every ounce of courage for her to say that. She had never felt so vulnerable in her life.

As though recognizing how raw the moment was for her, he reached out for her hand and clasped it firmly in his. "It would be my honor, Suzanne."

She almost cried and had to bite her bottom lip to control her emotions as she led him into her room. Climbing into bed, she realized she didn't even want him to make love to her. She felt like a young girl who needed comforting. She waited until he came into bed and held out his arms. Sighing, she slid into them, resting her head on his chest as he stroked her hair.

"I'm going to miss you so much," she whispered into the dark room, no longer able to hold back the tears.

"I know, Suzanne, and I'm going to miss you, too," he whispered back, stroking her shoulders.

"What am I going to do without you?" she sniffled.

"Shh . . . you're going to continue to be the strong woman you are, the great mother you are."

"I'm not a strong woman," she protested, unable to stop the tears from falling onto his chest. "I don't feel strong at all."

"Well, you are," he answered firmly. "I've watched you these two months and you are one of the strongest women I have ever known. You're going to be all right, Suzanne."

Hating that she sounded so pathetic, she simply nodded, even though her heart felt like it was breaking. She had lost so many people she'd held close. Her parents. Kevin. Ingrid. And now she had to let Charlie go. It felt too heavy, too much to carry and suddenly she was exhausted. Every muscle in her body just seemed to let go. Maybe it was the champagne, or the emotion.

He must have felt her surrender, for he whispered, "That's right. Just relax and close your eyes. You're going to be okay, Suzanne."

She snuggled next to him, inhaling the clean scent of him, feeling his strong muscles surrounding her. For this moment, she felt safe within his embrace. She wouldn't think about tomorrow. Right here, she felt like she was finally home.

He continued to stroke her hair and her shoulders, relaxing her until he could hear her steady breathing. Staring into the darkness, Charlie finally allowed himself to experience the emotions that were holding him hostage. He didn't know how he was going to summon the strength to leave her in the morning, when every instinct was urging him to awaken her with a kiss of invitation. But he knew that would be cruel to both of them. For the first time in his life he had experienced love, real love, and he had to leave it until he settled the unrest within his heart. His guilt was nearly suffocating. How could he love Suzanne so deeply and yet be so afraid of her son? She would never understand. He didn't understand himself. All he knew was that he needed space to figure it all out.

More than anything he wanted to make a life with Suzanne, yet to tell her that would be unfair. She had suffered more than her share and he wouldn't add another disappointment to it. Better to leave her now, than years later, if he couldn't straighten out his head. He knew it was him, never her and Matty. He was the one with the problem.

He just didn't know if he could raise Mitch's great-grandson.

Holding Suzanne close, he kissed the top of her head and whispered, "Forgive me, my love. I'm not the man you think. I'm not that strong."

She awoke the next morning to sunshine and a dull, throbbing headache. Squinting her eyes, she looked at the clock and couldn't believe it was almost nine. Throwing back the covers, she dragged herself out of bed and then stopped to turn back and look at it.

Charlie had slept with her, or at least she'd fallen asleep with Charlie next to her. Where was he? Why hadn't Matty woken up yet? She hurried into the nursery and saw the crib was empty. Knowing Charlie had taken him, she then turned back to her bedroom and quickly used the bathroom. Dressed in her robe, she walked down the hallway and stopped when she passed Charlie's room. The bed was neatly made. The room appeared empty of anything personal. So he was packed already. Ignoring the sinking feeling in her heart, she quietly made her way down the stairs and into the kitchen.

She could hear Charlie's voice in the sun room and tiptoed the remaining distance. Not wanting to disturb the scene, she leaned against the wall and watched the man she loved holding her son and talking to him.

"And remember when her nose starts to get red, she's about to cry, so be patient with her. She's got a lot on her shoulders now, but you're one lucky lad to have her for a mother. Watch out for her for me. Give her lots of love and make her laugh whenever you can. She's got the best laugh. She'll probably spoil you, but you'll have to be strong yourself. Don't give her too much trouble, for she has enough to deal with right now. Just be a good lad, all right?"

She sniffled and Charlie looked up with an expression of embarrassment. "See?" he asked the baby, holding up Matty. "Look at her nose."

Grinning, Suzanne walked into the sun room. "I can't believe he's being so good without being fed yet."

"Oh, he's had his breakfast. There was the other bottle of milk in the refrigerator. I heated it and gave it to him. He's quite content," he proclaimed, handing over the baby.

Suzanne held her son to her chest and patted him on the back. "Thanks," she said to Charlie and then smiled into his eyes. "I keep thanking you for everything and it still doesn't seem enough."

"It's enough," Charlie answered, standing up and straightening his shirt. "No more thanks. We both know how the other feels."

"Well then, I'll insert a final one for last night. It was wonderful to fall asleep in your arms."

He looked directly back into her eyes and said, "It was wonderful to hold you."

Neither of them said anything for the longest time, until he added, "Your nose is starting to get red again."

She laughed, realizing she would never be able to hold back her emotions from him. She turned toward the kitchen and spied a long green duffel bag in the corner. "When are you leaving?" she whispered with a feeling of dread.

"In a few minutes. I was waiting for you to awake."

"So quickly?"

"No point in dragging it out."

Knowing she had been doing exactly that ever since he'd told her he was leaving, she simply nodded as she held Matty closer. She watched as he walked to the foyer closet and picked up the leather jacket he had bought a month ago when they'd gone clothes shopping for him. Coming back into the kitchen, he dropped it on his duffel bag and then turned to her.

His smile was tender, yet sad, as he held his arms open.

She quickly filled them as she rested her head on his chest. "I won't say good-bye, Charlie. I can't." She didn't want to be strong. She wanted to rant and wail and beg him to stay.

His arms encircled her and Matty and he lowered his head to kiss the top of hers. "All right. No good-byes."

"Be safe," she whispered, blinking back the tears. "Find whatever it is you have to, and then come back for us."

His arms tightened around them. "Take care of each other." He released them and then gently cupped her chin to raise her face. Smiling down at her, he added, "You're the best woman I've ever known. That won't ever change."

In spite of everything, she grinned. "You just remember that, Mr. Garrity. We love you and we'll be waiting."

"Don't," he whispered. "I can't promise anything."

"So who asked?"

Neither of them said anything until Charlie nodded. He released them and turned to pick up his things. Slipping his jacket through the strap of the duffel bag, he hoisted the thing to his shoulder and looked back at them. "I don't know what to say," he whispered.

She could see he was trying to control his own emotions and realized she would have to be strong. "I know," she whispered back, hating the fact that no matter how hard she tried, tears were brimming at her eyes and she simply had to blink to clear them.

It was as though their hearts were speaking for them as they continued to stare into each other's eyes, conveying what the last two months had meant to them, how they had come to know each other as friends, as lovers, as soulmates, and how much it had affected them, how they would never again be the same. Love had altered them. Finally, as though verbalizing what each was thinking, he muttered, "In my whole and entire life, Suzanne."

Her lips were trembling as she whispered with a nod, "Mine too, Charlie."

He cleared his throat, nodded, and turned toward the door.

Suzanne wiped at her eyes and watched the most amazing human being, this gift of love, slowly open the front door and walk out of her life.

She held Matty closer, letting the tears come, feeling like her heart was splitting open as she nearly stumbled to the front window. She saw him walking down the driveway, not looking back, his shoulders straight, his gaze forward.

"Oh God," she muttered, clutching her son with one hand

and raising the other to the window for support. How was she supposed to let him go in her heart? She couldn't.

Matty started whimpering, as though sensing her emotions, and she patted his back while straining her neck to see the last glimpse of Charlie before the limbs of the trees obscured her vision. "I won't say good-bye," she murmured, nearly choking for the sobs that were demanding release.

When she could no longer see him, she continued to stare out the window feeling as though the sunshine had gone out of her life. Matty turned in her arms and reached out for her face. His hand touched her slippery cheek and he made a noise, an unintelligible noise, yet as she turned her face and looked at him smiling a toothless grin, she couldn't help but grin back. "We're gonna make it, sweetie. I don't know how, but we will. He'll come back. I know it. Someday he'll come back into our lives."

And she believed it with all her heart.

At that moment, she simply had to believe in something. Why not love? It had fooled her before, but this time she was willing to risk it all. Charlie was worth it.

He walked up to the shiny new red automobile that was parked around the block. The door on the passenger side was opened and the back of the seat pulled up. Without saying anything, he flung his duffel bag into the back and then got inside.

"Are you okay?"

He took several deep breaths to steady his nerves, to still his thudding heart, to stop himself from crying like a young boy. Leaving Suzanne was one of the hardest things he'd ever done, yet he knew it was for the best. At least he kept telling himself that.

"I'm fine, Jen. Let's get going."

"You got it, Charlie," the young woman stated, starting the powerful engine and slipping the transmission into gear. "California, here we come!"

As the car pulled away from the river, Charlie knew it was going to hurt. He'd said it to Suzanne. He'd known it, but he never realized how much of his heart he was leaving behind. God, he loved her.

21

"Geez, Charlie, we're almost halfway there, and you've said maybe a hundred words the whole trip. I didn't mind it the first three days 'cause I know you're hurting, but this is turning into one long ride if you won't talk about it."

"There's nothing to say," he muttered, gazing out the window at the scenery. Everything looked the same to him. Interstates filled with cars. Billboards lining the sides of roads in smaller towns. It was depressing, and with each mile that separated him from Suzanne he felt even more sick to his stomach.

"Of course there's something to say," Jen shot back, as she easily maneuvered her way around a slower car. "You don't just leave the woman you love and pretend to be all stoic about it. If you talked it out, you might just feel better."

"You talk enough for both of us," he mumbled, crossing his arms over his chest and staring at the flat landscape of Texas that seemed to go on forever.

"I heard that," Jen remarked. "And I'm not even going to

get mad at you for it, since you're in such a funk. I mean, how could I when you bought me this great car? I still can't get over it. Why won't you tell me where you got the money for it?"

"I've already told you. It was a business deal that finally paid off. Why do you have to question everything?"

"Because I'm female," she answered with a slight laugh. "Besides, we're friends, aren't we? Friends tell each other things."

"There are some things I would prefer to keep to myself." Maybe it would have been easier to take a train, he thought as he shifted his position and stretched his arms. At the time he had made the decision, it seemed rational to ask Jen to drive him. She wanted to get to California. It was far enough away from New Jersey. She had a driver's license and he had the money to make it happen. Now he was questioning everything, especially leaving Suzanne.

"Okay, so you'll keep it all to yourself, like that makes you strong or something. To me, it's just plain stupid to bottle everything up." She looked at him for a second. "It's going to come out one day, you know. Better to have it happen with me than in some bar fight where you'll really get into trouble."

"I don't fight in bars," he remarked, wishing she would just shut up, for he had seen his share of fisticuffs in his younger days and didn't want to admit it.

"Okay, we won't talk about Suzanne or how much you're missing her right now. Let's talk about something else."

"Thank you."

"What do you plan on doing when we reach California? You going to get a job?"

"I don't know." He really didn't. He had no idea what he was going to do. California was just the farthest he could get from the situation in New Jersey.

"How can you have no plans?"

"Easily. Do you have a plan?"

"Yeah. I've already told you I'm going to look for work as soon as we arrive. I don't care what it is. I'll even wait tables until I figure it out. You have to have a plan, Charlie."

"Why?"

"So you know what you're going to do. It's just the way it's done."

"Who said?"

She shrugged. "You can't go through life without a plan, without looking toward the future."

"Why?"

"Because then you'll just be—I don't know—drifting through life."

"Does having a plan make you feel safer?" he asked, suddenly interested in the topic for a change. He also felt a surge of impatience.

"Of course it makes me feel safer."

"Believe me, Jen, all your plans could change within a moment and then what will you do?"

"I'll make a new plan," she answered.

"I used to think that way once. Then I learned I'm not in charge."

"Who is, then, if not you?"

He shrugged. "I can't answer that. I only know that something, something I can't control, can enter my life at any time and turn it upside down. And there's not a damn thing I can do about it but go along for the ride and try to stay sane at the same time."

"What's happened to you, Charlie? You sound like a man who's lost faith in life."

"Faith?" He almost laughed. "I only know how to be faithful to myself now. When anything can change at any moment, I can only control the choices I make along the way."

"I can understand that, but something's happened to you, something that's shaken your world. What is it?"

"You wouldn't believe me if I told you. And I wouldn't blame you."

"Try me."

He shook his head. "You're a good woman, Jen, but I'd rather not discuss it."

She chuckled. "Darn, and it was turning out to be a good conversation." After a few minutes of silence, she said, "You know who you remind me of, Charlie?"

He knew the silence was too good to last. Sighing, he asked, "Who?"

"Luke Skywalker."

"Who?"

She laughed. "Don't tell me you've never seen *Star Wars!*"

"There's a lot I haven't seen. What is it?"

"It's a movie. You should see it. At least the first one."

He stared at the front window to the rows of automobiles, wishing they would get out of Texas and he could get out of this car. Finally, he said, "Okay, so why do I remind you of this person?" It was at least something to think about, besides what he'd left behind him.

"Well, technically Luke Skywalker isn't a person. He's a character in a movie," Jen said with a grin, obviously happy to enter into the conversation. "Anyway, he spends the whole time in the movie trying to discover something called the Force, and trying to learn how to use it. At the end of the movie, he's on this critical mission to save the planet. Don't ask me to explain the whole movie. Just rent it. So, anyway, he's in this hi-tech fighter and—"

"What's that?"

"What?"

"A high-tech fighter?"

She glanced at him. "A fighter plane. What planet are you from?"

"If I told you, you wouldn't believe me."

"Okay. Let's get back to the story," she said with a frown. "I'll think about that remark later. So Luke is in this fighter plane, trying to save the planet, when all of sudden he remembers the Force and he hears his mentor's voice telling him to trust it. So he removes all his high-tech equipment and starts flying by the seat of his pants."

"What does that mean, flying by the seat of his pants?"

"It means he begins to trust himself and his instincts. Everything he's depended upon in the past doesn't work anymore and so he's got to start trusting the Force within him. That's why you remind me of him, Charlie. That's what it sounds like you're doing now. Flying by the seat of your pants. Everything you once believed seems to have failed you, yet you said there is something, something you can't name, directing your life now. You don't have any plans. You're flying by the seat of your pants now."

He thought about her words for a few moments. "What is this force?"

She shrugged and grinned. "It's unnameable. Just *is*. Maybe it's the force of life. I don't know. I'm just trying to tell you the end to a movie and why you remind me of one of the characters."

He looked back out the window. "I'll watch the movie."

"Yeah, it will explain it better. You hungry?"

"I don't know. I guess I could eat something."

"Let's get off at this exit and find a place." She turned on her signal and changed lanes. When they were off the interstate, she drove for less than a mile when she pointed to the right. "How about The Singing Spurs Bar and Grill?"

"Sounds fine to me," Charlie answered, and his stomach tightened with hunger at the prospect of food.

Pulling into the parking lot, Jen shifted into park and looked up at the place. "Can you believe this name? Funny, huh?"

His shrugged as he opened his door. "It's Texas. Sounds about right."

They were shown to a table in the restaurant section and even before settling into a booth, he knew what he was going to order. The aroma of steak and fried potatoes was making his mouth water.

"What can I get you to drink?" the waitress asked as soon as they were seated.

Charlie glanced up at an older woman wearing a uniform with a fancy handkerchief on the left side of her chest. Smiling, he said, "I'll have a Guinness."

"Don't have no Guinness. Got Miller. Miller Light. Coors. Coors Light. Michelob. Michelob Light. Bud. Bud Light. Lone Star—"

He held up his hand. "Just bring me anything cold."

"Okay, and you, miss?"

"I'll have a Sprite."

"Got it," the woman said, writing it down and then sticking her pencil behind her ear. "Be right back with your drinks and then I'll take your order."

"Thanks," Jen said with a big smile, before opening her menu. "Feels good to be out of that car," she added, looking over her choices.

He sat back against the cushioned booth and stared at her. She certainly looked tired, yet she always sounded happy and fresh. Maybe it was her younger age. Maybe life hadn't sucker-punched her yet. "Sorry that you have to do all the driving, Jen. I know you're tired."

She looked up and grinned. "Hey, that was part of the deal. If you don't have a license I'll drive. Rather do that than get pulled over in some small town and try to talk our way out of a summons. I don't get it, though. You had to have had a license once, right? Did you lose it?"

He shook his head. "Never had one."

"That doesn't make sense for someone your age. How could you have gotten this far through life without one?"

He merely shrugged.

"So all those nights we met, planning this trip, you were illegal?"

"I suppose I was," he answered.

"Well, you drive good enough. You can get one when we're out in California."

"I can?"

"Sure. There's a whole new life out there waiting for us." She closed her menu and leaned her elbows on the table. Tapping her red nails, she added in an excited voice, "We're almost there, you know. Beyond the point of no return. A few more states and then sunny California." She sighed and her grin widened. "Thanks, Charlie. I can't say it enough."

"I hope you find everything you desire there, Jen."

"I just know I will," she answered as the waitress came back with their drinks. They gave her their order and then Jen picked up her glass. "To California!"

He raised his mug of beer. "To California," he said, wondering whether expectations were practical. Knowing he hadn't been much of a traveling companion, he added, "May all your dreams come true."

"Yours too, Charlie."

Halfway through their meal, a woman was seated across from them. She had a baby with her who was put into a high chair and she talked to it constantly. Charlie couldn't help staring and it wasn't until Jen pointed it out that he tore his gaze away.

"You're thinking about Suzanne again, aren't you?"

He just shook his head.

"Why don't you tell me about her? Talk about it, Charlie."

His jaw hardened. "I can't." He didn't want to say he was afraid if he did, what was left of his heart might just disintegrate.

She was seated in the sun room, holding Matty asleep in her arms, staring out the window to the garden and the birds, and she knew she had everything to be happy about, yet she simply couldn't stop the tears. She felt so miserable and had no one to turn to, to cry out her anguish to, to commiserate with now that she was alone. God, she was sick of crying. She'd started when Charlie had left and now, three days later, she was still at it. All she had was the memories and she wanted once more to kick herself that she'd never taken a single picture of Charlie, even though she had meant to dozens of times. Maybe it was best this way, she thought, as she placed Matty into his bassinet. At least she wasn't clutching some picture to her chest as she fell apart. Now that would really be pathetic.

"Right," she whispered to herself. "Like you're not pathetic now."

She walked into the kitchen and stood, staring at the refrigerator. She wasn't even hungry, yet knew she had to eat for Matty's sake. How was she supposed to nourish a child when she had no appetite? Maybe it was time to wean Matty. She'd wanted to wait a few more months, but she just didn't have the same enthusiasm now—for anything. Secretly, she knew she was depressed and it was unfair to her child, yet she didn't know how to get out of it. Everything she did, everywhere she looked, reminded her of Charlie.

Something inside of her seemed to say *get out of the house*. It would take such effort, she thought, and Matty was sleeping. Again, the urge came to get out. Shrugging, knowing she simply couldn't shut herself in any longer, she picked up her purse, the baby, and headed for the door. Maybe just driving would help.

She fastened Matty into his car seat. Bless his heart, he didn't awaken. Climbing into the driver's seat, she turned on the engine and stared out the window. Where was she going to go? What was Charlie doing right now? Did he catch a ride? It wasn't until after he'd left that she'd realized he had been walking. She could have offered to drive him to the train station.

Just go, the voice inside her urged, interrupting her self-recrimination.

Shifting into reverse, she backed out of the driveway not

knowing where she was headed. It wasn't until she had reached the bridge over the creek that she knew where she wanted to go. Having a destination, she felt determined to reach her favorite spot, the place where she had pulled Charlie out of the water. Her spirit felt lighter as she turned onto the bumpy back road. She took it gently so Matty wouldn't awaken, and it wasn't until she reached the water that she saw another car already parked there.

Then her brain refused to believe what her eyes were seeing.

Seated on a blanket was Ingrid, staring out at the water.

Oh, isn't this just perfect, she thought as the anger surged up within her. First this woman takes her husband, and now she takes her favorite place. It wasn't fair!

Ingrid heard the car's engine and turned around. When she recognized Suzanne, she stood up and stared at her, as though waiting for her to turn off the car and get out.

Suzanne took several deep breaths to calm down. How totally unfair was this? And she was about to tell Ingrid the same thing! Opening up her door, she got out and left it open so she could hear Matty if he awoke. She walked up to the woman who had once been her best friend and said, "This is my place, Ingrid. I resent you being here."

Ingrid nodded, and pulled down the white blouse she wore outside her pants to cover her pregnancy. "I know. That's why I've come here every day. I kept hoping you would show up."

"Why?" Suzanne demanded. "What can we possibly have to say to each other?"

Ingrid took a deep breath. "We need to make peace, Suzanne. We're going to be family in some fashion, and somehow I need to mend the breech between us."

Suzanne saw the tears brimming at her eyes and looked out over the water. "I don't know if that's possible," she murmured.

"I don't either," Ingrid said. "But I know I have to try."

Suzanne didn't say anything as she continued to stare out

at the water, watching as the sun's reflection became almost mesmerizing.

"I'm scared, Suzanne."

Blinking to break the spell, she turned her head and looked at Ingrid. Tears were streaming down her cheeks. "Scared of what? The pregnancy?"

"That too. I mean, here I am with this life inside of me and I can't seem to stop crying. I'm worried about everything. I keep gaining weight. I gained eight pounds by my last doctor's visit."

In spite of everything, Suzanne had to bite the inside of her cheek not to smile. "That's normal. Wait till the end."

"If I keep gaining weight like this, I'll weigh over two hundred pounds! Even Kevin says I'm gaining too much."

She had to grind her back teeth not to growl at the mention of his name. "Forget what Kevin says. He's never given birth to another human being, nor was he very supportive of me when I did."

"He's about ruined, you know."

"Ruined? How is that?"

"Not financially. Emotionally. You did a job on him, Suzanne."

"I didn't do anything. I followed the law and the paper trail. That land was never his to sell."

"I understand," Ingrid said, wiping away the tears on her cheeks. "In a way, I have to admire you, but that doesn't make him any easier to live with now."

Suzanne shrugged. "It's your choice, Ingrid," she said, not believing that she was actually standing here talking this long.

"He's the father of this child and—"

"So what?" Suzanne demanded. "There's no law that says you have to stay with someone who's making you miserable."

"I . . . love him. It's not his fault."

"Of course it's his fault. He was greedy. He's always been

greedy, and now that you can't fix everything in his life he's going to make you pay? Can't you see that he's like a vampire who will suck your energy because he doesn't have enough of his own to survive? That's not love, Ingrid. That's codependence. You want to spend the rest of your life trying to save him from his disappointments?"

Ingrid started crying again and Suzanne swallowed down the thick lump in her own throat. "I'm sorry," she whispered. "It's none of my business."

Shaking her head, Ingrid muttered, "You sounded like my friend just then, like you cared about me. I've missed you, Suz. I . . . I don't have any other friend now, not one I can talk to about this."

Suzanne almost laughed. "Well, join the club," she said, sniffling back her tears. "Ain't this pathetic? Friends of the friendless."

Amid her tears, Ingrid chuckled. "We used to call ourselves that when we first got to college."

"Well, this isn't college anymore, Ingrid. This is life, and sometimes, life is really, really tough."

"At least you've got Charles. He seems stable enough."

"Think again. He's gone."

"Why?"

She couldn't face her. Wrapping her arms around her waist, she sighed. "Seems he had to find himself after that mess with Mitch in the hospital. I don't know where he is, or if he'll ever come back."

"Oh, Suzanne . . . I'm so sorry. He seemed—I don't know—stable. And he was so protective of you. I mean, you could just see how much he loved you in his eyes whenever he looked at you."

"Well, he still had to leave, so I don't know anything anymore."

Neither of them said a word until Ingrid murmured, "I guess it was a lot to ask of any man."

Suzanne turned her head to look at her. "What?"

"Well, if he stayed with you he'd be raising Mitch's great-grandson, wouldn't he?"

"So?"

"So I don't imagine there's any good feelings between them, do you?"

She stared at Ingrid, watching the way the wind played with her hair, and yet her mind seemed to be working at warp speed as she put it all together. The way he looked at Matty, so sad. The way his muscles stiffened when she spoke about him. Charlie resented her son? It couldn't be possible, yet he really couldn't give her an answer when she'd asked why he had to leave. He wouldn't even discuss her and Matty going away with him. It was the only thing that made any kind of sense and as it rang true within her heart, she knew she couldn't even blame Charlie for it. Mitch had taken everything away from him.

"My God, Ingrid—what if you're right? I mean, I know he loves me. I know in some way he loves Matty, but there's no way to fix this. This is about genes, and I had to be the one to teach him about it!"

"Teach him?"

She shook her head, as though that didn't matter. What did was that she finally felt like she had an answer. She now knew why Charlie had to leave, what he couldn't tell her. She looked out to the water again and called out to him in her mind.

Take all the time you need to settle this in your heart. I understand.

"Suzanne?"

She blinked and looked to her side. "Thank you, Ingrid. You've helped me more than you'll ever know."

"So are we . . . friends again?" The question was hesitant, almost shyly asked.

Suzanne took a deep breath, feeling a weight lift from her

soul. "Let's say this is the beginning of something new. I don't know what it'll become, if anything, after today. I only know that I'm glad you were here."

"So am I."

"Be happy," she whispered. "Even if it means being alone. Think about it. We're healthy. We have abundance in our lives. Even without men, we have more than most. Why are we standing here by the water and crying?"

She didn't know if she was talking to Ingrid or to herself. It didn't matter. It was good advice, and she was taking it.

22

Jen slid into the chair across from him, looking tanned and healthy and happy. "Oh, sorry I'm late," she said with a breathless smile. "Last-minute catering party in Beverly Hills. Had to supply all the plants and deliver them and then got back to the apartment with just enough time to shower and change. So how are you?"

Charlie laughed. "I'm doing pretty well. I have to say California agrees with you. You look great."

Jen seemed to sparkle even more right before his eyes. "I met someone," she whispered.

"Someone?"

"You know . . . *some*one."

"Oh," he said with a knowing grin. "*Some*one. Who is he?"

"His name is Jeff and he's a screenwriter. Can you believe it? He writes for the movies!"

"Interesting," Charlie remarked, looking around the expensive restaurant for their waiter. Everything about Los Angeles seemed expensive to him, especially the hotel he was staying in. He should have rented an apartment, like Jen, but he didn't think he'd be staying over a month. It just took time to make the right contacts. "Where did you meet him?"

"He came into the nursery to buy a plant and I helped him."

A waiter appeared at their table and asked for their drink order. He asked for a Guinness and Jen ordered her usual Sprite. "Okay, so tell me about him. I'm still a bit protective of you, you know."

"Oh, Charlie—can't you tell I'm fine? Better than fine. I love it here. I love working outside, being surrounded by nature. A whole lot better than sitting in an office processing mortgages. Now, for my man—"

He grinned. "Your man? Sounds like you've made up your mind." She did look wonderful, dressed in a short skirt and a white top that showed off her tanned shoulders. He was glad she was so happy.

"Well, not yet, but who knows," Jen answered with a theatrical raise of her eyebrows. "We have our first date tomorrow night. He's got blond hair—like who doesn't out here—blue eyes that seem to look right into my soul, and dimples—the cutest dimples when he smiles."

"And where is he taking you?"

Her eyes widened, as though he was acting like her parent. "Dinner, and I don't know where yet. He's calling me later tonight and we'll discuss it."

"I'm happy for you, Jen. Have fun."

"I'm sure I will. Now, what about you? What have you been doing?"

"Besides talking to my investment broker? Not much. Studying my driving manual."

"When do you take the test?"

"Next week."

"Looks like you've been shopping too. That's a new suit."

Shrugging, he said, "I can't wear the same one all the time."

"You look very successful, Charles Garrity," she said, as the waiter brought their drinks. "And pretty handsome too," she added in a whisper.

"Why, thank you," he answered, laughing at her antics. She certainly was in a good mood.

They ordered their dinner and sat back in comfortable silence—that is, until Jen asked her question.

"Have you called her yet?"

He stared across the table and frowned. "No."

"Why not?"

"I'm not ready. I haven't really figured anything out yet."

"Well, what *is* it that you need to figure out? I can help you."

He shook his head and sipped his Guinness.

"You love her, right?"

"Yes, I love her."

"She loves you?"

"I believe she does."

"So what's the problem? I know it's a cliché, but doesn't love conquer all?"

"I don't know, Jen. I just don't know."

"You are so frustrating, Charlie Garrity! If it's not her and it's not you, then what is it?"

"There's more to it than that," he muttered, looking out the window to the tall skyscrapers. It still amazed him every time he saw them.

"The car seat!"

He turned to look at her. "What?"

"There's a baby, a child. I completely forgot about it. That's what it is, isn't it?"

His frown deepened as she added, "Come on. I finally figured this out, didn't I?"

He didn't say anything.

"So you can't accept her child. Sounds kind of shitty to me, but knowing you, you must have a good reason."

"Drop it, Jen."

"No, I'm not dropping it," she stated emphatically. "After all this time, we're finally getting somewhere. What is it, Charlie? What's holding you back? It's not like keeping it all to yourself has helped you work through it."

He didn't say anything, feeling all the hostility coming back to the surface. He didn't want to dissect this now, in a restaurant.

"Well?"

"The child is related on his father's side to my enemy."

She stared at him for a few moments, as though stunned. "Excuse me? Your *enemy*? Who the hell has time in this day and age for enemies? What century are you from?"

"The last one," he muttered through gritted teeth. "You don't know anything about this."

"I know that you're wasting precious time with talk about enemies, like it's some grudge you have to carry with you the rest of your life. Damn, Charlie. Life's too short for that."

He nodded, hoping to dismiss her. "Fine. Thanks for your advice."

She smiled at him, as though knowing exactly what he was doing. "Listen to me. You think I don't know about enemies? Think again. You know why I order Sprite now every time we're out?" She didn't wait for him to answer. " 'Cause I don't drink anymore. I stopped the night you talked to me about driving you to California. My old man is a drunk. So was my mother. And I was headed the same way until you walked into my life. I know what it's like to hate and to try and deny it. I hated my father. I hated him for what he did to my mother. She drank herself to death just to get through the day with that sonofabitch. I grew up knowing my parents hated each other, blamed each other for their miserable lives, and then he blamed me because my mother got pregnant and he missed his chance in the big leagues playing football because he had to marry her.

"Then after she died, he tried to do the same thing to me, to lay his guilt all over me, so I moved out when I was seventeen. But not before I learned how to medicate the pain away, just like they did. I learned how to hate from them too, but I'll be damned if I'm going to pass it on to my kids. I don't have time to hate anymore, Charlie. I'll bet my parents learned it from their parents and it probably goes back generation after generation. Somebody's got to stick their heels in the ground and say it stops with me. I'm not going to make the same mistakes. Because you know what? Life really is too short to waste time and energy hating anyone. Think about what it takes away from you, what it costs you. Is it worth your freedom? Your happiness?" She stopped and picked up her Sprite. "Anyway, that's what I've learned."

He was stunned. He didn't know what to say to her, how to respond to her outburst of emotion.

"Shocked you, huh?"

He nodded. "I'm so sorry, Jen. I never would have thought you'd grown up like that."

"Why would you? Take a look out there, Charlie," she said, pointing out the window. "See all those people? You think any one of them is normal? Normal's the illusion. We're all working on our stuff, whatever that might be, but we sure try like hell to pretend we're as close to normal as possible. Look, all I know is life is tough enough without adding the weight of hate to it, ya know? Lighten up, my friend. Start enjoying life again. I know of one woman in New Jersey who would really appreciate it."

"How did you get so smart?" he whispered, in awe of her wisdom.

She giggled. "I told ya. I watched *Oprah* and then did some independent reading." She sipped her soda. "And I'm not so smart, Charlie. If anything, I'm finally trying to be real, though I have no intention of laying any of this on my screenwriter just yet. Time will tell if he can handle it."

Their dinners arrived, as though on cue, and Charlie watched as Jen began eating with enthusiasm. His own appetite seemed to have disappeared as he digested everything his young friend had said. Where was all his hate getting him? What was it serving? It suddenly dawned on him that this way it was almost as though Mitch had managed to take away what was important to him again. Because of Mitch he was no longer with Suzanne.

He could feel a tiny crack in the wall of protection around his heart.

"You're not eating."

He looked up from his plate. "I'm thinking."

Jen smiled. "Good. I hope you're thinking about calling her."

"Not yet. There are some things I need to do first."

"Like what?"

"Like get legal. I need a passport."

"A passport? Where are you going?"

"I'm not sure, but I don't like the idea that I can't get out of this country without one. There are so many laws now."

"You've always needed a passport, so what's new about that?"

"You didn't always need a passport, Jen. Take my word for it. It's just going to be tricky to get one for me, but I've found that money can ease the way if you make the right contacts."

"Charlie, you're not on the run, are you? I mean, you're not wanted by the law, or anything. I know I asked that back in New Jersey, but—"

"No, I'm not wanted by the law," he interrupted with a chuckle. "Am I on the run? That could be true."

"You're running from yourself, huh?"

"You just love being right all the time, don't you?"

Shrugging, Jen stabbed a floret of broccoli and said, "I'm not always right. Wouldn't that be boring? I'm just hitting the mark with you 'cause you're easy. I told you when we first met, you're one of the good guys, Charlie. You just needed a little tune-up to remember that yourself."

Now he laughed. "A tune-up?"

"Sure. We all get out of whack from time to time, don't we? It helps if someone else can see us, like an observer. Someone who's not emotionally involved." She pushed her plate forward and leaned her arms on the table. "See, I don't have a stake in how your life plays out, except as your friend. I can see what you're too bogged down in emotions to realize. Now you can take my observation and stick it where the sun don't shine. Or . . . you can examine it and see how it feels inside of you, and then run with it. Your choice. The only difference it makes with me is that I'd like to see you happy."

He sighed deeply. "You're a good friend, Jennifer McGee."

Her grin was almost tender. "So are you, Charlie. Now when are you going to call her?"

The phone rang and Suzanne stared at it for just a moment as her heart clutched tightly in hope and expectation. Slowly, she picked up the receiver.

"Hello?"

"Suzanne, hi. It's Laura. I'm returning your call. What's up?"

"Hi." She suppressed the sigh of disappointment, wondering why she still believed in her heart that Charlie would contact her. It had been well over a month now and all she'd received was silence. "Thanks for calling me back, Laura. Fortunately, this has nothing to do with law. It's about a good cause."

"Well, that's a relief. What is it?"

"It's called Renewal. They collect clothing to help women re-enter the job market, to dress professionally for interviews. So I'm calling all my professional friends to see if they want to clean out their closets."

"I've heard of this," Laura said. "Sounds worthwhile and I've been putting off cleaning out my closet for over a year."

"Oh good, so then you might have something? I can pick

it up, or you could drop it off here. I've already collected quite a bit and I'm about to make a trip over to Philly to the women's center."

"Give me a few days and I'll drop off whatever I can."

"Thanks, Laura. It really is a good cause."

"No problem. Gives me an excuse to do some overdue housecleaning. So how are you? How's Charlie?"

She inhaled and said, "I'm doing well."

"And Charlie? How is he?"

Suzanne paused. "I hope he's doing well. He left over a month ago."

"Wow. I didn't know, Suzanne. Are you all right?"

"I guess so," she answered. "I'm keeping myself busy."

"Well, call me if you need someone to talk to."

"Thanks, Laura, but I'm okay." Not wanting to continue this thread of conversation, she added, "So you'll drop off the clothes by the end of the week?"

"Sure. Oh, and did you hear? Kevin is now living in Florida."

Suddenly, she became alert. "Florida?"

"Yes, his lawyer notified me last week. All your payments should still automatically be deposited in your checking account."

Suzanne wasn't even thinking about money. "I can't believe it. He's in Florida."

"Suzanne, I have another call. Do you want to hold?"

"No, that's okay. I'll see you at the end of the week."

She hung up the phone and slowly walked into the sun room. She sat down in a chair and stared at Matty, lying on a blanket playing with the dust motes that were illuminated by a ray of sun. Kevin was in Florida? Did he go alone? Was Ingrid with him? Was he living with his parents? She hadn't seen or spoken to Ingrid since they met at the creek.

Suddenly, as she sat watching her child, it all played out in seconds across the screen of her mind.

If Kevin and Ingrid had never done what they did, would

she have been at the water at that exact moment to pull Charlie out of it? Would they have ever met? Would they have ever become friends? Would she have experienced such a profound love with the most extraordinary human being to ever come into her life?

She didn't know, but she felt like it all happened perfectly.

She hadn't been really happy married to Kevin. How could she be, when he'd always loved another? Yet she knew she would have stayed in the marriage if Kevin hadn't told her the truth. She would have continued to try to make it work, all by herself, trying to fix everything, when it had always been beyond fixing. Now she was out of it.

Why, if she really thought about it, without all the tangled emotions, she was actually grateful to Kevin and Ingrid for the roles they had played in her life. Without them, she might never have met Charlie. She might never have known what it was to be loved by such an incredible man.

Was this forgiveness?

She wasn't sure. She only knew it felt right. It was as though a heavy weight had been removed from her heart. She could breathe easier. Her muscles were less tense. She felt like it was all finally making sense. She had needed the push to get out of a situation that no longer served her. In truth, it hadn't been serving her for some time. So a bomb exploded, a *big* bomb to get her attention and to move her past her fears. And what had she found on the other side when the debris cleared?

Love.

Incredible love.

"Hey, Matty," she called out as she stood up and walked over to her son. "Let's go for a ride in the car."

Within minutes, she and her child were out the door.

She knew where she was driving. A part of her thought surely she must be nuts. Probably anyone else who heard about it would think she was over the edge, but she found she didn't care any longer what anyone else thought of her or her life. She had spent too many years worrying, hoping that she would appear normal. Almost laughing at the thought, Suzanne turned down the familiar street.

She parked at the sidewalk and looked up to the farmhouse. It was empty. She could tell by the darkness inside, the way the flowers were dying from lack of attention. Once she had loved this place, envisioned a future there, and now it was just a shell, empty and cold. Sighing as she left the past behind her, she shifted the transmission into drive and headed for her next stop.

Less than ten minutes later she slowly drove up to Ingrid's home. Her car was parked in the driveway. Suzanne shut off the ignition and took a deep breath. Ingrid's house looked pretty unloved too. Her spring plants were dead and she hadn't replaced them. "Well, Matty, it looks like we're about to make a surprise visit." She gazed into the rearview mirror and grinned at her son, before opening her door and getting him.

She held Matty to her chest as she walked up to the front door. Biting her bottom lip, she rang the doorbell and waited. But she didn't care if it seemed crazy. Something within her had been urging her here.

The door opened and Ingrid looked shocked to see her on her doorstep. She also looked like she had been through hell and back. Her hair was in streaks and could use a washing. She looked like she had slept in her sweatsuit.

"Hi," Suzanne said with a tight smile. "Maybe I shouldn't ask how you're doing."

Ingrid tried to smile back, but her chin trembled as she muttered, "He's gone."

"I heard. Something told me you didn't go with him."

Shaking her head, Ingrid held open the door. "Do you want to come in?"

"Okay. We can't stay long. I . . . I guess I just wanted to see if you were all right."

"All right?" she asked with a sarcastic laugh as she closed

the door. "I don't know if having the father of your child leave is . . ." She stopped speaking and stared at Suzanne with a horrified expression. "I'm so sorry. I wasn't thinking."

Suzanne actually laughed. "It's okay, Ingrid. I know exactly how you feel. What did he do? Run down to mommy and daddy to nurse him while he licks his wounds?"

"He said he couldn't take the pressure any more. I guess I'm pressure and having another child is pressure, but I think it was losing that money that did him in." She led Suzanne into her kitchen. "Want a cup of tea?"

"Not really. We can't stay," she answered, shifting Matty to her hip.

"So, this is Matthew," Ingrid whispered, sniffling as she came closer.

"This is Matty," Suzanne whispered, smiling down at her son as she presented him. "He's my angel child."

Ingrid leaned closer, her face inches away. "Hi, Matty."

Her son reached out and grabbed a handful of Ingrid's hair and tried to take it into his mouth. "Matty! Let go," Suzanne warned, prying his tiny fist apart. Laughing, she added, "Okay, so maybe he's not always an angel child."

Ingrid smiled as she smoothed her hair back into place. "He's beautiful. He's also going to have a half sister. I found out last week."

"A little girl," Suzanne breathed, finding it remarkable that she wasn't resentful any longer. All of that had miraculously disappeared when she realized she was grateful, instead of hateful. "Congratulations."

Ingrid's eyes started to water again and she rubbed her fingers against them. "I don't know what to do, Suz. I'm all alone and—"

"Oh, sit down, Ingrid," Suzanne said with a hint of impatience as she and Matty sat at the kitchen table. She waited until Ingrid sat across from her and then added, "You're going to pull yourself together, that's what you're going to do. Not for you. Certainly not for Kevin. But for that child inside of you. You're a mother now. You don't have time to allow this depression to take hold of your life. You're going to have a baby in a few months, Kevin or no Kevin. And you'll do it."

Ingrid wiped at her nose with the sleeve of her sweatshirt. "If you think I'm depressed, you should have seen him. He stayed in bed for days and then started blaming *me* for all this, saying if it hadn't been for me his life wouldn't have been ruined."

Sighing, Suzanne said, "It wasn't ruined. He has plenty of money."

"He hates to lose, Suzanne."

"Yeah, well, that's life. We've all got to learn that lesson sometime. It's time for Kevin to grow up, and running back to his parents isn't exactly mature now, is it? The real question might be *why* you want him in your life. Don't you want an *adult*?"

"I . . . I love him."

"Really? Or is it habit, or you think you've been through so much you have to make it work? Come on, Ingrid. I've known you too many years to believe you ever could be happy with a man who isn't responsible for his actions and his choices."

Ingrid didn't say anything, so Suzanne continued. "Look, it makes no difference to me. The reason I came over here when I heard Kevin took off was actually because I wanted to thank you."

"Thank me?"

Laughing, Suzanne nodded. "I know it sounds crazy. Two hours ago I would have thought so too. But it suddenly hit me that without you and Kevin doing what you did, I still would be married to that man and . . . well, quite frankly, in your position, trying to fix everything just so his life runs smoothly. Everything revolved around his moods. I cringe now when I think of it. I was almost hostage to them, hoping he'd be in a good one when he came home at night. I didn't have to live like that, but I was so blinded by this image of a family that I would have made myself miserable and murdered my soul trying to do it."

Ingrid just stared at her, as though shocked by her words.

Suzanne figured she might as well say it all. "By your choices, I was forced to make some of my own. It was terrifying at first, but when I calmed down I found I liked who I was without Kevin. I liked the peace that eventually came into my life. And I'm eternally grateful for the love that came into it too."

"Are you saying you forgive me?" Ingrid asked hopefully.

"I don't know about forgiveness. I'll have to think about that in more detail. I'm not a saint. I'm doing this for me, not for you or Kevin. Because it makes me feel good about me. All I know is that I'm not angry with you any longer. If I feel anything for you right now, it's compassion."

"Pity," Ingrid mumbled, starting to cry again. "I am pathetic."

"Ingrid?" She waited until Ingrid looked up. "Shut up."

Ingrid stared at her.

"I don't pity you. I feel compassion for you. I know what it's like to be in your shoes. And I'm telling you, you'll make it if you stop feeling sorry for yourself and get out of this house. Why don't you have any flowers planted yet?"

Ingrid's eyes widened. "Maybe because I've had a few things going on here and gardening was put on the back burner?"

"Go get your purse."

"Why?"

"Matty and I are taking you out of this house. We're going to pick up a few flats of bedding plants and then get our hands into the earth."

Ingrid was shaking her head. "Oh, I don't know if I'm up to it yet and—"

"Look," Suzanne interrupted. "You can sit in this house and become a pitiable woman, doing God knows what to that poor life inside of you, or you can come with us back into the sunshine and let mother nature begin to heal you." Standing up, she added, "It's your choice. Just make one."

As Suzanne watched Ingrid rise to get her purse, she realized she didn't know what it was that was prompting her to open up once again to Ingrid. Maybe it was the power of healing old wounds. Maybe it was compassion. Whatever it was, she only knew it felt right.

23

He walked up the green hill and stood still, staring out to the water before him. It was a majestic sight and it took his breath away for a moment as all the memories seemed to rush across his mind with lightning speed. The ocean. The sight of it never failed to move him. A strong summer breeze caressed his face, lifting his hair. He inhaled the clean scent of it, feeling it move down into his body, renewing him, making him whole again.

Below him was a beach and he watched as a man and a child walked hand in hand, stopping to examine shells and then adding their find to a bucket the man held. A lump formed in his throat and he allowed the tears. Here, on this land he had just purchased, he could allow all the sorrow, all the pain, all the memories to play out. He could let the wind dry his tears. The ocean to accept his sorrow. Here he could be made clean again.

Watching the man and child, he thought of those he had left behind. Suzanne and Matty. How he wanted to bring them here now, now that he had settled it all in his mind. Yes, Matty was Mitch's great-grandson. But he was also Grace's. He had forgotten that. And Matty was also a part of Suzanne—two of the most gracious, lovely women he had ever known. How had he let his hate obscure something so obvious? There was more of Grace and Suzanne in the boy than there was of Mitch.

Watching the man pick up the boy and swing him around struck Charlie's heart. The tears flowed without censure and he felt like such a fool for walking away from Suzanne and Matty. He loved them. Both of them. His fears were unfounded.

Would her heart still be open to him? Had his silence conveyed a message he hadn't meant to send? So many recriminations assailed him and, for the first time in his life, he wondered what kind of man he was. How could he have turned away from such an incredible love?

He now realized it was his own foolishness that had caused all this sorrow in his life. Ever since he had been carried to this time, he had harbored such hatred for the man who had caused him to lose everything. But now he saw that the life he had left in the past wasn't what he wanted. He didn't want to plant orchards. He didn't want to marry Grace.

He wanted Suzanne. He wanted Matty. He wanted to bring them to this place, stand with them on this hill, walk with them on the beach. He wanted to swing Matty in his arms, to show him by example how to be a man, to teach him what he knew of life and to learn along with him what he didn't.

He wanted to be a father.

He wanted to be Matty's father.

And most of all, he wanted Suzanne.

He pictured her in his mind, the way she had looked the day he'd left. Again, his throat felt tight. Never again would he cause her pain. This he vowed. He would spend his life making sure she was happy. If she would still have him.

Suddenly he was gripped by the urge to get back to her, to beg her to forgive him. He took one last look at the spectacular view and turned away to walk down the hill. In the distance was the house. It was in need of major repairs, but they would do it together, build a life and a home.

He knew in his soul it was the right thing to do. He could feel it in every part of him. Opening the car door, he got in and turned on the ignition.

"Home," he whispered, gazing with love at the land. Maybe he would never hold on to anything tightly again, but it was time to replant his roots.

"Tell me the truth, Suzanne. I've signed up for the classes, but I really want to know. Is it as bad as all the old wives' tales?"

She laughed and reached out to pull Matty toward her in the water. He was sitting in a floating seat and loving every minute of being in Ingrid's swimming pool. "You seriously want the truth?" she asked, making sure his cotton hat was shading his face. "You're sure?" she added, pointedly looking across the water.

Ingrid visibly swallowed and nodded.

"Okay, I can only answer for myself. Labor and delivery were the hardest work I've ever done. But it's worth it. Look at him." She spun her son around.

"It hurts, then."

"Of course it hurts, especially at the end. But you can do it, Ingrid. And if you can't, then ask for drugs. No shame in it, as far as I can see. Matty's birth just went fairly quickly."

"I'm scared, Suzanne."

She splashed her with water. "Get over it. Women have children every minute of every day. It's natural, Ingrid. But I'll hold your hand and you'll do fine."

"I wish I was so sure."

"Look, you're birthing new life, your body is contracting, helping it move down the birth canal. You've got to expect some pain." Suddenly she thought about her own life and said, "You know, Ingrid, maybe that's what we've been doing. Life presented us with some contractions, pushing and squeezing us toward a new life. It was painful, sometimes so much that we wanted to scream out to resist it. But we made it through, didn't we?"

Ingrid pushed Matty back toward her. "But you still won't trust me, will you?"

Sighing, Suzanne said, "I don't know. Give it time. Like I said, this is a new life we're living. Let's not push it. I don't know about you, but I've had enough pushing to last several lifetimes."

"Amen, sister, I'm ready to float for a while." And she swam out to the deep end and turned over onto her back. "No remarks about whales!"

Ingrid did look pretty funny, with her belly jutting out of the water. She stared at her friend. Yes, she could once more call Ingrid her friend. Not best friend. It wasn't the same relationship. This was different, more guarded. It was something new and Suzanne had no idea where it would lead. She just knew she felt better about having Ingrid in her life again.

Maybe this was forgiveness?

Her cell phone rang and she yelled out to Ingrid, "Watch the baby," as she hurried up the pool steps. Grabbing a towel with one hand, she scurried over to the chaise lounge where she had dropped her purse. She picked up the phone and flipped it open.

"Hello?"

There was nothing but static. She spun around, trying to find clearer reception. It didn't work. She hit the phone a few times with the palm of her hand and tried again. "Hello?"

Same thing. Shrugging, she closed the phone and threw it back on the cushion. "Where's Matty?" she yelled out, watching as Ingrid whispered in his ear. "I'm coming to get you!" She walked to the deep end, seeing her son follow her every move. "Here I come," she called out, right before diving in the water and coming up right in front of him.

His mouth opened in surprise and then he laughed.

"Did you hear him?" Suzanne spurted, wiping her face and staring at her son. "He laughed! A real laugh!"

"Well, I would hope so. That was one of the worst dives I've ever seen."

Ignoring Ingrid's remark, she said, "The other day, I swear I heard him say 'mama'. It sounded just like mama. Say mama, Matty. Come on."

Ingrid ducked down behind Matty and whispered, "Mama. Promise when I'm older you'll send me to a professional to learn to dive."

"Oh, give me my son," Suzanne demanded, twirling Matty's seat and watching the pleasure on his precious face. "I will remind you when your daughter is born that payback is a . . . no fun," she corrected in deference to her son's sensitive ears.

"Oh, Suzanne, you'll never tell her about . . . well, about what happened between us, will you?" Ingrid appeared terrified.

"Of course I won't. Why would I ever do such a thing?"

"Do you think Kevin will? I mean, if he ever wants to see her?"

She could only answer honestly. "I don't know, Ingrid. I guess that's part of taking responsibility for your choices. It's a risk."

"I wish I could keep him away forever. I never want him anywhere near either of us again."

"I understand."

The phone rang again and Suzanne pushed Matty back toward Ingrid. "Watch the baby," she called out, hurrying toward the steps. By the time she got out of the pool and reached the phone it had stopped ringing. Knowing her service would pick up, she said, "That's the last interruption I'm allowing."

As she re-entered the water, she asked, "So when do you feed us? I'm starving."

Ingrid laughed. "Soon. The chicken is roasting. I promise you won't starve." Her mood suddenly became serious. "Hey . . ."

Suzanne stared at her while untangling Matty's fingers from her necklace. "What?"

"We're doing okay, aren't we? Without men in our lives?"

"Hmm, speak for yourself. I miss my man."

"I know you do, but we're all right, aren't we? We're actually happy. We can do this single motherhood thing."

Suzanne nodded. "We can do it, but let's be honest, Ingrid. We're wealthy women. It's a heck of a lot easier when you don't have to worry about money. How many women are trapped by security, or lack of it? I don't even want to think of the numbers."

"You're right," Ingrid murmured.

"I wish I wasn't," Suzanne answered. "That's why I got involved with Renewal. Most of those women are single mothers. Imagine the courage it takes to restructure your life and enter the business world. How scared they must be."

Ingrid was shaking her head. "Don't get me started with women's issues."

"I won't," Suzanne said with a laugh. "I remember in college when you organized that protest rally for the ERA. You had me carrying banners and raising my fist—"

"And it *still* hasn't passed Congress!" Ingrid interrupted. "Maybe I should get involved in civic movements again. I'm going to have a daughter. What will it be like for her?"

Matty started whimpering and Suzanne pulled him closer. "I think he's hungry."

"You feed him and then we'll eat," Ingrid said, wading toward the pool steps. "Yes, I think I'll get involved again. It's been too long."

Suzanne smiled at Ingrid's back. She was going to be okay. She was interested in life again.

An hour later, Suzanne pushed away from the table and groaned. "I'm stuffed, and I feel like I'm pregnant again. Look at my stomach!" she declared, standing up and patting her skin. "Heaven forbid anyone but a friend see me in this bathing suit!"

"You look great. You've gotten your figure back. I pray I'm so lucky."

"Run around after a baby and you will. I can't believe how active he is. I'm telling you, I'm exhausted when I get to bed." She looked at Matty asleep in the portable crib and sighed. "But it's worth it."

"You keep saying that."

"Believe it," she whispered bending over her son. "I hate to eat and run, but I've got to bathe him and get him down for the night. Thanks for everything." She picked him up and cradled him in her arms. "Can I leave the crib and get it tomorrow?"

"Sure. It will be fine out here on the patio."

Ingrid walked her to the car, carrying her diaper bag. When she had Matty in his car seat, she closed the door and looked at her friend. "I really enjoyed myself today. Thanks for the invite."

"Any time, Suz. Thanks for coming. It . . . I don't know, felt like old times."

Suzanne nodded as she placed a towel on the front seat. Even her shirt was still damp. Turning, she said, "Take care of yourself, Ingrid. And take care of my son's half sister."

Ingrid sighed. "Who'd have believed our children would be related?"

"Ingrid, if I told you everything that's happened in the last six months, you wouldn't believe that, either. Let's just accept the unexplainable. It's so much easier."

As she drove home, Suzanne felt pretty good about the day. She was glad she had accepted the invitation to swim. Matty had been near ecstatic with the pool and it did feel like old times with Ingrid. Only better now that Kevin was no longer in the picture. She still wasn't completely comfortable with Ingrid, but it was a work in progress and she had no idea what the final result would be.

When she came to the river, she made the turn toward her house and was startled to see a car parked in her driveway. Who could be waiting for . . . Her breath caught in her throat. Her heart started pounding against her rib cage. She felt like time was suspended as she pulled up behind the car and watched him get out.

She could only stare at him through the front window as he stood staring back at her. Dear God, it felt like her soul was reaching out to him. He looked so handsome dressed in a light blue tennis shirt and navy slacks. Immediately, she was aware of how she looked. Why in heavens name had she chosen *this* day to wear a two-piece bathing suit!

He started to walk toward her car, and she pulled the edges of her shirt together, wishing she had the time to button it. Releasing the door handle, she pushed it open and slid her legs down to the ground.

They stood, staring into each other's eyes, neither of them saying a word. She felt her eyes start to burn, and she blinked to stop the moisture. "You came back," she whispered, still stunned to see him before her. She had imagined it, prayed for it, and now here he was.

"I had to," he murmured.

It felt like his eyes were devouring her, every inch of her, and she pulled the shirt around her. "Why?" She had to hear this, to put all her fears to rest.

"I missed you," he whispered, looking toward the back of the car. "And Matty. And I realized I couldn't live without you," he added, gazing back at her. "No matter where I went or what I did, my life felt empty. I'm so sorry, Suzanne. I . . . I didn't realize what my . . . my ego was costing me."

She couldn't help smiling. "Your ego?"

"I've been reading," he muttered with a sheepish grin. "I

was filled with hate and it nearly cost me you. You and Matty. Am I too late? Can you ever forgive me?"

Once more her heart was melting. "For walking away to straighten out your head? There's nothing to forgive. A phone call would have been appreciated, though."

"I know. I just had to work out some things." He jammed his hands into his pockets, and looked to the driveway. "Some things I'm ashamed to admit now."

"It was about Matty, wasn't it?"

He raised his head. "You knew?"

"Not right away. A friend helped me to realize it. You were afraid to commit to raising Mitch's great-grandson."

He nodded.

"What's changed?"

"Well, I had a friend help me to realize a few things too. The first was how stupid I was to allow my hatred for Mitch ruin what we had between us, all three of us—you, me, and Matty. I know now it was the best thing that's ever come into my life, Suzanne. You've got to believe that."

"I do, because I felt it too."

His eyes widened, as though he was trying to keep them from filling up. "And . . . well, I finally realized that Matty was also a greater part of you and of Grace and . . . I love the lad, Suzanne. I can't deny what I feel. I promise you I'll be a good father to him. You'll not want for a better man to father your son and to be your husb—"

Crying with gratitude, she reached out and put her fingers to his mouth. "I believe you. Now, will you please stop talking and kiss me?"

She could see his whole body relax with relief as he reached for her hand.

"I'll not kiss you until I've asked you this."

"What? Dear God, what? I forgive you. I believe you," she said, placing her hand in his and watching as he reached into his pocket.

He held up a ring, a magnificent square-cut emerald ring surrounded by diamonds.

"You were right when you said maybe love is the only thing that can last forever. And I love you, Suzanne Lawrence," he said with tears in his eyes. "Will you marry me?"

She could barely see with the tears in her own eyes. Out here, on the driveway, dressed in a bathing suit, she felt like the luckiest woman in the world. "I will," she whispered, and waited for him to slip the ring on her finger.

"There's more."

"Oh . . . more. Okay." Sheesh, she could have waited for him to finish, but she wanted to get that "I will" in as quickly as possible!

"I've bought land."

"All right."

"I want us to live there. At least part of the time."

"Okay."

"It's in Ireland."

"Ireland!" She was stunned.

"I bought back my family's land," he said, pausing for a moment as though steadying himself before beginning again. "Will you come with me to Ireland, to the green hills and the running waves? Will you marry me, be my wife, and raise our son amid the deep peace of the flowing air and smiling stars? Will you honor me by allowing me to cherish you both for all my days and nights?"

Her jaw dropped.

"You want more?"

"I want *you,* wherever you are. I want to be with you, Charlie."

He slid the ring onto her finger and then pulled her into his arms.

"Now you'll kiss me?" she breathed in anticipation.

"Now I'll kiss you, lass. Soundly."

And he did.

Suzanne felt her body melt into his while such joy rushed through her body that she almost couldn't contain it. "I love you, Charlie Garrity," she murmured against his lips when the kiss broke. "I will love you until the end of time. We are meant to be together, you and I. I'll live in Ireland or anywhere else you want—just as long as we're never apart again."

He held her close to his chest and kissed the top of her head. "I traveled seventy-five years to find you. I'm not about to let anything ever come between us again."

"Technically, *I* found you, but that doesn't matter."

She felt his laughter in his chest. "C'mon, let's get the sleeping boy into the house. I have a burning need to see you in better light. That bathing suit. I shall make short work of removing it, for this time, Suzanne, neither heaven, nor earth nor even time itself can keep me from claiming you."

"I like the sound of this," she said with a giggle as Charlie opened up the back door of the car. She watched as he leaned in and unbuckled Matty and then held him to his chest as the baby whimpered at being disturbed. "Come along, Matty. Go back to sleep now. Your mother and I have unfinished business. She will never know how hard it was to hold her that last night we were together. Ever since then I have been dreaming about making her my own. But you'll understand these things when you get older, lad."

"Such talk for a baby."

"He's sleeping. He knows I'm back," Charlie whispered, and kissed Matty's forehead.

With one arm around her and the other holding the child, he walked them up to the front door. Suzanne felt like her feet were barely touching the ground as happiness moved her along. They were together. A family. Sighing with contentment, she knew the truth of the old saying.

You are where you are meant to be at any given moment.

All they had to do was realize that moment was here and now.

AFTERWORD

Come to the edge
Life said.
They said:
We are afraid.
Come to the edge
Life said.
They came.
It pushed them . . .
And
they
Flew.

GUILLAUME APOLLINAIRE
1870~1918

ACKNOWLEDGMENTS

I would like to acknowledge the staff of HarperCollins, especially Lyssa Keusch, my editor; Helen Breitwieser, my agent; and Cristopher Sterling, my partner. Their contributions have been invaluable and always appreciated. And thanks also to Colleen Quinn Bosler, sister of my soul, for her encouragement and her gift of friendship.

Six Tips for Finding Mr. Right
From the Avon Romance Superleaders

Meeting Mr. Right requires planning, persuasion, and a whole lot of psychology! But even the best of us needs help sometimes . . . and where better to find it than between the pages of each and every Avon Romance Superleader?

After all, Julia Quinn, Rachel Gibson, Barbara Freethy, Constance O'Day-Flannery, Cathy Maxwell, and Victoria Alexander are the experts when it comes to love. And the following sneak previews of their latest tantalizing, tempting love stories (plus a special bonus from Samantha James) are sure to help you on the path to romantic success.

So when it's time to find the man of your dreams (or, if you've already got him, to help your friends find equal success) just follow the lead of the heroines of the Avon Romance Superleaders. . . .

Tip #1:
Ballroom dance lessons really can pay off.

Miss Sophie Beckett longs to believe that her dreams can come true. However, this Regency miss seems destined to be at the beck and call of her wealthy relations. But when she secretly attends Lady Bridgerton's annual masked ball, she's swept into the strong arms of handsome Benedict Bridgerton. Sophie knows that when midnight—and the unmasking—comes she must leave or risk exposure. But she won't do so before she accepts . . .

An Offer From a Gentleman

Coming July 2001
by Julia Quinn

Sophie hadn't seen him when she'd first walked into the room, but she'd felt magic in the air, and when he'd appeared before her, like some charming prince from a children's tale, she somehow knew that *he* was the reason she'd stolen into the ball.

He was tall, and what she could see of his face was very handsome, with lips that hinted of irony and smiles and skin that was just barely touched by the beginnings of a beard.

His hair was a dark, rich brown, and the flickering candle-light lent it a faint reddish cast.

He was handsome and he was strong, and for this one night, he was hers.

When the clock struck midnight, she'd be back to her life of drudgery, of mending and washing and attending to Araminta's every wish. Was she so wrong to want this one heady night of magic and love?

She felt like a princess—a reckless princess—and so when he asked her to dance, she put her hand in his. And even though she knew that this entire evening was a lie, that she was a nobleman's bastard and a countess's maid, that her dress was borrowed and her shoes practically stolen—none of that seemed to matter as their fingers twined.

For a few hours, at least, Sophie could pretend that this gentleman could be *her* gentleman, and that from this moment on, her life would be changed forever.

It was nothing but a dream, but it had been so terribly long since she'd let herself dream.

Banishing all caution, she allowed him to lead her out of the ballroom. He walked quickly, even as he wove through the pulsing crowd, and she found herself laughing as she tripped along after him.

"Why is it," he said, halting for a moment when they reached the hall outside the ballroom, "that you always seem to be laughing at me?"

She laughed again; she couldn't help it. "I'm happy," she said with a helpless shrug. "I'm just so happy to be here."

"And why is that? A ball such as this must be routine for one such as yourself."

Sophie grinned. If he thought she was a member of the *ton*, an alumna of dozens of balls and parties, then she must be playing her role to perfection.

He touched the corner of her mouth. "You keep smiling," he murmured.

"I like to smile."

His hand found her waist, and he pulled her toward him. The distance between their bodies remained respectable, but the increasing nearness robbed her of breath.

"I like to watch you smile," he said. His words were low and seductive, but there was something oddly hoarse about his voice, and Sophie could almost let herself believe that he really meant it, that she wasn't merely that evening's conquest. . . .

Tip #2:
Mothers across America proven wrong— sometimes looks _do_ count!

The gossips of Gospel, Idaho, all want to know—who is Hope Spencer and what is she doing in their town? Little do they suspect that she's a supermarket tabloid reporter on the run from a story gone terribly wrong . . . all they can learn is that she's from Los Angeles, which is plenty bad. Even worse, she's caught the eye of Dylan Taber, Gospel's sexy sheriff—the only good looking man in three counties. He's easy on the eyes and not above breaking the laws of love to get what he wants. And before you know it, there's plenty to talk about in the way of . . .

True Confessions

Coming August 2001
by Rachel Gibson

"Can you direct me to Number Two Timberline?" she asked. "I just picked up the key from the realtor and that's the address he gave me."

"You sure you want Number Two Timberline? That's the old Donnelly place," Lewis Plummer said. Lewis was a true gentleman, and one of the few people in town who didn't outright lie to flatlanders.

"That's right. I leased it for the next six months."

Sheriff Dylan pulled his hat back down on his forehead. "No one's lived there for a while."

"Really, no one told me that. How long has it been empty?"

"A year or two." Lewis had also been born and raised in Gospel, Idaho, where prevarication was considered an art form.

"Oh, a year isn't too bad if the property's been maintained."

Maintained, hell. The last time Dylan had been in the Donnelly house thick dust covered everything. Even the bloodstain on the living room floor.

"So, do I just follow this road?" She turned and pointed down Main Street.

"That's right," he answered. From behind his mirrored glasses, Dylan slid his gaze to the natural curve of her slim hips and thighs, down her long legs to her feet.

"Well, thanks for your help." She turned to leave but Dylan's next question stopped her.

"You're welcome, Ms.—?"

"Spencer."

"Well now, Ms. Spencer, what are you planning to do out there on the Timberline Road?" Dylan figured everyone had a right to privacy, but he also figured he had a right to ask.

"Nothing."

"You lease a house for six months and you plan to do nothing?"

"That's right. Gospel seemed like a nice place to vacation."

Dylan had doubts about that statement. Women who drove fancy sports cars and wore designer jeans vacationed in nice places with room service and pool boys, not in the wilderness of Idaho. Hell, the closest thing Gospel had to a spa was the Petermans' hot tub.

Her brows scrunched together and she tapped an impatient hand three times on her thigh before she said, "Well, thank you, gentlemen, for your help." Then she turned on her fancy boots and marched back to her sports car.

"Do you believe her?" Lewis wanted to know.

"That she's here on vacation?" Dylan shrugged. He didn't care what she did as long as she stayed out of trouble.

"She doesn't look like a backpacker."

Dylan thought back on the vision of her backside in those tight jeans. "Nope."

"Makes you wonder why a woman like that leased that old house. I haven't seen anything like her in a long time. Maybe never."

Dylan slid behind the wheel of his Blazer. "Well, Lewis, you sure don't get out of Pearl County enough."

Tip #3:
If he's good to kids,
he'll be good to you.

Most men, when confronted with a baby, do one of two things: run the other way or fall for it. When a beautiful baby girl is left on journalist Matt Winters's doorstep, he turns to his neighbor, wedding gown designer Caitlyn Deveraux, for help. After all, she's a woman . . . shouldn't she know everything about babies? Soon, Caitlyn and Matt must confront their deepest desires—her longing for a child, his wish for a family—and a passion for each other that's . . .

Some Kind of Wonderful

Coming September 2001
by Barbara Freethy

"Oh, isn't that the cutest outfit?" Caitlyn ran down the aisle and pulled out a bright red dress that was only a little bigger than Matt's hand. "It has a bonnet to go with it. You have to get this one."

"This was a big mistake," he said, frowning at her unbridled enthusiasm. With Emily nuzzled against his chest and Caitlyn by his side, he felt like he was part of a family—a husband, a wife, a baby. It was the American dream.

"It's one cute little dress," Caitlyn said, putting it in the cart. "Diapers, we need diapers." She walked around the corner and tossed several large bags into the cart, followed by baby wipes, bottles, formula, bibs, socks, a couple of sleepers, a baby blanket, and a pink hair ribbon that she couldn't resist. By the time they headed down the last aisle, the cart was overflowing with items Caitlyn insisted that he needed.

"You know I'm not a rich man," he told her.

"Most of it is on sale."

"And most of it we don't need—I don't need," he corrected. "She doesn't need," he said finally finding the right pronoun.

Caitlyn simply offered a smile that told him she could see right through him. To distract her he stopped and looked over at the shelves, determined to find something else that they didn't need so she would coo over it and focus her attention anywhere but on him. That's when he saw it: an enormous chocolate brown teddy bear with soft, plush fur and black eyes that reminded him of Sarah.

"Emily would love that," Caitlyn said.

"It's bigger than she is," he replied gruffly.

"She'll grow into it." Caitlyn took the bear off the rack and sat it on top of the growing pile, daring him to take it off.

"Fine," he said with a long-suffering sigh.

"Oh, please, you don't fool me."

"I don't know what you're talking about."

"I'm talking about that sentimental streak that runs down your back."

"You're seeing things with those rose-colored glasses again, princess."

"And you're a terrible liar."

Tip #4:
Sometimes it's good to
take charge!

Charles Garrity is a man out of time . . . one moment it was 1926, the next, 2001! But he doesn't have a single minute to figure out what's happened, because he's faced with rescuing his rescuer—a very beautiful, very pregnant woman who says her name's Suzanne McDermott. Charles quickly realizes that all has changed except for one thing: Love is an emotion that can transcend time, and that nothing else matters but what you feel . . .

Here and Now

Coming October 2001
by Constance O'Day-Flannery

"Who are you anyway?"

"Charles Garrity, ma'am. And thank you again . . . for pulling me out of the river." He didn't know what else to say to this confusing female, and he certainly had no idea what to do with a woman about to give birth.

"I'm Suzanne. Suzanne McDermott. Now let's just make it to the car so both of us can get some help."

Charles kept looking at the odd automobile. "You drove this?"

"Of course, I drove it."

Charles shrugged, then reached down behind her legs and, with a grunt, swept her up into his arms.

"No! Wait! You'll drop me!" she yelped.

"Just stay still, ease up, and we'll make it," he gritted out.

As they approached the machine Charles took one last step and set her down as gently as he could next to it.

He pulled on the metal latch on the automobile and stared in wonder as the door opened easily and exposed the luxurious interior.

"You're going to have to drive us to the hospital," she said.

"I am?" he asked.

"Yes, you are. You have driven a car before, haven't you?"

"I've driven an automobile," he insisted, straightening his backbone.

"Good," Suzanne answered. "Let's get out of here. I want a doctor when my baby arrives."

"Let me help you," he said, wrapping his arm around what was left of her waist and assisting her. When they managed to get her onto the back seat, he stood panting.

She felt like she was instructing a child as she patiently began rattling off instructions. A wave of relief swept over her as the engine cranked and the motor began humming.

"This is astounding," he said with a breath of awe.

Suzanne knew now was not the time to ask questions.

The car lurched forward. He must have hit every single rut on the back country path, and he stopped when they finally came to the main road, even though there were several times when he could have safely merged.

"What's wrong?" she asked.

Charles Garrity stared at the unbelievable spectacle before him. Automobiles of every color and size whizzed past him with more speed than he'd ever imagined. Something was wrong—*very* wrong—for this was no place he'd ever been before.

Tip #5:
Sometimes men like it
when you play hard to get.

When pert, pretty Mary Gates gets her chance for a London Season, she sets her cap on someone far more lofty than Tye Barlow, the local rake. The insufferable man thinks he's the world's gift to women! But though he drives her crazy when they're together, she finds herself longing for him when they're apart. Then a daring bet between them ends in matrimony, and Mary must decide whether she's lost—or won . . .

The Wedding Wager

Coming November 2001
by Cathy Maxwell

Tye Barlow's hand came down on top of hers, pressing it flat against the horse's skin. He held it in place. In spite of the beast's impressive height, Barlow glowered down at her from the other side.

Mary wasn't one of his silly admirers. She knew better than to trust a man who could make a woman's brain go a little daffy. But when he was angry like this, she had to concede he was rather good-looking. He boasted sharp, cobalt blue eyes, straight black hair, broad shoulders, and a muscular physique that made other men appear puny.

However, Mary knew what sent female hearts fluttering was not his perfections, but his imperfections. His grin was slightly uneven, like that of a fox who had raided the henhouse. A scar over his right eye added to his devil-may-care expression, and there was a bump on his nose from the day years ago when he, Blacky, David, and Brewster had brawled with a neighboring village.

They'd won.

Now her face was inches from Tye's, and she could make out the line of his whiskers and smell a hint of the bay rum shaving soap he used. For a guilty second she was tempted to blurt out the truth . . . then pride took over.

How *dare* he manhandle her. And the state of her affairs was her business, not his.

She gave his black scowl right back at him. "I can afford the horse, Barlow, and I've bought him. He's mine. And you are a sore loser."

Her words hit their mark. His hold on her arms loosened as if she'd struck a physical blow. She jerked away. Two steps and she could breathe easily again.

"Your stubborn arrogance will ruin you, Mary."

His accusation stung. She wasn't arrogant. Proud, yes; arrogant, no. Calmly, forcibly, she said, " 'Twas a business decision, Barlow. Nothing personal."

The daggers in his eyes told her he didn't believe her. "And how do you think you are going to find the funds to pay the horse's price?" His low voice was meant for their ears alone.

"I have plenty of money," she replied stiffly.

"God, Mary, stop this pretense. You're done up. It's not your fault. Your father—"

"Don't you dare mention my father. Not after what your family did to him—"

"I did nothing and if you think so, then you're a fool."

His blunt verdict robbed her of speech. They were back in each other's space again, almost toe-to-toe.

"If I was a man," she said, "I'd call you out and run you through."

"But you're not a man, Mary. Yes, you are good with horses, but damn it all, you are still a woman. . . ."

Tip #6:
Sometimes fainting isn't such a bad idea.

Lady Jocelyn is no shrinking violet, but even she knows that sometimes a lady has to fall into a swoon—and if you're caught in the arms of sexy Randall, Viscount Beaumont, so much the better. Of course, Jocelyn had always dreamed she'd be marrying a prince . . . or at least a duke. But Randall's strong embrace and tempting kisses are far more enticing than she'd ever imagined. And then a surprising twist of events makes it possible that she just might become . . .

The Prince's Bride

Coming December 2001
by Victoria Alexander

He caught her up in arms strong and hard and carried her to a nearby sofa. For a moment a lovely sense of warmth and safety filled her.

"Put me down," she murmured, but snuggled against him in spite of herself.

"You were about to faint."

"Nonsense. I have never fainted. Shelton women do not faint."

"Apparently, they do when their lives are in danger."

Abruptly, he deposited her on the sofa and pushed her head down to dangle over his knees.

"Whatever are you doing?" She could barely gasp out the words in the awkward position. She tried to lift her head, but he held it firmly.

"Keep your head down," he ordered. "It will help."

"What will help is finding those men. There were two, you know. Or perhaps you don't." It was rather confusing. All of it. She raised her head. "Aren't you going to go after them?"

"No." He pushed her head back down and kept his hand lightly on the back of her neck. It was an oddly comforting feeling. "I have my men searching now, but I suspect they will be unsuccessful. One of the rascals is familiar to me. I was keeping an eye on him tonight. He is no doubt the one who threw the knife."

"Apparently, you weren't keeping a very good eye on him," she muttered.

He ignored her. "I have yet to discover the identity of his accomplice and I doubt that I will tonight. It's far too easy to blend unnoticed into a crowd of this size." He paused, the muscles of his hand tensing slightly on her neck. "Did you recognize him?"

"Not really," she lied. In truth, not at all. They were nothing more than blurry figures to her and dimly remembered voices. "He could be anyone then, couldn't he?"

"Indeed he could."

It was a most disquieting thought. Well matched to her most discomforting position. "I feel ridiculous like this."

"Quiet."

It was no use arguing with the man. Whoever he was, he obviously knew what he was doing. She was already feeling better.

She rose to her feet. "Who are you?"

He stood. "I should be crushed that you do not remember, although we have never been formally introduced." He swept a curt bow. "I am Randall, Viscount Beaumont."

The name struck a familiar chord. "Have we met then?"

"Not really." Beaumont shrugged. "I am a friend of Lord Helmsley."

"Of course." How could she forget? She'd seen him only briefly in a darkened library, but his name was all too familiar. Beaumont had taken part in a farcical, and highly successful plan to dupe her sister, Marianne, into marriage with Thomas, Marquess of Helmsley and son of the Duke of Roxborough. "And an excellent friend too from all I've heard."

"One owes a certain amount to loyalty to one's friends." He paused as if considering his words. "As well as to one's country."

At once the mood between them changed, sobered. She studied him for a long moment. He was tall and devastatingly handsome. She noted the determined set of his jaw, the powerful lines of his lean body like a jungle cat clad in the latest state of fashion. And the hard gleam in his eye. She shivered with the realization that regardless of his charming manner, his easy grin, and the skill of his embrace, *this* was a dangerous man.

And because you can never have enough handy tips
when it comes to meeting a man,
we give you a bonus!
In case you missed it, it comes from
The Truest Heart
by Samantha James
Available now from Avon Books

Bonus Tip #7:
A good man is hard to find . . . and
sometimes a bad man is better.

When Lady Gillian of Westerbrook discovers a near-mortally wounded warrior, she takes him in and nurses him back to health. He has no memory of his past, but as Gillian tends to him he begins to remember . . . and she realizes he is none other than Gareth, lord of Sommerfield, the man sworn to betray her to a vengeful king. As Gillian succumbs to his masterful touch, she is forced to choose—between her family honor and her heart's truest desire.

"You are a man who knows little of piety and virtue."

There was a silence, a silence that ever deepened. "I do not know. Perhaps I am a their. An outlaw."

Gillian looked at him sharply, but this time she detected no trace of bitterness. "I think not. You still have both your hands."

"Then perhaps I'm a lucky one. Now come, Gillian."

Outside lightning lit up the night sky. The ominous roll of thunder that followed made the walls shake. In a heartbeat

Gillian was across the floor—and squarely onto the bed next to him.

He laughed, the wretch!

"Perhaps you are not an outlaw," she flared, "but I begin to suspect you may well be a rogue!"

He made no answer, but once again lifted the coverlet. Her lips tightened indignantly, but she tugged off her slippers and slid into bed. He respected the space she put between them, but she was aware of the weight of his gaze setting on her in the darkness.

"Are you afraid of storms?"

"Nay," she retorted. As if to put the lie to the denial, lightning sizzled and sparked, illuminating the cottage to near daylight.

She tensed, half-expecting some jibe from Gareth. Instead, his fingers stole through hers, as had become their custom. Comforted, lulled by his presence, it wasn't long before she felt her muscles loosen and her eyelids grow heavy. 'Ere she could draw breath, long arms caught her close—so close she could feel every sinewed curve of his chest, the taut line of his thighs molded against her own.

There was no chance for escape. No chance for struggle. No thought of panic. No thought of resistance, for Gillian was too stunned to even move . . .

His mouth closed over hers.